Praise for J. L. Langley's *The Englor Affair*

Rating: 5 Angels and a Recommended Read "...The whole milieu in this series shouldn't work well but Ms. Langley does it flawlessly, making a believer out of me."

~ *April, Fallen Angel Reviews*

"The Englor Affair does what sequels should – propel the series forward while improving on the last... Sexy, romantic, and fun...but what else would you expect from gay Regency romance in space?"

~ *Book Utopia Mom, Uniquely Pleasurable*

Rating: 5 Clovers and a Recommended Read "One of the most anticipated books for me this year is The Englor Affair and I must admit it was brilliant."

~ *Sandra, CK2S Kwips and Kritiques*

Rating: 5 Coffee Cups "All I can say is J.L. Langley has done it again, and I, for one, cannot wait for the next book to come out! You absolutely do not want to miss a single book by this author. She is one of the best in the business, and I highly recommend The Englor Affair."

~ *Regina, Coffee Time Romance*

Look for these titles by
J. L. Langley

Now Available:

With or Without Series
Without Reservations
With Love
(Also in print anthology Hearts from the Ashes)
With Caution

Sci-Regency Series
My Fair Captain (Book 1)
The Englor Affair (Book 2)

The Englor Affair

J. L. Langley

A Samhain Publishing, Ltd. publication.

Samhain Publishing, Ltd.
577 Mulberry Street, Suite 1520
Macon, GA 31201
www.samhainpublishing.com

The Englor Affair
Copyright © 2009 by J. L. Langley
Print ISBN: 978-1-60504-407-1
Digital ISBN: 1-60504-236-6

Editing by Sasha Knight
Cover by Anne Cain

First Samhain Publishing, Ltd. electronic publication: November 2008
First Samhain Publishing, Ltd. print publication: September 2009

Dedication

To Ally, Willa, Jet, Luisa, Brenda and Kimber. The best critique partners, writers and friends a girl could ask for. I love you guys. Thank you for everything you do: Your support, your encouragement, for entertaining me with fabulous stories, and kicking my butt and making me work when I don't want to. You guys are the best.

Special thanks as always to Andre, my life, my love, my friend. I'd be lost without you.

Prologue

October 3, 4820: Planet Englor: Fischer House in London, Moreal (The ruling country of Englor)

Bloody hell and imploding stars that hurt. He was going to be lame if this dance didn't end soon. Simon smiled tightly at his partner. How long was this set anyway?

"Oh dear! I'm so sorry, Your Highness." Lady Drucilla's bottom lip quivered and she ceased moving. The girl was heavy on her feet for such a gangly thing. Those dainty little pink dancing slippers were lethal weapons.

"Quite all right, milady, no harm done." Simon tugged her hand just enough to get her going again.

"But your foot..." Her big brown eyes brimmed with tears, reminding him how young she was.

"It was my fault, not yours." Glancing toward the edge of the dance floor, he spotted her mother, Lady Hemplewine, frowning. *Damn.* He'd have to ask Drucilla for another dance to keep her from getting in trouble with her mama. Galaxy, he didn't know if the tops of his feet could take the abuse, but to keep her from a lecture, he'd grin and bear it. "I'll allow you to make it up to me however. Perhaps you have another dance available on your card?"

Her eyes widened and her steps faltered. "You don't have to do that, Your Highness."

Simon glanced over her shoulder at her glowering mama and the line of debutantes staring at them. Gads, he hated

9

balls. They made him feel like a piece of meat thrown to a pack of starving dogs. "I want to."

She smiled suddenly, her whole face brightening. One day she'd be a real beauty...once she grew into her limbs. At barely sixteen she was an awkward thing, reminding Simon of a fawn. "She is glaring daggers at me, isn't she? Or are you hoping to escape the hordes of hopefuls vying for your attention?"

Oh, she was a smart one. Simon chuckled. "Both actually."

Drucilla giggled and promptly stepped on his foot again. "Oh dear. I'm really rather terrible at dancing, aren't I?"

"Nonsense. It's what? Your first season? You will improve by leaps and bounds. By next season you'll be the belle of every ball." Simon decided he'd make it so by dancing with her at every one of the blasted things he was forced to attend. He liked her. She didn't flirt outrageously or chatter nervously. That in itself was unique. Most of the ladies of the ton did both things in his presence.

"You are too kind, Your Highness. I volunteer to help you keep the ravenous ladies away, but please don't worry about Mama. She will forgive me. As you've pointed out, it's only my first season after all."

"Then I shall hold you to helping me fight off the marriage-minded ladies of the ton, milady." Simon grinned as the music ended and offered Drucilla his arm. "Thank you for the dance."

She leaned close, she was nearly as tall as he, and whispered, "What makes you think I'm not one of the marriage-minded ladies?"

The minx. Simon threw his head back and laughed. "Call it a hunch. Maybe because you hesitated so long when I asked you to dance. Your mother practically shoved you into my arms."

The crowd parted for them as he led Drucilla back to her mother. Simon couldn't help but notice the eager females close in behind Lady Hemplewine. Darting a gaze around the crowded ballroom, he searched for an escape route.

"Your Highness..." Lady Hemplewine began fluttering and

curtsying.

Drucilla let go of his arm as they drew close to her mother and said, "Isn't that your friend Lord Biltshire beckoning to you by the refreshment table, Your Highness?"

He owed the girl one for this. "It is indeed. Forgive me, Lady Hemplewine, Lady Drucilla, but I must see what he wants." He bowed, winked at Drucilla and dashed away. Now if he could just get to the card room without being stopped, he was in the clear. He'd done his duty and danced a few dances, now he could leave. Maybe after a stop in the card room, he'd find a nice young man to spend the evening with. Or maybe not since the scandal was the talk of the ton and prospective dates were lying low.

"Your Highness." Lords Tettering and Avery nodded as he passed.

"Milords." Simon dipped his head in greeting, but didn't linger. He was only a few yards from the ballroom entrance. *Almost there.*

"Did you hear about Lord Keller's youngest boy?"

Upon hearing the venom in his mother's voice, Simon stumbled, nearly plowing into a potted plant. He almost toppled. It took some work, with his shoes sliding on the polished pink marble, but he righted himself and ducked behind the large topiary. She too had apparently heard of the scandal and wasn't above gossiping about it.

She let out a sound of distaste very much like a snort. "Got caught with a footman. Disgusting! I tell you, those sodomites should all be executed. Deviants, every last one of them. We need to outlaw it and make it a mandatory death sentence. That will stop it. I've tried to get Howard to bring it up in parliament, but he hasn't. So I've elicited help from Lord Devonshire, Lord Brotham and His Grace the Duke of Paddock. That should show my dear husband. I'll get things done without his help."

Bile rose up the back of Simon's throat, and he hoped she hadn't noticed him. He'd always known how narrow-minded she was, but did she really think men should be hanged for preferring other men?

Sweat dripped from his temple and he wiped it away. Hopelessness overwhelmed him.

"Simon?"

Bloody hell. Simon's breath caught in surprise and he slapped a hand to his chest. When he whipped his head toward the voice, he came face-to-face with his uncle. "Dust, St. Albins."

Aldred Hollister chuckled. "Didn't mean to scare you, boy." He cocked one dark brow. "What are you doing hiding behind plants instead of enjoying yourself? This is a ball, you're supposed to be dancing and having a good time."

Simon willed his heart to stop racing and smiled at his uncle. He glanced around at the couples dancing and milling about. The music had faded into the background of his mind and he'd totally lost track of where he was, but now it came back with new clarity. Peering over his shoulder, he looked to make certain his mother hadn't noticed him.

Simon turned back to his uncle's inquisitive gaze. "I've just finished dancing."

"Hmm..." Aldred pursed his lips, studying Simon. He jerked his head toward the entryway of the ballroom. "Come join me for a drink. I doubt Westland will mind if we use his study."

It wasn't a surprise that his uncle picked up on his mood. Caught off guard as he was, Simon hadn't put on his poker face yet, but fortunately this was the one person he didn't need to pretend with.

As they made their way around the clustered groups of people in conversation on the edge of the dance floor, Aldred drew near to be heard over the orchestra. "What's wrong?"

Simon hesitated, only for a second. Aldred might even ease Simon's mind a little. Although he didn't see how. "Have you heard abo—?"

"Your Highness, Your Grace, good evening." Lord Dimplemore stepped away from a small cluster of lords and bowed to them. His gaudy bright purple waistcoat competed with the pale yellow and salmon colors of the Earl of Westland's

12

ballroom, hurting Simon's eyes.

Nodding, Simon acknowledged Dimplemore with a "milord", but kept going. He'd learned long ago, if he hesitated at all, he was doomed. Normally, he didn't mind, but the thought of his mother wanting to execute people for their differences had him off kilter.

Aldred echoed Simon's greeting and rushed to catch up to Simon. "Well done, my boy. Dimplemore is a windbag. We'd have been there for ages."

"You taught me well." Simon grinned. His parents would have simply cut the man, but that wasn't his uncle's way. It wasn't Simon's either. It was probably the reason Simon looked up to Aldred as his mentor rather than his father. Aldred had always understood Simon better than anyone. "Have you heard of the scandal?"

"You mean Keller's son?"

"Yes."

"Ah. Yes, I don't believe there is a soul in London who has not."

True, the ton had been talking about it for the last two days. The reactions ranged from horrified to sympathetic. Likely the news was all over the countryside by now, and possibly the entire planet of Englor. Simon found the whole ordeal quite tragic with the lovers being shunned as they'd been.

They reached the door and squeezed by several Lords and Ladies entering. Simon and Aldred both dipped their heads in acknowledgment as they passed.

In the hallway, Aldred stopped in front of a slim tall lady with graying brown hair piled high on her head. When she turned, Simon recognized her as Lady Westland, their hostess.

"Milady, might we borrow Lord Westland's study?" Aldred asked with a bow.

The countess practically fell all over herself, blushing and simpering like a chit right out of the schoolroom. "Why of course, Your Grace." She curtsied to Aldred and then Simon. "Your Highness."

Simon caught her gloved hand and brought it to his lips. "Lady Westland, you look lovely as always."

She giggled and her cheeks grew even ruddier. "Why thank you, Your Highness. Please feel free to use Westland's study as long as you need. I'll inform our butler, William, that you're not to be disturbed and that the room is not to be recorded."

"Thank you, milady." Aldred bobbed his head and continued down the hall to their right.

Simon hadn't been in the Earl of Westland's townhome enough to know where the study was, so he followed his uncle's lead.

When they reached the study, Aldred held the door open, allowing Simon to enter first before closing it. The small dark room was done in greens and blacks with a huge black marble fireplace. It had a masculine cozy feel to it, refreshing compared to the garish ballroom.

Simon sat in a black leather armchair in front of the fire as Aldred crossed to the small mahogany side bar and began pouring two tumblers of scotch. "Tell me, what's troubling you?"

Simon stretched his feet out in front of him, relieved to be out of the public eye. "My mother." Which was nothing new, his mother was a constant source of irritation. He hadn't reached eighteen years of age without learning that she cared more for her looks, clothes and social rank than she did anything else, including her only child. This time though, she truly disturbed him, her attitude was...*frightening.* "She's a dangerous woman."

"Ah. Yes, she is. Most people with access to a lot of power and very little intelligence are." The statement was delivered matter-of-fact, without even a touch of malice. Aldred crossed the room and handed Simon a tumbler. He sat opposite Simon and sampled his scotch.

Umm, the warm smell of scotch assailed his senses. Simon sipped his drink and used the moment to digest his uncle's statement. The scotch was good, musky and earthy. It replaced the sick feeling he'd been harboring since he'd overheard his mother's conversation. He'd never considered his mother an idiot, but it was true that she did not know a wide variety of things. "Why did he marry her? He could have had anyone. It's all a game to her, a power trip to ensure her own gains."

Aldred pulled a silver cigar case from his inside coat pocket, opened it and offered it to Simon, then took one for himself before putting it away. "I should think that would be obvious. Your mother is a very beautiful woman."

"So are certain species of snakes..." Simon took another drink. "Ahhh..." That tingling when it went down was something. A few more of these and he'd be fine with everything. Too bad he had a conscience that wouldn't allow him to overdo it and forget.

Aldred laughed. "Indeed, but don't be too hard on your father. You got your mother's looks, thank Galaxy. How would you've liked to have been cursed with the Hollister ears?" He smiled over his drink, his gray eyes twinkling in merriment.

Simon scoffed. His uncle was not an unattractive man. Simon would much rather have gotten the Hollister dark hair than his mother's fiery red. Besides, Aldred's ears weren't anywhere near as big as Simon's father's. Being single and only in his mid-thirties, Aldred was still considered quite a catch. "I look like a Hollister."

"A Hollister with a nice smooth freckle-less complexion and ears the right size for your head. But that's beside the point. What did your mother do now? And why were you asking about Keller's boy?"

Tapping the cigar against his glass, Simon sat back. "She wants to have homosexuality outlawed and punishable by death." Little did she know her own son would be at the gallows along with all the other—what did she call them? Deviants? "I'm safe from her hatred and bigotry, but other Englorians are not."

"Ah." Aldred pulled out a cutter and snipped the end of his cigar before lighting it. Tossing the cutter and lighter to Simon, he sat back and puffed on his cigar.

The pleasant, almost sweet-smelling smoke of Aldred's preferred vanilla-flavored cigars filled the air.

Simon frowned, catching the lighter but missing the cutter. *What does he mean, "ah"? He doesn't sound surprised.* Reaching down between his feet, Simon picked up the cutter off the emerald-colored carpet. He studied it then pushed the plunger down. It was like a mini guillotine. He winced, once again thinking about what his mother would like to do to people she considered freaks of nature.

"That again? I thought she'd given up on the homosexual issue."

"She's done this before?" Simon snipped the end of his cigar and stuck it between his lips. Sure she'd gotten on her high horse about other issues before, but she'd never tried to make something punishable by death.

Aldred shrugged and pulled his cigar out of his mouth, holding it and his scotch in one hand. "She does it every few years, depending on who she's associating with." He took a puff from his cigar and crossed one black linen-clad leg over the other. "Let's see, she's been seen with the Viscountess Griffon and the Marchioness of Whipple lately. Both are patronesses of the Church of Englor. So, yes it makes sense. Plus with the recent scandal... Can't let the morality of Englor suffer, don't you know?"

"Morality?" Simon winced. He hadn't meant to shout, but damn it, how was this a morality issue?

Aldred's left eyebrow rose. "So she says. So most people say."

Disgusted, Simon shook his head and removed the cigar from his lips. "It's no more a moral issue than some debutantes preferring orange to pink or some lords having a fondness for brandy over scotch. Morality is whether it's right or wrong to kill someone, whether it's okay to steal. Who one chooses to sleep with is not a moral issue nor should it be against the law. Isn't adultery against the law? And yet over half the people in that ballroom behind us are adulterers, including my mother. You don't hear her or her friends wanting to make that punishable by death." Simon finally took a breath and tried to relax. Shouting at his uncle wasn't going to help matters. Sticking the cigar between his lips again, he fumbled with the lighter.

Gads, he was never going to get used to these things. None of it, the oddities of politics or the habits of the ton. They all seemed so shallow. He lit his cigar and promptly choked.

"Put that out before you kill yourself. You do not have to smoke." Aldred took another sip of his scotch and a puff off his own cigar, before tapping some of the ashes off in the green glass ashtray on the small table between their chairs.

Simon swigged his drink, trying to calm his hacking. It helped a little. "I keep thinking it will get better. I mean there must be some reason you and Father smoke the damned things."

Chuckling, Aldred shook his head. "Put it out. You don't have to master everything."

Simon snubbed out his cigar and leaned back in his chair, smiling. His uncle knew him too well. "I don't like it, Uncle." His grin melted from his face. "A government should protect its people...all of its people. It's not fair."

Aldred leaned forward, his own smile fading. "Life's not fair, Simon."

"No, it's not." His stomach plummeted to his feet. Simon set his glass on the table then ran his hands down his face. "My friend Proctor is a perfect example of political unjust. Roc is being forced to join the IN and then the Englor Marines against his wishes because he is a commoner, from a wealthy family, but one without a title nonetheless. The flip side of that is my friend Wycliffe wants a military career but his father refuses to buy him a commission. He insists the future Duke of Amberley must remain out of harm's way. What better way is there to learn to be a duke?" Simon sat forward, bracing his elbows on his knees. The unfairness of it all ate at him. "How can we expect people to respect us and follow our lead when the laws don't apply to us?" Hell, Simon himself had entertained the idea of fighting for his planet, but he'd never brought it up, knowing he'd be advised against it. "Why can't leaders make laws to protect and help their constituents? Why is it they only do things to protect their own interests?"

"I've heard all this before, my boy. Nothing has changed.

This is the way it works. That is how it has always been done, you know that." His uncle's voice was soft, almost sad.

"I do, but I don't like it. I've never liked it and I never will." That footman and Lord Gerald should be able to be together if that was what they wanted. Instead the footman was thrown out on his ear without a recommendation and Lord Gerald was sent to rusticate in the country.

"Then change it."

Simon blinked and met his uncle's gaze.

Aldred stared right at him, just as serious.

Just like that, it all seemed so clear. Why hadn't he seen it before? Simon stood, heading for the door, his mind made up. "I *will* change it. I'll lead by example." Since graduating from school last year, he'd been contemplating his life, his destiny. Wycliffe's reasons for wanting to join the service were sound and made sense. He thought it would help him more effectively manage his estate when it was passed down to him. And Simon agreed. The future of Englor rested on his shoulders. He was going to do what he considered honorable.

"Where are you going?"

Simon stopped, his hand on the doorknob, and turned to face his uncle. "I'm going to enlist in the Intergalactic Navy, then serve my planet in the Englor Marines."

Aldred's eyes widened and he juggled his cigar, nearly dropping it in his scotch. Simon was fairly certain some ashes fell in the drink. "Simon, the royal family does not serve in the military."

"No, but the common man is regulated by law to serve two years in the IN and two years in the Englor Marine Corps. to protect the freedoms of Englor and its peers. That hardly seems right." He turned back toward the door. No one was going to talk him out of this. "Besides, where else am I going to learn to lead?"

As he closed the door behind him he thought he heard, "That's my boy."

Chapter One

My parents may never recover from the trauma of having to ask me to put my hacking skills to good use after dissuading me from using them all these years.
—from the journal of Payton Marcus Townsend

January 15, 4830: the Lady Anna: Two parsecs outside of the Englor System

"Hurry, hurry, hurry." Payton looked around the engine room then back to the monitors in front of him. Almost done, download ninety-eight percent complete. *Come on.* If he could just get into the IN mainframes...

Dust. His hands were sweating. No sooner than he wiped them on his trousers, a drop of perspiration dripped down his temple as well. He dashed it away. *Get it together, Pay. If you're going to spy for your planet you can't go around looking like a nervous ninny.* This was the perfect plan. Hacking into the Englor Marines' message database from the Lady Anna would make it nearly impossible to trace. Even if there were cyber footprints, they wouldn't be detected until he was on Englor. No one would suspect *him.* Unless, of course, he failed to get out of here and back to his room unseen.

His com-pad beeped, signaling it was done. "Yes." Payton closed the two screens together, with the displays facing out so he could see what the ship's cameras were seeing. He was going to need it to get back to his room undetected. Bypassing sensors and cameras to hide his whereabouts was simple, but sneaking past crewmembers—Nate in particular—unseen proved a little more challenging.

After punching the buttons on the halo keyboard of the ship to log off, he pulled up the Lady Anna's cameras on his com-pad. Nate had brought Payton on this trip to work on deciphering a message Aiden and Trouble had intercepted, but Payton wanted to get a head start on looking into Colonel Hollister, who was mentioned in an intercepted letter by an Englorian Spy on Regelence. This should prove once and for all that Payton's unconventional computer skills were a blessing.

Pulling up the first camera on his screen, Payton hurried to the door. He could turn the camera off remotely, but he needed to see if there was anyone outside the door first. He brought up the view immediately outside the engine room door and then the next hallway to make certain no one was walking into this corridor. The coast was clear. Nothing out there but the ugly purple carpet and stark metal bulkhead. Who used violet on a ship? The IN colors were black, white and gold. Why not black carpet?

He tapped the window on his screen and the corridor disappeared. Payton opened the door and closed it quietly behind him. As he rushed toward the end of the hall he pulled up the next camera. Still clear. With a couple of touches of his fingertip, he turned off the camera and opened a window with the next view in it. *Dust.* Two sailors were headed his way. Payton looked around. There was a hatch directly across where he stood now. He did some fast tapping on the screen and opened a map. The room across from him was an officer's apartment. That wouldn't work. Where was a broom closet when you needed one?

He had mere seconds to decide what to do. The two men were about to round the corner. What were the odds they'd mention to Nate that they saw him? Payton ducked his head and plowed forward, like he was where he was supposed to be. Really he had no other choice, just standing there looking for a hiding place would definitely make him stand out. *Note to self:*

next time steal—no not steal, a Townsend did not steal—borrow a uniform.

The sailors came around the corner. Both were privates, both a little taller than Payton's five feet six inches. He hadn't seen either one of them before. Of course that wasn't surprising, there were over two hundred crewmen on the ship. Fortunately, neither man paid Payton any mind. They walked right past him, still engrossed in their conversation.

Payton let out the breath he'd been holding and brought up the next camera view. That had been amazingly easy. But this was where it could get tricky. The corridor opened up into a four-way intersection. Two of the branches led to the public areas of the ship. The hall he was in led to the engine room, and the hall directly across from him led to his quarters. The problem was, the cross sections were usually busy. *Maybe the same trick would work?* At this point he had nothing to lose. The closer he got to his room, the antsier he became. On his screen the intersection appeared devoid of personnel, but Payton had no illusions that it would stay that way. He turned off the camera, put his com-pad under his arm and raised his nose in the air. *Nothing to see here. Just taking a stroll, stretching my legs.*

As Payton reached the halfway point of the intersection, a husky female voice said, "Aye-aye, Admiral."

Stardust and imploding planets, there was only one Admiral on board. Payton looked in time to see Nate turning away from Captain Brittani Kindros and toward the intersection. *Dust.* Payton took off running. He didn't stop until he got to his hatch. He darted inside and leaned against the smooth metallic panel when it closed behind him. He'd tell Nate what he'd done, but he wanted to wait until after he had some information to impart.

His hard-headed macho Admiral brother-in-law would throttle him if he got caught. Despite bringing Payton for his hacking talent, Nate was trying to keep Payton's involvement to a minimum. At least that's what Payton suspected.

He took a deep breath and pulled himself together. Using

his screen, he brought the cameras back up.

Nate turned down the hallway that led to Payton's room. Even Payton had to admit how sexy the commanding air surrounding Nate was. The man really was something. Even though he was so big and masculine, he moved with an elegant grace that spoke of his upbringing. And he looked every inch the earl right this second in his crisp brown morning coat, brown pinstriped waistcoat and cream-colored cravat. Aiden was a lucky man...and any minute Payton would be a dead one.

He'd told Nate he was going to nap after Nate had soundly beaten him at chess. His black leather case sat by the chaise he'd deserted to go play spy. He raced toward it and deposited his com-pad into it. He needed to look like he'd been here the whole time. As he sat down he reached into the outer pocket of his case. The knock came just as Payton grabbed his leather-bound journal and pulled it into his lap. He scrambled for a pen.

Payton took a deep shuddering breath, trying to slow his racing heart, opened the book and held his pen like he was writing. "Come in."

Nate met Payton's gaze and smiled almost reluctantly. "You've been writing in your journal?" The hatch shut behind him.

"Yes." Payton smiled. *Please don't let him see how hard I'm breathing.*

Nate's brows pulled together, his forehead furrowing. "Okay, I thought I— Never mind. So, tell me, how is it someone as computer savvy as you records his journal on paper rather than his computer? You've rarely been without that thing"— Nate dipped his head toward Payton's computer bag, which lay beside the chaise—"the entire trip. You're nearly as bad as your brother with his sketchscreens."

Payton shrugged. "I know better than anyone how easy it is to hack into computers."

Nate's face went comically blank. "Are you telling me that your personal computer is not secure?"

No computer is secure with someone who knows what he's

doing. Payton laughed, hoping it didn't sound nervous. "Of course it is. If you are concerned about household computers breaking in, you need not, even Jeffers can't get into my compad and I've programmed him to be able to take a peek at other computers that enter the castle."

"Good." The tension in Nate's shoulders eased and he came further into the room. He smelled good, smoky and kind of sweet, like he'd smoked a flavored cigar. Payton had always liked that smell. Taking a seat on the edge of the chaise, Nate crossed one leg over the other, stretching his feet out in front of him. He gestured toward Payton's journal, making a "give it here" motion.

Payton's mouth dropped open. He shook his head and clutched it to his chest. What was wrong with Nate? Surely he didn't expect Payton to allow him to read his journal.

Nate sighed and held his hand out. "I'm not going to read it."

"Then why do you want it?" Admiral, brother-in-law and guardian at the moment not withstanding, there was no way Payton was turning it over. Nate would have to physically take it from him, and for all Nate's brute strength Payton didn't think the man had it in him. He was so gentle with Aiden. Not that Payton didn't think Nate could be rough and dangerous, the man exuded danger from every pore, but Payton didn't think Nate would, not over a journal anyway. He'd overheard his brother tell Nate to keep Payton safe. And as silly as Payton thought that was—he could take care of himself after all—he knew Nate would never break a promise to Aiden.

"Flip to a blank page and give it here." Nate's eyes narrowed. He was serious.

Payton shook his head so hard he felt like Muffin being told to get her bath. He inched his way to the side of the chaise, preparing to run. Childish and cowardly it might be, but *no one* read his journal.

Moving surprisingly quick for such a big man, Nate snagged the leather-bound book and the pen out of Payton's arms.

Mine. Gasping, Payton lunged at him.

Nate caught him easily and shoved him back to his seat.

Payton landed on his arse with a jolt, even on the soft cushion.

Flipping to the back of the book, Nate wrote something. Within seconds he offered the book and pen to Payton.

What in the bloody hell? Maybe Nate hadn't lost his mind. Payton snatched the book from his brother-in-law's hand, giving him a glare for good measure.

Nate smiled. "I'm impressed. Your brother probably would have attacked me if that were him and his sketchscreen."

Payton didn't bother mentioning that he *had* tried to attack Nate, but Nate had pretty much swatted him away like a pesky fly. Being small rained meteors. Still frowning, he looked down at the journal.

On the unlined paper was a surprisingly elegant scrawl. *Can you secure this room so we can talk privately?*

The tightness in Payton's chest eased. The Lady Anna, like Jeffers, had listening capabilities in the private quarters. Nate wasn't losing his mind, he just didn't want to take a chance of the IN being alerted that he had silenced the ship.

Nodding, Payton reached over the side of the chaise, stuffed his journal into his bag and grabbed his com-pad. He hadn't turned it off, so all he had to do was flip it open. In seconds, he had the computer locked out of this room and the adjoining suite that belonged to Nate, just in case the speakers were ultra sensitive. He glanced up at Nate. "Okay."

"Okay? That was quick."

Yeah, it was, since he'd already been inside the ship's computer, but he wasn't going to tell Nate that. "I'm good."

Nate chuckled. "You are indeed, I'm impressed. I wanted to talk to you about our plan. You're going to Englor as my aide and an IN lieutenant."

Huh? Payton's jaw dropped open for the second time in minutes. "Beg pardon?"

"I've had Brittani fake your records. No one will know but

the two of us...and Brittani."

"And Captain Kindros is trustworthy?"

"Absolutely." Nate said it so quickly and with such confidence. "But you trust no one but myself. Understood?"

"Yes, sir. What if someone recognizes me?"

"I doubt that will be a problem. But if they do you will just pretend to be flattered and tell them thank you, being a Regelen it is quite an honor to be mistaken for Prince Payton." Nate grinned. "You *are,* however, not Payton Townsend, but Lieutenant Payton Jeffers. You answer only to me. I have uniforms for you with my things. We will change on the space station before going down to Englor. Do you think you can act like a soldier?"

"Jeffers?" Jeffers was the name of his family's computer butler. Payton smiled. This was going to be fun. "Aye-aye, Admiral, I think I can handle it. Are you forgetting where I was raised and how revered soldiers are on Regelence?" He gave Nate a crisp salute. Pretending to be a soldier would be simple.

Nate chuckled and shook his head. "Good. I'll have to talk to my family to make certain they don't give you away, but other than that I believe we are set."

"Not quite."

One of Nate's dark brows rose. "Oh?"

They were fairly certain the IN was behind the stolen weapons stash and the kidnapping of Payton's brother Aiden a few months ago since Nate had identified the spy as an IN Intelligence Agent, but even after Aiden's return they weren't certain if Englor was involved or, if so, to what extent. Englor could be a great ally in a confrontation with the IN, but first they had to be certain Englor wasn't in bed with the enemy. "What other sources do you want me to try? Should I get into IN Intelligence and Colonel Hollister's computer for a peek around?"

Payton was nearly positive the encoded message Nate's son, Trouble, had intercepted a few months back had been a stolen message intended for Colonel Hollister from his spy Benson.

Benson had been Aiden's valet for several months but no one had realized he was a spy until after he was killed trying to protect Aiden.

After some digging around Payton had ascertained that the code was Englorian, but since he didn't know Englorian encryption, that still left him with a lot of work to do. Hopefully, his recent adventure, breaking into the Englor message system, would aid him in figuring out the code. "We still need to learn what Benson was doing on Regelence," Payton reminded Nate.

"I'm going to ask around...discreetly. And if that doesn't work, we'll ask a little more forcefully."

Yes. "Like an interrogation? Torture?" Payton leaned forward. The danger of getting caught was exciting. It would be like shutting down Jeffers, their butler at Townsend castle, only more intense, more like setting up the program to hack Englor's mainframes.

Nate laughed and shook his head. "No. Well yes, but you aren't going to be with me if it comes to that."

Dust. Payton sat back in his seat, his shoulders slumping. *Wait.* He leaned forward again. "You can't do it by yourself, you'll need back up." Nate shook his head again, but Payton didn't wait to be turned down. "I'm an excellent shot with a fragger and competent with a sword. I'm also trained in hand-to-hand combat, although admittedly I haven't a lot of practice with it."

"No. You're here to help me decipher that coded message. There's no way I'm going to put you in the line of fire. Any information I need you to decipher, I'll *bring* to you."

Oh bloody hell. Payton slumped back into the chaise. "What good is all my schooling if I'm never going to use it?"

"Are you not using your computer skills?"

"I wasn't taught the particular computer skills I'm using, I learned them myself. I was referring to the different survival techniques all young lords are forced to learn. Like fencing and martial arts." Here he was away from home and he was still going to be coddled like a child. At least Nate did want him using his more controversial technological knowledge. That was something.

"What exactly does your education consist of? Aiden thinks the majority of it is useless, that it's all about obtaining a consort and running a household."

"Some of it was. I suppose for Aiden a lot of it was a waste of time. After taking his first art class, all he ever wanted to do was draw. He only did enough of the other stuff to keep from getting in trouble so he could get back to his art. But for the rest of us..." Payton used a little of all of it. "We're taught math and English of course, French, Latin and Italian. The basic computer skills, economics and diplomacy are touched on as well as history and science. I don't see myself ever using music or art and I wish I didn't have to use dancing, but all of those were included as well as basic self-defense. We probably learned more self-defense than most lords do. Cony thought it was very important. He still makes us spar with him on occasion just to make certain we remember."

Nate seemed to consider it for a moment. "Very well, should the need arise I'll include you on the breaking and entering."

Payton smiled. This trip was promising to be quite an adventure. "Perhaps this is a good time to tell you I've hacked into the Englor message center."

January 15, 4830: Planet Englor: Hollister House in London, Moreal (The ruling country of Englor)

Please let there be word on Benson. Simon slid off the saddle, so wrapped up in his thoughts he nearly missed the greeting from his groom. Handing Cirilo's reins over, Simon smiled and mumbled thank you. He climbed the steps to his townhouse, turning his attention back to his missing informant. He'd first sent Benson to Regelence after overhearing his mother arguing with a man in the Earl of Clifton's garden during a ball the earl and countess were throwing to celebrate their youngest

son's commission into the Marines. Simon normally bowed out
of social events, but the earl's son was a friend and had served
with Simon in the IN.

His mother was always into something—she went through
lovers like most people went through tissues. Her arguing with
a lover wasn't surprising, but there had been a desperation to
her voice Simon hadn't heard before. It had raised enough red
flags to make him conceal himself and listen. Upon hearing the
man's demand for schematics, Simon had known he'd better
find out what was going on.

"Stop right there, Colonel."

Damn. Simon froze, his foot hovering over the threshold of
his front door. What now? He was cold, wet and—was that him
that smelled so foul? He dipped his head toward his chest and
sniffed. His nose twitched. Yeah, that was him. The ride home
on Cirilo wasn't bad, but having handed the thoroughbred over
to his groom the wind was no longer breezing past him. Instead,
it was at his back, blowing the stench toward him. "Dunston,
it's freezing out here, I smell horrible and Roc and I have to get
ready to meet Wycliffe for dinner at White's. I have to shower."
From the appearance of the horizon, a storm was moving in at a
rather fast clip.

"According to my sensors your boots are covered in mud
and all manner of vile substances. The staff has just cleaned
Hollister House from top to bottom and I'll not have you
defacing the mansion with that filth. Remove the boots,
Colonel," the smooth deep voice ordered evenly.

Knowing better than to argue, Simon groaned as he
reached down and tugged on his right boot. His hand covered
slime. *Ah yuck.* "Stupid computer," he mumbled under his
breath.

"I heard that."

Of course he did. Dunston heard everything, Dunston saw
everything and Dunston *knew* everything. One of these days,
Simon was going to reprogram him.

"Whatever happened to you, Colonel?"

Simon reached for his other boot. Oh galaxy, something

28

squishy wiggled between his toes. "I rescued Lady Eleanor Pimpernickle's new puppy from the Serpentine in Hyde Park."

"Ho there, out of the way, Si. What's the hold up? It's cold out here." Roc jostled Simon aside and stepped onto the polished green marble foyer of Simon's townhouse with sludgy, pond-mucked boots.

Simon let go of his own boot to keep from falling on his arse and caught his balance on the balustrade of the porch steps. "Roc..."

"Outside, Major Bennett. If you track up this mansion you *will* clean it."

Roc's shoulders slumped and his head drooped as he backed out of the foyer. He frowned at Simon, his tawny brows pulled together, looking for all the world like a petulant child.

Simon bit his bottom lip to keep from laughing. At least Dunston was an equal opportunity tyrant. "Dunston, send Henderson out after our boots."

"Damned butler is worse that an IN drill sergeant," Roc grumbled as he used his right boot to toe off his left.

"I can hear you from outside, Major," Dunston said. "Henderson is on his way with some towels."

Roc's mouth dropped open and a piece of brown pond scum slipped down the shoulder of his gray morning coat and went splat on the concrete steps.

Simon couldn't hold it in. He chuckled and returned his attention to his other boot. It came off with a slurping sound and he held it upside down. A piece of brownish green slime and what looked like a couple of tadpoles fell onto the steps. The moldy smell intensified. *Ewww...* What was in that lake water? He wiped his dirty hand on his trousers and grinned up at Roc.

"Oh laugh it up. That's the last time I let you talk me into playing the hero. Stupid dog was only taking a swim. Don't know why the silly chit was shrieking like a harpy. She shouldn't have let go of his leash."

"You wouldn't be the least bit out of sorts if it were a pretty little lord." Simon tugged off one stocking, then the other. Roc was all talk. He was always up for a good heroic adventure.

Thunder clapped, startling a hop out of both of them.

Roc frowned up at the sky. "Looks like we'll be taking a lift to White's." He reached for his other boot. "I'm not walking bare arsed into the house, Si."

"I doubt that will be necessary. And she did thank us."

"She thanked *you*." His Hessian came off and Roc started on his stockings. Glancing up at Simon, Roc fluttered his eyelashes. "Oh thank you, Your Highness," he mocked in a high voice.

Simon threw his sock, hitting his friend in the chest with it.

"That is disgusting." Dropping his own soaked stocking, Roc peeled Simon's off himself with his finger and thumb. He looked up at Simon with a wicked gleam in his eyes.

Oh shit. Simon laughed and hightailed it into the townhouse. The beeswax and lemon scent of furniture polish washed over him before the putrid pond odor overpowered it. He dashed toward the stairs and nearly knocked the armful of towels out of his footman's arms. "Sorry, Henderson."

Henderson sputtered, "Colonel," then there was a spat and a loud shriek.

Simon turned around, his hand slipping on the polished banister. Thunder cracked outside, echoing in the marble and wood foyer.

The stocking Roc had intended to throw at Simon slid down Henderson's face before falling to the marble foyer with a splatter.

Simon burst into laughter as Roc raced forward, apologizing profusely. *And Aldred wonders why I have a hard time keeping servants since I moved out of military housing.* He was going to have to give Henderson a raise again.

As Simon stepped out of the shower, Roc entered the room, brushing a towel over his chestnut hair. They'd never been more than friends, nor did Simon want to be, but Simon still took the time to admire the view.

Roc wore black trousers, his shoes and an unbuttoned white shirt, with a snowy cravat hanging loose around his neck. Tossing his towel at the hamper next to the bathing room door, he picked up one end of his cravat and let it fall. "Can you tie this bloody thing or loan me your valet?"

Simon grabbed his own towel and began drying off. "Tell Dunston to send Adams up. I thought you were wearing your dress blues."

"I was, but your footman got even for the stocking mishap and brought back evening wear when he went to retrieve them from my apartment." Roc scoffed. "Who is Adams?"

Chuckling, Simon wrapped his towel around his hips. Henderson was a worthy opponent. Maybe he'd stick around longer than the others had. "Adams is my new valet."

Roc's mouth dropped open. "You're jesting. What happened to Patterson?"

"Wycliffe clocked him with a water balloon and a bag of flour." Simon retrieved his comb, nudging Roc out from in front of the mirror. "The two of you are going to have to stop assaulting my staff."

"Don't go blaming Wycliffe and me. As I remember it, you're the one who made Tinkerton quit." Roc turned and leaned against the bathroom vanity, watching Simon comb his hair.

Simon groaned at the reminder. He hadn't meant to dunk the under butler in the fishpond in back of the townhouse. It wasn't like Simon knew that Cook had dropped her handkerchief in there on her morning walk. And really, Simon couldn't be held accountable for the man looking like Wycliffe from behind.

A loud clap of thunder rattled the windows and immediately after rain pelted the townhouse. Roc winced. "Dust, can't remember the last time we had one like this. Sure hope the leak in my roof was fixed. Damned military housing."

"Why do you think I bought myself a townhouse? Marine housing implodes planets and no way in hell was I staying in the IN barracks." Simon tossed his comb onto the counter and went to his dressing room. *Uniform or evening dress?*

"You really should talk to your father about more funding for military living quarters." Roc picked up Simon's discarded comb and followed him into the dressing room.

"Talked to my uncle about it when I moved out of my apartment on base. He was going to draft a bill to present it to parliament." Simon opened the closet and took out his IN dress blues. "The problem is, since we share the base with the IN, parliament wants the IN to help with the costs." Turning toward Roc, he took his jacket and shirt off the hanger.

Roc dropped the comb on the chaise in front of the closet.

"That doesn't belong there." Simon laid his jacket and pants on the back of the chaise and put his shirt on. Once again he contemplated the Benson problem. Where was the man and why hadn't he checked in?

Groaning, Roc snagged the comb off the chaise. He took it back to the washroom, then leaned against the doorframe. "Are you going to Gentleman Jackson's tonight?"

"I hadn't planned on it." Simon began buttoning his shirt as he crossed to the dresser to retrieve underclothes. "Was going to go workout tomorrow evening after work. Why?" He tossed his towel aside and pulled on his short drawers. "Don't tell me you're ready to step back into the boxing ring."

Roc snorted, rolled his right shoulder and clutched it with his left hand. "I should say not. My arm still hurts from pummeling Wycliffe."

Last time they'd gone to Gentleman Jackson's, Roc had challenged Wycliffe to a match and neither had fared well. Or perhaps both had? At any rate neither was fit for public viewing for several days, and they'd both cried off working out with Simon. Simon retrieved his trousers from the chaise. "If I remember correctly, Wycliffe nailed you in that shoulder."

"Colonel, there is a lieutenant here to see you. He says he has an urgent message for you," Dunston said. "Shall I have him seen to your study?"

Simon stepped into his trousers and pulled them up in a hurry, nearly hopping toward the door. "Is he an Englor soldier or an IN soldier?" It could be either, but he hoped for the former.

"He is in an Englor Marine uniform, Colonel."

Yes. It was information he'd been waiting on.

Roc raised a brow. "Benson?"

He sure hoped so. Tucking in his shirt, Simon fastened his trousers. "Dunston, please make the lieutenant comfortable in my study. I'll be right down." Maybe Benson had found more information. Perhaps even some that would paint his mother in a better light, although he highly doubted it.

"When is the last time you heard from him?"

Simon grabbed his shoes from the closet and sat on the edge of the chaise to put them and his socks on. "It's been several months since his last message." And *that* message had been way too brief, containing only two letters, *IN.* Which could mean anything or nothing. Simon was an IN soldier as well as an Englor Marine. Their base was both IN and Englor Marine. The message was not the damning evidence Simon needed. He finished tying his shoes and stood. "You coming?"

Roc nodded. "You bet. This concerns me too."

It did indeed. It concerned all of Englor if Simon's suspicions were correct.

When they entered the study, the gangly blond lieutenant stood and saluted. His hair and uniform were wet from the rain, but Simon recognized him as the messenger assigned to pick up Benson's messages every week.

"Colonel Hollister, Major Bennett." Boyd was fresh out of the IN, starting his first year with the Englor Marines.

"Lieutenant Boyd." Simon motioned the younger man toward the fireplace to the right of his desk. "Dunston, leave the room please and secure it, until I call your name again. Boyd, stand in front of the fire and get warm."

"Yes, Colonel." The study door clicked shut.

Roc took a seat in the chair in front of Simon's desk, his

cravat still untied. "Where is the message, Lieutenant?"

"There has been no recent news. Our go-between hasn't heard from Lieutenant Benson in over three months."

Damn. Something wasn't right. And why hadn't Benson sent any other messages? What had happened to Benson? He'd been instructed to check in every two weeks, whether he had information or not. Simon glanced past the lieutenant at Roc.

Roc met his gaze and frowned, obviously coming to the same conclusion as Simon.

Damn it. What if they'd been found out? This situation was getting more and more complicated. What if Benson were being held captive...or worse?

Simon crossed to the bar and poured himself a scotch. First, he needed to send someone to locate Lieutenant Benson. "Lieutenant Boyd, how'd you get here?"

"I walked, sir."

Thunder echoed through the study, followed by a loud crack of lightning. Simon and Boyd both started. Roc mumbled, "Damn," under his breath and stood. He walked to the window and pulled the curtain aside, peering out. "It's really storming out there."

Simon tossed back the rest of his scotch and set the tumbler on the bar. "Dunston?"

"Yes, Colonel?"

"Please have a lift brought around to take Lieutenant Boyd back to the base."

Boyd rubbed his hands together in front of the fire. "Thank you, sir."

"Colonel, the lift is on its way," Dunston announced.

Simon nodded and crossed to his desk. "When you get back to base, change into a dry uniform, Lieutenant. You're dismissed."

Boyd saluted before leaving the room.

"Stardust and imploding planets." Simon dropped into his chair, leaned back and put his hands over his face. "Dunston, secure the room again." Interlacing his fingers, he put his hands behind his head and stared up at the wood-paneled ceiling.

"Any idea what Benson meant by IN?"

"I have no idea." Did he want Simon to go to the IN for help?

Roc shrugged. "Do you still have the message before last?"

"Yes." He had all the messages memorized.

"Tell me what it said again."

"Benson overheard his fellow valet telling someone that he thought he had their man set up to get the cloning technology once he married into the family. He said the royal bitch, which we have deduced to be my mother, only knew that she would get the money when she gave him the schematics."

"Right. What schematics? And why would she need money?"

"Gambling debts would be my guess. My father refuses to support her gaming." Simon closed his eyes and shook his head. "And I wish I knew what schematics. I haven't been able to find out. I've been discreetly asking around to see if the IN or the Englor Marines have developed a new ship or weapon or...anything." Maybe they needed to take their Marine commander, General Davidson, out for drinks and see if they could get him to talk.

Simon sat up and scanned his thumb on the desk scanner, opened his top drawer and pulled out Benson's last note.

Roc frowned. "I haven't heard anything either. Admittedly, I haven't devoted much time to it. I've been hoping Benson would come through with more information."

"You and me both." Silently, Simon read the next line. *The valet said that Azrael has no idea I am here but I think he might suspect us. And remember, we always have her child to use if we have to.* "Who is Azrael?" he wondered aloud. Did the note mean Azrael's child or the queen's? Simon couldn't imagine what anyone could have on him. The only possibility would be his being gay, but it would be very hard to prove.

"I suspect we'll have an easier time figuring out what

cloning technology and schematics they're talking about." Roc shrugged and let go of the curtain. "Azrael is an angel, isn't he?"

"Right, he was the angel of death. It's a code name, but for who?" Simon asked.

"That is a good question. Do you think Benson wants us to go to the IN with the info we have?"

"I'm not doing anything until I find out more."

"Good plan."

"Maybe we can skip White's and go straight to Jackson's. A good fight might make me feel better."

"I'm only boxing with you if you promise not to hit back." Roc let go of the curtain and turned to face Simon. "We need to find Benson, and figure out what the bloody hell is going on."

Lightning crackled and the lights flickered. Simon sat forward, resting his elbows on the desk.

In the foyer, right outside the study door, a deep male voice yelled, "Bloody hell." Then Dunston announced, "Colonel Eason is here to see you, Colonel."

What was Wycliffe doing here? They were supposed to meet him at White's. "Let him in, Dunston."

Wycliffe stepped into the study, bringing the scent of rain with him. His Marine uniform was crisp and dry as was his black hair. He held his cover in his hand, his lips pressed tight in a grim line. Closing the door behind him, he sought out Simon's gaze, then Roc's. "Admiral Hawkins is coming to inspect the base."

The lights flickered once again before going off. Immediately, the hum of Dunston's backup generators whirled, and the lights came back on.

Simon groaned. "When it rains it pours."

Chapter Two

It has occurred to me that on Englor I will have no need for a chaperone, and as far as I know Nate has not procured one for me. And to think...all it took was a spy to kidnap my brother and his stepson.

—from the journal of Payton Marcus Townsend

Payton put his journal away and retrieved his com-pad when it beeped. He'd been waiting to see a likeness of Colonel Hollister for the last fifteen minutes. With all the excitement last night—arriving on the base and moving his things to his new room—he hadn't gotten a chance to search for a picture of Colonel Hollister. When he'd begun his search this morning, he'd found it a lot harder than he'd expected. Hollister's files were highly classified, probably due to his royal status. He had a high military rank, but as an admiral's aide, Payton should have had access to it. He didn't, but that hadn't stopped him from obtaining it. He grinned and flipped through the file.

The picture was blurry, but Simon Hollister wasn't at all what Payton expected. He was tall and thin. Very young looking. It was hard to tell what color his hair was because of the short military buzz cut, but it looked dark. Sadly there was no date on the picture. Payton dragged his finger across the screen, flipping pages. There was an impressive war record, but no more photos. Why had the heir to Englor been in action? That couldn't be right. Payton frowned. Hollister had joined the IN as a private and worked his way up to lieutenant. He'd served on a space destroyer for most of his IN career then joined the Englor Marines as a colonel in the cavalry. He'd then been given honorary rank of colonel in the IN and command of the Englor Base. His career in the military did not appear to be ornamental. *Interesting.*

Payton closed the file and turned off his com-pad. He'd have to search for another photo of Hollister. He'd never recognize the man if he ran into him.

Going to the washroom, he added locating another picture to his mental list. *Break in to the IN intelligence and see if I can find anything on the IN spy who'd kidnapped Aiden, under the name Caldwell. Find a better picture of Hollister. Crack that damned code.* Galaxy, he had a lot of work ahead of him.

Upon spying his reflection in the mirror, Payton smiled. He almost looked...handsome. No one would dare call him cute in IN dress whites. This was a uniform that inspired power and authority, not cuteness. The uniform also made him look...bigger. He turned sideways, trying to see his back. He really *did* look larger. The shoulder boards and gold cords made his chest look wider and not so adolescent, more like a man. His height, however, was a lost cause. He was short and no way was he wearing high heels to change that. Smoothing his hands down the front of his uniform, he stepped away from the mirror. He'd always thought military uniforms were dashing.

Payton walked away from the mirror and out of the tiny dark-blue-tiled washroom. His small room had stark white walls, a twin bed with iron headboard and footboard. It had a simple iron and wood desk and chair opposite the door and an oak dresser across from the bed. The only real color was the navy carpet, single curtain over the window across from the door and the bedspread. It wasn't at all what he was used to, but it wasn't bad. The room had a simple, masculine feel to it. He kind of liked it. It was...normal.

The knock at the door made Payton jump. That must be Lieutenant Tavis, to take him to his office.

Late last night, Lieutenant Tavis had shown him and Nate to their quarters. This morning, Nate was touring the base with

Colonel Hollister, aka heir to the throne of Englor, aka the man Payton and Nate were investigating, while Payton scoped out the computers in their offices and made certain everything was secure. He and Nate hadn't said much last night, being unsure of their privacy, but Nate had made it clear that Payton was supposed to familiarize himself with the surveillance situation on the base and in their offices in particular.

Payton crossed to the door, opened it and came face to chest with a pristine white navy uniform with shiny gold buttons covering an impressive torso, standing at attention. Lifting his head, he finally found the officer's handsome face. Mmm...the man smelled fresh out of the shower. Yes, his brown hair was still a little damp. He must have come directly from his own housing.

Payton fought back a wince—he hated lying about who he was—and smiled instead. "At ease."

Lieutenant Tavis's coppery eyes danced with merriment as his stance eased. The man was very cheerful, Payton noticed it last night as well. "Good morning, Lieutenant." He stepped aside, allowing Payton to exit. "Did you sleep well?"

"I did, thank you. I appreciate you showing me to my office." Payton turned back to the desk where his black com-pad bag lay. "Just a moment, I need to get my computer and I'll be ready to go." He grabbed his bag, slinging the strap over his shoulder. After letting the door close behind him, he pressed his thumb to the scanner on the door and locked it.

"Have you eaten breakfast, sir?" Tavis dipped his head to a fellow soldier in passing before glancing at Payton.

On Regelence during the season, breakfast began at ten o'clock or later. Payton wasn't accustomed to eating so early. Nor was he accustomed to getting up so early. There were times when he and his brothers were just getting home from a ball at five in the morning. "Please, call me Payton. I'm not much of a breakfast person. I'm supposed to meet Admiral Hawkins for lunch later."

"Then please call me Edward. Mind if I ask you a question, Payton?" Tavis sounded so serious. His gaze darted around and the look on his face grew hesitant.

"I can't say until you ask me." Payton grinned, trying to ease the tension and encourage the man to talk. Anything he learned and any friend he made while here on Englor could potentially benefit him.

"Yes, I suppose you're right." He chuckled and continued to lead Payton outside the glass doors at the end of the hall and into the bright sunlight. It was chilly and windy out, though thankfully the uniform was nice and thick. If he went a great length he'd need to get his coat, but judging from last night's quick observation when they'd arrived, his office wouldn't be far. Tavis wasn't wearing a coat.

Payton tried not to look at Tavis, not wanting to pressure him, but he was curious what the man was so reluctant to ask. Since it was daytime, Payton took the time to look around for anything he might have missed last night. There was a sidewalk meandering around a grassy campus. Each of the buildings were a good twenty to thirty feet apart and connected by the wide cement sidewalk.

Finally, the lieutenant broke the silence, nodding like he'd come to a decision. "What is he like? The admiral?"

Payton had expected something like that. Nate, being a native Englorian and one of the most powerful men in the IN, would definitely be a source of curiosity. Not to mention the soldiers thought Nate was here to inspect their base. Which he was. It just wasn't the only reason they were here. "He's a good man, fair, just don't get on his bad side. But most of the time he has a good sense of humor."

Tavis pointed at a set of brick buildings with several men going in and out, all in uniform, some blue, some white. "That's the mess hall."

Good galaxy, all the men were so big. Payton suppressed the urge to grin. It was always nice to have pleasant scenery. What, was it some rule you had to be over six foot and musclebound to be on this base? Not that Payton was complaining, he preferred big men, but it made him feel... Maybe he'd take advantage of the gym while he was here.

Shrugging his bag up on his shoulder, he made himself stop gawking. Heck, he needed to workout just to be able to haul his bag around. It was getting heavy. "Are you Englorian, Edward?"

Tavis nodded. "Yes. Admiral Hawkins is a bit of a legend around here. Did you know his family is part of the peerage of Englor? His father is the Duke of Hawthorne. Englorians are quite proud to claim him as one of our own. Most of polite society isn't even aware of his unfortunate marriage."

His unfortunate marriage? Nate married a prince, third in line to the throne of Regelence, if one didn't count Cony. How was that unfortunate? *Oh.* Tavis referred to the fact that Aiden was a man instead of a woman. Payton swallowed the lump in his throat. He'd known Englor was not like Regelence, Nate had warned him so, but the way Tavis said that... Payton's stomach clenched. Tavis hadn't sounded hostile, but it was clear from what he'd said some soldiers thought preferring men to women was a defect in one's personality. *What have I gotten myself into?* It was a stark reminder that he was on foreign soil.

"Ah, here we are. These are the IN offices. The building across the way"—Tavis pointed at a white building with a rounded portico with four Doric columns supporting it—"is the Englor Marine officers office building." They stopped in front of a red brick colonial-style building with white fluted columns on either side of the door. He opened the glass door and held it open for Payton to precede him. "Colonel Hollister, our base commander, has his office in the Englor Marine building— technically, he's both an IN officer and an Englor Marine officer—but everyone else you may need to contact should be in here."

Payton nodded. It was good to know. He'd have to pull up that building's surveillance cameras to get a look at Hollister.

When they walked in there were several people milling about, men and women, all in IN uniforms.

Payton swallowed hard, feeling like a phony. His heart sped up. There was such respect and tradition in the IN that he felt ashamed for deceiving these people. He consoled himself with the fact that it was necessary to protect his home, his family and his beloved Regelence.

A tall thin ensign stepped forward. "Permission to speak freely, Lieutenant?"

"Permission granted"—Payton glanced at the man's name tag—"Adams."

Adams smiled. "Were you with Admiral Hawk on Regelence when he was promoted to Admiral?"

Not only was there excitement in the ensign's voice, but Payton noticed he suddenly had undivided attention from the room as a whole. These men and women clearly looked to Nate as a hero, a sort of celebrity. It amused him further knowing his brother-in-law would grumble about the attention and his brother would beam proudly while encouraging the admiration of his spouse. He could almost hear Aiden bubbling over with details about the ceremony, and Nate mumbling at him to behave. "Yes, I was. I was lucky enough to have been present at the ceremony."

There were excited whispers about Nate's heroics and him in general.

Tavis dipped his head, not even trying to conceal his grin. "If you're ready, Lieutenant, I'll show you to your office. It's right next to the admiral's." He held out his hand, indicating the way to the offices.

"Yes, please." Payton followed Tavis toward a narrow hallway.

As they left, a man from behind them quietly said, "Too bad the admiral is a sodomite." A fair amount of hostility laced the voice, and Payton had to fight the urge to turn around to spot the speaker.

His spine stiffened in outrage and he had to remind himself to relax. He wanted to give them all a piece of his mind. The only thing that stopped him and made him continue down the hall was his resolve to finish this assignment, for the sake of his planet.

Bloody hell and imploding stars. Payton resisted banging

his head against the desk. He'd known hacking into the IN Intelligence agency would be tough, but it was bloody nerve-wracking as well. He had to take extra precautions to make certain his efforts to break in weren't detected. He'd been trying for the past few hours and gotten nowhere. A challenge was nice, but it was getting old. There had been nothing but challenges since he started working on deciphering the message Trouble had confiscated. His brain hurt.

At least he hadn't had to worry about the personnel on the base seeing what he was up to. His desk faced the door, with his computer out of eyeshot to anyone unless they came into the office and stepped up behind him. There wasn't even a window at his back that he had to worry about—it was to his side at the end of the office—so he'd elected to leave his door open hoping to pick up on some gossip. Unfortunately, he also spent the time before lunch pretending not to notice all the impressive men in uniform passing his open door. It was hard not to wonder about every one of them. Did they think his genetic makeup perverse? How many of them pretended to be fine with Nate but really weren't?

He shook himself out of his musings and got back to work. They knew Caldwell was an IN spy, thanks to Nate. If Payton could get into the Intelligence files, he might be able to see what Caldwell—or whatever his name really was—was doing on Regelence.

It was twelve fifty and Nate wasn't back yet. If it weren't for feeling so out of place among the musclebound, studly men, he'd go get his own lunch. He was getting a headache and his stomach was rumbling.

It was almost humorous. Here he was without a chaperone with all these super masculine men and not a one of them would want him. Not that he had any intention of compromising himself—he had been raised better than that—but even if he wanted to it wasn't likely to happen. He was having a hard time not gawking since he'd always had a liking for large men and men in uniform in particular. Hell, he'd been raised to have a preference for men in uniform. It was in his DNA, just as it was all the other lords on Regelence. It was disconcerting to say the least. He'd never had to hide who he was. Even on Regelence he'd been allowed to admire from a distance, with a chaperone of course. Now he understood why he wasn't assigned a chaperone here. He didn't need one.

Shaking himself out of his musings, Payton changed screens. While the program he'd designed continued to mask his presence and get into the Intelligence office, he'd copy surveillance vids and dog-tag registries to his com-pad. In the files was everything he could possibly want to know about everyone on the base, including their working hours and what they did. Every building had a registry which automatically tallied military personnel's presence by their dog tag. The program he'd set up to retrieve messages while he was still on the Lady Anna had turned up nothing. He'd yet to find any messages to Colonel Hollister, but he wasn't giving up. Maybe he'd find something out by watching surveillance videos. At the very least he should be able to find Nate on the videos from this morning and see what Colonel Hollister looked like.

When he typed in "S", several S names popped up. The "I" narrowed it down further, Sidell, Silsby and several Simon's. There were about twenty of them. Dust, Simon was a popular name on Englor. He finished typing in the "M", "O" and "N", then scrolled down to the H's he found *Hollister* in the building registries. Several buildings popped up. The mess hall, the Englor Marine building, the gym. Oddly, the building where the officer's quarters were located wasn't one of them. According to the registry, the Englor Marine office building and the gym were the two places the colonel frequented the most. Perhaps a trip to the gym was in order. Galaxy knew Payton could use the exercise.

"At ease." Nate's voice drifted into the office.

Payton glanced up to see Nate coming his way. He started to stand, but Nate shook his head and closed the door behind him, looking around the room.

Payton grinned, knowing exactly what his brother-in-law was asking. "There is no video or audio in this part of the building."

Nate came further into the room, peeking over Payton's shoulder. "Have you found anything of interest?"

He thought about mentioning that Hollister frequented the gym on base, but decided against it. Nate would never allow him to go there if he knew. "No, have you?"

Shaking his head, Nate crossed the room and lifted the curtain, peering out. "No. Needless to say Colonel Hollister wasn't very forthcoming with info. I did find out he doesn't like to be referred to as Your Highness."

"Can't say that I blame him. I've never been fond of the address myself. Makes it seem like I think I'm better than everyone else." He shrugged. He liked being a prince, he did. He loved Regelence and he was proud to represent it, but he couldn't help but wonder what it would have been like to be born a commoner and not be under constant scrutiny. He hated people always staring at him. It made him feel self- conscious. He'd always reveled in the fact that he was a great deal more intelligent than most men, but would rather inspire lust than be sought after for his family connections. "What do you have planned for the evening?"

Nate blinked. "Nothing, why?"

"I thought if it was okay with you, I'd go to the gym. My brain could use the break. Besides, it might be a good place to pick up stuff. Hear the latest rumors." That was the truth, if not the whole reason.

Nate grinned. "Good thinking. They're much more likely to talk to you than me."

Sitting on the bunk in his room, Payton put his running shoes and workout clothes in his duffle bag with a sense of dread. He swallowed hard and tried to shake the foreboding feeling. He was being ridiculous, but the thought of changing in front of anyone else had him terrified. It was just too weird, some habits died hard, not to mention his Cony would completely flip if he found out. Who was he kidding? Payton was self-conscious. Changing in front of others was strange and something he'd never be allowed to do at home.

Zipping up the bag, he considered once again waiting until nighttime, when the gym would be mostly deserted. He knew it would clear out around seven, because he'd looked at the gym log.

By going at five, he might pick up on some rumors that could help his and Nate's investigation. At the very least, maybe he could pick up something about Hollister—whether Hollister was there or not—that would shed light on his motives for sending a spy to Regelence. So far, everyone seemed to adore the colonel. It was suspicious. No one with the power Hollister had could be that liked, could they?

Payton stood, stretching out his neck and arms. Wiping his hands on his pants, he winced. He really didn't want to do this. What if they laughed at him? It wasn't just the changing clothes. What if he was so out of shape he couldn't lift even the slightest weight? Maybe he'd wait to lift weights until no one was around—surely they had machines as well as free weights—so he wouldn't need a spotter. He groaned, grabbed his coat off the back of the chair and put it on. *Stop being stupid, Pay. No one will even care if you're there, much less how much you can lift.* Picking up the bag, he threw it over his shoulder and headed to the door.

The wind blew against the door to the building housing the officer's quarters, so he had to put his whole body into forcing it open. Galaxy, he could use some more upper-body strength. After squeezing through the door, he winced and snuggled down deeper into his coat.

The chilly air whipped down the back of his neck as he turned the corner. The gym was located on the west side of his apartment, opposite where the offices and mess hall were. It was a bit of a trek but at least the wind was at his back.

"Lieutenant, wait up."

Payton turned to see an Englor Marine Sergeant running

toward him. What was his name? He'd shown Payton the grounds earlier today, after he and Nate had gone to lunch. The sergeant was a native Englorian who had just gotten out of the IN and started his service with Englor. *Lewis?* Yes, that was it. Danny Lewis. His father owned a millinery in Mayfair across from Hyde Park. He was close to Payton's age, but he seemed younger. He was so animated when he spoke it brought to mind an excited puppy. Payton liked him. "Lewis, where are you headed?"

"The commissary, to pick up a few things. You?" Lewis closed the gap between them and started walking in the same direction as Payton.

"The gym." A gust of wind assaulted them, blowing leaves around their feet and whistling through the buildings. Payton shivered.

"Brrr... It's supposed to snow tomorrow evening." Lewis stuffed his hands in his pockets. "I hope it does. Last year we had a huge snowball fight in the courtyards outside the mess hall. It was great. Colonel Hollister and Colonel Eason even took part."

"Were they the only officers to take part?" Payton fished.

"No, of course not, but they're both titled and most of the titled lords don't associate with us peons." Surprisingly, there didn't seem to be any animosity in the statement, just fact. "Colonel Hollister is our prince. He's heir to the throne of Englor. Colonel Eason is heir to the Duke of Amberley." His voice held an awed tone, like even he couldn't believe the men would engage in a snowball fight.

Payton digested that for a second. It spoke positively of the two men. Even on Regelence some of the lords in service didn't interact with the commoners any more than they had too. Payton had never understood that holier-than-thou attitude. The lords were there to serve and protect their people, they were responsible for giving the common man a voice in government, not the other way around. Maybe Hollister really was as wonderful as everyone claimed.

"Here's your stop." Lewis stopped in front of a two-story red brick building. "Have fun working out. Maybe we could have a drink together sometime while you're here?"

"Sure. I'd like that."

Lewis strode off, ducking his head down further into his coat. "See you, Lieutenant."

"Good evening." Payton waved. Dust, his hands were like icicles and his toes were numb. He glanced up at the gray sky. The weather changed so quickly here on Englor. It had been sunny this afternoon. He couldn't wait to get back to the more constant weather on Regelence.

The tiny set of lights above the door flashed to green as Payton approached. He averted his attention away from the lights and continued on toward the door. No one else would even think about the lights, but because he'd had to tape his own tag on, he couldn't help it. The IN injected the tiny chip into the shoulder of new recruits and could track anyone who had ever served, even those now retired from service, as long as the building they entered had a sensor. Since, like Regelence, men had to go into service with the IN first for training, the Englor Marines and the Regelence military branches also had dog tags. Well, everyone except those only pretending to be soldiers. He had the urge to reach back to make certain his tape was still there. But he knew it was, the green light on the building had meant he was being logged in.

Giving himself a mental shake, Payton walked through the automatic doors and into the lobby of the gym. He followed a sign all the way to the locker room, spine straight like it was no big deal, but his stomach decided otherwise. It felt like the butterflies were trying to break their way out. *Come on, Pay, you can do this. You're a lieutenant. They'll expect that you're used to dressing in front of other men.* Only someone forgot to give his body that memo. It still thought he was a sheltered prince back on Regelence where he would never be allowed in the locker room of a gym, even with a chaperone.

Payton hitched his bag up again, held his chin up high and strolled right into the locker room...and almost swallowed his tongue. Good Galaxy, men were just walking around naked.

Okay, focus, Pay. No blushing. Locker. You need a locker. Oh, right there past the man with the nice muscled arse and hairy legs.

He was staring and he couldn't afford to stare. These men weren't going to tell him anything or let anything slip if they thought he was different. Gritting his teeth, he moved toward the red metal grid lockers. The thought of what he'd heard today still chafed. Nate was top of the food chain here, and if people saw his sexuality as vulgar, then no way could Payton, a mere lieutenant, socially survive them all knowing. And if it ever got out that he was a Regelence prince? It was going to be tough enough getting them to be comfortable since they saw him as the admiral's eyes and ears when he wasn't around.

Toward the end of the bank of lockers a door was open, and blessedly no one was in front of it. Payton hurried over and pressed his thumb to the locking mechanism. The light above the thumb pad flashed green, signaling it registered his print. Just to make certain, he closed the door and tried it. It was locked. Pressing his thumb to the thumb pad again made the lock click open with a winding sound. Good, it worked. He unzipped his bag and turned around, searching for a place to set it. Big mistake. A nude man stepped out of a cloud of steam pouring from an opened corridor. The sounds of skin slapping tile echoed out along with laughs and conversation. The guy coming out of the shower room dried his hair with his towel, completely unconcerned about his nudity. Payton's cock started to fill. Good Galaxy, the man was hung like—

No staring.

Looking down, he found the blue plastic-coated metal bench and willed his prick to ignore the pretty man with the wet dripping muscles and washboard abdomen. This was proving to be a test of willpower. All these well-formed bodies parading around in the buff were going to be the death of him. It was going to bloody kill him to keep from gawking and blushing.

He sat, hunkering over his bag, and took a deep breath. The room smelled musky and faintly of muscle ointment, but the scent of sweat and raw male lingered there too, teasing his nose. None of those smells should be appealing, but his cock twitched, proving differently. He felt like banging his head against something. Pulling his bag into his lap, he reached into it with one hand and with the other pinched the inside of his thigh...hard. *Yeouch*. His prick got the message and softened again.

Once Payton was sure he had his errant body under control, he took out his clothes. Men were talking and laughing. He could hear water running from behind him in the shower room, but that wasn't the only water sound. It also sounded like... He glanced up and around. To his right was the entrance, more lockers and more men. One man popped another's arse with his towel and laughter ensued followed by playful threats. There was no one Payton recognized. Where was that sound coming from?

Payton pulled his shoes and gym shorts out of his bag. It sounded like someone—

He turned his head to the left and froze. His mouth dropped open and his eyes widened. *Oh galaxy, no*. It was someone relieving himself. To his right was an open doorway and along the wall a mirror. From his viewpoint he could tell exactly where the open doorway led.

In the mirror a man stood displaying his back and a wall of urinals in front of him. Payton gulped down air, his gaze shooting to his bag. He was having a hard time getting oxygen into his lungs. *Don't panic, Pay*. No way could he use the water closet in front of everyone.

In a daze, he blinked and dropped the bag back to the floor. Reaching for his shoes, he pulled one off, then the other. The butterflies in his stomach had turned into vicious snarling, biting bats.

"Lieutenant Jeffers?"

Payton stuffed his shoes into his bag and tried to ignore the water sounds. The shower just made him think of all the wet, dripping, hard bodies, the other... He swallowed. He was going to have to hold it until he got back to his room. Any water he consumed was going to have to leave by way of sweat.

"Lieutenant Jeffers?"

Someone sat on the bench next to him. A black duffle landed next to his green one.

Oh. Payton felt like someone slapped him upside the head. *He* was Jeffers. Stardust and imploding planets. He looked up and to his right.

Lieutenant Edward Tavis sat next to him. He smiled and began unbuttoning his shirt. "I thought that was you. How was your first day?" Tavis shrugged his shirt off and stuffed it into his bag before taking out another one.

For a second, Payton sat there stunned. The man was undressing so casually. *Which you should be doing, you ninny.* Payton began unbuttoning his own shirt, then remembered his taped-on dog tag. He paused. Oh well, it would look like a bandage, no one would realize what it really was. Working on his buttons again, he glanced over at Tavis. "It went well. This is a nice base. I'm anxious to see more of Englor."

Tavis nodded and stood. "Let me know when you have some free time and I'll take you on a tour." He unfastened his trousers, dropped them and sat on the bench to tug them off his feet.

Payton hurried and removed his shirt, quickly folding and stuffing it in his bag before retrieving his athletic shirt. Galaxy, these workout clothes looked like underclothes. The shirt was thin and loose with short sleeves, almost sloppy, but it was better than the ones with the sleeves cut out of them. It wasn't fit for polite company, but it would have to do. He pulled it over his head as the lieutenant fussed with his shoes. "I will. I—" His mind went totally blank.

The most gorgeous man in the entire universe walked up to the lockers just to the right of them, three lockers down. Payton would have sworn that everything in the room stopped. The fluorescent lights gleamed off the man's copper-colored hair. His angular jaw was shadowy like he needed a shave, but somehow it looked...dashing. His eyes were light, but from this distance Payton couldn't tell their exact color. The redhead was huge, six foot four at least, but it wasn't entirely his size that made him stand out. His shoulders were wide and his hips slim. Under his dark blue uniform trousers, the muscles of his thighs were evident. He had a beauty and grace about him one usually didn't associate with such a large man.

Payton stared, transfixed. His cock hardened, pushing against his pants. His fingers clenched into his palms, wanting to touch.

Dropping his bag, the man turned to his right, talking and laughing with the dark-headed man next to him. The pale blue shirt pulled tight across his back as he reached forward with both hands and began unbuttoning his shirt. His muscled arse flexed as he shifted his weight and a deep sexy rumble erupted from him as he laughed at something his companion said. It made Payton's cock jerk and his stomach clench. Bloody hell, those pants couldn't possibly be regulation, could they? They sure looked like Englor Marine uniform pants.

Payton's breath caught. The man was incredible. The trousers *were* regulation, the man was not.

Someone walked into Payton's line of sight, snapping him out of his daze. *Dust.* He was staring. Not only that, he had an erection and was practically drooling. He darted a quick gaze around him, realizing that the entire room had *not* stopped, and hoped no one had noticed his infatuation. Fortunately, Tavis was tying his shoes. No one else seemed to witness his sudden lack of brain activity either.

"Where are you headed first?" Tavis asked, turning his head toward Payton.

"Huh?" Payton swallowed and a drop of sweat slid down his temple. "Oh, the treadmills, I think."

"Me too. Let me go take a piss and we'll go." Tavis picked up his bag and stuck it into an empty locker before heading toward the water closet.

Payton gave him a jerky nod, not even flinching at the coarse language. "Okay." His heart was pounding so hard he could feel its pulse everywhere, his throat, his ears, his cock. *Okay, breathe and don't look back at the man. Just concentrate and the boner will go away.* Payton glanced back at the redhead. *Pay! You weren't supposed to look.*

The Adonis was now sans shirt. His back was wide and well-defined, mouth-watering really. His muscles were so nicely rounded and his skin so smooth—even if it was pale—that he looked fake. No, not fake, like a marble masterpiece, a flawless statue.

Payton snapped his mouth shut before the drool dripped out, willed himself not to look at the human masterpiece, and bent over like he was getting something out of his bag. Oh, that was awkward. The seam of his pants bit into his erection. He gritted his teeth and shifted on the bench, trying to appear as though he wasn't relieving the pressure off his prick. He probably looked like his arse itched. *Argh.* Payton stopped. Someone was going to notice if he didn't. He sat back up, pulling the bag into his lap. *Oh, better, sort of...*

"You're not ready."

"Huh?" Payton turned to find Tavis standing over him. *Think, think, think.* "I have a cramp." Payton stretched his leg out, being careful to keep the bag over his erection, and pounded on his thigh with his fist. "Why don't you go ahead and I'll meet you there. Where are they?"

Frowning, the lieutenant glanced at Payton's leg. "Are you okay? You look a little flushed."

Only a little? He felt a whole lot flushed...and flustered. "Sure, just an old injury, not used to this weather, I guess. Go on without me." *Pleeease, go on without me.*

"Okay. When you leave the locker room turn left and just keep going. The treadmills are all the way to the back left corner."

"Great, I'll see you there."

Tavis walked off and Payton's attention went right back to the redhead. *Guh.* What was wrong with him? The man was like a magnet, and Payton a helpless piece of steel.

The man was bent over pulling his trousers off his feet. Payton shook himself mentally. He had to snap out of it and get his own pants off. Which was going to be difficult with the hard-on he was now sporting.

Making sure to grab his large shirt and maneuver it over his lap, Payton put his bag back on the floor. He got his shorts out and laid them across his bag. Without standing up, Payton unbuttoned his trousers and shimmied them off with his arse only lifting from the bench for a second. He pulled them over his feet and replaced them with his shorts. After getting his shorts on his legs, he tugged them up as far as he could without standing. Once his shirt covered his problem, he stood quickly and yanked them over his hips. He impressed even himself sometimes. No way had anyone seen anything. Grinning, he reached for his shoes and lifted his head.

One crystal blue eye stared at him, the other covered by a red hank of hair before it was brushed back by a big hand. A set of full lips curved into a smile.

Dust. Payton jerked his head down, studying his feet. He fumbled with his shoes and swallowed. How much had the Adonis seen? What if he saw Payton's little, er, big problem? Sadly, the thought of being seen did nothing to alleviate *that* condition.

His hands were sweating, but he finally managed to get one shoe tied and his other on his foot. He fancied he could feel the man's gaze boring into him. *Please, let that be my overactive imagination.* Glancing up again, he caught the same clear blue gaze.

The man was bent over tying his own shoe. The lock of red hair fell back over his pale forehead. The dark-headed man who came in with him touched his shoulder and said something. The redhead grinned again and winked at Payton before looking back over his shoulder at his friend.

Payton did the only thing he could think of.

He ran...right out of the locker room, with his shoe untied and his bag still on the floor.

Chapter Three

The locker room was as deserted as the gym, except for the sound of running water coming from the shower room. Grinning, Simon ran the towel over his forehead before hanging it on his shoulder and taking a swig of his water. Glancing down to where the pretty little blushing soldier had left his bag two hours ago confirmed his suspicions about who was showering, and his prick hardened right up.

The bag sat on the bench where Simon had set it and zipped it up after the man had fled, but now it was unzipped with shoes and clothes lying next it. Oh, this had the potential to be a great evening.

Simon had spotted the kid as soon as he and Wycliffe walked in. He had to be a new transfer, because if he'd been anywhere on this base Simon was sure he'd have seen him before, and he bloody well wouldn't have forgotten that angelic face. The kid had to be around nineteen or twenty, barely out of basic. Even with a nice strong masculine jaw and bit of beard shadow, the raven-haired man was stunning...a real beauty. Funny, Simon had never thought of other men as beauties, but that's what the man was. He was slim and small, almost delicate looking. And that wide-eyed innocent stare? Simon chuckled. It brought to mind a kid seeing the inside of a candy store for the first time.

The blush had made him even more appealing. It was usually Roc who went for the pretty boys, but Simon had taken one look and decided against giving Roc, or Wycliffe for that matter, the chance.

Using his thumb, Simon opened his locker. He set his water bottle inside and tugged the towel off his shoulder. He'd had his eye on the beauty the whole time he'd worked out tonight, noticing how the kid lingered behind, not hitting the weights until the place was almost deserted. He was also fairly certain the man hadn't seen him watching. Simon had wanted to go over and talk to him so badly it had nearly killed him, but he'd restrained himself. He'd seen the kid first and he wasn't going to draw Wycliffe's attention to him. Wycliffe was a competitive bastard, but if Simon said he'd met him first, Wycliffe would respect that. Even so, he'd sent Wycliffe ahead of him to go meet Roc at White's.

The dark-headed soldier had tried like hell to hide his interest, but Simon had seen right through it. The way those yellow eyes had followed him... Simon shivered and pressed the heel of his hand against his throbbing cock. Those amber eyes were amazing. They were practically a feline yellow. *Damn and bloody hell*, his prick jerked against his hand. He couldn't remember the last time he'd been so hot for a man without even speaking to him first. Not since he was a starry-eyed teen.

After giving his erection one last rub through his shorts, he pulled his sweaty shirt over his head and dropped it to the floor. This was going to be fun. As far as he could tell he and the little beauty were the only ones in the whole place.

Simon toed off his shoes and brought his foot up to tug off his sock. His cock hardened even more, wanting to go see if that body was as stunning as the face. Simon glanced toward the shower room again and groaned. Hurrying, he took off his other sock, removed his shorts and jockstrap, then grabbed the soap and shampoo out of his locker. He made himself walk instead of run to the shower room door. He already looked like an idiot smiling and walking around with a stiffy. Speaking of...

He got a towel off the laundry cart beside the shower room. Setting the shampoo and shower gel down, he wrapped the towel tight around his hips. It didn't do a whole hell of a lot to disguise his erection, but at least it didn't look like he was flaunting it. Picking up the two bottles and a washcloth, he headed in to find the object of his interest.

Simon's quarry stood at the very back of the shower room, in the right-hand corner. Steam billowed around him and water ran in rivulets down his slender body. He looked ethereal. Unfortunately, a low pale blue tile wall with two bottles and a towel on top covered his lower half, but what Simon could see of the upper half lived up to his imagination. There was barely any muscle tone in those small shoulders and arms, even flexed to wash his neck like they were, but he was all man. The washcloth was held in his left hand as he scrubbed his neck and other arm. Was he left handed?

Simon moved forward, mesmerized by the suds slipping over the pale smooth back. He strolled silently toward the shower nozzle just on the other side of the low tile wall. The closer he got, the better the view became. The soap bubbles slid down the shallow indention of the man's lower back and oozed over the nicest round arse Simon had ever seen. His breath caught. The kid was exquisite, with legs fairly long for his size, even if he barely reached Simon's shoulder.

It also occurred to Simon that those slim limbs were going to be sore tomorrow. There wasn't an ounce of fat on him, in fact, in places it was easy to see his ribs. As fragile looking as he was, it didn't seem possible that he worked out on a regular basis. Maybe Simon should offer a rubdown. The thought of his hands on that sleek body, massaging the pert little arse, had his balls drawing up. Simon had the insane longing to trace those ridges with his tongue. He was pretty sure his prick was leaking on the front of his towel, but he couldn't feel it because of the steam. *Bloody hell.* He was so close he could reach out and touch. Would the milky skin feel as soft as it looked? His empty hand tightened into a fist, then relaxed.

The kid dropped his hand and leaned forward, hanging his head under the water. Simon noticed a bandage on his left shoulder, right above his sharp shoulder blade. He was hurt?

Simon frowned and set his shampoo and shower gel down on the wall. "What happened to your shoulder?"

"Ack!" The beauty sucked in a harsh breath and spun around, his left hand, complete with soapy washcloth, slapped to his narrow chest. His ebony hair was slicked back with the water. The already big yellow eyes got bigger. He darted a glance at the towel on the wall and then at the shower room door before looking back to Simon.

Simon grinned. Damn, the man was even more beautiful up close. "Sorry, I didn't mean to scare you."

A hank of black hair slid down over his forehead as he bobbed his head, and his Adam's apple moved as he swallowed. His washcloth hand inched toward his groin and his other arm came across his chest. It was adorable, like he was trying to hide himself.

Simon couldn't help himself. His gaze followed the rag, down the trail of dark hair, past the bony hipbones, over the dark curls, to the thick limp cock, before the white sudsy washcloth covered most of the black hair at his groin and the nice prick. The man shifted his weight from one foot to the other.

Simon was willing to bet his cock was fairly long when erect. Raising his gaze, he smiled. "What happened to your shoulder?"

"Um..." Reaching back with his right hand, the man touched the spot then crossed it over his chest again. He dropped his hand further to cover his middle. It was like he didn't know what to do with his hand. Finally, he just let it hang at his side. A nice blush spread over his face and neck as he shrugged. "I got stabbed by a foil while fencing with a friend." The last word lilted a little, making it almost sound like a question. "Um." He caught his bottom lip in his teeth. "I'm Payton." He held out his hand, palm facing down, before turning it sideways.

Simon chuckled. *Payton.* It was a good name, it fit him, elegant. Simon captured Payton's offered hand and didn't let go. "I'm Si."

"Sai? As in the weapon?" Payton's voice was soft, drawing out the "I" like a caress.

Simon fought the urge to moan. Payton would probably sound incredible in the heat of passion. His voice was soft, not very deep, but it had a seductive quality to it. Simon cleared his throat and nodded. "No, as in Simon, but I like that." He didn't think Payton had any clue who he was, and if he did he didn't show it. For some reason Simon didn't want him to. He wanted to get to know Payton without him wigging out about Simon being a prince or the colonel in charge of the base. He'd never really cared before, but there was something about this angelic-looking man that made him want to be just an average guy.

Payton tugged his hand back, making Simon finally have to release it. "Nice to meet you, Si." His gaze traveled over Simon's body. He licked his lips, then jerked his head back up when he reached Simon's towel. His yellow eyes looked like they were about to pop out of his head, and his Adam's apple bobbed again.

Some inner demon inside Simon cheered. Oh yes, Payton was definitely as interested as he was.

"I thought I was alone. You gave me a start."

Uncaring about his very large, very evident erection, Simon pulled his towel off and laid it on the wall.

Payton hissed in a breath and tried to cover the noise by turning around toward his own shower. "I need to hurry and get back to my quarters, but it was nice meeting you."

Quarters? Not barracks. He was an officer. Simon gave Payton's arse one more glance and focused on his own shower. He pushed the button below the nozzle. "One hundred and two." The water came on, making him flinch. It was nice and hot, felt good. "Sorry for scaring you, Payton. How about I make it up to you? How about a drink?" *Or a nice long fuck?*

Payton pushed the button on his own shower, shutting the water off, and grabbed his towel off the wall, but not before Simon caught a glimpse of a nice erect prick reaching toward Payton's navel.

Simon grinned. He was right, it was long and fairly thick. Payton wasn't small all over it would seem.

Still holding onto the wet washcloth, Payton wrapped the

towel around his hips, not even bothering to dry off. The adorable blush remained on his face and neck, but was now spreading over his shoulders. "I—" His voice cracked and he cleared his throat. "I can't, but thank you for the offer."

Damn. A lump formed in Simon's stomach, his cock shrinking a tad. "How ab—?"

"I've really got to go. It was nice meeting you." Payton's voice trailed off as he darted for the exit, his bare wet feet slapping on the tile.

Well, bloody hell and damnation. Simon groaned. What had he done wrong? Payton was definitely interested. Maybe he'd never— *Oh.* What if the kid was still deluding himself that he was straight? Simon frowned, then shrugged.

No way was Payton straight, with that kid-in-a-candy-store look he'd worn earlier, or the nice once-over he'd given Simon, but maybe he was extremely shy. He *was* shy, that was obvious, but not straight.

He peered down at his cock, which stuck straight up toward his belly. "Looks like it's just you and me tonight." He grabbed the bottle of soap off the ledge and poured some into his hand. Wrapping his hand around his length, he stroked upward. Oh yes, that was good. Imagining long, slender, elegant fingers gripping him instead of his own large calloused hand, he set up a steady rhythm.

Closing his eyes, Simon braced himself on the wall in front of him with his left hand. His balls drew tighter and his breath hitched. He pictured that round arse and Payton's soft voice begging. That dark head bent over his lap would be a hell of a sight. He wondered if Payton would blush while sucking cock. *Probably.* And dust wasn't that a pretty picture.

Simon's heart sped up along with his breathing and his hand. His red pubes would look dark against Payton's ivory little arse as he drove into Payton. "Oh fuck." This wasn't going to take long. Hot water continued to pour down over him and steam surrounded him. The slapping sound of flesh on flesh echoed in the empty room. *His hands speared through dark wet hair as he thrust into swollen pink lips. Those big yellow eyes looked up at him as the perfect rounded nose buried in Simon's curls.*

His arse clenched tight and a tingle raced up his spine. Simon's eyes flew open. Creamy white semen covered his hand and splashed on his stomach before washing away in the hot water. Simon groaned and let go, forcing his breathing to go back to normal.

Releasing his cock, he flattened both hands on the wall in front of him. "Bloody hell." Simon sighed. Tomorrow night he'd come later. Hopefully he could catch Payton by himself again. He grinned. It appeared he needed to coax the shy beauty a bit harder next time. This was going to be fun. Payton was his, whether he realized it or not.

Chapter Four

"You're late, is everything all right?" Dru stood on the porch of Blake House in a dark green riding habit and ermine collared tan coat.

Simon winced. He hadn't meant to worry her. He and Dru had started Monday morning rides three years ago whenever he was on planet and weather permitted. In that time, he had never been late. "My apologies. I moved back to the base for a few weeks." Swinging down from Cirilo, he offered her his hand.

"Why ever would you do that?" She wrinkled her nose as she took his hand and allowed him to lead her to the mounting block where her horse, Cleopatra, waited. "Is there something wrong with Hollister House?"

"No. Hollister House is fine. Minus a few less servants, but fine." His townhouse also lacked an amenity the base currently had. A pretty little raven-haired officer named Payton. But unfortunately, that particular feature didn't come standard with Simon's office either.

Dru giggled. "You really need to lay off the pranks, darling."

"Me?" Simon waited for her to step up on the block. "It's not me. You need to talk to Wycliffe and Roc."

Settling herself into the sidesaddle, Dru rearranged her skirt and coat. "Forgive me if I don't believe you're completely innocent." The ivory-colored feather on her cap fell into her eyes and she shook her head to dislodge it.

Simon chuckled and slapped a hand to his chest with flare. "I'm wounded."

"Nonsense. Get on your horse and take me for a ride in the park, you silly man. It's a beautiful day. I don't want to waste it. We aren't likely to have many more like it." She collected her reins and steered her pretty bay horse forward to stand by Cirilo.

As Simon climbed into his saddle, Dru tsked. "Is that the best you can do? As dramatic as you are this morning, I half expected you to vault into the saddle from behind."

"You don't think I can?" If he weren't sore from sleeping on the couch in his office, he'd have been tempted to try it just to amuse her.

"Si, I've known you long enough to know you can do anything you put your mind to. I've always admired that about you."

He hoped she was correct, because out of the several things he wanted at the present, Payton was likely to be the easiest to obtain and Simon wasn't sure that task would be all that easy.

"Ready?"

Studying the gray clouds, Simon secured his uniform cape tighter around himself. Thankfully, it wasn't that cold today, but the forecast predicted bad weather tonight. Dru was probably right, it had been a mild winter so far, they may not get much more riding in for awhile and he needed to talk to her. "I'm ready. Lead the way, Your Grace."

Dru flicked her reins to get Cleo moving. "Tell me why you're staying in those horrid accommodations. I know it's not something you'd do unless something dire had happened, so what is going on?"

"I can't get anything past you, can I?" Simon grinned. He loved that about her. She had always been sharp and forward. She'd also turned into an exquisite woman as he'd predicted. Until last night, he'd never seen anyone, woman or man, who compared to her. "Actually, I'm glad you asked." Talking to Dru would get his mind off Payton. "I wanted to speak to you about it."

"Me?" Clasping a gloved hand to her chest, she turned her head toward him then back to the front, making the long feather on her cap land over her left eye again. She blew at the feather, but it didn't leave her forehead. "I assure you I had nothing to do with you being booted out of Hollister House." Grinning, she finally batted the feather away. "Stupid hat."

It *was* a ridiculous-looking hat, with its wide brim, shallow crown and the enormous matching green bow tied under her chin. It looked like a top hat someone had sat on, but it was the height of fashion.

Smirking, Simon turned Cirilo toward the Stanhope Gate. "Now who's being silly? I know why I'm sleeping in my office. I'm staying there to make certain things run smoothly with Admiral Hawkins here." *And hopefully to get close to a handsome new officer.* "What I want to know is if you have any gossip on the admiral."

"Darling, I always have gossip." She snorted. "It's amazing how many people try to share gossip with me to get in my good graces." And Dru was cunning enough to use that gossip to her advantage, listening to anything that would guide her investments. She may have married a wealthy man, but after his death she doubled his fortune.

"Well? What is the ton saying about Hawkins?"

As they entered the gate several gentlemen called out hellos.

"Good morning." Dru fluttered her fingers at them. "Deverell. The admiral is the Earl of Deverell."

Simon tipped his hat to Lords Rumpledust and Turner. "Good morning, gentlemen."

"Let's ride around the Serpentine, then we can walk a little before we go down Rotten Row." She pointed toward the walk closest to them. "My understanding is that Lord Deverell is primarily here to inspect the base. Do you think differently?"

"No. He's definitely here for that. I was just wondering what else you've heard about him."

"He ran away from home to join the IN nearly twenty years ago. There was a duel over a Lady Appleton, only she was Lady Seagraves then. Supposedly Deverell killed her fiancé and the duke disowned him. Although to hear Hawthorne tell it, he never disowned his son. Hawthorne is quite proud of Deverell."

Simon had heard all of that about the admiral. "Something doesn't sound right." If Hawthorne didn't disown his son, why hadn't the admiral been back to Englor in all those years? There was more to the duel than people knew. It gave Simon hope that maybe it was the reason the admiral was here and not because he'd caught Lieutenant Benson spying? Or perhaps it really was only to inspect the base? No. Simon didn't think so.

"There have also been a few murmurs about Deverell being married to a man, a prince or something. That has caused more than a few raised eyebrows and talk of moral reform."

Wonderful. Simon would bet his right testicle he knew who was leading that cause for reform...again. "The prince's name is Aiden Townsend. He's the third in line for the Regelence throne." They reached the Serpentine and reined to a halt.

"It's true?"

"It is." Simon had learned that much from his informant on Regelence. The fact that Hawkins was married to a man made his visit even more puzzling. Hawkins had to know Englorians weren't going to overlook it, even if he was a war hero. Simon swung his leg over the saddle and dropped to the ground. Gathering Cirilo's reins, he waited for Dru.

She slid to the ground, gripped the reins and fell in beside him. "Do you expect trouble?"

Simon started walking, adjusting his stride to match hers. "I always expect trouble." It paid to be cautious, especially where powerful men like Admiral Hawkins were concerned. "If you mean because of public outcry over Hawkins's marriage, no. The admiral is a powerful man because of his status in the IN. The ton might not like it, but they can't do anything about it. And I seriously doubt a man like Hawkins gives a bloody damn if he's cut by society."

Dru snorted. "He"—she turned her head toward him, meeting his gaze—"nor anyone else should care about being unpopular over such a thing. It's not against the law, last I heard."

Simon ignored her taunt. There was no use in repeating the same argument. He was *not* marrying a man. "No. It's not against the law." And it would remain that way if Simon had anything to say about it. "But that will not stop certain members of the peerage from trying to make it so."

Mumbling something undoubtedly unladylike under her breath, Dru shook her head. "Fine. Do you want to hear the rest of the gossip?"

Does it involve a very handsome and shy soldier? What he wanted was to find out if Payton was going to be at the gym tonight, but that wasn't something Dru would know and unfortunately neither did Simon. He didn't even know Payton's last name.

Several peers passed them going the opposite direction, some on horseback, others walking.

"Si? Where are you? You're a million miles away." Dru waved to a couple of ladies walking by with a groom in tow.

"Sorry, I was thinking about something else. Tell me what other rumors are making the rounds this week."

"Oh no." She smiled brightly. "You aren't getting out of it that easily. Who is he?"

"What?" No way was he telling Dru anything. She'd badger him for details and start making wedding plans. Besides, there was nothing to tell...yet. "I was just thinking about work. It's a little hectic with this base inspection going on."

Dru looked like she would argue for a moment, then she nodded. "Lady Carston is having an affair with Lord Grafton."

"I thought she was seeing the Earl of Hopkins."

"That was last month. Lord Paterson compromised Lady Sarah Foley and refused to marry her. Poor thing was sent to rusticate in the country."

Sarah was a nice girl. He'd have to see if he could set her up with a fellow soldier. "Anything else?"

Pursing her lips, Dru touched a gloved finger to them. "You were seen sneaking out of my townhouse at three in the morning last Wednesday." She waggled her eyebrows.

A smile tugged at his lips. Last Wednesday he'd been at White's with Wycliffe. Sometimes the ton and their idiotic rumors annoyed him, but this wasn't one of those times. The stories always amused Dru and as long as they didn't hurt her—which wasn't likely with her status in society—they helped quiet the more damning whispers about him. "Was I?"

"Apparently."

"Was I any good?"

"I don't know, you tell me." Dru chuckled.

He stepped closer and lowered his voice. "The best piece of arse in Englor." His lips twitched, but he kept from breaking into a smile.

Dru, on the other hand, failed miserably. She threw her head back and laughed. "Oh good. It's nice to know I can still pick them."

Simon lost it then and joined her guffawing.

When the mirth finally subsided to a few giggles, they'd made it to the wooded part of the trail. The cement path had narrowed and there was less traffic, but the sounds of people enjoying the park were all around them. "Are you ready to ride again?"

Dru stopped her horse. "Sure, if you can give me a boost up."

Flipping his reins back over Cirilo's head, Simon walked around the stallion to Dru's side.

"Thank you for taking me riding."

"My pleasure."

"You're the only one I go riding with nowadays." Dru bumped his shoulder with hers. "Well, you and Wycliffe. But Wycliffe would faint dead away if I even considered galloping, so I don't go with him often." She got quiet for a few moments, petting Cleo's nose. "Anthony used to be terrified I'd fall. Do you know he even tried to get me to ride astride?" She handed him her reins. "And my parents think *I'm* scandalous."

Taking the leather straps, Simon laid them over the horse's neck and waited for Dru to come to him. His heart hurt for her.

He'd always envied her relationship with Kentwood. He'd never have anything like it. He'd marry one day, but it wouldn't be for love. "You miss him."

She met his gaze. "Terribly." With a sad smile and teary eyes, she sidled up next to him, holding her arms out for him to lift her.

As he raised her, a loud thundering of hooves came from behind them, drowning out the rustling leaves and distant voices. Cleopatra backed away. "Whoa, girl." Setting Dru back on her feet, Simon held his hand out to Cleo. "Easy, girl."

He glanced toward the trail a few yards behind them, but because of the sharp turn and the stand of trees concealing the road he couldn't see anything. The rapid clip-clop of hooves grew louder and Cirilo huffed out a breath, throwing his head up.

Simon caught Cleo's bridle. "Drucilla, get out of the middle of—"

A large chestnut horse came barreling around the corner headed straight for them.

Simon dove at Dru, knocking her out of the running horse's path.

They careened into the trees at the other side of the trail and ended up on the leaf-littered ground in a tangle of arms and legs with Dru on top of him.

"Bloody hell." Simon pulled Dru up with him, dusted her off and swept the leaves from his uniform. "Are you hurt?"

She shook her head and the ridiculous feather, now broken, flopped over the bridge of her nose. "No, I'm fine. What the galaxy? Who was—? Oh no, your horse." Her shoulders slumped as she stared down the road.

Damn. Cirilo had run back toward the front gate. And the reckless rider had kept going, with his dark greatcoat flapping behind him. He never even looked back. *Bastard.*

Cleo danced in place, snorting and flipping her head.

"You're sure you're fine?" Simon picked up his cover off the ground and brushed it off before putting it back on his head.

"Yes. Thank you." Dru fussed with her riding habit and hat. "I'd love to get a hold of that rider and give him a piece of my mind."

She wasn't the only one. But Simon was likely to do more than introduce the man to the sharp side of his tongue. After giving Dru a once-over and assuring himself she was truly fine, he stepped back onto the concrete path. He needed to calm their remaining horse before she bolted.

Holding out his hand for the mare to smell, Simon inched his way closer. "It's okay, girl. Easy now."

A soft breeze blew leaves across the path, making them rattle and crackle. Cleo backed up a few steps, but Simon followed her. When the wind stopped, a steady clip-clop of hooves headed their way from around the blind corner. "Dru—"

"I'm out of the way," she said softly, and her hand touched his shoulder.

Simon continued to gentle the bay. "Easy, girl." Out of his peripheral vision, he spotted a dark blur and the clicking of horseshoes stopped.

"Markham and Baymore." Dru sounded like she was gritting her teeth.

"Ah, Your Grace, up to mischief again I see," a man chided. Leather creaked and boot heels hit the ground. "I assume this horse belongs to your friend?"

"Yes. Give him to me," Dru said, just as Simon got close enough to grab Cleo's bridle.

"Shh..." It took only seconds before she was standing in place allowing Simon to pet her nose. "Good girl." Once he was certain she was calm, he turned.

Dru held on to Cirilo, her other hand on her hip, glaring at two men. Both were tall and appeared to be peers of the realm. One wore a light gray coat and held the bridle of a big roan horse. He wasn't much older than Simon, perhaps in his mid-thirties. He had dark hair and a large nose, but not big enough to distract from his handsomeness. The other gentleman was as tall as the first but thinner. His short mousy brown hair curled around the brim of his tan hat. He had piercing hazel eyes but was otherwise quite plain looking.

Expressionless, the first man studied Simon from top to bottom, sizing him up. There was such an air of spoilt aristocrat to him that Simon half expected the man to pull out a quizzing glass. After several seconds a slow smile spread across the lord's lips and he bowed slightly. "Your Highness. A pleasure to make your acquaintance."

So the man recognized him. Simon dipped his head. "Please call me Colonel. And you are?"

"Markham, the Earl of Markham. And this"—he indicated the thinner man—"is my associate, Lord Baymore."

Baymore bowed. "A pleasure, Colonel."

Markham glanced at Dru, then back to Simon. "I trust you and Her Grace are well?"

"We're fine. Thank you, milord," Dru said dryly.

Markham dipped his chin. "Good, good. You could've been seriously injured. People have been trampled to death by horses, you know. You're very lucky." He met Simon's gaze. "Beautiful horse you have there, Your High—excuse me, Colonel." He smiled and looked over at Cirilo.

"Thank you. And thank you for bringing him back."

"Not a problem. Baymore and I were just turning onto the path by the lake when we saw him bolt out of the trees. I caught him easily enough, assuming we'd meet up with a horseless rider down the road. I see I was correct. Now if you will both excuse us"—he mounted his horse—"we've got to get going if we're going to make it to the House of Lords on time."

"Thank you again, Lord Markham, Lord Baymore."

Baymore tipped his hat. "Glad to be of assistance, Colonel." Completely dismissing Simon and Dru, he heeled his horse, taking off in a gallop toward Rotten Row.

Markham followed.

Dru bristled, huffing out a breath. "Pompous jackanapes."

Simon chuckled. They did seem a little self-absorbed, but no more than most men of their ilk. "They seemed nice enough."

Scoffing, she handed Cirilo's reins to Simon. "They are two of the lords calling for moral reform."

He led her toward her horse, "Up you go," and lifted her into the saddle. "Baymore must be a fairly new title. It doesn't sound familiar."

"He bought his barony. He was in trade. I don't know the specifics but I believe your mother was behind him getting his title."

That figured. The Baron probably held his mother's gambling markers. "What happened to the old Earl of Markham?" Simon swung himself into his saddle and waited for Dru to join him.

"The old Earl took ill and died when you were fighting on Lorgania last summer." She heeled her horse and led them toward Rotten Row. "It was quite mysterious. No one was even aware the Earl was sick, until the new Earl showed up to take care of his uncle. As soon as he took the title, he became quite active in parliament. He's a big supporter of the morality laws and the Church of Englor," Dru scoffed. "He and Baymore are part of those right-wing bible thumpers convinced all of us are sinners and headed for hell. Needless to say, they don't approve of my more daring approach to life."

Perhaps that prudishness was what Simon had sensed earlier.

Dru turned her head, making the silly broken feather fall forward. "Dust." She brushed it back. It fell again.

He edged his horse closer to Dru's. "Allow me to assist you." He snatched the feather from the hatband. "Here." He handed it to her.

Dru's jaw dropped open, but quickly gave way to a smile. "Si. You broke my hat." Swatting at him, she dropped the feather, allowing it to float to the ground. "You blackguard, you."

Simon heeled his horse and took off in a run to keep from being smacked.

Laughing, Dru gave chase, following him right out of the

front gate of Hyde Park.

"Someone kill me," Payton grumbled as he studied the chair across from Nate's desk. He was tired and sore. Someone should put him out of his misery. Last night he'd been haunted with dreams of Si. Not just any dreams, dreams he shouldn't be having. Of course, it never stopped him before, but this was different. It was borderline obsessive. The intimate get-together with his hand last night should have banished Si from his thoughts, but it hadn't. He'd been thinking about the redhead all day—oh it hurt to breathe—in between bouts of agony. "Working out rains meteors." The walking had gotten easier, but the sitting? Oh, this was going to hurt. One good thing about it, none of his Si-induced erections had lasted long today. Pain was good for something.

Nate chuckled. "What did you do with the liniment I gave you?"

Ignoring Nate in favor of getting into the chair, Payton turned around and scooted until the backs of his thighs touched the cushy leather chair. He took a deep breath. *One, two, two and a half, oh dust, three.* He fell backward, bouncing a little when he hit the seat. His legs flew straight out in front of him and the chair cushion made a whoosh sound. "Ow." So much for not bending his legs. It had hurt anyway.

"You should go soak in the hot tub at the gym if you aren't going to use the liniment." Nate shook his head and went back to his computer.

Payton wrinkled his nose. No way was he using that vile stuff Nate had given him earlier after laughing at Payton's stiff-legged entrance. "Have you smelled that stuff?" Galaxy that had stunk. He couldn't possibly use it. When he went back to the gym tonight, everyone would know. He was going to make a big enough cake of himself going all stiff and aching. Maybe the hot tub wasn't such a bad idea.

No, no he couldn't... Even if he had a bathing suit, it wasn't something one wore in public. Of course, he'd been naked last night in the shower with Si. Oh dust, that man was handsome. All those bulging muscles and... That wasn't the only thing bulging on him. Payton's face heated at the memory of the lovely, thick erection Si had done nothing to hide. His own cock stirred.

"I like the smell," Nate said.

Payton started and looked up at his brother-in-law. Rubbing his thigh, he winced. That really didn't help, but it did deflate his prick. How could he have forgotten where he was? If Nate saw him blushing like a ninny, he'd start asking about what happened at the gym. No way did Payton want to get landed with a chaperone. "It smells like that stuff Aiden uses to mix paints."

One of Nate's dark brows rose and the goofy, sappy grin he always got when Aiden was mentioned slid into place.

Payton could have kicked himself. Here he was daydreaming about Si when he should be helping speed things up so he and Nate could go home. "That's why you like the smell."

Nate shrugged. His brother-in-law was such a sap where Aiden was concerned and Aiden was just as bad. "Did you learn anything at the gym?"

"No. I actually met a Simon."

"Simon is a popular name. Many Englorians name their sons after the prince just as, I'm sure, there are Regelens named after you and your brothers. I want you to stay away from Hollister though." Nate leveled a stare at him. "We still don't know for sure what he was doing with a spy on Regelence."

"No. I'd love to talk to whoever wrote Englor's code. It's genius. I've spent most of the day trying to crack it and going through new emails I've confiscated."

"Anything interesting in the emails?"

"No, just departmental stuff." Which quite frankly rained

meteors. He wanted this to be over with. Why couldn't Hollister put stuff in his emails like everyone else did? There was no mention of Benson, Regelence or anything related. The only thing of interest— "Oh, Hollister moved back on base for your visit. He's staying in his office. You think he's on to us?"

"I don't see how. Me coming here is perfectly legitimate. I'm supposed to be checking out the bases under my command. More than likely he wants to make certain everything is running smoothly while I'm here."

Payton considered it for a second. Nate was right. It wouldn't do to make a bad impression on an IN Admiral.

"There's a dinner at Hollister Palace in my honor this Saturday. Make sure you're available."

At the palace? This could work out well. "I will be there *with* my com-pad in tow."

Nate nodded. "Good. You will of course make sure your com-pad is not detected."

"Of course."

"Good. Now go get the liniment. It will—"

"Admiral, you have a call from Regelence," the computer interrupted. "It's your very lonely, very tired, but extremely talented consort."

Nate chuckled and glanced up at Payton.

Payton smiled back, shaking his head. The computer obviously quoted Aiden word for word.

"Put him through please." Nate leaned back in his chair, resting his hands on his stomach, still smiling. Payton could tell the exact moment Aiden's face appeared on the screen because the expression on Nate's face softened. The tenderness and longing playing over his features made Payton feel like a voyeur, and also kind of sad. Nate missed Aiden. The determination to speed things up by helping Nate with this investigation overcame Payton. He should get back to work on the code instead of going to the gym.

"Come home," Aiden nearly whined.

"I can't. Not yet. I really want to, but—" Nate frowned and

exhaled loudly. "Tell me, what did you paint that you're so pleased with?"

Aiden chuckled. "Hold on and I'll show you. Hey wait. Are you by yourself?"

"No, Payton's here." Nate met Payton's gaze and one side of his mouth curled up. "Why?"

"Well, because I was going to show you the absolutely dashing painting I finished today."

"What does that have to do with me being here?" Payton wondered aloud. "I've seen your work before."

"Not this one you haven't. It's, uh...um...never mind." Aiden's voice trailed off. "How are you, Payton?" he asked with renewed enthusiasm.

Oh ho, someone was painting naughty pictures. Payton bit his lip to keep from laughing.

Nate wasn't so restrained. He did laugh. "Now I've really got to see this painting."

"Uhhh, are you sure you want to see it now?" Aiden sounded incredulous.

Payton decided to take pity on his younger sibling. "I've started working out. I'm terribly sore."

"Eeeew." Aiden's tone made it easy for Payton to imagine the horrified look on his brother's face. "Why ever would you do that?"

Payton was beginning to wonder that himself, even though he had the insane urge to go back tonight. Would Si be there? "I'm going to get all buff and when I come home you won't even recognize me." Si's buff body came to mind and he nearly groaned again. *Concentrate, Payton, you are trying to help speed up going home, not find a paramour.* Maybe Si could give him info on Hollister and Englor in general. "And speaking of which, I should get back to work." Payton took a deep breath, grabbed the armrests of the chair and scooted his feet in. This was going to hurt. He shoved himself up out of the chair and groaned. "Oh ow."

"Rubbish. You've been working all day. Go to the gym, soak

in the hot tub. Take a break. That's an order." Nate glowered. "And don't stay up all night studying code."

Payton waved his hand dismissively. "Talk to your consort. I'll see you tomorrow morning and give you an update on what I've found." Which wasn't much.

"Bye, Payton," Aiden said.

"Goodbye, Aiden."

As soon as Payton closed the door, Nate hissed out a breath and said, "Bloody hell, boy."

Payton chuckled. He was going to have to hack into Nate's computer to get a peek at that painting.

He walked through the deserted building, back to his own office. The lack of activity didn't surprise him since it was after seven o'clock. All the normal people were at home or out having fun, yet, here he was. Who wanted to be normal anyway?

Damn it, he did. His brain was tired. He didn't want to work anymore. Maybe going back to the gym wasn't a bad idea. He could go to the gym, work out his upper body and come back and study the code some more. *Give it a rest, Pay. Admit it, you want to see Si again.*

And why not? As soon as he got home, he'd have to go back to being watched constantly. He wasn't going to go running into his consort's loving arms like Nate.

He grabbed his coat off the back of his door and put it on. A trip to the gym then back here to get his com-pad and he'd work in his quarters. He shut his office door and pressed his thumb to the scanner to lock it. "Stupid conscience." He strolled right past Nate's office and walked to the front of the building. Huddling into his coat, he pushed open the door and headed to the gym.

Chapter Five

Six. Payton grunted and hefted the bar up again. He hadn't worked out his upper body yesterday and now he knew why. *Seven.* His upper body strength was next to none. After hoisting the bar back onto the stand, he left his hands on it. "Eight." At least no one was here to witness him struggling with such miniscule weight. Pulling his feet up onto the bench, he lay there staring at the staggered white tile and fluorescent light ceiling. It was ugly. The gym looked like a gym, not the pristine workout room at home.

Good grief, he was becoming a whiner. He huffed out a breath, making the hair on his forehead flutter, and closed his eyes. First, he was melancholy over not having a consort. Which was stupid, he didn't *want* a consort. It was just from watching Nate talk to Aiden, and witnessing how happy they both were. Second, he didn't want to work, which he really needed to do. The guilt was gnawing at him. That was also stupid because as soon as he figured out why Benson was on Regelence, he was going to go home and back to being under constant surveillance. He actually had a bit of freedom here...and he was using it to lift weights. Yeah, he was whining, most unbecoming, but he couldn't seem to help it.

"Lifting free weights by yourself is a very bad idea."

Payton sucked in a breath, dropped his feet back to the floor and opened his eyes.

Si stood at the end of the bench, his hands on the bar. How had Payton not heard him come in? He loomed over Payton with his brow furrowed over crystal blue eyes. "No more lifting weights on your own. It's dangerous." A couple strands of auburn hair fell onto his forehead.

Payton let go of the bar and suppressed a shiver. His mood was suddenly looking up. This was the reason he'd come here in the first place. To hear that voice again and see if the man was as handsome as he remembered. Last night, he'd dreamed of that smooth sexy voice whispering unspeakable things in his ear while they did unspeakable things to each other. Good grief, he was getting aroused. He was obsessed. How pathetic. All it took was a perfect body, a handsome face and someone to be nice to him for no particular reason.

Si crossed his arms on the bar, leaned over toward Payton and grinned. "How many are you doing?"

Galaxy, the man was every bit as gorgeous as Payton remembered. The clothes emphasized his masculinity. Red hair peeked out from under his arms, not concealed at all by the white sleeveless shirt he wore. His gray shorts were practically threadbare and very short, the hair on his legs visible right up to his upper thighs. There was almost nothing covering him. Unlike Payton, Si didn't seem the least bit embarrassed by wearing so little. He seemed quite secure and sure of himself.

That confidence made Payton's cock even harder. He swallowed the lump in his throat and hurried to sit up. He barely noticed his aching thigh muscles as he turned toward Si, hoping he hadn't spotted Payton's growing erection. "I— You— you don't have to help me. I'll slow you down. You— I—" He groaned and bit his bottom lip. There was just no way to get around it. "I'm not up to your"—he waved his hand, searching his brain for the right word—"standards."

Chuckling, Si darted a gaze down Payton's body then back up. "You are definitely up to my standards." The gleam in his eyes made it clear he wasn't talking about working out and weight limits. "Besides, I need a workout partner, my friends abandoned me tonight." Si pushed himself upright and grabbed the bar, ready to spot him. "Now lay back down and finish your set. How many?"

After hesitating for only a second, Payton decided the hell with it and lay back down. Si hadn't even tried to hide his erection yesterday in the shower. Either he'd ignore Payton's or— Payton didn't know what, but he was willing to take the chance. He knew he wasn't reading Si wrong. The man was definitely interested in him and Payton had nothing to lose. After all, wasn't this what he'd come here hoping for? It wasn't like anyone would find out. What was a little flirtation? "Three sets of eight, I've done one set." He got his hands on the bar on the outsides of Si's and pushed up.

Si didn't let go of the bar until Payton held it steady above him.

Payton brought the bar down then back up easily.

"One." Si's hands hovered above the bar. His legs were so muscular and—*dust, his shorts are short.*

Doing another rep fairly easily, Payton let his attention stray upward.

"Two."

Si's prick was right there, in his face. Payton couldn't *not* look.

"Three." Si stepped closer, his legs against the edge of the bench. He wore something white under the loose gray shorts. Underclothes, but none like Payton had ever seen. It only covered the genitals, with bands around the waist and each leg, leaving the arse bare. "Four." The garment cupped Si's testicles and outlined his prick.

Payton's cock twitched.

"Five." Si dipped toward Payton, his hands ready to catch the bar. His groin was scandalously close to Payton's face. "Come on, Payton. Three more." Was his voice more raspy than before?

Shoving the bar up, Payton ignored the burn in his arms. That was really not the way to get him to do three more. He had the insane urge to nuzzle his face into Si and see if he smelled as good as he looked. Whoa, where had that come from? Thankfully, his face was already heated from the strain of moving the weights, because after that thought he was surely blushing. He shouldn't think things like that, but dust if his cock wasn't throbbing and straining against his shorts.

"Six. Two more."

The weights were getting really heavy. His heart was thrumming in his ear.

Si scooted forward, his legs now straddling the edge of the bench. Payton could feel the heat of Si's thighs on his ears as Si took some of the weight of the bar, making it easier on Payton. Sweat and a musky warm scent teased Payton's nose as Si dipped again, following the barbell.

"Seven. Come on, do one more." His blue eyes glittered down at Payton, and his voice was definitely lower and huskier than before.

Gulping in a breath, Payton steeled himself for one last rep. He was not going to notice the thick cock outlined in those strange underclothes. He wanted to bury his nose there and— oh galaxy, he wanted to know how Si tasted. Payton gasped, shocked at the admission. He wanted to taste and touch and do whatever Si would— *Oh.* Payton's arms buckled.

The bar never touched him.

Si hauled the bar up like it weighed nothing, making the veins on his forearms obvious, and set it on the stand. He leaned his forearms on the bar and looked down at Payton.

At least Payton thought he did. His attention stayed focused on Si's erection, outlined through the thin gray shorts. Payton made a noise halfway between a gasp and a growl. He reached up, his hand hovering in front of Si's groin, before he came to himself and stopped.

Groaning, Si caught Payton's wrist and pressed his palm against the hard length of Si's cock.

Payton curled his fingers, and Si's cock jerked under his hand. It was so odd touching someone else like this. He squeezed.

Making a strangled noise, Si tugged upward on Payton's wrist. "Sit up."

Payton let go, loathe to do so. Turning around, he straddled the bench and scooted closer.

Stomach pressed against the barbell, Si leaned forward and hooked his thumbs in his waistband. He dragged the nearly transparent gray material down, revealing a scrap of white barely covering his prick. The white undergarment was nearly as threadbare as the gray shorts and yellowed with sweat and age. A damp spot dotted the material where the tip of Si's cock lay just under the elastic waistband. It was the most erotic thing Payton had ever seen. It was mesmerizing, fully capturing his attention.

Si's right hand slid behind Payton's head, urging him forward. His left hand tugged at the band of the white underclothes, but all Payton could concentrate on was that wet spot on the material.

He caught Si's hand, moving it aside, and leaned forward, pressing his open mouth to the damp material over the tip of Si's cock.

The tangy taste burst over his tongue as the sweaty smell flooded his senses. He sucked at the material and the head of Si's cock through it. It was so warm and firm, different than anything he'd ever had his lips against. Closing his eyes, he gripped Si's hips and pressed his face against Si's hot, hard prick. He smelled so good, not all cologney and sweet, but masculine and real.

"Payton, you're killing me. Suck my cock," Si growled and tugged at the waistband of his underclothes again.

Moving back, Payton watched as Si's cock bobbed free of the cotton undergarment. Payton just stared. It was amazing, long and reddish, different than Payton's yet the same. He swore he could see the blood rushing through the long vein down the front, even though he knew it was his imagination. The head flared slightly, then went back to normal, and a bead of clear liquid collected on the tip.

Payton licked his lips, his own cock started to leak and his testicles drew closer. He may have even moaned, he wasn't sure, but he knew Si did. The sound was pure sex and traveled right to Payton's prick.

Tightening his fingers in Payton's hair, Si pushed Payton's head closer, leaving little room for doubt about what he wanted. His other hand gripped the base of his cock. "Suck me."

Leaning forward, Payton flicked his tongue over the end, swiping off the drop of almost sweet precome.

Si grunted and tapped Payton's lips with the tip of his cock.

After a few tentative licks Payton opened up and took the head into his mouth. The very idea of what he was doing had Payton moaning around the thick cock.

Thrusting his hips softly, Si began to fuck Payton's mouth. The smooth skin caressed his lips, causing them to tingle. It was surreal, and Payton let himself get lost in the sensation. His fingers dug into Si's arse, urging him closer.

Dropping his hand flat against his stomach with his thumb and forefinger still around his cock, Si surged forward. His cock hit the back of Payton's throat, making Payton pull away and gag. Tears stung his eyes. He pushed back for a second, his hands still clutching Si's hips, to collect himself and catch his breath.

"Sorry." Si ran his fingers through Payton's hair, petting.

A trickle of sweat ran down Si's belly into the red curls at the base of his cock. Payton followed it with his eyes before catching it on his tongue. The tangy taste had him reaching down to press the heel of his hand to his erection. "Mmm..."

"Bloody hell." Si grabbed a handful of Payton's hair and pulled him forward again. He fisted his cock, reducing the length Payton had to suck.

The grip on Payton's hair was almost painful, but it was exciting. Payton dove back in and swallowed Si's cock. He managed to keep from gagging and bobbed his head at a nice steady rhythm. Si's grunts and Payton's own wet slurping sounds went to his head.

He slipped his hands around to Si's arse. With every thrust the muscles tensed, and sweat trickled down the small of his back onto Payton's hands. It was so primitive, not the polite distant sex Payton envisioned went on between most lords. His testicles were so tight, his cock throbbing. Those throaty sounds Si made drove Payton mad.

Payton's whole body tightened, his orgasm taking him by surprise. He pulled back, eyes wide, staring up at Si, and came in his shorts.

"Oh fuck." Si let out a hoarse yell above him and something hot hit Payton's cheek, then his nose and chin. It ran down his neck.

Payton blinked and dropped his head, trying to take it all in.

Si released his cock and grabbed Payton's chin, tipping it up. He bent over the bar and licked a long line up Payton's neck, then his chin and cheek, cleaning the semen off.

With sudden harsh clarity, reality came back to Payton. He was in a gym with a near stranger. He'd just— "Oh galaxy." If he got caught...

Panic flared to life and his stomach clenched painfully. His heart started hammering in his chest, trying to beat its way out. He had to get out of here. Jerking his chin out of Si's grasp, he ignored the surprised gasp. "I've got to go. I—I gotta go."

"Payton, wait." Si tried to grab his arm.

Payton shook his head. He had to get out of here. He couldn't do this. Turning, he ran for the door, not even caring that he was making a cake of himself.

Wind and snow hit him with a gust when he opened the door, but he didn't stop. He needed to be alone, to hide, to think. The freezing wind helped clear his mind. He would just stop going to the gym. He hadn't seen Si anywhere else on base. Si wasn't going to tell. If anyone found out he'd be in as big a trouble as Payton.

Payton took a deep breath and exhaled it. Steam blew out of his nose and mouth, and he realized he was halfway to his quarters, still in his gym clothes.

Chapter Six

The day was as bleak as his mood. Simon wrapped his cape around him tighter as he steered his horse toward Mayfair. He hadn't slept very well last night after Payton's abrupt departure. It had really galled that he couldn't go track Payton down then and there and talk to him, so he'd asked one of his aides to find out who Payton was first thing this morning. But before he could learn anything he'd gotten a summons from St. Albins.

"Good morning, Your Highness." George, St. Albin's groom, bowed.

Simon tried not to glower at the boy as he swung his leg over the saddle and hopped to the ground. He hated being called "Your Highness," it sounded so pompous. "Good morning, George, and it's Colonel," he corrected, and handed over Cirilo's reins.

George bowed again, his face going a little pale. "Yes, Colonel. Sorry, sir."

Simon stepped over a pile of snow where it had been shoveled out of the walkway and onto the street. He was being an arse. It wasn't the groom's fault Payton took off last night and Simon couldn't get the haunted yellow eyes out of his head. Stopping on the bottom step, Simon turned. "George."

The boy looked up. "Yes, Colonel?"

"I'm sorry. I didn't mean to snap at you."

George's mouth dropped open for a brief second then snapped shut and smiled. He dipped his head in acknowledgment. "My fault, Colonel, I won't forget again."

84

Ascending the steps, Simon let his mind drift to last night. Had he pushed Payton too far? Honestly, he was surprised things had gone as far as they had. He'd known how shy Payton was from the beginning. But damn, he hadn't expected that heat between them. Payton made him ache like no one had in a long time. Simon hadn't meant to be so overbearing, but he totally lost control with those stunning lust-filled eyes following his every move. Payton had been aroused from the moment Simon had walked in last night and it had gone right to Simon's head. Simon was just mourning the loss of experiencing it again, since he'd likely scared Payton off.

He strolled up to the mansion, taking his gloves off, then raised his fist to knock on the door.

The door opened before his hand made contact. The smooth deep baritone of Aldred's butler Jaxon greeted him. "Welcome, Colonel."

The under butler bowed and held out his hands for Simon's gloves, hat and cloak. "Good morning, Colonel. His Grace is waiting on you in the breakfast room."

"Thank you, Dudley." Simon took off his cover and coat, handing them over before following the scent of food down the hall.

As he reached the open archway, Clayton, Aldred's valet, gave him a warm, fond smile and stepped aside. "Your Highness, welcome. His Grace has been expecting you."

Simon couldn't not smile back, even if Clayton had called him by that dreaded address. Clayton had been with Aldred since he'd lived at the palace, since Simon was still in the nursery. Simon had had quite the infatuation with him as a teen, but more than that he considered Clayton a friend of sorts. As a kid Simon had spent many hours with the man, taking refuge in Aldred's room until Aldred returned from whatever ton event he'd been attending.

Simon grabbed Clay's hand before he could leave. "Nice to see you, Clayton. How are you?"

Clayton smiled even wider, his green eyes twinkling with merriment. "I'm fine, and I see you still haven't learned to ignore servants. It's very un-noble of you, you know," he teased, then tipped his head toward the breakfast room. "Get in there, it's important."

"Yes, sir." Chuckling, he let go of Clayton's hand and slapped him on the back. "And you spoke to me first," he called back over his shoulder as he entered the room.

Aldred sat at the head of the table with a plateful of eggs, bacon, kippers and beans. It lay untouched in favor of reading the newspaper.

"He's still handsome."

"Back off, boy." Aldred grinned over the morning news. "Get your own valet."

Laughing, Simon held his hands up in surrender. "Have no fear. I'd never subject Clayton to my friends. Although I suspect he could handle anything Roc and Wycliffe dish out. It would be them running for the door, instead of Clayton."

"Right you are, my boy. Clay put up with enough of your antics as a child, I suspect he can survive anything. Fix yourself a plate and come sit down." Aldred frowned, his face suddenly very serious. "I've got something you've got to hear, before it's splashed all over the front page this evening."

Great. "That doesn't sound good. Should I go fetch the scotch from the study?"

Aldred set the news aside and tried to give him a stern look. He failed miserably, his lips twitching. "It is entirely too early for you to be in your cups."

Shrugging, Simon fetched a plate from the sideboard. "Yes, God forbid my mother should hear of me getting sloshed before noon. I'd rather not have holy water flung at me every time I step outside, nor do I think my commanding officers would approve of the base being picketed over my sins."

"Oh come now, a little holy water never hurt anyone and our most righteous lords would never picket...they'd send their servants to do it for them."

Simon grinned as he filled his plate. That would be a sight to see. A rainbow of livery holding signs, yet bowing and saying milord to everyone who entered the gates. "I actually have an update for you as well. So give me your bad news and I'll give you mine."

"There is a movement in parliament to have the Englor Marines disbanded."

Simon spun around so quickly some eggs fell off his plate. "I beg your pardon?"

"You heard me correctly." Aldred took a drink of his orange juice.

Setting his plate down, Simon glanced at Aldred. "Who? Who is pushing for it and why?"

"Markham and his cronies."

"Markham?" What a strange coincidence.

His surprise must have shown, because Aldred cocked his head. "Mmm...yes. He's the main one championing the cause. You know him?"

"Yes. No. I only met him yesterday briefly. Dru and I were nearly run down by a rider in Hyde Park. Cirilo bolted in the confusion. Markham and Baymore caught Cirilo and brought him back. Markham seemed nice enough. What do we know about him? And how much support does he have?"

"About half of the House of Lords from what I gather. He wants to appropriate funds going to the Marines for interplanetary trade and moral reform." Aldred took a bite of his bacon.

"Moral reform? Yes, Dru mentioned that. She didn't think too highly of him." Simon pushed his eggs around his plate. "She was under the impression Mother had something to do with Baymore getting his barony."

"I believe so, yes. Gambling debts if I had to venture a guess. Baymore doesn't say much, just follows Markham's lead."

"Hmm..." That was the impression Simon had as well. "What's Markham against? Drinking, gambling or sodomy? Or all of the above?"

Aldred met his gaze. "I don't know."

"Have they no sense? Do they not realize how vulnerable Englor will be without their own defense?"

"They claim that is what the IN is for. Hawthorne, Oxley and I are rallying support against the proposal. Your father has not weighed in yet. With Hawthorne's help I plan on cornering the king at the dinner Saturday night in honor of Admiral Hawkins. You will be in attendance, won't you?"

Simon groaned. He hated formal dinners. "If I must. But in the meantime, we need to find out everything we can about Markham. I'm not above blackmail." Simon set his fork down, his appetite gone. Whatever he ate would likely sour in his stomach. He should have pressed Dru for more information about the man.

"I've already got people on it, and for the record, neither am I, my boy...neither am I." Aldred lifted his glass of juice and took a drink. "Tell me your news. Does it concern your man Benson?"

"Yes. I'm sending someone to look into his disappearance. There's been no word from Benson in several months."

Aldred thought about it for a moment, his dark brows pulling together. "Do you suppose Admiral Hawkins has learned something and that's why he's here?"

The thought had crossed Simon's mind. Admiral Hawkins was in deep with the Regelence royal family. He would not take kindly to finding a spy in the palace. "I don't know. I wish I knew more. If I could figure out who, why and what mother was trading..." Simon shrugged. "You haven't heard of any schematics, have you?"

"No, I've asked around. If we have something in the works, it's top secret and no one outside of the Marines knows about it." Aldred raised his glass and gave Simon a pointed look. "And that is your field, my boy. I believe it's time to start talking to generals."

Simon groaned and slumped back in his seat. "Are we really ready to let it be known that the queen may or may not be a traitor?"

"Are we ready to let the security of Englor be compromised?

Assuming that this asinine proposal goes through, it would be." Aldred picked up a piece of bacon. "Do you trust the IN to protect us? Are you certain it is not they who are involved in this mess on Regelence?"

Nothing was certain, but Simon couldn't shake the feeling that Admiral Hawkins was here for more than to inspect the base. The question was, who was Hawkins loyal to? Regelence, the IN or Englor? "I don't know, Uncle. I don't know. Benson mentioned the IN in his last message, but he didn't say anything about them." Simon pushed back from the table and stood. "Do you think it might have something to do with this new movement in parliament? Maybe Benson got wind of the IN wanting to take over the Marines?" That didn't make sense though. As base commander, if the IN were negotiating with the Marines, Simon would have heard of it already. Wouldn't he?

He shook his head and sighed. "Find out what you can about Markham. I'm going to send someone to look into Benson's disappearance. In the meantime, I'll keep trying to find out what schematics the note was referring to." As he turned toward the door, a thought occurred to him, making him pause and look back over his shoulder. "Don't trust anyone until we find out what's going on, Uncle."

Aldred shook his head. "I won't. Be careful, boy."

Simon nodded. "I'll be in touch. You know where to find me."

He met Dudley at the front door with his belongings. "Thank you, Dudley. Will you call someone to bring Cirilo around?"

Dudley dipped his head. "I already have, Colonel." He tossed Simon's cape around his shoulder and handed him his gloves.

"Thank you." Simon fastened the frog on his cape and put his hands in his gloves. He needed to know more about Admiral Hawkins. Instinct told him if he found out why Hawkins was here the rest of the unanswered questions would fall into place.

As he opened the front door of St. Albins House, the wind whipped across his body, bringing forth a shiver. He glanced down into the startled eyes of his aide, Jonah, who was making his way up the steps.

"Colonel, I have that information you wanted. I thought you'd want it immediately so I brought it here."

Information? What information had he asked— *Oh. Payton.* Bloody hell, he'd nearly forgotten. He closed the door and stepped outside. "Who is he?"

"Admiral Hawkins's aide, Sir."

Payton frowned down at his screen, then leaned back in his chair and rubbed his eyes. He was tired. After the Si-induced, mind-numbing, orgasm at the gym last night, he'd returned to his quarters and gotten back to work on cracking Englor's encryption. Sadly, he hadn't accomplished a lot because his mind kept drifting back to Si. Payton was in way over his head and didn't feel as panicked as he should, which scared him. What had he been thinking last night? They could have gotten caught.

Stretching his arms over his head, Payton turned his attention back to his computer. He'd made no progress with the encrypted message Trouble had stolen from the ship he and Aiden had been held hostage on. It seemed to be a message to Colonel Hollister from Benson that Caldwell the IN spy intercepted, but Payton wasn't positive. Damn, he wanted to meet the man who wrote this code. *I'll either propose marriage or run him through.*

A series of beeps sounded, startling Payton, then a window popped up on his com-pad that read, *IN Intelligence access granted.*

"Yes!" Payton laughed, a thrill of excitement shooting through him. He'd been working on getting in for the past three days. The program he'd had running in the background had finally managed to find a password for the login, he guessed. He'd tried *Caldwell*—the last name the IN spy who had

90

kidnapped Aiden and Trouble was using—Daniel—the man's supposed first name—and as many variations of the two combined names he could think of as logins. None of those had worked. So, on a whim, this morning he used *The Valet*. Who would have thought it would be something so obvious? Or maybe that was the point, it was too obvious, so no one would guess it.

Bouncing in his seat just a little, Payton checked the spy's email. Several recent ones appeared on the screen. Which meant the man had not been killed when The Marchioness self-destructed in space after Aiden and Trouble were recovered.

Someone named *Vretiel* corresponded several times with *The Valet*.

By five o'clock in the evening and with a lot of snooping Payton learned the schematics the IN spies referred to had not been obtained. There was nothing definite, but several obscure references to the schematics belonging to the EMC. Most of the mails were times and places for meetings. They obviously didn't feel secure enough to discuss things in their mail. Smart of them, but really aggravating for Payton. Was EMC the Englor Marine Corp? He frowned and leaned back in his chair. He couldn't think of anything else EMC might stand for even though he'd never heard the Englor Marines referred to as EMC.

Stretching out his stiff neck, he got busy again. He needed to know who *Vretiel* was and see if he could pinpoint his or Caldwell's location.

Payton became so immersed in trying to answer those questions that he'd have missed the door clicking open if it hadn't been followed by a brief knock. He glanced up just as Nate's head popped through the doorway.

"Have you seen this?" Nate came in holding a cup of something steaming—probably tea, it was teatime—and a paper and closed the door behind him. Tossing the paper onto Payton's desk, he sat in the chair across the smooth mahogany surface from Payton and took a sip from his cup. "Ah..."

The headline read: Parliament proposes IN absorb Englor Marines.

"Why?" Payton picked up the paper, skimming the article. "Do you think The Englor Marines are in league with the IN?" This didn't fit with what he'd found out today. Why would Englor allow this? Was this an attempt by the IN to obtain those schematics—whatever they were of—by other means?

Nate sampled his drink and shook his head. "I don't know, but I can't imagine Englor being stupid enough to disband their only armed force. The article says it's for appropriations to be allocated elsewhere."

"Did you know about this?" Payton set the paper down.

"I'm glad you asked." The smile Nate gave him was downright evil. "I read it in the newspaper this morning like everyone else. It seems to me though that someone in the IN must know something about it. Which in itself is suspicious, one would think as an admiral I'd be consulted. Think you can figure out who knew and what they expect to gain from the situation?"

Payton grinned, thinking maybe he already knew. "Would EMC by any chance stand for the Englor Marine Corp?"

"It's rarely called that by anyone but IN. But yes, EMC *is* the Englor Marines."

Feeling ten feet tall, Payton chuckled, stretched his legs out under his desk and crossed his hands behind his head. *Go me.*

"What?" Nate frowned. "What did you find?"

His victorious, I-know-something-you-don't-know pose lasted all of two seconds. Payton sat forward and told Nate what he'd found today, barely holding in his need to shout with excitement. When he finished, Nate sat back, staring at him like he'd seen a ghost.

"You are scary. I may have to make you my aide for real."

Now that was an idea. It would certainly give him something to do. More to the point, something he enjoyed doing. Payton bit his bottom lip. Could he talk his parents into it though?

Nate took another sip from his cup, his face unreadable. "How about the message to Hollister? Have you made any headway with the encryption?"

"No. Any chance you'll let me break into Hollister's office?"

"Absolutely not. Your investigation is limited to what you can pick up on the computers here and from other officers. If I put you in danger, your sire would have my head."

Damn. At least he'd tried. If he couldn't find anything through those channels he was going to break into Hollister's office—with or without Nate's permission—but he'd play it Nate's way first. "Okay."

"I'm thinking about sending you home next week. You already helped so much and I'm not sure what else you can learn being here. You can continue to work on decoding that message at home." Nate crossed one foot over his knee, getting comfortable.

No. You can't. Payton took a deep breath and pushed the panic aside. He knew he would have to go home sooner or later. Really, Nate was right. If Nate wasn't going to allow him to break into Hollister's computer, then there wasn't much he could do here. But the pang of regret wasn't for missing the chance to hack into computers like it should be. The ache in his chest was from giving up Si so soon.

"How is the working out going?"

"Uh. Good."

Nate lowered the cup he'd just raised without taking a sip. "Have you met anyone?"

What? Did he know? Payton's mouth felt like he'd swallowed cotton. No, Nate couldn't possibly know, he was only asking if Payton had found any info from other soldiers. If Nate had suspected anything, Payton would have already found himself with a chaperone, likely Nate himself. "No, not really. I've been going late and it's been pretty cleared out." *Please drop it.* Technically it wasn't a lie, he had waited until nearly everyone else had left. Payton's stomach clenched almost painfully. He didn't want to lie to Nate. Nate had been so fair to him, treating him like an adult and even allowing Payton to help defend his planet with this investigation.

Nate stared at Payton a few more seconds, in which Payton swore Nate could see right through him, then he stood. "Let me know as soon as you find anything else on the IN and Marine merger."

"Yes, sir." Payton wiped his sweaty hands on his pants under the desk.

Stopping with his hand on the door, Nate turned his attention back to Payton.

Payton's heart rate kicked up a notch.

"Don't forget about the dinner Saturday night." Nate opened the door and left.

Sagging into his chair, Payton made himself relax. Maybe Si would know something about the IN and Marine merger. Nah, probably not, if Nate didn't know. Si would have to be really high up in the Marines and Payton didn't think he was. Besides, Payton shouldn't go back to the gym. He was leaving soon and going back would do nothing but make him mourn the loss of his freedom. Nothing could come of his and Si's relationship.

Speaking of the gym... He should check the gym log from last night and find out if Hollister had been there. Actually, come to think of it, he really ought to find out more about Si. Just in case he ran into Si on the base during the day. *Yeah right, Pay.*

It only took seconds to log into the base computers. Pulling up the gym log, Payton searched for Hollister's name. It registered at the gym seventeen minutes after twenty hundred hours. That was after Payton had gotten there. *Hmmm...*

Payton put his elbow on the desk and leaned his chin on his hand. Should he go back? Maybe he could meet Hollister. Not to mention, he really wanted to see Si again. If he was leaving so soon, would it really matter if he saw Si one last time? Payton shook his head and groaned. No, he really shouldn't go. Scrolling down, he noticed he was the second to last person to leave the gym yesterday.

The last person to leave was *Col. S. Hollister.*

Chapter Seven

Not only did I manage to accidentally meet the man I'm investigating, I managed to accidentally have sex with him. I'm either the luckiest man alive or the unluckiest. The verdict is still out as to which.

—from the journal of Payton Marcus Townsend

Standing outside the gym door in the cold, he watched his breath rise into a steamy cloud and debated with himself. Payton was pretty sure the IN was playing Englor just as they were Regelence from what he found today, but he didn't know for certain. Si could be in with the IN...although everything he'd heard so far made him think otherwise.

Why did Si have to turn out to be Simon Hollister, heir to the throne of Englor? Payton reached for the door, then let his hand drop. He sighed and turned away from the gym.

Leaving and never coming back would be the best thing to do, yet here he stood. *Damn you, Si.*

The snow glistened in the light from the streetlamps. In the distance horse hooves clacked and the low hum of lifts carried through the base gates, but the base itself was quiet. Smoke billowed out from the tops of the different buildings and lights glowed in windows. Everyone was locked away inside, oblivious to him. No one knew he was there. No one *would* know. Why shouldn't he go in? Maybe Si could help him figure out what was going on. Perhaps Payton could learn something from him.

He turned back toward the door with his stomach in knots.

He *wanted* to go in. It would be foolish, but a little voice in his head whispered that he'd never get the chance again, at least not until he was twenty-five, and he was leaving soon anyway. The fact that Si was Hollister should eliminate the prospect of a fling, but it didn't. "Bloody hell, I'm doomed."

Mind made up, he opened the door and stepped inside. What was it about Si that made him so irresistible? No, it wasn't just Si. It was the freedom, the ability to do what he wished, to rebel.

He tried to convince himself it was a prime opportunity to find out what Englor was up to, but even he wasn't buying it. In fact, he was going to have to tiptoe around that.

Hurrying to his locker, Payton changed. His mind drifted back to last night. He'd never dreamed it would be so intense, or that he'd enjoy it so much. Masturbating by himself in the dark didn't compare. He'd give almost anything—including going against his better judgment—to feel that at least once more.

Wait. What if Si doesn't come back? "Would you come back after you ran out like you did?" Payton groaned and finished dressing in a hurry.

Upon leaving the dressing area, he discovered there was no one in the main weight room with all the free weights, nor was there anyone in the treadmill and cardio area upstairs in the open loft. Payton's mood fell. He hadn't checked out all the rooms, but he felt certain that if Si were there he'd be in one of those rooms. After checking the room with all the weight machines downstairs, opposite of the free weight room, he headed back toward the cardio room. This was for the best, he knew it was, but he couldn't help the disappointment he felt.

Since he was here he might as well work out. He could certainly use the exercise.

As he climbed the stairs again, he heard a thudding sound coming from the opposite direction as the treadmills. Frowning, Payton turned around and spotted a narrow corridor he hadn't noticed before. There were two doorways. Both doors were open. *What is that noise?* He turned down the corridor toward the thuds.

The first open door revealed a large space with a mirror along two walls. In the back corner of the room Si punched a heavy bag. Sweat dripped down Si's wide muscular back, soaking his white sleeveless shirt. Gauging from the dampness of the shirt, he had probably been there for some time.

Payton nearly swallowed his tongue and stood there silently, in awe of the raw power in that big body.

Si was pure male. His voice was cultured and aristocratic, but looking at him now, it was hard to believe he was royalty. He didn't seem like a man to conform to society's dictates. It was one of the things so appealing about him.

Payton's cock filled instantly, remembering how uncivilized they'd both been last night. He could almost feel Si's hands pulling his hair and telling him to suck his cock. Payton shivered.

After hitting the black bag so hard it bounced on its chains and made a clanking sound, Si stopped.

Stepping inside the room, Payton closed the door behind him. "Hello."

Si spun around, his eyes wide for a second. "I didn't think you'd show up tonight...Lieutenant." His gaze slid down Payton's body, lingering on his erection before returning to his face. "Does the admiral know you're meeting with me?"

So, Si knew who he was. "No." *Act casual, Pay. Like it's no big deal that he knows.* Now wasn't the time to chicken out. "When did you find out?"

"This morning."

Payton nodded. "I'm sorry about last night." Making his way into the room, he walked slowly down the length of the back wall, which held racks of swords, foils and rapiers.

"If you're talking about leaving so abruptly, there's nothing to apologize for." Si grinned. "I've been there, it's a bit overwhelming at first, but I assure you no one will find out."

Unable to meet that knowing grin, Payton pulled one of the foils with a rubber tip on the end off the wall. Si knew he was here as Nate's aide, but did he know they were investigating him? His confidence wavered a bit, but he didn't show it. Swinging the foil a few times, he tested its weight and balance.

"You know who I am, don't you?" Si walked a few steps closer to Payton and took a foil off the wall.

Payton swallowed hard and bobbed his head. "I found out this afternoon."

"Then you didn't set out to meet me?" Si slashed his blade through the air.

"No."

Simon stared at him for long seconds, his expression unreadable, then finally he nodded. "Do you fence?"

"On occasion, when my sire can't persuade any of my brothers to spar with him."

Si's smile was downright wicked, his attention drifting to Payton's groin again. "Winner names his prize." He lurched forward, not even waiting for an answer.

"Uh!" Even as surprised as Payton was, his training took over and he parried easily.

"Well done." Si went on the attack, backing Payton up several yards. "Why is the admiral really here, Payton?"

Oh, so this was going to be an interrogation. Si knew or at least suspected they were here to investigate him. "For a routine inspection of the base."

Si stopped dead in his tracks, his eyes narrowing slightly, then one red brow arched before he came at Payton with unrelenting determination.

By the time Payton got his bearings and was able to counterattack, he was breathing heavily and working up a light sweat. Thank galaxy Cony insisted he be well trained in swordplay, otherwise he would have already been soundly beat. Si was an excellent swordsman, nearly as good as Cony and Rexley. Payton was thoroughly impressed.

"Are you sure that's the story you want to stick to?"

Advancing, Payton moved Si back to the middle of the room. "Why else would Admiral Hawkins be here?" No way was

Payton giving him anything, not until he knew he could trust Si.

"Hmm..."

They went back and forth several times, well matched, but Payton couldn't help but notice he was more winded than Si.

"When you lose, I'm going to spread you out on this floor and—"

Gasping, Payton crossed out of the way of Si's foil. "That's cheating."

Si chuckled, not looking a bit repentant. "Nonsense. How is talking cheating?" He lunged.

Payton knocked his foil aside and went on the attack. "You're trying to distract me."

"Trying?" Si backed up several steps, tossed his foil into his other hand, pulled his shirt off one arm then switched back. His chest gleamed with sweat as he tossed the shirt aside then lunged again.

Blast, Si is gorgeous. Payton groaned. Caught up in the play of perfectly chiseled arm muscles, he nearly missed parrying. His cock took notice once again, not that it'd ever fully lost interest.

Taking advantage of the distraction he created, Si knocked the foil out of Payton's hand, stepped forward and pressed the tip to Payton's throat. "Strip."

"S-strip?" Payton panted, trying to catch his breath.

"Strip," he repeated.

Payton's cock jerked at the demand and his heart raced. Glancing down Si's body, he saw the bulging erection against Si's thin gray shorts. Once again Payton's stupid conscience tried to warn him against dallying with Si, but he ignored it. He wanted Si. He'd worry about the consequences later, right now...

Payton grabbed the hem of his shirt and whipped it over his head. It took every ounce of restraint he had not to cover himself with his arms once the shirt was gone, but he managed.

Si stepped back and flicked the material of Payton's shorts

up with his foil. "Shorts. Off."

Swallowing the lump in his throat, Payton hooked his thumbs in the waistband of his shorts and slid them down. He got them to mid-thigh before Si interrupted him.

"Mmm...nice. Lie down." Tossing his foil aside, Si knelt.

Payton's stomach clenched in anticipation as his cock grew harder. He got to his knees before Si helped him the rest of the way to the ground.

Once Payton's arse rested on the thin black rubber mat covering the floor, Si tugged Payton's shorts and smallclothes off over Payton's shoes. He put his palm on Payton's chest. Si had to have felt how hard his heart was pounding, but he didn't say anything. He pinched Payton's nipple, then pushed. "Lay down on your back."

Easing onto his elbows, Payton nodded. He was nervous, but his body didn't seem to realize that because his testicles grew tighter.

Si crawled between his legs and leaned over, resting his weight on one hand beside Payton's hip. Sweat dripped off his chin onto Payton's belly and his biceps flexed as he bent his arm a little. With his other hand he gripped Payton's cock.

Hissing out a breath, Payton squirmed. No one had ever touched him like that. He wanted it, but it was strange, his mind's first inclination was to yell no. Not only was he new to this, but Si could be Regelence's enemy. *Why do I want this so badly? I've become a complete wanton.*

He must have flinched, because Si grinned up at him. "Relax, I'm not going to hurt you." His eyes held a sincerity that inspired trust. Whatever was going on between their planets, it didn't affect them, their attraction, not right now anyway. They *both* wanted this.

Dropping his head forward, Si held Payton's gaze as he took the head of Payton's cock into his mouth.

"Oh!" It was the most amazing thing Payton had ever felt. His arse muscles clenched and his legs stiffened. A tingle raced down his shaft to his testicles, and he forgot all about espionage and who might or might not be involved. Even his nipples tingled. They seemed to be attached to his cock.

Slowly, Si slid down his shaft. His blue gaze fairly twinkled at Payton. His cheeks hollowed out as he applied suction, before slipping back up Payton's prick.

"Oh galaxy." Payton closed his eyes and dropped his head. It was pathetic, but already he was having to concentrate on not climaxing.

Si didn't relent though. He dragged his hand up with his mouth, creating a wonderful friction that had Payton's head spinning. He went deep, taking Payton all the way to the back of his throat.

The heat closed around the tip of his prick and Payton saw stars. "Oh bloody hell. More. Oh please."

Si bobbed his head, getting to work.

The wet sounds added to Payton's excitement. He couldn't believe this was actually happening. He'd gotten so aroused by doing this to Si last night, he'd never imagined how much better it would be having it done to him. His cock jerked in Si's mouth, his stomach clenching as tight as his arse and thighs. "Please don't stop." Rocking his head back and forth, he stared at the white ceiling tiles, trying to focus. Trying not to come.

Moving his hand off Payton's cock, Si slid it to his testicles, pulling gently as he deep throated Payton's prick.

"Dust." Payton arched up into Si's mouth, his back bowing off the mat, and came. He lay there panting for several seconds. His whole body tingled.

Si got to his knees abruptly, his ab muscles rippling. "Get up here." He jerked his shorts and the odd underclothes out of the way and began pumping his cock.

Still dazed from his orgasm, Payton sat up, not understanding what Si wanted until Si grabbed a handful of Payton's hair and drew him closer. He smelled of sweat, sex and something uniquely Si.

"Open your mouth."

The tug on his hair should not have been sexy or

intoxicating. Payton whimpered and opened his mouth. His prick slapped against his stomach as he wiggled nearer. He loved the feeling of helplessness when Si held his head like that. It took the choice away from him, freeing him. Payton couldn't imagine anyone who knew who he was treating him as a sex object. It was a huge turn-on.

Thrusting into his own fist over and over, Si dropped his head back and his eyes closed, but he didn't let go of Payton's hair. The red tip of his cock peeked out from his hand, already glistening with precome. Moaning, Si snapped his head up. His big body shuddered and he pulled Payton closer, giving him no choice but to dip his own head back.

Payton scrambled closer, licking his lips. He wanted Si to come on him again. He wanted to taste this time. Galaxy, his own cock was still hard as stone.

Roaring, Si met his gaze. It went straight to Payton's cock, making it throb and leak at the tip.

Come splashed over Payton's cheek then into his open mouth. When he closed his mouth to swallow, Si tapped his face with his cock, splattering spunk onto his nose and beside his eye. The musky smell invaded Payton's senses and his own body jerked.

Si's grip on Payton's hair loosened and Payton fell to the floor, grabbed his own throbbing prick and pumped twice before shooting for a second time.

Dropping forward, Si caught himself on his hands next to Payton's head. His breath panted out, fanning over Payton's cheek. He stared into Payton's eyes for several seconds. "That was amazing, but we still need to talk, Lieutenant."

Simon was biding his time. He didn't want to scare Payton off, but he wanted to know what Payton knew. Payton was either an exceptional actor or he had told the truth when he said he hadn't known who Simon was. Simon was pretty good at reading people and he chose to believe the latter. But now that they knew who each other was Simon wanted answers. He wasn't buying the "routine base inspection" bit.

Caressing Payton's ankles with his thumbs, Si glanced over the younger man's knees into his red face. "One more, Payton."

Payton struggled to rise back up. "Ugh. Easy for you to say, you can probably do this in your sleep." Payton got all the way up to a sitting position and fell back on the mat, letting his arms flop over his head.

Chuckling, Si let go of Payton's ankles and stood. "Come on." He offered his hand. "Shower."

Taking his hand, Payton pushed to his feet. He was quiet the whole way to the locker room, but Simon could tell he wanted to ask something. His bottom lip was caught between his teeth as he began undressing in silence.

Simon watched for a few moments, his prick getting hard again, then he turned away and got to work on his own clothes. He wanted to talk and if he didn't concentrate he'd get sidetracked again. It was easy to do with Payton around. He drew not only Simon's attention but his lust. "Are you from Regelence, or did the admiral pick you up elsewhere?"

"I'm Regelen." Payton sounded cautious as he got soap and towels then hurried off toward the showers. At least he wasn't trying to cover himself. Although Simon had to admit, the trait was endearing.

Simon followed. The shower was a better place to talk anyway. There were no cameras or microphones in the gym, but the shower seemed more private.

When he got inside, Payton was standing under a spray of water, his head bowed at the far end of the room. The half tile wall was to his left and another showerhead to his right, with a low wall opposite the other one.

"One hundred degrees," Simon told his own shower before setting his gel and shampoo on the ledge.

They spent the first several minutes in silence. It was an awkward quiet, not the comforting silence he was coming to know with Payton, which made Simon even more convinced that Payton knew something.

Simon poured shampoo into his hand, closed the lid and

set it back on the tiled wall. Winking at Payton, he rubbed his hands together before lathering his hair. Taking a deep breath, he dipped his head under the water. What did he have to lose? He was certain Payton could help him find Benson. If Payton had anything to do with Benson's disappearance, or knew who did, Simon wouldn't be telling him anything he didn't know. Benson wouldn't be missing if his cover weren't blown. If Payton didn't know anything, he'd think Simon was making small talk. "I had a friend on Regelence..." The white bubbles slid away down the drain. Simon brushed his hands through his hair and shook the water out. When Payton didn't answer, Simon turned toward him. "Let's help each other out here."

Shaking his head, Payton began soaping his hair. "I don't know what you mean."

Biting back his frustration, Simon clenched and unclenched his fists. "My friend's name is Ralph Benson."

If Simon hadn't been watching closely, he'd have missed Payton's spine stiffening. It was a minute gesture that he covered quickly. "I don't know a Ral—"

"Tell me about my friend, Pay."

Payton stood there for several seconds before his shoulders slumped and he let out a breath. "He's dead." He turned around slowly, his face blank and his eyes watchful.

With his gut twisting, Simon nodded, trying not to show a reaction. He'd suspected as much, but Ralph Benson was not only under Simon's command, he was a friend. "Damn." It hurt. "How was he killed?"

Payton's face paled a little, rivulets running down his temple. "Why was he on Regelence?"

Simon's jaw clenched. *Damn it to hell.* "Who killed him?"

With his gaze boring into Simon's, Payton stood there, stance rigid. He was so damned stubborn. At any other time Simon would have admired it, but his friend was dead and he wanted answers. Answers he was sure Payton had. *Galaxy, Ralph, why did you go and get yourself killed?* Simon exhaled deeply and closed his eyes. When he opened them he had to blink back threatening tears. "He was my friend."

"I—I'm sorry." There was another awkward silence and Payton turned toward the spray. Dipping his head, he let the water rinse the shampoo away.

"How do you know that we aren't looking for the same answers?"

For several moments Payton didn't say or do anything, he just stood there with his back to Simon, letting the water rain down over him. Then he met Simon's gaze. He looked...wilted. "A man named Caldwell killed your friend."

What? Simon sucked in a breath out of surprise. "Caldwell? Bloody hell and damnation!" He punched the wall.

Payton gasped and stepped back, his eyes wide.

Fuck. Pain radiated along Simon's knuckles, shooting up his arm. Shaking his hand, he turned away. "Damn it." He knew the name from one of Benson's messages. "Benson knew Caldwell was in the middle of things. Why wasn't he more careful?" Caldwell was the key in all this. If Simon could figure out whom Caldwell really was... "How? Why? Who the fuck does Caldwell work for?" Simon shouted.

"Benson was shot trying to keep Admiral Hawkins's consort and son from being kidnapped."

If Payton were telling the truth, Caldwell was indeed their common enemy. Simon studied his face. Payton was weary looking as though he was preparing to run, but he wasn't lying, Simon was sure of it. He made himself calm down. The apprehension he read on Payton's face hit him in the gut and the urge to comfort came over him. He took a few deep breaths and ran his fingers down Payton's cheek.

Payton flinched, but didn't move away. He stared at Simon for several seconds then shook his head, closed his eyes and leaned into Simon's caress.

"Who did Caldwell work for? You've already told me enough to know we're on the same side here, Pay. Let's help each other out." He dipped forward, his face hovering above Payton's. Not because he was trying to force information out of Payton, but because he couldn't seem to help himself. He closed his eyes and a puff of breath brushed his lips.

Payton's hands wrapped around his wrists, his forehead touched Simon's. He whispered something, making Simon pull back and open his eyes.

Simon gazed into the weary yellow eyes. "Tell me."

Darting a glance around, Payton clutched Simon's wrists tighter. When he spoke Simon wasn't even sure Payton said it aloud, but his lips formed the words clearly. "The IN."

Simon dropped his hands, stepping back. His stomach felt hollow and his mouth suddenly dry. "That's what Benson's last message meant," he said more to himself than Payton.

"What message?"

Turning away, Simon grabbed his washcloth and soap. His movements were quick and sure as he washed himself. Why was the IN involved? What did they stand to gain by pitting Regelence and Englor against each other? How did the IN and Englor Marine merger fit into this? And what about—? "What about Hawkins? He *is* IN."

"He had nothing to do with it." Payton stepped between Simon and the wall. He put his hand against Simon's chest. "Why would he kidnap his own consort and son?"

Nodding, Simon glanced down at the pale elegant hand on his chest and closed his own over it. Could Payton feel his heart thudding? Did he know how scary the idea of going against the IN was? Simon's stomach grew queasy. He slid his hand up Payton's arm and tugged him so close their chests touched. If Payton was lying... Simon shook his head. Payton wasn't lying. It was the one thing Simon had faith in.

Payton blinked back the water droplets falling into his eyes.

Even with the realization that his planet could be in real danger, Simon couldn't help but be drawn to this man. He dropped the washcloth and brushed the dark hair off Payton's forehead. "What do they want?" he whispered.

"I don't know," Payton whispered back.

Standing there holding Payton against him, Simon rested his cheek on top of the head of dark wet hair and closed his eyes. Sweat dripped down his temples and his chest heaved to bring in the steamy air. He may want to protect this man, but he couldn't help but think that Payton would, despite his size, stand by Si's side and fight the IN with him...for both their planets.

Chapter Eight

Simon groaned and rubbed his temples. Staring at the computer was giving him a headache. "What schematics?" He'd been researching it for two bloody days. "I just want to know what the fucking schematics are for." Whatever they were, it was very top secret. He had fairly high clearance, but he couldn't access the Englor Marine's Research and Development office. Dropping his head to his desk, Simon closed his eyes.

Okay, think, Si. Payton thought the cloning technology Benson referred to was Regelence's artificial reproduction method, although he didn't know why the IN would want it. They were equally certain that the schematics were something that belonged to the Englor Marine Corps. Simon banged his head against the desk and sat back up. The IN was going to great lengths to get these two pieces of information and draw the suspicion away from themselves. It had almost worked.

Beep. Beep. Beep.

Simon started. Damn, he'd forgotten about setting the alarm on his computer. He closed his workstation down and pushed back from his desk. If he was going to return and meet Payton for a night on the town, he should go and get dressed. After two days of going over and over their information, they both needed a break.

They'd done nothing but work at solving the remaining puzzle pieces. Even at night they hadn't managed to finish a full workout or have sex because they'd been too busy going over things. Not that Si was complaining...*much*, because he was getting to know Payton better.

He enjoyed working with Payton. It was amazing how the man's mind processed and analyzed information. If anyone could help Simon figure this out, it was Payton. Smiling, he stretched his hands over his head and yawned.

Simon felt slightly guilty about not telling Payton about his mother's involvement, and wondered briefly if the information would help Pay, but he didn't see how. There was nothing to gain by dragging his mother through the dirt. It would make the entire royal family look bad. Besides, it looked like she was a pawn in this IN game just as everyone else was.

Grabbing his uniform cape, he slung it around his shoulders and headed out of his office.

By the time he got back to the base the snow had stopped. The continuous snowfall throughout the day accumulated a good eight inches on the ground. It was pretty and reminded Simon of playing in the snow as a kid with Aldred and some of the servants. Those were fun days, before he realized what kind of responsibility lay on his shoulders, before he had to worry about the very entity that trained him to lead trying to take over his planet.

He looked at his watch. It wasn't quite twenty hundred hours, so Payton wasn't late, but in the back of his mind Simon wondered if Payton would come. He'd sent Payton a message this morning asking him to meet outside of the gym in civilian clothes. The man was a workaholic.

Asking Payton out killed two birds with one stone. It gave Simon the potential to discuss what they already knew, and it gave both of them a much-needed rest. They were at a standstill until they figured out what the IN wanted. Maybe time away from the issue would help. Then there was Payton... Simon would be lying if he said he didn't want to see more of Payton.

As if Simon's thoughts conjured him, Payton walked around the corner of the building. When he drew close he smiled. "Hello." His hot breath formed a cloud of vapor when he spoke.

Simon's cock hardened, like it seemed to always do when he saw Payton, and tension he hadn't realized he had seeped out of his shoulders. "Good evening." Simon pushed away from the wall.

Payton looked every inch a lord in his greatcoat and top hat. Regency dress suited him, right down to his white gloves. He wore black trousers over shiny black ankle boots and as he drew close his wool coat fell open revealing a charcoal evening coat, cream-colored waistcoat and snowy white cravat. His cravat was tied to perfection in a complicated knot, as though a valet had dressed him. "You look exceptional."

"Thank you. You look quite dashing yourself."

Simon smiled at the once-over Payton gave him. He was dressed similar to Payton, only his waistcoat was black and he'd forgone a hat. "Thanks. Did you dress yourself?" Motioning toward the front of the base, Simon waited for Payton to fall in beside him.

"Yes. I— Yes. I told you I was Regelen."

Waving to the guard in the guard shack, Simon stepped through the wrought-iron gate. "Yes, but you look... Do you have a title?" It was doubtful. Regelence was like Englor in that very few titled gentlemen went into military service, but Payton learning who Simon was hadn't seemed to change how he treated Simon. Not that he was complaining, but it was unusual. It spoke of someone familiar with the gentry.

"Your message said you wanted to discuss what we learned last night."

Hailing a hackney, Simon faltered. He'd said that because he knew Payton wouldn't have come otherwise. "I thought we both deserved a break. We can discuss things over a game of cards and a few drinks." Why had Payton changed the subject?

"So you haven't learned anything new either." Payton sighed. When the lift pulled up, he strolled up to it and ordered the door open. As the steps slid down, he stepped aside waiting on Simon.

"No," Simon mumbled, transfixed. The moonlight glaring off the snow-covered ground cast Payton's pale skin in an ethereal glow. He was devastatingly handsome. Instead of being stiff with military precision, he stood with an elegant and refined posture. He had a regal bearing. Lined up against the peers of Englor, one would be hard-pressed to say Payton wasn't one of them. He looked every inch a lord of the realm. Simon started to ask once again if Payton held a title on Regelence, but it wasn't important. Likely Pay just didn't want Simon to know he wasn't a lord. Simon would have to assure him it didn't matter, but for now, he let it go and held his arm out toward the coach. "After you."

Taking his hat off, Payton climbed into the coach and took the seat riding forward.

After joining him, Simon ordered the door closed. When he was certain the door was down and no one could see them, he slid close and rested his hand on Payton's knee. *Mmm...* This close Simon could smell the sweet and spicy aftershave. Even Payton's scent was appealing. It was going to be hard pretending they weren't lovers in public.

Payton's gaze shot to Simon's hand and he swallowed audibly. The demureness was charming. He still wasn't used to Simon touching him. Or was it that he wasn't used to anyone touching him? Simon was fairly certain he was a virgin as far as other men were concerned, but was he like this around women too? He knew homosexual relationships were acceptable on Regelence, according to what Benson had told him—the king was married to a man—but were they the norm or just among the aristocracy?

He pushed back a spark of jealousy trying to creep in. Why couldn't Englor be all right about same-sex relationships? Hiding who he was got old. It wasn't so bad on base—lots of marines played around, whether they were gay or not—but out in society? Simon had always had to pretend interest in women so no one would know. It rankled. Giving Payton's leg a light caress, Simon studied the flawless jaw line in the dim coach lights. Payton was truly exquisite.

Licking his lips, Payton swallowed again. His teeth worried his bottom lip for a split second. "Where are we going?"

Simon leaned forward, focused on those full kissable lips. He hadn't kissed Payton yet. Most of the time he didn't kiss his lovers, it was so intimate, but he really wanted to kiss Payton. What would those lips taste like? Were they as sweet as the rest of him? *Wait. What did he say?* "What was that?"

"Where are we going?"

"To a new gaming hell down the road from Brook's." *Oh.* He hadn't informed the hackney computer. Payton had him preoccupied. "Take us to Apollo's Den on St. James."

The lift started moving.

"Are all your streets named after historical England?" Payton asked.

Oh, he was a smart one. Simon grinned. "Most are. Our founder, James P. Moreal, was a historian and due to the similarity of our river to the Thames, he made the capitol of Moreal, London and named the river and streets accordingly. We even have a Hyde Park, Vauxhall Gardens, Drury Lane, Covent Gardens, White's, Almack's, Gentleman Jackson's...several of historical England's Regency Era landmarks."

Payton worried his lip again.

Simon was beginning to realize it was something he did when he was nervous or thinking. Simon didn't want him to do either at the moment. He moved his hand up Payton's thigh and leaned forward, only inches from the delectable mouth. "Are you a history buff?"

Payton blinked. "No, why do you ask?"

"Even a lot of Englorians don't realize the similarities to historical England." He inched closer to Payton, focusing on his lips.

"Oh. No. Well yes, sort of. I enjoy history, but it's not my hobby or anything. I suppose I'm just well educated." He said it without a hint of arrogance, tilting his head slightly. "I was raised in a Regency-type society too, remember?"

Simon's cock jerked. He did remember and bloody hell, that self-confidence was sexy. He'd known Payton was bright, having worked with him the past couple of days, but now Simon wondered just how smart Payton was. Squeezing Payton's thigh, he gazed up into those bewitching yellow eyes. *"Vous avez les yeux étonnants,"* he said in French.

"Avete sorprendente occhi anche," Payton breathed across Simon's lips in what sounded like Italian before he touched their mouths together briefly.

That would never do. Growling, Simon cupped Payton's jaw in his hands and sealed his lips to Payton's. He slid his tongue along the seam of Payton's lips, tasting and teasing.

Payton opened almost hesitantly. For several seconds he did nothing, just let Simon explore his mouth. It occurred to Simon that he hadn't done this very often. Why that thought made Simon's cock throb he had no idea. He'd never cared for purity, but Payton's was amazingly erotic. Maybe it was because all the men Simon had been with had never truly been virginal. They'd all been with women, if not other men.

Clutching Simon's wrists, Payton pushed sweet moaning noises into Simon's mouth along with his tongue making Simon's world tilt on its axis. He wanted to get to know Payton better. Even the last couple of days where they'd done little but brainstorm together he ached for Payton. Simon wanted to keep him. Which was utterly ridiculous. It was too risky. Someone sooner or later would figure out Simon had a male paramour stashed away. But damn it was a nice fantasy.

With his eyes still closed, Payton pulled back and licked his lips. He was the study of innocence. He made a little humming sound that had Simon's cock jerking to attention.

He sat there staring at Payton for several moments, just soaking in the beauty of the man before him, then his brain clicked back on enough to ask, "Was that Italian?"

Nodding, Payton leaned into the caress. "I said you have amazing eyes as well. So blue..."

Simon moaned and ran his fingers down Payton's jaw, marveling in how smooth it was. He really was a handsome man...and smart. Most Englor Lords spoke French as well as English, it was even taught in the IN because several planets used it, but Italian wasn't a common language.

Galaxy, Si wanted this man. He considered detouring to his townhouse. His cock was throbbing, wanting Payton so badly. The need to bury himself in Payton's lissome body had been riding him hard since the first night he'd seen Payton. It didn't seem possible but Simon wanted him more every time they saw each other. He was almost mad with the need to fuck Payton. Surely no one would think anything of it if they saw them entering Simon's townhouse? Wycliffe and Roc went home with him all the time, everyone knew they were friends.

Payton's eyelids fluttered open. He stared into Simon's eyes for several seconds then closed his eyes again, tilted his head and parted his lips.

Bloody hell. He groaned and shifted forward, focused on Payton's now-swollen lips. He cupped Payton's jaw and drew him forward again. This time when their lips met, it was hungry, almost violent. Simon slid his hands down Payton's body, wrapping them around Payton and hauling him closer.

Payton landed against him, knocking them back onto the seat. Groaning at the delicious weight of Payton's body on his, Simon grabbed two handfuls of tight linen-clad arse and squeezed. He pressed their erections together, grinding up against Payton.

Lifting his head, Payton moaned and thrust his hips against Simon. "I want—"

The lift stopped. "Sir, we have arrived at your destination." The lift door began to open.

Shit. It was like being doused with ice water. Simon sat quickly, bringing Payton up with him. He couldn't afford for anyone to see him like this. He had enough to deal with at the moment without adding a scandal into the mix. So much for going to the townhouse.

Fixing his jacket, Payton looked away. He cleared his throat and gathered his stuff, but his blush deepened.

Damn. Si pressed his thumb on the scanner next to the door. "Put it on my tab." As they exited the coach, Si looked around. People were going in and out of clubs all up and down the street. The sidewalks were busy, but no one seemed to have noticed them. He touched Payton's arm, stalling him for a second. "I'm sorry. It's just that things are...different here than on your planet. And on base. On base there is more tolerance of—" Si looked around again to make certain no one was listening.

"It's okay, I know. And it was as much my fault as it was yours." Nodding, Payton gave Simon a wobbly smile and headed toward the door of the gaming hell.

Somehow that didn't make Simon feel any better knowing Payton understood. It wasn't okay, not really.

Simon glanced up at the discreetly lit sign above the door and the small group of gentlemen entering in front of them. Smoke and the sound of laughter exited along with a few patrons. Maybe this wasn't the best place to take Payton. What if his wide-eyed innocence gave him away as it did in the locker room? The military was much more forgiving toward gay men. The ton, even the more disreputable members, was not. Had Simon recognized Payton for what he was because he was looking for it? He didn't want some dust for brains teasing Payton.

Someone slammed into his shoulder, hard. A twinge shot down his arm.

"Pardon me, Colonel. I didn't see you there." The voice was familiar.

Rubbing his shoulder, Simon turned. He felt Payton brush against his other arm as he fell in beside Simon.

Markham dusted his own coat with a flick of his fingers and a snarl of his lips. "Gaming, Colonel? I wouldn't have thought you the type to participate in such vulgarities." His polite tone warred with his words.

He had some audacity chastising Simon for entering the very same establishment the man himself had just left. No wonder Dru disliked this man.

"I assure you I have many bad habits, milord. What brings *you* to this side of town?"

Completely ignoring the question, Markham turned his attention to Payton. "I see you've traded partners in crime." He raised his head just high enough to look down his nose at them. "A fellow soldier, I assume. Do they not have entertainments on base?"

Simon bit back the urge to laugh at the haughty action. It was exactly what he expected of a moral leader. The Earl thought himself better than a mere soldier. The attitude had always disgusted Simon. "They do, but I think it's quite fitting London offers better entertainments to the men who fight for Englor's freedoms, don't you?"

"It was nice talking to you again, Colonel. I've an appointment to keep and I find it quite rude to keep my friends waiting." He tipped his top hat. "Good evening, I leave you to your pursuits."

Clenching his teeth, Simon forced himself to relax as Markham left. Funny, the very organization Markham wanted to do away with was the one that kept Simon from beating the man to a bloody pulp.

"Who was that?" Payton asked.

"The Earl of Markham, the man spearheading the movement to have the Englor Marines disbanded."

"What an arse."

"No. He's the lead arse. Come along. I have no intention of allowing the moral leader of the ton to spoil our debauchery."

After handing over their coats, gloves and Payton's hat to the doorman, they entered the loud and smoky Apollo's Den. Wycliffe and Roc had invited Simon to the grand opening of the hell earlier in the week, but he'd been distracted. Pleasantly so. He glanced over at his distraction and found Payton gaping like a fish. Apparently, his embarrassment from the lift was fleeting, thank galaxy.

"Stars." Payton studied the place with his mouth hanging half open.

Chuckling, Simon grabbed Payton's arm and steered him out of the way of a passing footman carrying a tray of drinks, before letting go. On Englor, brothels and gaming hells were the normal stomping grounds for young men when not being dragged by the ear into a ball or the theater. But it was obvious from the response that Payton had never been to a gaming hell. Why not? It seemed odd that he wouldn't have gone. Were only the ton allowed in on Regelence? That didn't seem right. Simon had started familiarizing himself with Regelence when he'd first decided to send Benson there, but he clearly needed to double his efforts.

As gaming hells went, this one was a tad on the ostentatious side, but Simon supposed it was as good an introduction as any. There were gaming tables scattered all over the room and it was carpeted wall-to-wall in a deep green. The wainscoting was white and the wallpaper above depicted pastoral scenes. Every ten feet or so was a white marble column along the wall as well as several in the middle of the room. The ceiling was painted to look like the sky at dusk, complete with big puffy clouds, and the curtains covering the windows and sectioning off the rooms were gold velvet. It was packed, loud and smoky, like every gaming hell Simon had ever been in.

"I say, Si, are you going to introduce your friend?" Wycliffe strolled up with a drink in one hand and a cigar in the other, eyeballing Payton suspiciously. He was turned out much like Simon, all in black except for his white shirt and cravat.

"Wycliffe, may I present Payton Jeffers. Payton, this is my dearest friend, Ansley Eason, The Earl of Wycliffe."

Payton's eyes widened slightly then he bowed like it was the most natural thing in the world to him. "Pleasure to make your acquaintance, milord."

Wycliffe tipped his head to Payton, still looking him over. "A pleasure to meet you as well, Payton. Tell me, where did Si find you?" Wycliffe always had been a suspicious bastard, but it was on the tip of Si's tongue to tell his friend to lay off, when Roc strolled up to them grinning ear to ear.

Roc joined them in looking Payton up and down before smiling and elbowing Wycliffe aside. He darted a glance around and leaned in to whisper, "It suddenly becomes clear why he's ditched us the last couple of nights."

Simon groaned. "Payton, this jackanapes is Roc."

"Proctor Bennett." Roc stuck out his hand.

Looking at it for a few moments, Payton grabbed it and shook, but not before Simon saw the slight furrow of his brow. "Payton—Jeffers."

"Where did Si meet you?" Roc asked, in no hurry to release Payton's hand.

"On base, Payton is an IN lieutenant." Simon flicked a glance at Roc and Payton's hands.

Roc blanched and dropped Payton's hand like a hot potato.

Giving Roc a pointed stare, Simon let his friend know that Payton was off limits. Perhaps he should have staked his claim when he'd agreed to meet his friends here. He hadn't even told them what he'd learned about Benson, wanting to talk it over with Aldred first.

"You're no fun a'tal, Si," Roc hissed quietly as a group of people jostled their way past them.

Squinting against the glare of Roc's bright red waistcoat, Si ignored the taunt. "Wherever did you get that waistcoat?" The rest of Roc's ensemble consisted of a classy black evening coat and a white cravat tied in a much simpler knot than Simon's, Payton's or Wycliffe's, but that scarlet was blinding.

"Do you like it?" Roc actually preened, before snagging a drink off the tray of a passing footman. He took a sip then made a face. "Brandy."

"I tried to talk him out of it." Wycliffe extracted the brandy from Roc's hand, took a drink and turned away from them. "Come. I've secured a private room. Delany and Sexton are joining us."

Simon watched Wycliffe stride off like he owned the place and shook his head. That sounded about right. Likely that was why Roc bought the waistcoat in the first place, because Wycliffe objected to it. The two of them took great delight in annoying the other, and Simon too for that matter. "Are you ready, Payton? Pay?"

Payton had maneuvered himself slightly behind Simon and was peeking around him at something toward the back corner. His face was pale and his eyes wide. Simon frowned and looked in the direction Payton was staring. There was only a group of young lords playing cards. It looked like Lord Jared Hawkins, Lord Timothy Gratham and... *Oh.* There was a flamboyant demi rep with a low-cut dress perched on Lord George Seaton's lap. She was laughing at something Lord Jared said. It was rather obvious what she was by her bold-colored clinging dress and makeup on her face. That must be what Payton was so stunned about. It was endearing. Once again he was reminded of Payton's lack of experience and it went right to his cock.

He touched Payton's elbow, bringing him forward. "Are you coming?"

"Oh." Payton flinched then looked up at him. "Yes. Sorry, I was just looking around. Where are we going?"

"Wycliffe reserved a table." Simon started them moving. He stopped a footman a few feet from them. "Bring cigars and a bottle of scotch to Lord Wycliffe's table." He glanced at Payton. "Scotch okay with you?"

"Sure." Payton didn't seem certain. He kept peering over at the prostitute, while trying to conceal his interest by keeping Si in the line of sight. He appeared shocked. Simon wondered briefly if he were going to run off like he did the first few times they'd messed around.

The footman bobbed his head and bowed. "Yes, Your Highness, right away."

Payton seemed to relax once the demi rep was out of sight, but he kept glancing back.

As they walked Simon reached out to grab Payton's arm and escort him, then realized what he almost did and jerked his arm back. He too looked around, hoping no one noticed. "Tell me more about Regelence."

"What would you like to know?" Payton hurried toward the room where Wycliffe and Roc went, walking ahead of Simon.

Simon's gaze landed on Payton's arse before he even thought about it. He lifted his head. Tonight was going to test his self-restraint. Galaxy help him should anyone see him groping Payton in public.

Payton was certain Nate's brother hadn't seen him when they'd arrived, but Payton had yet to let his guard down. Every time that curtain moved, it drew Payton's undivided attention. He'd been so careful sneaking off base, making sure to tell Nate he was turning in early and leaving the dog tag in his room. If Jared saw him... Payton took another sip of his drink and looked down at his cards.

"Tell me, Payton, where are you from?"

Payton fought the urge to squirm under Viscount Delany's steely gaze and set his cards on the table. Delany didn't smile much and Payton couldn't decide if Delany disliked him or if he was just a serious gambler. "I'm from Regelence."

Delany's lip turned up in a snarl, and he tossed his cards onto the table.

Aware he was on foreign soil, Payton met Delany's stare. His throat tightened and his stomach clenched, but he refused to let his nervousness show. Would his admittance mean trouble? It didn't matter. Spurning his planet wasn't in him. If admitting his patriotism meant a fight, so be it.

"Oh?" Arching an arrogant ebony eyebrow, Wycliffe glanced at Si.

"Regelence? Isn't that the sodomite planet?" Sexton asked, his gaze boring into Payton.

Roc choked on his scotch.

Pounding on Roc's back, Simon addressed Sexton. "I suggest you mind your tone, Sexton. I'll remind you that Payton is an IN officer and my guest."

Sexton pushed back from his chair so hard it clambered to the floor. "I beg your pardon, Your Highness. If you gentlemen"—he sneered at Payton—"will excuse me, I've remembered something I have to attend to." He strode to the curtain, knocking it aside so hard Payton expected it to come tumbling down into a heap on the floor.

Roc finally stopped coughing and took another drink. Red in the face, he cleared his throat and mumbled "Thank you" to Simon.

Wycliffe raised his attention from his cards, darting a glance toward the door. "Good riddance." He grinned at Payton. "I hear Regelence is a lovely planet, much like our own."

Payton nodded, deciding immediately he liked Wycliffe. "It is—"

"Excuse me, gentlemen. I just remembered Sexton is my ride home." Delany dipped his head in a pretense of politeness and left so quickly he nearly ran over a footman coming back in the room with a fresh decanter of scotch.

Dust. Was this going to cause Simon problems? Was Si mad? Suddenly, Payton missed Regelence, his chaperones and all the restrictions of being a prince.

"Hmm, I never figured Sexton for a bigot." Si stared at the curtain, a look of complete shock on his face. Shaking his head, he turned back to his cards and shrugged. "Fuck 'em."

Maybe being sheltered wasn't so bad after all. Payton's chest hurt. He didn't like feeling...different? He'd never thought of himself as *different*, but here he was.

"You didn't tell us Payton was from Regelence." Wycliffe laid his hand on the table, took a swig of his drink and stared at Si expectantly.

"No, you didn't," Roc added.

Did they know about Simon's investigation? Or was it the liking-men thing? No, they knew about Si, Payton was positive. They'd just defended Payton and Roc's remark when they first arrived...

"Payton has given me some important information we've been after, perhaps we can all discuss it later." Simon smiled at Payton.

"Ah." Wycliffe nodded and picked up his cards again. "Your turn, Roc. Relax, Payton. You're among friends."

Then it was the investigation they were curious about. Payton inhaled, finally feeling like he could get air.

Roc played his hand and took a drink from his tumbler. "Si, have you—?"

The rest of Roc's question was lost on Payton. The heavy gold velvet curtain blocking their private room from the rest of the gaming hell opened, and Payton's gaze flew toward it expecting Jared Hawkins to walk in, or worse Sexton and Delany returning. It was only a footman. Payton turned his attention back to the table without really listening.

"I'm still looking into it," Si said.

Payton blinked and looked down at his cards again, hoping someone would say something to give him a clue what they were conversing about. He tried not to be nervous but Delany and Sexton's abrupt departure had him way off kilter. What had Roc asked? *Please don't let anyone ask my opinion.*

"I'm out." Si tossed his cards down and picked up his drink. "I've got a meeting with General Davidson next week. If anyone knows about the proposed merger, he will."

Ah, the IN and Englor Marine merger. Sipping his own drink, Payton glanced toward the curtain again. The gaming hell wasn't at all what he'd expected. Men played Hazard, Whist, Faro and Poker—like Payton, Si, Wycliffe and Roc—with an occasional game of blackjack. There were one or two roulette tables as well. All in all, it was a little disappointing. Unless one considered the gambling, and Payton didn't see why that would count. The gym locker room was much more risqué. For the life of him he couldn't understand why unmarried men were not allowed to go on his planet. Was it different at home? Maybe they *did* have wild orgies in Regelence gaming hells. At least at home no one would act as if Payton were some oddity.

"Payton, tell us more about the cloning technology on Regelence. Are all children on Regelence created in such a way?" Wycliffe asked without looking up from the cards in his hands. He set another chip in the middle of the table.

Payton frowned at his cards. Was Wycliffe merely curious or was he going to insult Payton as well? Tossing his cards down, he slid an ante chip over it and went out this hand. He'd give Wycliffe the benefit of the doubt. He'd said Payton was among friends. "I'm out. It's not cloning. It's just a basic artificial reproduction process."

Wycliffe tossed another chip out, raising Roc. "But aren't all Regelens alike?"

"No, of course not."

"But all the infants are male, aren't they, with other similar traits?" Wycliffe glanced up, meeting Payton's gaze. "Call, Roc."

He meant the preference for men. "Well yes, most are male unless specifically requested otherwise and have a preference for their own sex. But Regelence does not allow designer babies and pretty much only the gentry use the process. A little over half of the children on Regelence are created the old-fashioned w—"

"Si? Darling? Are you in here?" A tall willowy woman in a green dress and a green and gold feather demi mask swept through the curtain into their room.

Everyone jumped to their feet.

Breathe, Pay, it's just some lady. Payton stood as well. Who was this woman? Good Galaxy, the start she gave him had his heart racing.

"Oh sit. Sit. I heard you were in here and had to come say hello." She walked over to Si, kissed his cheek and grabbed his hand.

Si kissed her back, a huge smile on his face, before taking both her hands in his and looking her over from her perfectly coifed black hair to the dainty gold slippers peeking out from under her elegant evening gown. "Dru, sweetheart, you look beautiful as always. But if you are going to wear a mask, the point is not to let everyone know it's you."

Dru waved a dismissive hand. "Oh, Si, you know people will know it's me whether my face is covered or not, so why shouldn't I speak to my friends?"

Wycliffe took the hand Dru was waving, bowed over it and kissed it. When he let go he shook his head and offered her a smirk. "Your Grace, you scandalize me, you truly do."

"Oh please, Wycliffe. Nothing I do can compare to yours

and Roc's antics. Where is—?" She turned and spotted Roc. Her face lit up under the green mask. "Tell Wycliffe I'm not scandalous, will you, Roc?"

Roc chuckled, before focusing his attention on Wycliffe. "Her Grace is not scandalous." He leaned forward and put his hand to his mouth like he was whispering, but his voice stayed the same. "Besides, she's the top of the food chain, she can get away with being scandalous."

"Dru, sit, join us." Si pushed the empty chair out so Dru could sit.

The three men took their seats.

Payton stood there for a second stunned. Who was this whirlwind and why hadn't they introduced him to her?

Si looked up at him and the laughter vanished. "Oh. Oh, Pay, I'm sorry." He stood and gestured toward Payton. "Dru, this is Lieutenant Payton Jeffers. Payton, this is Her Grace the Duchess of Kentwood."

The duchess stood and offered her hand and a big smile to Payton. "A pleasure to meet you, Lieutenant." She put her other hand beside her mouth much as Roc had and whispered rather loudly, "But I'm not Her Grace the Duchess of Kentwood." Her gaze darted around. "Because my mother would be scandalized. A duchess would never go to a gaming hell."

Payton grinned and bowed over her hand. "It's a pleasure to meet you, not the Duchess of Kentwood."

Everyone laughed as Payton, Si and Dru took their seats.

Payton couldn't help but notice the duchess sat closer to Si and immediately engaged him and Wycliffe in quiet conversation. The three were clearly old friends. Payton suddenly felt like an outsider.

Si laughed at something she said and rested his arm on the back of Dru's chair. They looked comfortable together. Si apparently held Dru in high esteem. A jolt of something very much like jealousy hit Payton, making him frown.

Roc leaned in close, getting Payton's attention. "Drucilla is a doll. Her husband died shortly after they were married. She was with child at the time and after the new Duke of Kentwood's birth, Dru was pretty much set. Dru, being widowed and holding one of the most vast estates in all of Englor, does as she pleases. No one would dare snub her."

Payton nodded, watching Simon take a drink from his tumbler and offer it to Dru. She shook her head and continued talking. They were sitting so closely together, Payton's stomach fell to his feet. Simon had never offered him a drink like that.

"Rumor is Dru is Si's mistress and that the new Duke of Kentwood is really Si's son." Roc shook his head and chuckled. Grabbing his drink from the table, he tossed back the rest of it.

What? Pay sucked in some air rather loudly, he couldn't help it.

"Yeah, you know how the ton is. They love to gossip." Roc nodded. "I'm guessing we're done playing." He shrugged and leaned back in his chair, watching the other three chatter merrily.

Relax, Pay. He said it was a rumor. Not true. He couldn't help the jealousy that surged into him. It had been building since he'd seen Dru walk in and kiss Si's cheek. But now... Dust, his hands were fisted and his teeth were clenched together so hard his jaw was beginning to ache.

Payton flexed his fingers, wiggling them a bit. He was being a ninny. So what if it was true. Si hadn't made any promises. Payton was going back to Regelence in a matter of days and— He sighed and grabbed his glass off the table. He tossed it down in one swallow, making his eyes water. He was being stupid. He knew better than anyone about rumors. Hadn't his family been the target of enough of them? Like the rumor about Muffin being Rexley's love child from a tryst with an upstairs maid? Or the one about Tarren wanting to be an opera singer? Or the one about Colton being in love with Lord Hasti— Okay, that one was true, but most rumors weren't. Payton took a deep breath and relaxed, feeling much better now that he had it all worked out.

Dru stood, and the rest of the men, including Payton, popped up as well.

"Gentlemen, it was nice seeing all of you, but I'm afraid if

I'm seen with all of you my cover will be blown." Dru chuckled.

"Darling, I've got news for you, your cover is blown. Everyone knows you on sight," Roc said, as he took her hand and kissed it.

"Yes, well, I'd just assume not add to my notorious reputation. I don't think I can stomach another lecture from my father. Besides, I have the most gorgeous man waiting for me at Blake House."

Si nodded. "Ah, I see we're being tossed aside for a five-year-old."

"Exactly." Dru turned to Payton. "Lieutenant Jeffers, it was a pleasure. I hope we meet again. Don't let these fellows drag you into trouble."

Payton clasped her hand and kissed it. She really was a pretty lady. If Payton liked women that way— He could almost see how Si might— "The pleasure was mine, Your Grace."

Leaning back against Si's chest, she moved her head without letting go of Payton's hand. "He's awfully pretty. Should I be jealous?"

Gasping, Payton tugged at his hand, but Dru held fast.

"No, of course not. Now let go of him." Si caught Payton's gaze over Dru's shoulder and winked.

Oh. Oh Dust. Payton looked around and noticed the footman had left and it was only the five of them in the room. Still, the statement caught him off guard.

While Payton tried to get his mouth closed and his heart to slow down, Dru left, waving to them all one last time.

They all sat. "Shall we resume our hand?" Roc asked.

It got quiet as everyone picked up their cards from the last hand. Payton looked at his cards, realized he'd gone out and set them back down. Si's comment had thrown him. Did he and Dru have something together? No, Roc said rumor. And Roc would know if it were true or not. But...would he tell Payton? *You're overanalyzing, Pay. Si winked at you. It was a joke.* Maybe he shouldn't have gulped down that scotch. Funny, he hadn't thought of that until his head felt swimmy.

By holding up the decanter, Si caught his attention from across the table. "More?"

I shouldn't.

Roc handed Payton's glass over to Si.

Okay, maybe just a little more.

Si filled Payton's glass and passed the decanter to Wycliffe, then took a sip, tipping his head back just a tad. His long throat worked as he swallowed and Payton had to fight the urge to moan. It reminded Payton of the kiss they shared in the lift and his cock hardened. Galaxy, just remembering that kiss was making Payton's head spin. He'd been kissed before, but nothing like that. It had been pure torture, knowing exactly what else Si could do with his tongue. Payton shivered, his cock throbbing. Dust, he was dizzy with wanting Si.

"What was that?" Roc asked, looking right at Payton.

Had he said something out loud? "I didn't say anything."

"It sounded like a moan." Wycliffe puffed on his cigar. "You haven't had too much to drink, have you?"

I think so. He didn't remember moaning though. "No, I'm good." Just to prove it, he took another drink of his scotch. He was going to have to stop thinking about Si apparently. Payton glanced up at the man worth moaning over and got another wink. He tried to wink back but he couldn't seem to get his eyelids to work—it ended up being more of a blink. Whatever it was, it earned a heartwarming grin from Si.

The rest of the card game went by rather quickly and they abandoned the gaming hell. There were no further run-ins with bigots, and Nate's brother had left before them, so Payton didn't have to worry about being seen. Which was good, because he wasn't walking all that straight. He'd nearly run into a footman with a tray full of drinks on their way out.

By the time they were walking down St. James looking for more entertainment, Payton felt wonderful...floaty almost. Wycliffe had suggested they all go to White's, and Payton was looking forward to it. White's was *the* club back in historical

England. Roc had assured Payton that it was made to look like the original club.

Roc and Wycliffe were bang-up guys. Well Roc was and Wycliffe was getting there. Payton was beginning to suspect that the cold façade was just Wycliffe's personality.

"Payton, what do you think of Englor?" Wycliffe asked as they passed Boodles.

I think the biggest thing it has going for it is Si. Looking up from his feet, Payton stumbled.

Si reached out to steady him. "Pay, I believe you're quite foxed, old man."

Payton didn't feel foxed, at least he didn't think he did. He felt...happy. Did being foxed feel happy? "'S very similar to Regelence, 'sept you can go where you wanna." *Come on, Pay, concentrate, you're slurring.*

Wycliffe chuckled. "At least you aren't suffering from culture shock. Most new recruits are stupefied."

"'Tis cause I'm from ah Regency planet too." Payton nodded, his head tilted to the side a bit. "Whoa."

Roc grabbed his arm to steady him and nearly toppled both of them. Roc had surely indulged in twice as many drinks as Payton.

Catching Payton under the arm, Si righted him and held on. "Steady. You okay?"

He liked Si touching him, even if it weren't sexual. He seemed to be doing that off and on all night. It made Payton smile.

"Maybe we should go to Hollister House, or back to base?" Wycliffe peered around Roc.

Roc looked at him, then back at Payton, wobbling.

Wycliffe grabbed Roc, chuckling. "Si?"

Leaning in, Si kept a hold of Payton's arm. "You want to go back to my place, Pay?"

Payton rested his head on Si's arm. "Mmm... Go anywhere you want me to go."

"Bloody hell."

Uh-oh, maybe he shouldn't have admitted that. Payton lifted his head.

Si stopped, giving Payton no choice but to stop too.

Several yards in front of them two men and a woman were getting into a lift.

Grabbing Payton with his other arm, Si steadied him but never looked away from the trio getting into the lift. "Wycliffe, do my eyes deceive me or is that who I think it is?" he asked quietly.

Blinking, Payton tried to focus on the couple. The woman was petite with red hair swept up in a neat chignon. She wore a blue evening gown that showed off a nice trim figure and large bosom. Like Dru had earlier, this woman was also wearing a demi mask, except hers had blue feathers to match her gown. Both men were of a size. One man was tall and slim, with brown hair. He wore buff-colored breeches with white hose and black shoes. He was the first one in the lift and Payton didn't get a good look at him. The other man wore all black. His evening coat was dark and he wore a black top hat over his dark hair. He looked familiar.

Wycliffe groaned softly. "It is indeed."

"Whoose wit her?" Roc asked.

"Bloody hell." Si stiffened. "That's Markham and Baymore."

Chapter Nine

If I never drink scotch again, it will be too soon.
—from the journal of Payton Marcus Townsend

His head was going to explode right out of his dry, scratchy eyes. Payton stretched forward, leaning closer to his desk, and glanced at his reflection in the glass covering it. His eyes were bloodshot and his face pasty looking. *Wonderful.* He'd drunk coffee, taken some anti-inflammatories and even tried some home remedies he'd heard of, but he still looked like he'd been in his cups.

In ten minutes he was supposed to meet Nate in his office with a daily update and Payton had nothing new he could share. The bloody message continued to elude him. *Stupid encryption.* Maybe he should inform Si about the message and see if he could tell what it said. He scrubbed his hands down his face and leaned back in his chair. No, he needed to keep something only he knew about. It would be foolish to give up everything he'd learned. He was certain he and Si were on the same side, but he felt more secure hanging on to some of his info. But maybe Si...

Argh. He couldn't stop thinking about Si. Every time he tried to work, he got sidetracked. He was losing sight of what he was here for. *Someone shoot me.*

He'd actually gone to a gaming hell and gotten drunk. He never thought he'd enjoy those sorts of pursuits, but he had. Despite seeing the prejudice against Regelens firsthand, it was nice to go out and meet other people without having a chaperone hanging over his shoulder. Grinning against his will, he leaned back in his chair. He'd had a bang-up time, except for... Was there something between Si and the duchess? Payton couldn't seem to shake the idea. They'd seemed so comfortable together. Payton couldn't really blame Si, given the world he lived in. If Payton preferred women, knowing his fellow Regelen peers would see him as an oddity, he'd pretend not to. Wouldn't he? He'd never considered it. Until last night he'd never felt...different.

It would probably be just as well if there was something between them. Payton was going to leave in the next couple of days and then... He sighed. Leaving Si and Englor wasn't going to be an easy task. He was becoming too attached to Si. He never should have gone off base. Not only had he risked getting caught, but it just made him want things he couldn't have. Like that kiss. It was the most amazing kiss he'd ever had, not that he'd had all that many—three very chaste ones to be exact. The kiss he'd shared with Si had gone straight to his head. It was much, much more than a kiss and it kind of frightened him.

Payton looked at the smooth mahogany surface of his desk and thought seriously about banging his head against it. Unfortunately, that would be counterproductive, not to mention make his headache worse. The idea was to look like he hadn't gotten foxed and cast up his accounts. And the close call? Payton suppressed a tremble. He was pretty certain Jared hadn't seen him, but if he had... There was nothing for it. Either Nate would call him on the carpet or he wouldn't.

He closed down the program he was using and saw the beautiful Regelence rose painting that Aiden had done several years ago which doubled as his com-pad wallpaper. *Aiden.* Payton was here having fun and Aiden was home missing his consort. Payton frowned, thinking he might just understand how his brother felt. He was going to miss Si and he didn't like that feeling at all. Groaning, he shoved back from his desk, gathered up his bag and put his com-pad in it.

Hauling his bag strap onto his shoulder, Payton locked his

office and went next door to Nate's office. Maybe being morose was part of the whole hangover process. He rapped his knuckles on the door.

"Enter," Nate called.

Payton stepped into the office and closed the door behind him. Taking a seat, he busied himself with his com-pad, getting it out of his bag, and hoped Nate wouldn't notice how hungover he was.

"Find anything, new?" Nate asked casually.

Shaking his head, Payton ventured a glance up. "No. There's no mention of the IN taking over the Englor Marines on the IN's end. I'm still looking through IN Intelligence, but so far nothing about the merger."

Nate sat behind his desk, his hands folded behind his head, looking at the ceiling. "Well, keep trying. I've got one of my former crewmembers from the Lady Anna monitoring the docks. A marine met with a courier off of a Regelence ship the day before we arrived. I think Hollister knows Benson is dead." Nate dropped his hands and glanced at Payton. He frowned. "Are you feeling all right?"

"Me?" Great. That had come out so squeaky it hurt his own ears. Payton cleared his throat. "Why?" *Don't blush, don't blush, don't blush. Look sober and don't let him know you know Si.*

One of Nate's dark eyebrows rose.

Payton's hands began to sweat. He hoped with all his might Nate couldn't see his pulse throbbing at his throat, because it sure felt like it was pounding hard enough to be obvious. Dust, he really wanted to tell Nate Si wasn't their enemy, but he couldn't, not without letting Nate know he'd met Si.

"Your eyes are bloodshot."

Damn, damn, damn. Payton swallowed the lump in his throat. Did Nate know he was hungover or was he fishing? Oh Galaxy, maybe Nate's brother *had* seen him last night. Payton didn't know what to say. He wasn't a liar. Sure he'd stretched the truth a little now and again, and he omitted information, but he'd never outright lied, and he didn't want to start now. If

Nate asked, he'd just have to fess up and take it like a man.

Narrowing his eyes again, Nate appeared for all the world like a stern parent. Payton suddenly felt sorry for his future nephews. Nate shook his head, letting out a long-suffering sigh, and leaned back in his chair. "Go get some sleep, Payton. Stop staying up all night trying to crack that encryption. You killing yourself and burning your candle at both ends isn't going to help."

Payton closed his eyes and took a deep breath. His shoulders shuddered with relief and he hoped it looked like he was trying to collect himself to agree. He hadn't had to lie. Opening his eyes, he nodded and stood, securing his com-pad in its bag and putting the strap over his shoulder again. He couldn't stay any longer. If he did he was liable to either toss his cookies or confess everything. He felt so guilty, but he was going to take the out Nate gave him...and that made him feel guiltier.

"Oh, and, Payton?"

Stopping at the door, Pay turned toward his brother-in-law. "Yes."

"I mean it, take a break from work tonight. You've done a hell of a job so far." Nate smiled. "I couldn't have done this without you. You've taken the brunt of this investigation while I've been busy with base operational stuff and I really appreciate it. You'll crack the code if anyone can. But for now, go get some rest."

Nodding, Payton headed for the door as fast as he could without looking like he was making a break for it. When Nate spoke again, he nearly jumped out of his skin.

"Oh, and don't forget the dinner at Hollister Palace tomorrow night. We need to leave here shortly after eighteen hundred hours."

"I'll meet you at your quarters by eighteen hundred sharp." As soon as he shut the office door he leaned against it and let out a breath. He felt about two feet high. Tears blurred his eyes, but he blinked them away. This was his fault. But he knew what he had to do now. Short of going back in there and begging Nate's forgiveness, only one thing was going to make things right. He had to find a way to prove Englor was on their side without letting Nate know he knew Si.

Pushing away from the door, Payton went and grabbed his coat out of his office and locked up. He had work to do. No more gym, he couldn't trust himself to be alone with Si. There had to be another way they could share information should the need arise.

He pushed open the outside door and the crisp wind slapped him in the face. He struggled to close the door and took off toward his quarters with his head down.

His fun was well and truly over. It was better this way for everyone. Si could go back to Dru, and Payton would have fond memories to last him a lifetime. He couldn't play second fiddle to anyone, even if the relationship could never go anywhere. Still, the thought of giving up Si made his stomach tie in knots. It felt just like it had when his grandparents had died, like he was losing someone, but he knew it was the right choice. As it was, he was gambling, just waiting to get caught. He had a responsibility to his planet and his family. The time spent with Si could be spent figuring out what the IN wanted and how to stop them. Besides, he'd known all along it couldn't last.

Getting himself together, Payton hurried his steps. He glanced around at the snow-covered ground and the empty sidewalks and wondered if it was snowing at home. Then his mind wandered without his permission. What was Si doing now?

He shook his head. At least he had some fond memories to take back to Regelence. That was more than he would have had if he hadn't met Si.

Chapter Ten

Formal dinners are a pain in my arse under normal circumstances. These are not normal circumstances.
—from the journal of Payton Marcus Townsend

"So tell me, Admiral, were you to have a child would it call you Mummy or Daddy? Will you tell the child it was designed to love other men instead of women as nature intended?"

Payton nearly choked on his bread. His gaze shot to the end of the table, where the queen sat, waiting for an answer. *Did she really just say that?* He'd decided not to let the ignorance of others bother him again after the run-in at the gaming hell, but— *Wow...just wow. She isn't just ignorant, she actually thinks I'm an abomination.*

Everyone began eating more...noisily? Yes, there was definitely more clinking of silverware and more rustling.

The king cleared his throat and made all sorts of racket at the head of the table. His rather prominent ears turned red. Dropping his fork on his plate by "accident" rather loudly, he hurried to set it on his plate with a clang and dinged his wineglass stem against his water glass as he picked it up. If he blushed any more his face was going to explode. Payton almost felt sorry for the man, almost. He did marry the harpy, after all.

His Grace the Duke of Hawthorne, Nate's father, glared at the queen with open hostility, as did His Grace the Duke of St. Albins.

Lord Markham smirked at the queen.

Payton kept his head down. So far Lord Markham had given no indication he recognized Payton. Markham seemed to have dismissed Payton as a commoner and completely ignored him after he was introduced as Lieutenant Jeffers. Payton wanted to keep it that way. All he needed was for the man to mention he'd seen Payton with Simon. Gads his palms were sweaty.

"Won't you feel guilty for lying to your child and not letting them know how God intended them to be before man stepped in and tinkered with their DNA?" the queen continued.

Payton tried not to look at Simon, but the clank of silverware as Simon tossed his fork onto his plate made Payton flinch and gape directly at him. *Dust, I can't believe he did that. Too bad he didn't throw it at her.* Surveying the table, Payton noticed everyone, including the queen, pretend not to see Si's pique of temper. It was obvious they had though by the sudden silence and sidelong glances. What was up with that? Did this kind of thing happen so often that no one cared?

Si scowled at his mother before sitting back in his chair. Even mad, he looked stunning. His black evening coat and white cravat were simple, yet classy. It showed off his wide shoulders. He was a big man and the clothes emphasized that. The candlelight made his red hair appear like flames, like the strands would be hot to touch. Turning his head, he caught Payton's gaze.

Abruptly, Payton averted his gaze to his own plate. *Blast.* He tried to concentrate on the tangy smell of beef and herbs wafting up to him, but it was no use. The only thing on his mind was wondering whether or not Si continued to study him. It was an unnerving thought, not just because Payton was afraid someone—Nate—would notice, but the idea that he'd never be able to touch Si again tore at him. And he wanted to so badly. Especially right now. He wanted to soothe away the anger the queen's comments caused. He'd hoped not seeing Si would make his desire for the man go away. It hadn't. It seemed to make it stronger.

"It is custom on Regelence for young lords to refer to their parents as Father and Sire, Your Majesty." Nate smiled and ignored her other comment, handling the insult like he had all the others, with grace and poise that made her seem idiotic and childish.

Payton admired Nate's restraint, because he was about to bust. The queen was a vicious bitch. What must Si have endured as a child? Did she realize her son also preferred men as lovers? Or was that why Si did nothing to quell the rumors about him and the Duchess of Kentwood?

A footman approached the queen with another serving of something in a steaming silver dish. She turned her perfectly coiffed red head and spoke briefly in a clipped tone to the servant.

Drop it on her. Payton took a bite of his potatoes, trying to stop thinking about the queen and how her being Si's mother may or may not have affected him. Payton suspected Si was waiting to get him alone to ask why Payton wasn't at the gym last night. They'd been introduced before dinner, but they had yet to find themselves alone where they could speak. If Payton had his choice that moment would never come, but by the looks Si kept giving him, he doubted he'd be so lucky. He just hoped Nate wasn't around when it happened.

"Do you know what is wrong with our universe, Admiral?" The queen tipped her elegant nose in the air and stared down the table at Nate, who was sitting on the king's right.

A smirk crept onto Payton's face, in spite of his resolve to remain annoyed. She was a piece of work. It was funny really. The table was set in the height of elegance, with white lacy tablecloth, the finest crystal glasses, beautiful china and silver candelabras, but the queen's venom offset all that. "No, but I bet she's going to tell us," Payton mumbled.

Jared, Nate's brother who was seated next to Payton, chuckled but quickly recovered by taking a drink.

Oh no, he'd said that out loud.

The Duke of Hawthorne raised a brow at both Jared and Payton from across the table as he took a bite of beef Wellington.

"Oops." Jared turned his attention back to his plate.

Payton flushed. He truly liked Nate's dad, but he was entirely too perceptive for Payton's piece of mind. He reminded Payton of his own father. Had he seen the looks between Payton and Si?

"Our universe has a complete lack of morals," the queen continued. "Gambling, drinking, horse racing...it's all contributing to our downfall."

"Quite right, Your Majesty. Well said," Lord Markham added.

"You forgot evil, vile, sinful queers," Jared whispered with sarcasm.

Payton choked in an effort not to laugh and fetched his napkin out of his lap to cover his mouth. Fortunately, it wasn't loud enough to make a scene, but Hawthorne apparently heard. He gave his youngest son *the eye*. When Payton recovered, he nudged Jared under the table with his foot.

A lock of wavy brown hair fell onto Jared's forehead as he smiled at his father. Jared had a dimple in his right cheek. It was charming and Payton wondered if Nate had the same dimple hidden under his beard. The brothers looked nearly identical except for Nate's beard. "Oops."

Payton took a drink of water. It was a small gathering with several lords, ladies and a few high-ranking IN and Marine officers, including Payton and Nate. The guests made small talk in between eating their dinner, except Si. Si peered at Payton, an auburn brow cocked.

Payton turned his head away in time to see the queen give an over-exaggerated mock shudder. "Those poor beasts. Men bouncing up and down on them, slapping their behinds and demanding they perform."

Jared leaned closer to Payton, bringing with him the scent of cinnamon and the wine he'd been drinking. "We *are* still talking about horse racing, aren't we?"

This time it was Nate and Jared's father who choked discreetly into his napkin.

The smile froze on Payton's face.

Si was scowling at him or...no, he was scowling at Jared.

Payton frowned. Si couldn't have possibly heard, and besides, they hadn't said anything that would upset him, had they? Sure she was his mother, but Si was clearly in the same boat as Payton and Nate. *Or maybe Si's frowning because you won't acknowledge him.* Payton went back to his food. *Shut up, Pay.*

"I can't wait to see what she has in store for dessert," Jared whispered.

Payton grinned without humor. "Nate's head on a plate?"

"If she could manage it."

"Is she always like this?" Payton asked, watching the queen, who was laughing at something the lady to her left said.

Jared nodded. "She's not the only one calling for moral reform, but she's the one with the most clout. Englor has always been conservative, but she takes it to the extreme."

Poor Si. How had he managed to be such a kind and caring man with a mother like that? They were nothing alike in temperament. Simon had his mother's hair and eyes, but that was where the similarities ended. Simon not only looked like his father and his uncle, but apparently shared more of their personality traits as well.

Payton took a drink and glanced Si's way. He was deep in conversation with the man to his left. Payton's heart hurt. His resolve to not see Si was crumbling. What was he going to do?

Turning his head, Simon caught his gaze and smiled as he continued to talk to the gray-haired man.

Payton smiled back and Simon's eyes nearly twinkled. His eyebrow raised slightly. For several seconds he held Payton's gaze before turning back to his conversation.

With his heart in his throat, Payton picked up his wine goblet and took a swig. *It's way too late, Pay. You've already fallen...hard.*

✧

Shutting the door, Simon hurried outside. *Come on, Payton. Where are you?* He was certain this was where Payton had gone when he'd slipped out of the library five minutes ago. Maybe he was wrong, but he'd gotten the impression Payton wanted him to follow. It didn't matter, Simon was going to see him tonight if it was the last thing he did. He got the feeling Pay was avoiding him and he didn't like it.

All throughout dinner Simon had watched Payton flirt with Lord Jared Hawkins. Even having to sit at the same table as his mother and her cohort, listening to the queen spew hatred, hadn't distracted him from Payton. It had really put his teeth on edge. He couldn't ever remember feeling like that over any other lover. Normally he'd have simply called the relationship to a halt and gone his own way, but with Payton he needed to know there was nothing between Payton and Jared. Why hadn't Payton been at the gym last night? Simon rolled his eyes at himself. What was wrong with him? He was acting like a jealous idiot. Payton probably just got caught up in working and forgot about their meeting. Maybe he'd found something new.

The snow crunched under his feet as he stepped off the veranda. He couldn't help but grin as he took in his surroundings. This had always been his favorite part of the palace. What did Payton think about it when he came out here? Simon wanted to know. He wanted to share this *with* Payton.

It was beautiful. The lawn was immaculate as usual, even covered with a blanket of snow. In the spring it would be lush and green with grass so thick it felt like walking on plush carpet.

Simon started across the lawn toward the series of slim rectangular pools cascading away from the palace. One pool drained into the next until finally ending in a large round pool with a huge fountain in the middle. It was so quiet and peaceful out here. The only sounds were his own footfalls and the water. The serenity of it eased the apprehension inside of him a little. Beyond the fountain lay a massive hedge maze with footprints in the snow leading up to it. *Ah.* That's where Payton had gone.

Simon followed the footprint trail into the maze. It shouldn't take him long to find Payton. The maze was well thought out, but Simon knew it by heart.

There were benches with arbors over them at each dead end, but this was not some easy trysting place for lovers, it was actually made to challenge. Payton had likely analyzed the maze. The man would take very few wrong turns. It wouldn't surprise Simon if Pay had studied it from the veranda before heading in. He was probably wandering around the maze this very minute with his bottom lip caught between his teeth.

Weaving around the maze, Simon smiled. Had he ever realized the little quirks of his other lovers? He didn't think so. None of them had held his interest enough to make him notice.

When he reached the middle of the maze he became aware of the crunching of snow while he stood still. Payton was close. Should he call out? Simon hurried around the corner. The next turn was to the dead center of the maze where the fountain was. The small pool with the fountain came into view and he stopped dead in his tracks, staring at the vision in front of him.

He'd thought once before that Payton looked handsome in evening wear, but once again Simon was taken by surprise at how perfect he looked, even in knee britches. Simon hated knee britches, and generally thought they were effeminate, but on Payton... They looked elegant. Even the white hose managed to emphasize his calf muscles instead of looking foppish. The heavy black wool greatcoat covered his stylish black evening coat and delectable arse, but Simon knew they were there. His cock stirred, hardening, remembering how the gold waistcoat had made the yellow of Payton's eyes practically glow in the candlelight. Simon had had a hard time not staring at Payton during dinner. Like the night they went to the gaming hell, Pay's white cravat had been tied in a complicated knot, making him appear quite distinguished. The urge to rumple all that sophisticated perfection along with Payton's refusal to acknowledge him earlier had set Si's teeth on edge. Now there was no reason Simon couldn't take what he wanted. Demand answers and—

Payton turned and spotted him. Quickly, he averted his eyes to the ground and his teeth caught his bottom lip.

—and kiss the life out of Payton. Simon began walking forward. When he was within two yards of Payton, Pay looked up at him again, his amber eyes heavy lidded.

"Pay?"

"I can't." He shook his head. "I shouldn't..."

Can't what? Shouldn't what? Simon opened his mouth to ask but Payton let out a deep, shuddering breath. His perfect posture collapsed, his shoulders slumping.

The need to comfort came out of nowhere. Simon frowned. When had he become so in tune to Payton's moods? When had he started wanting Payton to be nothing but happy? He wanted answers but instead of demanding them, he wanted to take Payton in his arms and tell him it'd be all right.

"Pay, whatever it is—"

Shaking his head, Payton turned and looked at the fountain, his white gloved hand trailed around the edge of the small pool. "I have to leave in a few days."

It felt like a physical blow, like someone had clocked him one. Simon shook his head without thinking. "No." He didn't want Payton to go, not yet. "We're working together. You can't leave."

Payton turned back to him, a sad smile on his face. "I need to find a way to tell Nate that we're on the same side."

Nate? Oh, the admiral. "I'll tell him. I'll tell him I want you to stay and help."

"No!" Payton's eyes went wide, his face drained of color. "He can't know we know each other."

Why not? Simon frowned. Even if the admiral told Payton to stay away from him, eventually he was going to learn that they were working together. "Pay, I—"

Taking one step, then another, Payton groaned, sounding defeated, then launched himself at Simon. His arms and legs wrapped around Simon's body.

Surprised, Simon caught him out of instinct and staggered backward. He lost his footing and landed on his butt in the snow. Collapsing onto his back, he brought Payton with him. "What—?"

Payton glanced down at him, his black hair falling into his face.

Staring into those yellow eyes, Simon forgot all about the admiral and the IN and Payton leaving. There would be time to talk later. He cupped the back of Payton's head and urged his chin down.

"Oh." Payton licked his lips and met him halfway.

Simon took Payton's mouth with all the ferocity he felt. He was lost. By now Simon had normally tired of other lovers, but his attraction for Payton had only increased with every new thing he learned. He shouldn't care so much, but he couldn't seem to help himself.

As was becoming his habit, Payton moaned, pushing the noise right into Simon's mouth along with his tongue. He was still awkward, obviously not having much practice, but he made up for it with enthusiasm.

Whether it was the sounds Payton made or the way he threw himself into the kiss, Simon couldn't say, but his cock grew hard instantly. He rolled them over until he was on top and pressing Payton into the snow, mashing his erection into Pay's hip. Rising up, he studied Payton.

The glare from the snow cast an ethereal glow over Payton's pale skin. His lips were already swollen and red. Growling low in his throat, Simon nipped the bottom one, before going back to cataloguing the beauty beneath him. Payton's dark hair made such a contrast to the white snow. His pale skin was only a couple shades darker than the ground. The ladies of the ton would die to have such smooth milky skin.

Licking his lips again, Payton raised his head for a kiss. Simon felt the erection pressed against his hip. Payton let out a ragged breath, making a cloud around them, and shivered.

"Are you cold?" Simon asked.

"Yes, and we shouldn't do this here."

Shit. How could he have forgotten where they were? They were concealed by the hedges, but if anyone came looking for them... It was pretty stupid on his part. Simon jumped to his feet, holding his hand down to Payton.

Taking Simon's hand, Payton got up. He shook his hair, making the snow fly from it, and huddled into his coat. His cheeks flushed pink and he glanced down, his inherent shyness surfacing.

Simon wondered if it would ever truly disappear. He sure hoped not. "I'm sorry, Payton, I lost my head. I seem to do that a lot when you're around."

"I know the feeling." Payton didn't sound too happy about it either, or maybe it was just because his teeth were chattering.

At least he wasn't alone. Grinning, Si reached out and rubbed Payton's arms through his coat. He liked touching Payton, it was becoming harder and harder not to whenever they were near. "I missed you last night. Where were you? Did you find something new?"

"No, I didn't find a blasted thing." Payton chewed his bottom lip and mumbled, "I missed you too."

Simon chuckled and ran his finger down Payton's forehead, soothing out the furrow. He had to have Payton. His body screamed at him to rush them away to his townhouse right now. The only thing that stopped him was knowing that Payton would never follow. If Payton were leaving— *No,* Simon was going to do his best to convince him to stay. "Meet me at the gym at twenty hundred hours tomorrow. Dress in civilian clothes again."

"Why?"

"Payton?" A shout came from the front of the garden.

Who was that? Simon turned to look, but stopped short when he noticed Payton's startled expression. His eyes were wide and his face had drained of color. "That's the admiral. I've got to go." He started toward the palace but Simon grabbed his arm.

"Wait." Simon wanted to ask so many things, but what came out was, "Meet me tomorrow?"

Glancing toward the veranda, Payton swallowed then glanced back at Simon. "Okay."

Simon let go of Payton's arm and watched him race off like someone was chasing him. He frowned and followed at a much slower pace. *How odd.* How did Payton think he would keep the admiral from learning they knew each other when they were ultimately working together? Eventually Hawkins was going to have to be brought up-to-date on what they'd found out.

What are you hiding, Pay?

Chapter Eleven

Starry night, leaving Englor and Si is going to kill me.
—from the journal of Payton Marcus Townsend

"Where are we going?" Payton looked out the lift window, biting his bottom lip. He really shouldn't be doing this, but his resolve to stop seeing Si had flown right out the window yesterday when he'd seen Si in the maze. He'd been so handsome, and the expression on his face when he'd spotted Payton... Payton shivered. It was possessive and warm and even nearly getting caught by Nate hadn't stopped him from meeting Si tonight. *I'm either brave or stupid. Or maybe both.* He only had a few more days and he was going to enjoy them. And he needed to figure out how to get Simon and Nate talking without involving himself.

The lift stopped.

Across from him, Si grinned. "We're here."

"Where is here?"

"You'll see." Si got out of his seat and moved toward the door. "Door open, steps down." When the door raised, Si alighted and reached back inside. "Come on."

Payton took his hand and climbed from the carriage. He'd noticed since the other night after they'd gone to the gaming hell that Si had been treating him a little differently. He couldn't put his finger on how, but it wasn't in a bad way. At first he'd thought it had to do with Dru. Simon hadn't said anything about his relationship with her, but he hadn't acted like there was anything to the rumors either. So Payton hadn't thought any more about it. The change had to do with them. Si was more attentive, or at least he was trying to be when Payton let him. It made him feel...special.

They were in front of a standalone townhouse. It was a lovely Italian styled home with pinkish stucco. Like the townhouses back home it had a narrow width and the other houses were very close to it. It looked to be four stories. The entry had a heavy wooden door and intricate wrought-iron rails on each side of the entry steps. "Are we going to a party?" The house didn't look as if there was a party going on inside.

After dismissing the lift, Si led him to the steps. "No. This is my place."

Payton's steps faltered. His world tilted on its axis. Maybe he really was more than a casual fling for Si. He smiled, his heart in his throat. Si didn't seem the type to admit something like that if it weren't true, nor did he seem the type to bring men home.

"Welcome home, Colonel," a smooth deep voice said as the door opened. "Don't forget to wipe your feet on the doormat. I'll not have the foyer all wet for the staff to slip and slide all over the place."

Colonel? Not Your Highness? The rest of what the butler had said hit Payton and his lips quirked. Even Jeffers, his butler at home, wasn't bold enough to talk to the family like that.

Growling, Si wiped his feet. He mumbled something about reprogramming and ushered Payton inside. Closing the door behind him, he looked at Payton and shook his head. "It does no good to argue, he'll just come up with something else to annoy me with. Dunston, send the lift around at oh three hundred hours and give me a wake-up call."

Payton wiped his own shoes on the rug, glancing around the marble entryway.

"Oh, I like him. So polite. Not at all like Major Bennett and Colonel Eason," Dunston said in a cheery voice.

Payton liked the butler already. Dunston had character and

147

regardless what Si said, the butler amused him. He'd had a grin on his face when he spoke of reprogramming.

Si chuckled. "Come on." He led Payton up the stairs.

The house was beautiful. The floor was a dark hardwood, as was the wainscoting. The walls were covered with dark green and burgundy striped wallpaper. It was very masculine, yet elegant. Much more humble than Hollister Palace. "Why are we here?"

Reaching the last door on the left, Si pushed it open and stepped aside, waiting for Payton to enter.

A bedroom. *Si's bedroom.* Payton stood there in awe. He'd never been in another man's—who wasn't a relative—bedroom before. It was in the same green and burgundy tones as the hallway wallpaper, with dark wood. There were candles lit around the room. The massive four-poster bed was turned back revealing silky cream-colored sheets. A fire blazed in the green marble fireplace across from the bed, casting a romantic glow.

Arms snaked around Payton's waist from behind, then Si's warm breath tickled his ear. He kissed Payton's neck, leaving goose bumps in his wake. "Why do you think?" His voice was soft and sultry.

Shivering, Payton closed his eyes and leaned back against Si's warm chest. The fire crackled in the fireplace and the smell of wood burning invaded his senses. He couldn't have imagined a more romantic setting. Part of him wanted to run and get as far away as he could, the other part never wanted to leave. He could never undo what was about to happen, but he didn't care. No one would find out. Why shouldn't he have this?

Si licked a long line up Payton's neck to his ear as his hands moved from Payton's waist to unbutton his greatcoat. When he got it undone, he pulled it off Payton's shoulders and tossed it away. "Tell me, why did you leave Regelence? Isn't it like Englor in that lords are not required to serve in the military?"

Payton nodded, keeping his eyes closed. He didn't want to talk about Regelence.

There was a rustle and then Si was back, pressing close to

148

Payton, with his own greatcoat gone. His wide chest rested against Payton's back and his hands slid forward and tugged at Payton's cravat. His lips trailed up Payton's neck, nibbling and biting. It felt wonderful. "Why? Why me, Payton? I know enough about you to realize you've never done anything like this. Why now?" His voice was soft, barely a whisper, rasped against Payton's neck as his cravat came free and was disposed of.

"Because you're the first person I've ever been this attracted to." It was the truth, if not the whole truth.

A low groan sounded as Si tugged off Payton's evening coat. "You make me want things I can't have." Si nipped his shoulder and turned him around.

Payton opened his eyes. His heart thundered in his ears and his throat felt like he'd swallowed rocks. His cock grew hard and his pulse raced. Did that mean if things were different, Si would want him for keeps?

The firelight caught Si's red hair, making it shimmer nearly gold. The man was very handsome. He took Payton's breath away. Si's blue eyes were heavy lidded and his focus was on Payton's lips. Self-conscious, Payton licked his lips.

"Mmm..." As he fussed with the buttons on Payton's waistcoat, Si dipped his head and nipped Payton's lip, making his teeth tap lightly against Payton's. He threw the waistcoat aside and made quick work of Payton's shirt, all the while licking and nibbling at Payton's lips.

Tilting his head, Payton rested his hands against Si's chest. His lips caressed Si's as he too began ridding Si of clothes. After he got Si's cravat, evening coat and waistcoat off, Si began moving them backward.

The backs of Payton's thighs hit the bed.

"Sit." Si trailed his fingertips down the side of Payton's cheek then ran his thumb over Payton's bottom lip.

As soon as Payton sat, Si knelt and began removing Payton's shoes and stockings. He did so in silence, and Payton ran his fingers through the thick auburn hair, unable to help himself. Si leaned into the touch, his eyes closing briefly. Quickly, he stood and divested himself of shoes and stockings, before sitting on the bed next to Payton.

Payton had to glance up to catch Si's gaze, even with both of them sitting. When he did, Si caught his lips in a gentle kiss that grew heated almost instantly.

Caressing and soothing, Si's hands were all over him. The only sounds were of their breathing, the fire and the rustling of clothes. It seemed like a strange thing to notice given the circumstances, but as long as he lived, Payton would never forget this moment.

The next thing Payton knew he was sans shirt, on his back in the middle of the bed, with Si resting his weight on one arm and staring down at him.

Si ran his other hand down Payton's chest. His eyelids fluttered, then his head lifted and those blue eyes focused on Payton's face. "You have a great body."

"Me?" Oh, that had come out kind of squeaky. Payton frowned.

Nodding, Si chuckled. "Yes you."

Si was the one with the marvelous body. Payton reached up and flicked the top button of Si's shirt open, wanting to see that incredible body.

"It would be rather boring if we all looked like me."

Speak for yourself. Payton snorted and kept revealing the strong godlike torso he'd come to crave. "You're insane."

"No, I'm not. You are a beautiful man. How can you not know that?" Si bent and captured Payton's lips in a quick kiss, then slipped down and flicked his tongue over Payton's nipple.

Arching his back, Payton hissed out a breath, and all thoughts of his body being inadequate fled.

"Oh, you like that." Si's voice dropped into a seductive whisper. He closed his mouth over Payton's nipple and sucked.

The sensation zipped through his body right to his cock, making it jerk against his trousers, begging for similar treatment. Who would have thought that would feel so good? He arched again, bucking his hips up and into Si's stomach.

Si smiled against his nipple, then rose and unbuttoned

Payton's trousers. "Lift." He caught Payton's smallclothes and took them off along with his trousers.

His cock slapped against his belly when it came free of his pants. Payton moaned. He swore even the air felt good. His testicles drew tighter along with his abdomen. Si and the things they did together were becoming an addiction. His body craved it.

Si stood at the side of the bed and began removing his own clothes. He was breathtaking with the firelight casting shadows over the plains of his chiseled body. The man was so gorgeous he looked...fake. No human could be so perfectly sculpted, yet he was. Payton's fingers itched to touch and his mouth watered to taste.

"Damn, I love that. You're so responsive. I love those sweet little noises you make."

Who could blame him with such a fine specimen of manhood standing in front of him, mostly naked?

Si threw his trousers aside then hooked his fingers in his smallclothes and pulled them down. Invitingly, his cock jutted out from his body. This time Payton was very aware of the moan that crawled out of his throat. He felt like he was going to burst. He sat up and reached for Si.

Putting his knee on the edge of the bed, Si pushed him back down, but not before Payton got a handful of hot, hard, leaking cock. Si groaned. "Bloody hell, Pay." He caught Payton's wrist in his hand and came down on the bed. His weight settled on Payton, mashing their pricks together.

They both moaned.

Si's lips crushed his, his tongue thrusting inside. In and out it moved, caressing Payton's tongue and lips. He nipped Payton's lips and slid down, trailing kisses in his wake.

Goose bumps raced up Payton's arms and legs, but he lifted his hips, all but begging Si to touch him where he most wanted it.

"In good time, Pay. We're taking this slow. I took the effort to make your first experience in a bed. I'm not about to spoil it by rushing." Without allowing him to respond, Si captured a nipple between his teeth then sucked.

Payton gasped. Partly because of the feel of Si's lips on him, but mostly because of what Si had said. Si had taken an extra effort to make this special for him. His throat tightened and a warmth that had nothing to do with sex pulsed through him. Nervousness threatened to overtake him when he thought of Si's cock in his arse, but he squashed it down. So far Payton had loved everything they'd done together.

A hand closed around his prick as Si kissed down his stomach.

Fisting his hands in the comforter, Payton lifted his head and watched as Si guided Payton's prick to his mouth.

Wet heat slid down his shaft, making Payton moan. It was as nice to watch as it felt. This time was so different. Before it had been fast and demanding, but apparently Si was serious about taking it slowly. He lingered over Payton's prick, gliding up and down in a leisurely pace, until Payton thought he'd lose his mind.

Removing his mouth from Payton's cock, he moved lower, nuzzling Payton's testicles. He licked and took them into his mouth, sucking lightly.

Payton pulled his feet up, planting them on the bed, giving Si more room. It was so wanton, but he didn't care.

Si pushed Payton's legs up, exposing him more, and swirled his tongue around Payton's hole.

To think, a week ago this would have shocked Payton to his core, but after what he and Si shared? Not much surprised him now. Oddly, he wasn't the least bit embarrassed either.

Lifting his head, Si let go of Payton's legs and glanced up. He met Payton's gaze and slid one finger into Payton's arse.

It felt strange. Not painful, but foreign. Payton tensed a little.

"Relax, love." Si's breath brushed over Payton's thigh, then he kissed it. He pushed in further, wriggling it around. He hit Payton's gland and grinned when Payton gasped. "Mmm...like that?"

Payton nodded jerkily. *Wait,* had Si said love? Payton melted. Si really was going all out to make this special.

Thrusting in and out a few times, Si tipped his head to the side and gripped Payton's cock again. "Beside you on the bedside table is an automatic lube dispenser. Get some in your hand and give it to me."

Turning his head, Payton found the dispenser. He'd seen them in bedrooms before, but never used them himself. He held his hand out and a dollop of clear gel fell into his palm. A warm clove scent filled the room. As he maneuvered his hand down toward Si, trepidation tried to creep back in. What did Si need lube for so soon?

"Relax, Pay. You're stiffening up again." Si dropped a kiss to his stomach, right above the black curls over his prick, and dipped his fingers into the lube, then smeared it around the outside of Payton's hole.

Payton didn't know what to do with the sticky residue left in his hand, so he just lay it palm up.

Si eased another finger in alongside his other one.

It burned. Eyes going wide, Payton froze. His cock flagged a little.

"Shh..." Si kept his fingers still. "Easy." His tongue slid up the length of Payton's prick on one side and back down on the other.

"Unh." His cock went right back to fully hard and leapt up, reaching for Si's mouth. Closing his eyes, Payton relaxed.

It was still awkward, but not bad. It didn't sting now, and the sensation on his prick was mind-numbing. Moving his fingers slowly, Si took the head of Payton's cock in his mouth. He kept it up, sucking and fucking Payton with his fingers, grazing Payton's gland every now and again.

It felt incredible, better than Payton would have thought. He found himself pushing into those fingers. Wanting more. Wanting everything.

Si added another finger and took Payton all the way into

the back of his throat.

"Ah." Panting, Payton couldn't decide whether to move away or closer. It felt good and not quite painful at the same time. As it was, the fingers moving in his arse probably kept him from climaxing when Si deep-throated him. Si didn't stop this time, he kept working Payton's cock, and thrust his fingers in to hit Payton's prostate.

Blast. Payton bucked up into Si's mouth, a tingle shooting up his spine. His cock throbbed and began to leak. He was so close. His head thrashed back and forth. "Yesss..."

Abruptly, the fingers in his arse were gone and Si was on his knees between Payton's legs. He bent forward, kissing Payton's chin, his lips. "Ready for me, Pay?"

Payton nodded, his hand drifting down to his cock.

Si rested his weight on one hand and reached toward the table with the other. Sitting back, he rubbed the lube over his cock, stroking it. A drop of clear liquid beaded up on the tip when his hand rose. He leaned forward again, his chest hovering over Payton's face. His collarbone looked so lickable.

Groaning, Payton gripped his own cock. Squeezing, he stuck his tongue out and swept it across Si's shoulder and neck. It earned him a drawn-out sexy groan.

When Si moved back this time, he rested one hand on Payton's upraised knee and the other pushed warm, slick fingers into Payton's hole. He stared at Payton the whole time. Inserting one finger, then two and three. After pumping in and out a few times, he removed his fingers and scooted forward. His thighs cradled the backs of Payton's. His other hand dropped down, tugging on one arse cheek. "Are you ready for me? Ready for this?" His gaze stayed locked to Payton's, his expression serious and tender at the same time.

Payton had no doubt if he said no, Si would stop, but he didn't want that. He nodded.

Si glanced down. The hot tip of his cock touched Payton's crease, dragging up and down before inching in. Si's eyes closed. "So fucking perfect." He let out a long, jagged breath and pushed steadily in. The hair on his legs tickled Payton. Once he

154

was fully inside he stopped. His eyes opened and his gaze bore into Payton's. His hands slid up Payton's chest and stomach, petting, feeling. "So good." He gripped Payton's cock and stroked slowly. "Feels so good."

The sting was back. Payton's breath caught, but he remained perfectly still hoping the discomfort didn't last long. The constant drag on his prick made the ache in his arse subside. He couldn't believe he was losing his virginity. He was glad it was Si.

Si's cock slid back then thrust in. He didn't rush, just let Payton get used to the new sensation.

It didn't hurt, but Payton couldn't quite make it comfortable either. His erection didn't dwindle though. If he concentrated on the delicious drag over his prick, it felt almost good.

"Oh fuck, you're beautiful. I love when you bite your lip like that." Si dropped forward, and his hand continued working Payton's cock. He gave Payton no time to think. His hips thrust again as his mouth seized Payton's. Si gave no quarter, just kept fucking Payton with his tongue as well as his cock. He pulled back, his lips barely touching Payton's. "Like my cock in your arse? You like me fucking you?"

Payton's whole body was on fire. He couldn't breathe. He loved it when Si talked to him like that. His body melted into a trembling mass of sensation. This is what had been missing. Si had been such a gentleman, and while Payton liked it, he liked this too. There was something about Si's growly voice whispering naughty things that really got to him. And Si knew it too. He grinned against Payton's lips. "I've been wanting to fuck you since I first saw you. Couldn't wait to get my fat prick into your tight little virgin hole."

"Dust." Payton gasped and nipped Si's lips. *Bloody hell.* He was close to coming.

Finally, Si pulled back. Sweat dripped down his chest, over the sparse matt of red-gold hair. He sat up on his knees and looped his arms under Payton's legs. A piece of his gorgeous red hair fell into his eyes and he tossed his head to get it out. Si grunted and slammed forward.

Payton went wild, trying to buck up against Si. He was vaguely aware of the sound of their skin slapping together, Si's grunts and his own moans. The uncomfortable feeling was long gone. Payton's cock dripped onto his chest, spurting a little. His testicles drew closer as Si's cock hit just right on every thrust. It was the most amazing feeling, like little sparks traveling up and down his spine. He clenched his arse tight and his thighs tensed. Eyes squeezing shut, he came. His cock jerked and hot semen shot out, hitting him in the chin, the chest and cheek.

Si roared above him and stopped moving.

Payton's body relaxed slowly. His breath was still ragged, his heart still racing, but he felt utterly boneless. His muscles were no longer tense. It was the best orgasm of his life.

Lowering his legs, Si slipped from his body.

It sent a shiver up Payton's spine. He opened his eyes to find Si staring at him. Dipping, he licked off the semen dripping down Payton's cheek. "You are amazing. Thank you." He took Payton's lips in a gentle caress of lips, sweet and...loving. He lingered, placing little kisses along Payton's jaw. He left the room and came back with a towel.

His fingers tickled over Payton's side and up under his arm. "What's this?"

Raising his head, Payton looked at the place Si touched.

Si traced his birthmark. "It looks like a rose."

"It's my birthmark. All Regelens, those of us born of artificial procreation, have it."

Bending, Si kissed the mark. He wiped off Payton's chest and chin and ran the towel down Payton's crease. Tossing the towel away, Simon lifted the edge of the comforter and climbed into bed. "Come on, Pay, get under here."

He really did not want to move, but Payton scooted up and under the covers anyway.

Turning on his side, Si wrapped Payton in his arms, putting his back to Si's chest. His breath tickled Payton's ear.

Payton was almost asleep when Si asked, "How old are

you?"

Payton blinked, surprised by the question. He'd never thought of that. He knew so many things about this man, knew his body intimately but he didn't know how old Si was. "Nineteen. How old are you?"

"Twenty-eight." Again he got very quiet. Payton thought he was asleep when he squeezed Payton tighter and kissed the back of his neck. "Thank you for letting me be the first, Pay." After that Si's breathing evened out.

Lying there with Si spooned around him snoring softly in his ear, Payton realized his life was never going to be the same. He cuddled back against Si, gripping the arms that held him, and tried not to think about the change in his life. His stomach ached and a pain started in his chest. He couldn't go back to the way he'd been before. He was falling in love with Si. Regelence was going to be a lonely, lonely place.

"Colonel," Dunston exclaimed, followed by a loud bang downstairs. "Colonel, wake up, St. Albins is on his way up."

A heavy thud of footsteps advanced rapidly on the stairs.

The Duke of St. Albins? The king's brother? Si's uncle? Payton shot into a sitting position. He looked down at blinking blue eyes.

"What?" Si asked.

Dread clawed at Payton's stomach, and he darted a glance around the room. Where could he hide?

The door flew open and St. Albins stepped into the room. "Simon, get up!"

Si shot up in bed, his eyes wide. "Uncle?"

Payton felt like he was going to vomit, and his heart raced. How could he have messed up this badly? What if...?

St. Albins never even looked at Payton. He leaned against the doorframe, trying to catch his breath, his shoulders drooping. "There's been an accident." His voice was barely a whisper. "The king and queen have been killed."

Chapter Twelve

Simon raised his head off his forearm where it rested on the window frame, pushed away from the wall and let the curtain fall. The lift carrying Payton back to base had driven away two nights ago. Staring down the street wasn't going to make it come back, nor was it going to change the situation. Funny, he'd buried his parents yesterday and all he could think about was that he hadn't wanted Payton to leave like that.

Payton had been mortified at being walked in on, but even still, he'd tried to see to Simon and make sure he was okay before he left. That's when Simon realized he was falling in love with Payton. Somehow Payton had slipped past his defenses. He'd only planned on a good time. The challenge to debauch the innocent had been too tempting to turn down, but somehow it had become more than that.

He strongly suspected that Pay was a Regelence lord even if he didn't have a title. Even the second son of a baron would be an acceptable match. Other than being a man, he would be a perfectly fine mate. He was highly intelligent, refined, elegant, came from a Regency society. He was also fun and caring. Simon loved how everything Payton felt was written on his face. Even having lived among the peerage, it hadn't ruined his innocence.

"Are you all right?"

Nodding, Simon turned. "I will be."

Aldred paced back and forth in front of the study fire. "He was important to you, wasn't he?"

Simon didn't have to ask who, Aldred had always had an uncanny ability to read Simon. He'd known as soon as Simon packed Payton into a lift to take him back to base the other night that Simon cared for Payton. The strange thing about the whole ordeal was he really didn't know a lot about Payton, but it didn't matter, his heart didn't seem to mind. What he did know was enough. He knew what type of person Payton was, he knew what he was like deep down where it counted. "I wanted him to be, but it doesn't matter now. I can't have that, I've always known it."

Aldred stopped pacing and glanced at Simon. He stood there for several seconds, an odd look in his eyes, then shook his head and began pacing again. "Are you sure? You're King now."

Simon swallowed the lump in his throat at the reminder. He felt nothing but numbness. He hadn't been all that close to his father in many years and never had he been close to his mother. Even at the funeral their absence hadn't sunk in. It would probably hit him later, but right now all he could think about was Englor was his to rule. He didn't know if he was ready. His mind swam with the things he needed to do, nearly taking his breath away. He chose to ignore his uncle's optimism and concentrate on the other problem. His parents had been assassinated. "It was military." Civilians would have a difficult time getting the components to make a bomb.

Aldred nodded. "I thought the same thing."

Simon's first thought was IN. It was on the tip of his tongue to deny that the Englor Marines had anything to do with it, but he couldn't possibly guarantee that with the current move in parliament to have the Marines disbanded. "Who can I trust, Aldred?" He took a seat in front of the fire. He felt defeated. He'd been going over this question since the night his parents were killed. There were only three people he knew he could trust and one of those people was in this room with him. He needed parliament members to advise him. The only thing he was certain of was that he didn't want his father's advisors. He'd released them of their duties yesterday, but he had yet to choose their replacements.

Simon caught Aldred's gaze. "If you were king, who would you choose as advisors?"

Aldred shook his head. "I don't know, I haven't thought about it."

"Do you trust Hawthorne?" Having Hawthorne as an advisor would give him an upper hand in gaining an alliance with Regelence, given Hawthorne's son's ties to the planet. He also admired Hawthorne's intelligence and political savvy. He thought the duke would make a great advisor, but he wanted Aldred's input.

"Hawthorne is a dear friend and an honorable man. He too thought the idea of Englor going without its own military unit was preposterous and told your father so." He gave a crisp nod. "I'd trust Hawthorne with both of our lives."

Dipping his head, Simon rose to pour himself a scotch. "Dunston, send someone around to Hawkins House and Bradford House and let His Grace the Duke of Hawthorne and the Marquis of Oxley know I request their presence as soon as possible. And locate Colonel Eason and Major Bennett and tell them I need them post-haste."

Simon sat quietly sipping his scotch with Aldred next to him, staring into the fire for what seemed like hours but was probably only twenty minutes or so.

They were really gone. A tear ran down his cheek. He'd hoped to get to know his father again, maybe try and change some of his mother's radical views. He'd thought he'd have years. He'd wanted to get to know them better, to care for them...have them care for him. He glanced over at his uncle, the man who'd been a parent to him most of his life, and smiled. Maybe it was awful to think, but he was glad it was them and not Aldred. "Uncle...I'm glad you're here."

A tear streaked down Aldred's cheek, gleaming in the firelight, then he turned to face Simon. "I wouldn't be anywhere else, my boy. I don't have to tell you how important you are to me." He patted Simon's hand where it rested on the arm of the chair. "Besides that, he was still my brother."

Simon nodded. He knew exactly what Aldred meant. As horrible and self-centered as his parents could be, they were family. He supposed like him, Aldred mourned the past and what could have been more than the present.

Taking a nip of his scotch, Simon closed his eyes and leaned back. He thought about the other night, having Payton in his bed. He'd never brought a lover to his home before, but it had felt like the right thing to do with Payton.

When he'd learned about Regelence's artificial reproduction, he'd actually let himself hope a permanent relationship with Payton was possible for just a brief moment. He'd known of such processes on other planets, but none where the female DNA was completely removed like on Regelence. Not only was it not done on Englor—no artificial procreation was done on Englor—but Simon didn't know of it being done anywhere. It was an amazing concept. It was— "Uncle." Simon sat up straight and set his tumbler on the table next to him. "The cloning technology that Benson spoke of. Do you remember?"

Aldred sat up straighter, giving Simon his undivided attention. "Yes, you said he'd overheard someone speaking of the mysterious schematics and some cloning technology. What about it?"

"On Regelence, the lords are born of an artificial procreation process that removes the female DNA entirely. Do you suppose there are benefits that come with that? Something that would make them more appealing to the military? More testosterone or something?"

Aldred frowned. "Are you certain? Removing the egg donor's genetics is not possible."

Simon sat forward on his chair. "I'm positive. I just don't know why the IN would want that information."

"Your Highness, His Grace the Duke of Hawthorne, the Marquis of Oxley, Colonel Eason and Major Bennett have just arrived."

"Show them in, Dunston." Simon jumped to his feet, his mood lifting for the first time in days.

Roc came in first. He bowed. "Your Majesty."

Simon had the insane urge to slap him on the head, but refrained.

"Your Grace." Roc bowed briefly to Aldred as well.

Aldred dipped his head. "Major Bennett."

Hawthorne was next. He bowed, then came forward and grabbed Simon's hands. "I'm very sorry, Your Majesty." Then he went to Aldred, clapping him on the back in a brief hug.

Oxley mimicked Hawthorne almost to a T, then Wycliffe came in. By that time Simon had had enough.

"Don't do it. I swear if you know what's good for you, Wycliffe, you won't even think about it."

Wycliffe grinned and caught Simon in a hug. "You okay?"

Simon hugged him back. "I will be." He turned to the other men. "Dunston, secure the room again please. Milords, Roc, please have a seat." As the men sat in chairs about the study, Simon propped himself on the desk. "I've a favor to ask. I need advisors. You men share my political views and are better informed of happenings in parliament than I. I need people I can trust." He looked at Hawthorne and Oxley. "You two are some of my uncle's dearest friends and he trusts you. Therefore I trust you. Both of your intelligence speaks for itself." He looked at Roc and Wycliffe. "I know neither of you are as versed in politics as Hawthorne and Oxley, but I've no doubt if I need anything you will both be there. You will do your best to learn the things I need to know to rule this planet. I'm not asking you to give up your positions in the Marines."

"I'm honored, Your Majesty, and I accept," Hawthorne said.

"I am as well, Your Majesty," Oxley added.

"I'm in," Roc announced.

"Me too." Wycliffe got up and poured himself a scotch.

"Uncle?" Simon crossed his arms over his chest, unsure of why his uncle hadn't yet accepted.

"Me?" Aldred sputtered.

Simon frowned. *Who else?* "Of course you."

Aldred's eyes practically sparkled, but he didn't smile. "I'm honored, my boy."

"Good. Now everyone stop calling me Your Majesty. It's Simon or Si," Simon groused. "Wycliffe, pour everyone else a scotch as well, then come sit down. We have things to talk about." He looked right at Hawthorne, who was gazing at Oxley. It was an odd look, almost... Simon glanced at Oxley, who sat on the small love seat with the duke. He wasn't any closer to Hawthorne than need be, but his crossed leg was touching the other man and his arm rested on the back of the seat. Were his fingers toying with Hawthorne's collar? *Well, I'll be damned.* Simon smiled. Like father like son it would seem.

Roc got up and helped Wycliffe with the drinks. After he handed one to Simon he sat down.

Simon cleared his throat. "Hawthorne, how well do you know the King of Regelence?"

"Call me Leland. And quite well actually. Not only are our sons married, I've become friends with Steven and his consort Raleigh. Jared and I spent Christmas at Townsend Castle this past year."

"What do you think of them and Regelence in general?"

"I think they are great men and Regelence is a wonderful planet." Hawthorne's brow furrowed. "Why do you ask, Your— Simon?"

"It's come to my attention that Regelence and Englor may have a common enemy."

Hawthorne nodded. "Ah. You should speak to my son. He's of much the same opinion."

Hawthorne knew about the IN trying to pit Englor against Regelence? Simon frowned. "Okay let us start from the beginning. Tell me what you know, Leland, and I'll tell you what I know."

Simon told them about Benson and what he knew of the queen's involvement, leaving out that he and Payton were working together. Payton had asked him for more time to tell the admiral. Simon couldn't imagine the admiral would be that mad, but Pay had disobeyed a direct order even if he hadn't known who Si was at first.

Leland nodded. "You really need to talk to Nathaniel. Let me know when and I'll arrange it."

Simon had had Roc check to make sure Payton was still on Englor, so Simon would talk to Payton before he met with the admiral.

"Colonel," Dunston interrupted, "if you are going to make it to the abbey in time for the coronation ceremony, you should get ready now. Your armed escort will be here in thirty minutes."

"I guess that's our cue. Leland, please talk to the admiral and see if he can meet with me. We need to see what we can do about opening talks with Regelence about a possible alliance." Simon stood, ran his hands down his face and straightened his shirt. He dipped his head at his advisors. "Gentlemen, I'll see you at the ceremony." He hated the palace, but he supposed he really should move into it. His entire life had just changed. He was now facing the moment he'd always prepared for...ready or not. He felt better about the Regelence situation, but he still had to get through this ceremony and stop Parliament from disbanding the Marines. He'd figure out what to do about Payton later.

A gust of wind nearly toppled Payton on his way up the abbey steps. Or maybe he just missed the step entirely since his mind was on Si.

A hand caught his arm in a firm grip, steadying him. Turning his head, he saw a marine in his dress blues. The man smiled and gave him a crisp nod. "Watch your step."

Hoping he wasn't blushing, Payton dipped his head in thanks and kept going. Snow pelted his cheeks and swirled all around him. A storm was kicking up again. A storm that no one in their right mind would be out in. But out they were. The place was packed with royal guards dressed in red and gold and marines in their dress blues. They made the gray day look colorful, but they were also a stark reminder why everyone was here. The king and queen had been assassinated and Simon was being crowned the new king. Payton's heart hurt. He missed Si already. He should be worrying about St. Albins seeing them together but he couldn't help but mourn his loss. This would be the last time he saw Si since Payton was leaving tomorrow.

"Payton?" Nate looked back at him. "Everything okay?"

Payton nodded and hurried to catch up to Nate, Nate's brother and Captain Kindros. He hadn't realized he'd lagged so far behind. The past few days his concentration had been shot. He hadn't seen Simon since that night. After St. Albins barged in on them, Payton had stayed. He shouldn't have, but he couldn't leave, not until he'd made sure Si was okay. Payton's stomach knotted up. Out of all the men on the base, how had Payton wound up with the one he needed to stay away from? The one he could never have a future with? He'd actually hoped for just a moment that night that maybe he could make their relationship work. He'd even had the temerity to wonder if Si would wait for him to turn twenty-five and come back to Englor. Conveniently, he'd forgotten Si would one day be King of Englor and his planet would never accept their relationship.

"Father is to be named one of King Simon's advisors along with St. Albins, the Marquis of Oxley, the Earl of Wycliffe and Major Proctor Bennett of the Englor Marines," Jared said to Nate as they entered the abbey.

What? Nate's dad, the Duke of Hawthorne, was one of Si's advisors? What if St. Albins told Hawthorne what he'd seen?

"Payton, are you all right? You look a little pale, dear." Captain Kindros looped her arm through the crook of his elbow. "Oh no, that wasn't very proper of me, was it? I'm sorry, Your Highness." She began to pull her arm away.

Payton stopped her, tucking her arm into his. "It's quite all right, Captain." It was actually nice to have someone walking with him. He was feeling a little lonely of late. And he liked Captain Kindros. She was nice, but very commanding. She sort of reminded Payton of his old nurse, Christy, only prettier. "And it's Payton or Lieutenant, remember?"

Smiling, she nodded. "Thanks, Payton, and call me Brittani. I'm not here as an officer, remember? Englor society frowns on female military personnel." She wrinkled her nose, showing her disapproval. "I much prefer Regelence society. There I'm a hero just like the men, I just don't get flirted with as much." She sighed. "Most of the men on Regelence only want to hear about my battle record. I guess at least here they see me as a woman."

Payton chuckled. Unlike Nate and Payton, she was out of uniform. She looked every bit the lady at the moment with her dark hair swept up and wearing her lovely burgundy court dress that Nate had procured for her. "I don't know, Brittani, I think I'd rather be seen as a war hero than a piece of meat."

She laughed. "So says one of the hottest catches on Regelence." As they entered the cathedral, she lowered her voice. "What's it like for you here? Is it hard getting used to not being royalty?"

"Not at all. I love it actually. I think I prefer the IN lieutenant to the prince."

There were five aisles with four sections of pews in the center, and stands along the walls of the abbey. Payton escorted Brittani down the center aisle after the Hawkins brothers. The cathedral was huge, with beautiful stained-glass windows casting color all over the place. The gray stone floors were covered with red runners leading to an enormous altar. The center platform had pillars at each corner, with a cross and candles lining the back wall. The barrel-vaulted ceiling was at least ten stories high. Its oppressiveness was a stark reminder of why they were here.

Nate and Jared stopped in front of them, indicating the second row of seats on the right of the center section of pews.

Good galaxy, how had they gotten so far inside? Payton let go of Brittani and entered the row first. She slid in beside him and then Nate sat next to her with Jared on the outside.

Glancing up at the altar where the throne sat, Payton swallowed the lump in his throat. They were so close. He would be able to see Si really well this last time, even if he wouldn't be able to talk to him. Somehow that didn't make him feel any better, just lonely.

Jared leaned past Nate. "Payton, have you ever been to one of these things? This is a first for us."

"I was at my father's when I was eight. I don't remember a lot. Mostly I just remember being bored." He wished he could obtain the same nonchalance he had then. His stomach was tied in knots. Just like his father's coronation, he didn't want to be here. No, that wasn't exactly true, he wanted to see Simon crowned King, but he hated the thought that this would be the last time he'd see Si.

Brittani touched Payton's arm. "Do they have a ball to celebrate the crowning?"

"Yes. I wasn't allowed at my father's, I was too young, but under the circumstances of why Colonel Hollister is being crowned, I doubt it will be right away. My father's coronation was under similar circumstances and there was a mourning period before the ball."

The music started and a hush fell over the entire assembly. The archbishop entered from the side of the altar in his white and gold robes and pontifical hat. He stood facing the back of the abbey.

The doors opened and sunlight poured in. It was dull due to the storm, but even still it painted the red carpet a shade brighter where it landed. The archbishop began reading a psalm, but everyone stayed focused on the back of the cathedral.

Payton knew the exact moment Simon entered. Everyone stood and the tension among the crowd seemed to ease. It was hard to explain, sort of like the crowd had been holding its breath, waiting for their leader. Payton held his breath too. His lover was being crowned King. Si was Hollister and his parents had been killed. It was nearly as surreal a thought as thinking that Payton actually had a lover.

The door shut with a loud boom and Payton's heart raced as he waited for his first glimpse of Simon in days. He rose up on his toes trying to see, but it didn't do much good. Nearly everyone was taller than him. It seemed like several minutes passed, but it was probably only a second before Simon walked past them on his way to the altar.

Si wore a thick, blue velvet robe lined with ermine over his Marine uniform. His shoulders looked even wider than normal in the heavy fur-lined robe. His posture was as sure and commanding as it was regal. His auburn hair looked blood red and his pale skin appeared tanned in the many chandeliers of candles lighting the abbey. He took Payton's breath away just as he always did, even with the somber look on his face.

Simon's advisors followed him in, with St. Albins in the lead carrying the crown. Hawthorne followed carrying a scepter, Oxley was next with an orb, and Wycliffe and Roc walked side by side in Englor Marine dress uniforms. Wycliffe carried a sword. They each presented the regalia to the archbishop then sat in the front middle pew opposite the center aisle from Payton, Nate, Jared and Brittani. Simon stood beside the throne.

After placing the regalia on the altar, the archbishop held out his arm toward Simon. "Sirs, I here present unto you, King Simon. Your undoubted King."

As one the crowd said, "God save King Simon," and trumpets heralded the occasion.

Simon sat on the throne and the archbishop proceeded to take his oath. Sweat dripped down Simon's temple and his hands clutched at the arms of the throne as Simon responded loud and clear to each of the archbishop's questions.

Payton's chest swelled with pride for Si, while a pang of regret hit him in the heart. He'd miss their working out together, and their working together as much as the sex. Dust, who was he kidding, he'd miss just looking at Simon.

Payton lost himself in Simon's deep voice, and the rest of the ceremony passed in a blur. He remembered how that voice sounded in his ear. His cock stirred at the reminder and his hands began to sweat. He couldn't believe that this powerful man had been his, if just for a little while.

When the archbishop picked up the crown, Payton scooted slightly to his left to get a better view, wanting to see the exact moment Si was crowned. As the crown was placed on his head, Simon peered up under a fall of red bangs.

Payton got a sense of déjà vu as Si's head lifted. The piercing blue gaze swept past Payton, then returned. Si smiled for the first time throughout the entire ceremony.

Dust. Payton felt like he'd swallowed rocks. His whole focus narrowed to tunnel vision as he caught Simon's gaze again. His eyes began to water and he looked away. *Better to have loved and lost...*

"I heard from the Marchioness of Whiltshire that His Majesty asked the Duchess of Kentwood for her hand," a whispered voice said behind Payton.

It felt as though a knife stabbed him in the stomach, or what Payton thought that would feel like. It hurt. The air grew heavy, making it hard to draw breath.

"It's about time he made an honest woman of her," another voice whispered.

Payton met a pair of wide brown eyes and realized he'd turned in his seat.

Offering a wavering smile at the ladies, he quickly looked back toward the front.

He watched the rest of the ceremony without really paying attention to it. Then the rumors had been true? Payton's eyes blurred, making him blink away tears. Why should he care? He knew there could never be anything between himself and Si. He knew this, so why did it still hurt?

Payton glanced around the abbey, looking for the duchess. At the very moment he spotted her, she turned her head as though she sensed Payton was thinking about her.

Grinning, Dru winked at him.

Payton returned her smile before looking away. Hopefully

she hadn't read the tightness in his face. Now he and Si were well and truly over.

Chapter Thirteen

Simon paced back and forth in the deserted locker room. Payton was late. What if he'd already gone back to Regelence? He'd asked Roc to deliver a message to Payton this afternoon and Roc swore he had. Wouldn't Payton have told Roc if he were leaving today?

Sitting down on the bench, Simon dropped his head into his hands. How had everything gotten so messed up?

"Hi." Payton's voice was low, with a hint of sadness in it.

Simon smiled, feeling relieved and tense at once. This would be the last time he saw Payton.

"Why did you want to see me?" Payton shoved away from the lockers. He wore a casual IN uniform and black greatcoat. A five o'clock shadow graced his normally smooth cheeks and his black hair was mussed with snow glistening on it. His eyes were red and heavy lidded as though he was tired, but he looked utterly delicious.

"To tell you goodbye," Simon growled, hating himself for wanting Payton even now. "It's too risky for us to be meeting like this. I can't afford the scandal if we're found out." He'd had a hell of a time leaving Hollister House. It was hard to be inconspicuous with two royal guards following his every move. With his parents being murdered, security was heightened. He and Aldred were both suffering the affects, but it was necessary until they figured out who'd assassinated his parents and why. He'd left his armed escort at the front gate of the base despite their protests.

Payton's shoulders slumped and he walked forward until he stood in front of Simon. "I know." He looked down at his feet and exhaled audibly. "I'm leaving tomorrow morning anyway."

"I'm going to have Hawthorne set up a meeting with the admiral and I'll discuss things with him personally. I'll leave your name out of it if you like and just tell him I know Benson was killed trying to save his consort."

Payton glanced up, his eyes sad. "I'll talk to Nate and tell him what we've found. He doesn't need to know anything else, just that we met and started working together." He nodded almost absently, his jaw tight. "This is a good thing." He didn't sound convincing.

Simon grabbed Pay's hand and pulled him onto the bench beside him. When Payton sat, Simon didn't let go. Turning his body, he faced Payton and tilted his chin up. Simon meant to tell Payton how Simon had to start looking for a wife and father an heir, that this was for the best, but what came out was, "You could stay on Englor." Galaxy, what was he saying? Now that he was King his days of freedom and fun were over. With the death of his parents no one was going to rest easy until he had another heir besides Aldred. Right now if something happened to him and to Aldred...

Payton laughed. It wasn't a nice sound. "You want me to be your paramour?"

"It's all I can offer you. I have to get married and beget an heir, you know that." Dipping forward, Simon brushed a kiss across Payton's nose, his chin, his lips. "Talk to me, Pay. I'm not trying to insult you." Payton was pulling away from him, he could feel it.

Shaking his head, Payton dropped his gaze to Simon's chest. "I know you're not trying to, but you have. I know how things work here, but on my planet..." Payton exhaled noisily. Lifting his chin, he gave Si a sad smile. "The answer is no. Go marry Dru."

Oh damn. Simon's stomach felt like it was lodged in his throat. That hurt. Even knowing that letting Pay go was the right thing to do, Simon couldn't quite make himself. Gathering

Payton closer, Simon rubbed his face against Payton's neck. He smelled so good, so fresh and so...Payton. Galaxy, Si's cock was already hard. How was he going to forget this man? "No one would know." They'd make certain of it. They had to. Nuzzling Payton's neck, Simon let out a grunt of frustration. This could work if only Payton would agree. Simon could marry Dru, keep Payton and no one would find out.

Payton moaned and pressed closer. "*I* would know. I won't live like that, Simon."

If Payton was go— *No, don't think like that, not yet.* "Stand up, Pay. You have way too many clothes on."

"I—" Payton stood as directed and caught his bottom lip between his teeth. He looked hesitant, but there was no mistaking his interest. His erection pressed against his uniform pants, and his face was flushed with need. "Once more," he whispered and shrugged his coat off.

Simon groaned. Unbuttoning Payton's shirt, Simon let the "once more" go for now. He pushed the linen from Payton's shoulders then drew him to straddle Simon's lap. He nipped the lip Payton had between his teeth. "I love when you do that." After tugging Payton's shirt off, Simon snuggled him closer.

"It's a bad habit." Payton arched his back, putting his hands on Simon's shoulders, and mashed their pricks together.

"Fuck, Pay." Latching on to the delicious Adam's apple mere inches from his face, Simon unsnapped Pay's trousers. He nibbled and sucked on Payton's neck as he fished Payton's cock out. It was hot and hard in Simon's hand, throbbing at his touch. "Want you." His other hand slid around and down the back of Payton's pants, grabbing his tight little arse. He was still slim, but their working out together had definitely had an affect. Payton's arse was firmer, more muscled.

Payton started making the mewling sounds he always made and bucked up into Si's hand. "Then take me." Lunging forward, Payton took Simon's lips in a deep, demanding kiss. His tongue thrust in and held him close.

Simon matched him, caressing his tongue against Payton's until he had to come up for air. Standing, Simon took Payton with him and set him on his feet.

Toeing off his shoes, Payton kicked them aside and reached out, but Simon ignored the elegant hand in favor of tugging down Payton's pants.

Bloody hell. Pay's pretty cock bobbed free, wet tipped and shining in the harsh fluorescent lights. Simon's mouth watered right along with Payton's prick. Opening up, Simon swallowed Payton down until pubes tickled his nose.

A harsh groan escaped Payton and he wrapped his fingers in Simon's hair.

Pulling back just enough to get his finger in his mouth, Simon sucked. He got his finger good and slick then slid it behind Payton's balls, searching for his hole. Simon was always desperate for Payton, but knowing this could be the last time made it worse.

When Simon pushed in, Payton gasped and pushed back.

Simon's finger hit Pay's gland and his breath hissed out. "Simon, please." He rocked back and forth on Simon's finger.

He pulled his mouth off Payton's cock with a pop. "You're not ready, be patient." Payton had only done this once.

"Don't care. *Pleeease...*"

How could Simon resist that breathy little plea and Payton fucking himself on Simon's finger? He pulled out, stood and grabbed Payton's discarded clothes. Placing them on the bench for padding, Si pushed Payton's shoulders, turning him toward the bench. "Put one knee on the bench."

Hurrying to comply, Payton looked over his shoulder. His yellow eyes grew hazy, then he closed them and his head fell forward, showing off the pale, slender back.

Damn, that sweet arse and back were a sight to behold. Simon dropped to his knees behind Pay. He ran his tongue up Payton's crease, grabbed his balls with one hand and fumbled with his own buttons with the other. Payton tasted salty and tangy. *Mmm...*

"Oh fuck."

Oh fuck, was right. Simon had never heard Payton use that

kind of language. It went straight to Simon's cock, making it jerk and his balls pull tighter. He wanted so badly to be inside Pay's body and at the same time Simon's mind screamed at him to slow down and savor. His insistent body won out.

He stood and tugged his pants to his knees. Gripping Payton's hip in one hand and his own cock in the other, Simon put the head against Payton's hole. Damn that was a nice sight. Steadily he pushed in as Payton pushed back toward him. This time it was he who bit his lip as the heat enveloped him.

Payton stopped suddenly, tensing up. "Oh dust." His voice shook.

"Breathe, Pay. Push out. Relax."

Payton's head bobbed and his back rose and fell. "Trying."

Try harder, please. Rubbing his hand over Pay's spine, Simon held still and gritted his teeth. It felt so bloody good. Payton was so damned snug and hot. Simon's stomach clenched and his knees felt weak with the effort to wait until Payton was ready. Sweat dripped down his temples, but no way would he hurt Payton. He'd known it was too soon, despite Payton's protests. "Want me to stop?"

Payton shook his head. "No, just give me a minute." His voice sounded steadier than before. His muscles contracted around Si's cock, clamping tight.

Finally, when Simon thought he was going to go insane from the effort to not move, Payton pushed back, nestling his arse against Simon's hips.

"Ahh..."

Payton's head bobbed again. "Move, please."

"Oh thank galaxy." He gripped Payton's hips and moved cautiously.

A long, drawn-out, pleasurable moan left Payton, and Simon thrust with more confidence. He leaned forward, his lips finding Payton's spine, his shoulder, his neck. A tingle ran down Simon's body. His sweat dripped onto Payton's pale back and ran down. The musky smell of perspiration and semen permeated the air as their skin slapped together. Simon groaned and reached for Pay's cock, knowing it was already dripping.

Payton turned his head, searching for Simon's mouth.

Thanks to their height difference Simon was able to lean forward and cover Payton's mouth with his. "Mmm..." Bloody hell, Simon loved this man.

"Motherfucker," a deep voice growled, echoing in the empty locker room.

Simon jerked away from Payton so fast a wave of dizziness hit him. His heart crawled up his throat, but instinct had him shoving Payton behind him.

Admiral Hawkins stood inside at the end of the bank of lockers, wearing regulation gym clothes, sweat soaking his massive chest. A tick started in his jaw and his neck muscles tensed. He looked like he wanted to pound someone to a bloody pulp.

Payton's forehead landed on Simon's back, rocking back and forth, and a soft, steady refrain of "dust" drifted up to Simon's ears.

After hitching his trousers up and tucking his still-hard cock back into them, Simon fastened them. *What the fuck?* And why the hell couldn't he find his voice? Bloody hell, the admiral looked fierce.

"Payton?" Hawkins gritted out.

Reaching back, Simon locked his arm around Payton's naked back.

"Yes, sir?"

The admiral's jaw tightened and he glared daggers at Simon.

Enough was enough. Simon opened his mouth to give the admiral a piece of his mind. Admiral or not, he had no business in Payton's private life. Payton was off duty and—

"Don't." The admiral pointed at him. "In my office in ten minutes." He strode to a locker a few feet closer to them, scanned his thumb and opened it without another word.

Reaching past Simon, Payton grabbed his clothes and

began putting them on. Simon did likewise and snagged his shirt off the ground. "Admiral, I—"

Hawkins buttoned his shirt and turned. "Not another word, Hollister." He shoved his shorts over his hips and stepped out of them, then took his trousers out of his locker, dismissing Simon.

Simon's jaw clenched. *Son of a bitch.* Yeah, he and Payton should have already talked to the man about what was going on, but Hawkins was blowing things way out of proportion. Hawkins should know enough about Payton to realize Payton wouldn't be with Simon if he thought he was working with the IN. No way did Hawkins have a problem with gay— Bloody hell, were Payton and Hawkins lovers? No, no, they weren't, Simon was being ridiculous. But— Payton's reaction that night in the garden came back to Si. He took a step forward and Payton caught his arm, turning him.

Payton's face was white, his eyes as round as saucers, and he shook his head.

A locker slammed, drawing Simon's attention back to the admiral.

"My office in ten minutes or there will be hell to pay." With that Hawkins slung his black greatcoat over his shoulders like a cape and exited the locker room.

"What the fuck?" Simon asked, retrieving his own coat from the ground next to the bench.

"I'm so dead." Sitting down on the bench, Payton dropped his head into his trembling hands.

Payton's hands were still trembling when he reached Nate's office. He stopped at the door and looked up at Simon. A lump formed in the pit of his stomach. Galaxy, his throat was dry.

Reaching up, Simon touched his cheek. "The IN has no rules about soldiers fraternizing off duty, whether they are on base, a ship or whatever. We'll tell him what's going on and once he realizes we're working together, it'll be okay. He might still be mad at you for not reporting to him, but—" Si shrugged.

"Unless there's something else going on you aren't telling me about."

Oh dust. Simon still thought he was an IN lieutenant. He'd meant to tell the truth, but he'd gotten so caught up in the investigation he'd forgotten. He leaned into Simon's hand and closed his eyes. "I'm not—"

"Payton!" Nate bellowed through the door. "Get your arse in here."

Simon smiled. "Stop worrying. It will work out."

Swallowing back a protest, Payton grabbed the doorknob. "Let me do the talking, okay?"

"Now," Nate yelled again.

Taking a deep breath that shuddered when it came out, Payton opened the door. Maybe he should have called Aiden first and had him talk to his consort. No, Payton was not going to cower behind his brother, he'd face this. He walked into the office and waited for Simon to shut the door and follow. This confrontation would make Payton's leaving easier. Now that their relationship was out in the open, he could tell Nate they'd been working together and that Simon was in the same boat they were in with the IN.

The door snicked shut and Simon's hand landed on the small of his back.

Nate stared at Simon's hand. "Sit. Both of you."

They took a seat and Simon started right off. "Admiral, you're overreact—"

Nate stood, slamming his hands onto the desk. "No, Colonel, I am not. If I remember correctly you are still an IN officer and under my command, are you not?"

His jaw hardening, Simon dipped his head in acknowledgment.

"Then I suggest you shut your face." He looked at Payton and pointed. "What in the bloody hell do you think you're doing? I told you not to get close to him. You are in my charge. Your parents are going to have my head over this. I-am-responsible-for-you." His voice climbed with each word. "What have you got to say for yourself?"

Simon bristled beside him, and Payton felt like smiling until he realized Si's reaction would likely be different if he knew. Maybe, just maybe, he could keep Si from finding out. The best defense was an offense.

Payton sat up straighter and patted Simon's thigh. "This is my fault. He has nothing to do with it. I honestly didn't know who he was when I first met him."

"Is that supposed to make me feel better?" Nate's eyes widened and his mouth dropped open. "You have compromised yourself. I let you go unchaperoned and what do you do? You find the one goddamned gay guy on the entire fucking planet besides the two of us."

Payton snorted. "I'm pretty sure we aren't the only ones on—"

Nate's fist smashed down on the desk. "Payton!"

Fury slammed into him, overriding his fear and good sense. He'd had enough. He was not going to sit here and be chastised like a child in front of Simon. Jumping up, planting his own hands on the oak desk, Payton stared up at his brother-in-law. "I wanted to. All right? I met him and couldn't help myself. It's the first time I've ever been tempted to actually do something like this. I fell for him and I don't care what anyone else thinks. It's my business and my business alone."

Simon stood, his voice calm. "That's enough."

"No, that is not enough." Nate turned on him. "Do you have any idea who *he*"—he jabbed his finger in Payton's direction—"is, Colonel?"

"No!" *No please don't.* Payton rambled on trying to get everything out, hoping it would make a difference. "Nate, it doesn't matter. This isn't his fault. The important thing is what I've learned about our common problem. We are all on the same side. The two of you need to talk about the IN situation, not this"—he gestured to he and Simon—"this is stupid and insignificant. After I leave here no one but you, Si and me will know. The important thing is that our planets can help one anot—"

It didn't make a difference. Ignoring him, Nate looked directly at Simon. "He is second in line to the throne of Regelence."

Actually, he was third, after his sire and older brother Rexley, but Payton suspected correcting his brother-in-law at the moment would not help matters any. Payton's anger evaporated and he sank back into his chair.

"What?" Simon turned to him, a look of shock on his face. "Payton?"

Payton leaned back, closed his eyes and covered his face with his hands. *Please, make this all go away.*

"*Prince* Payton Townsend," Nate corrected. "King Steven's second child and my consort's older brother. Are you familiar with Regelence's customs, Your Majesty? Did your spy tell you about unmarried lords and how they are off limits?"

Dust, dust, dust. Payton blinked away tears, trailed his hands down his face and ventured a glance at Simon.

His complexion was nearly as red as his hair. Without taking his eyes off Payton, Simon answered Nate. "Yes, Admiral, I am familiar with Regelence customs and as such I will marry him to save his reputation."

"What?" *Since when? When did Simon learn that?* He sure hadn't told Payton he knew it. Then the second part of what he said sank in and Payton jumped up, already shaking his head. Simon had lost his mind. "No! No you can't." He looked at Nate. "Nate, this is a mistake. No one will know. You won't tell. I won't tell. And he"—he pointed at Simon—"he *can't* tell. His people will go against him." *Oh Galaxy, my chest hurts.* Payton clutched a hand over his heart.

Dismissing Payton, Nate looked down at the vid screen and began talking to someone, but Payton had no idea who. It was like he was in a well. He couldn't breathe. No matter how hard he tried, he couldn't get enough air into his lungs. Nate's voice filled the room, but Payton had no idea what he said.

Simon touched his shoulder. "Breathe, Pay."

Nate finally looked up. "I've called Brittani and told her

we're on our way. You'll be married on the Lady Anna."

There was a string hanging on the curtains covering the lift window. Payton yanked it, intending to pull it off, but instead it unraveled. *Kind of like my life.* Payton let go and leaned his head back on the leather bench, studying the roof. He was a married man. A consort to a very angry man whose planet would not approve of their relationship. For all Payton knew, their marriage would not even be recognized by the laws of Englor, much less the citizens. *Guess I need to get a copy of Englor's Constitution or Parliamentary Sovereignty or whatever it's called.* He wondered if Englor was a constitutional monarchy like Regelence, or if it was an absolute monarchy? He suspected the former.

The anger at being caught and having to reconcile the situation had passed. Now he was numb. He wanted to be something, anything—mad, scared, confused, something—but his brain had apparently shut down all emotion for the moment.

Nate had spoken to him on the way to the Lady Anna, telling him it was the right thing to do. And for some reason, Payton couldn't help but think Nate was acting more surprised than he was. He hadn't seemed all that angry after Simon agreed to the wedding. Could he have known? Why was he at the gym, anyway? He hadn't gone before. Nah, Nate would have said something sooner.

Payton rubbed his forehead. His chest pain had turned into a gigantic headache. He felt guilty. He felt like he'd trapped Simon into marriage. The man had more or less asked him to be his paramour. He'd planned to marry Her Grace the Duchess of Kentwood and relegate Payton to dirty little secret.

He winced, feeling a jolt of embarrassment. It was what he'd wanted, wasn't it? To be wanted for himself and not because he was a prince? Then why did it make him feel...dirty? His shoulders slumped. It didn't matter now. It was a moot point. He was Simon's spouse, not his paramour. He'd tried to let Simon off the hook, but Simon had been determined to do the honorable thing.

"You lied."

Oh, we're talking now. Payton straightened and glanced across the lift. Simon hadn't spoken to him in over an hour, not since gritting out his wedding vows through clenched teeth.

"This is why you were so anxious to keep Hawkins from finding out we were working together. This is why you ran the other night at the dinner." Si sat with his ankle propped on his opposite knee, lounging back in the seat with his arms spread out along the backrest. His head was turned with his attention out the window rather than on Payton. The heavy coat made his shoulders look impossibly wide and masculine. There was even stubble on his cheeks. It was as red as the hair on his head and would probably be missed in daylight, but in the lamplight of the lift there was a nice shadow covering the lower part of his face. He appeared withdrawn, untouchable, yet there was a firmness to his jaw line that wasn't normally there. He was angry. "I trusted you."

Guilt swamped Payton, but he brushed it away. He wasn't mad at Simon, exactly, but he couldn't help feeling...trapped? He'd said he didn't want a consort and Simon had ignored him. "I didn't lie. I just didn't tell you everything."

"Why did he bring you?" Simon's voice was flat, devoid of emotion.

Payton rested his head back on the headrest and closed his eyes. There was really no point in lying. They *were* on the same side. "Because I'm good with computers."

There was a rustle from across the coach.

Payton cracked an eye open to find Simon studying him, a frown on his face.

"You've been hacking into computers?"

"Yes." Payton closed his eye again. Should he tell Si about the message he was trying to crack?

"My computer on base?"

"No, Nate wouldn't let me break into your office."

Simon growled. "Not only have you lied to me, but now

you're patronizing me?"

Galaxy, I can't win for losing. Payton sat up again, a feeling of indignation swamping him. "I am not patronizing you." Simon acted like Payton was the only one who'd lied through avoidance. He sure as hell hadn't told Payton about Drucilla Blake. Oh galaxy, had he already asked Dru to marry him?

Leaning forward, Simon clenched and unclenched his fists. "Don't—"

The lift stopped. "Your Majesty, we are at Hollister House as you requested."

Payton didn't wait for Simon. He was in no mood to deal with this at the moment. Standing, he moved to the door. "Door open, steps down."

The lift door slid up into the frame with a swish sound and the steps descended. He alighted and walked up the porch to the townhouse. There were two royal guards on either side of the door. They moved to stop him, but paused upon catching sight of Si. One of them rapped on the door and it opened.

Payton nodded his thanks and continued into the house. He needed sleep. He could think better after a good night's sleep.

"Payton. Don't walk away from me, I'm talking to you." Simon's footsteps echoed behind Payton.

Dunston greeted them but before Payton could acknowledge the butler, Simon grabbed his arm and spun him around. "I think you're forgetting something." His grin was downright evil, sending a shiver down Payton's spine. "By Regelence law, I'm your legal guardian until you're twenty-five."

Chapter Fourteen

Simon stared down at his half-eaten breakfast. What he'd eaten felt like a brick in his stomach. Taking one last drink of juice, he pushed away from the table and left the breakfast room. He had a meeting with his advisors in ten minutes and what he really wanted to do was talk to Payton. Maybe he'd gone too far with the guardian remark. When he'd gone up to bed last night, he'd found Payton curled up in his bed sound asleep—or doing a great job of pretending. They hadn't spoken at all and Payton was still in bed this morning. "Dunston, is Payton awake?"

"No, Colonel. At least it doesn't sound as if he is. Shall I call out to him?"

"No. Let him sleep. When he wakes send up some breakfast."

"Yes, Colonel."

Wandering down the hall, Simon made his way to his office. He had no idea why he'd said what he did. Revenge maybe? Pay's refusal to marry him had rankled. Simon had gotten the feeling that he'd only gone through with it because of something the admiral had said to him in the transport pod on the way to the Lady Anna. After that Payton had ceased to argue.

And Simon knew Payton well enough to guess the guardian comment would make him mad. It hadn't had quite the affect he'd envisioned though. Instead of starting a fight, Payton had turned so pale Simon had feared he was going to pass out. Then he'd walked away without so much as a retaliatory remark, disappearing into the depths of Hollister House. Simon had drunk himself into a stupor. Sometime after oh five hundred hours, he'd dragged himself up to bed. He'd been surprised to find Payton there in his room rather than another room, given their last exchange.

"Dunston, when Payton wakes you may admit him wherever he wishes to go. He's my—" What the hell was he? Same-sex marriages weren't illegal on Englor, but they were extremely rare and not at all accepted thanks to the Church of Englor's refusal to sanction them. The only such marriage Simon even knew of happened when he'd been eighteen, right after he'd gone into the IN. Lord Keller's son had been embroiled in a scandal with one of the footmen. The two had been wed a week afterward and fled to the countryside. The earl had disowned his son and told everyone he was dead. "I married him last night."

Simon entered his study and even with his stomach in knots, his gaze narrowed in on the tumbler of scotch sitting on the bar in the corner of the room. It was so tempting, but Aldred would have his head, and since Aldred was due any minute...

"Good choice, Colonel. I really like him. I believe the proper term for him would be consort."

Yes, now he remembered, that was what spouses were called on Regelence, Payton's home planet. He wasn't ignorant to Regelence's customs since they were very much like Englor's. He'd done his homework. He'd known as soon as he found out Payton was a lord and only nineteen what compromising him meant. It had been obvious that Pay was looking for a good time with no consequences, so Simon had given him that. It's not like anyone on Regelence would have found out, if Payton had been a regular old run-of-the-mill lord. And why would Simon expect him to be anything else? Who would have thought a prince would be so far away from home on the front lines of an investigation?

"He will make a fine one, I suspect. He has a regal bearing about him, and I imagine he can even charm the populace into approving of him."

Simon grinned. "That's probably because he is the son of a king." As for his charm? Simon suspected Dunston was correct. Payton's good looks and charisma had won Wycliffe over immediately. Wycliffe was not a trusting guy. It took him a long time to warm up to people, which was why Roc and Simon were two of his very few friends. Regardless, Payton wasn't going to go anywhere without a guard or four. Until Simon figured out who had his parents killed... No even after that. Payton could very well be a target just because he was a man and Simon's consort. Like it or not, Payton was going to have to cope with it, because Simon was not going to risk Payton's life.

"Perhaps he can keep you and your friends in line," Dunston quipped. "Your guests are here, Colonel, shall I send them in?"

"Yes, please." Walking over to the fireplace, he leaned against the mantle and stared down into the flames. He'd either made the biggest mistake of his life, or his greatest triumph. He had what he wanted—well almost, he didn't have an heir yet—but Hawkins had assured him that Regelence procreation would be open to him. To Simon it was the ideal set up. He would secure his succession without having to marry an unwanted woman and pretend interest. Now to see if his advisors agreed with him. Crossing to his desk, he pulled out his chair and sat. He leaned back, resting his hands over his stomach in a confident relaxed way he did not feel at the moment.

"Good morning, Si." Roc came into the study followed by Wycliffe, Oxley and Aldred.

Simon felt a sting of regret upon seeing his uncle. He shouldn't be telling his uncle about his marriage like this. It should have been done beforehand, not here in front of everyone.

"Simon." Hawthorne entered, dipping his head, with his son on his heels. The admiral stood a good four inches taller than his father. He wore IN dress whites, his cover in his hand. If he weren't so damned big and intimidating, he'd be a really handsome man, just as his father was. Both had the same swarthy coloring, brown eyes and dark brown hair, though Hawthorne had the sexy graying at the temples and no beard like his son. Leland also had laugh lines at the corners of his eyes that his son lacked.

"Colonel," Admiral Hawkins said as he met Simon's gaze. He was an enigma. If not for his reaction to catching Simon and Payton last night, Si would have thought the admiral planned their getting together. It was obvious the man held Regelence and its royal family in high regard and would do anything to protect the planet and its people, even going against the IN, but Simon had to wonder if that also included marrying off one of the princes to ensure an alliance.

It would benefit Englor as well, but Simon couldn't rule that possibility out. To do so would underestimate Hawkins, and Simon wasn't about to do that. The man hadn't gotten his military record and reputation from nowhere. He was a hard man. Simon felt sorry for Payton's brother.

"Gentlemen. Please be seated. I have some important news." He waved his hand toward the admiral. "And I've invited Admiral Hawkins to join us."

Hawkins sat on the love seat next to his father. "Please, call me Nate." A soft almost-smile flitted across his face. Thankfully, he looked much more relaxed and in a better mood today than he had last night.

Dipping his head, Simon acknowledged the request. Nate had asked him to call him by his first name last night when they spoke on the way to the Lady Anna. "Dunston, secure the room."

The door closed and the lock snicked shut.

Simon took a deep breath and let it out. He'd best get it over with. "Last night I married Nate's aide, or rather his brother-in-law, Payton Townsend."

The room was silent for all of five seconds then burst into chaos with Roc and Wycliffe being the most vocal. Both his friends jumped to their feet, shouting about not being forewarned and formulating a plan to deal with the predicted public outcry.

Simon hadn't expected that. He didn't know whether to be annoyed or relieved they were doing their job as advisors.

Oxley looked like someone had slapped him, and Hawthorne turned to his son and started talking.

Shaking his head, Simon tuned them all out and met his uncle's gaze. "I'm sorry, there wasn't time to call you."

Aldred sat there for several seconds in silence, then a slow smile crept across his face. "Congratulations."

"What? This is not a good thing," Wycliffe interrupted. "Look, Si, I like Payton, but the citizens of En—" His eyes widened and he turned toward Nate. "Payton is your brother-in-law?"

A long, low whistle escaped Roc and he returned to his seat. "I'm beginning to see the whole picture."

Arsehole. Simon was going to take a ribbing for compromising Payton and getting caught, no doubt about it.

"Okay, let's look at this another way." Oxley leaned forward, resting his forearms on his knees. "He's a Regelence Prince, right?"

Simon nodded. "Yes, the second oldest."

Oxley nodded. "Even better." He turned toward Nate. "I assume you've spoken to Simon about the mess with the IN, Nathaniel?"

"Yes, Kit. We spoke last night." Nate stretched his arms over the back of the maroon leather love seat and crossed his ankle over his knee. "Simon and I have shared information. He's informed me of his mother's possible involvement. And I'm helping to investigate the king and queen's murders as well."

"Good." Oxley smiled and turned his attention to Simon. "This will make getting an alliance with Regelence a given. Oh, and congratulations, Simon."

Hawthorne groaned. "Kit..."

One of Oxley's dark brows lifted, but the smirk on his face remained. "Don't growl at me, Leland. Politically, this puts us in a great situation. There's no sense in not acknowledging that.

And besides, who knows? This could start a new trend here on Englor."

Simon smiled without humor. He somehow doubted Oxley's optimism.

"We can only hope," Wycliffe mumbled.

"You could always go to Regelence to find a spouse, Wycliffe," Nate said.

Wycliffe slapped a hand to his chest. "Bite your tongue, Deverell. Not only am I not in the market for a wif—consort, Amberley would disown me, should he survive the shock."

Simon chuckled. He'd nearly forgotten that Nate was the Earl of Deverell. *Oh damn. Amberley.* Wycliffe's father would be one of the most vocal against Simon's marriage. "Something tells me you should prepare yourself for Amberley's wrath anyway, Wycliffe. He will not be pleased if you remain my advisor or my friend."

"He can say what he likes, Si, but I'm behind you a hundred percent." Wycliffe stared him right in the eye.

"So am I," Roc added.

Oxley nodded. "As am I."

Aldred caught Simon's gaze. "You know where I stand, so I won't bother announcing it. However, I want to point out that in light of this new event—happy as we may be about it—others will not be. You will lose votes we need to make certain that the Marines remain Englor Marines and not the IN's. Some lords will vote against anything you're for, whether they believe in it or not, on principle."

The same thought had occurred to Si last night when he'd weighed the advantages and disadvantages of marrying Payton. Simon sat forward, resting his arms on his desk. "I'm aware of that. And I assure you, the Marines *will* remain on Englor and under Englor command." Meeting each of the gazes of the other men in the room, Simon kept his face blank, letting them read the seriousness of his statement. He believed in allowing the people to choose for themselves, but he was a military man. He *would* do whatever it took to protect his people if it came down to it.

No one spoke for several seconds, but everyone in the room nodded their agreement.

"You said last night that Payton thinks the cloning technology referred to in the message you received from Benson is the Regelence Procreation Process?" Nate finally said.

"Yes, he does. Neither of us can figure out why the IN would want the technology." Simon leaned back once again and crossed his ankles under his desk to get comfortable. He was anxious to get the admiral's take on this.

"From what I've witnessed of Regelence men, in general, they are highly intelligent, extremely agile and have an underlying aggression." He frowned. "Even Aiden, as refined as he is, can be quite ruthless when riled. Trouble, er, my son Jeremy, is Regelen. When I found him on a space station in the Regelence system, he was nearly feral. And Raleigh? The king's consort is a scary man. Come to think of it, from what I've seen, the rest of them have that potential for violence as well. Makes me wonder what they'd be like without the trappings of polite society. I wonder if it's a trait. If something the scientists do to create them makes them..." He shrugged. "They don't allow designer babies. I don't know how—"

"No, I see where you're going with this," Hawthorne interrupted. "Every Regelence Lord I've met has been in top physical condition. They all seem to have that agility and quick reflexes you were speaking of. Maybe there is some side effect that makes them that way in the process that makes them prefer men or removes the female's DNA."

Bloody hell. Like the perfect warrior? It was a scary thought, but it made sense. Even as small as Payton was he was quick and...strong. When they'd fenced at the gym, Payton had protested to be an amateur but even still, Simon had had his work cut out for him in beating Payton. Actually come to think of it, he'd resorted to trickery. Plus, the amount of weight Payton lifted was rather impressive for his size. "Nate, when are you going back to Regelence?"

"Today. Which means I'll be back on Regelence in a week's

time."

"You'll look into this when you get back? Talk to the scientists?" Simon asked.

Nate uncrossed his legs. "Absolutely. I was thinking the same thing."

"Although I have to tell you the idea that you find Payton's father frightening does not make me eager to inform the man I compromised his son."

"Sire. Raleigh is Payton's sire, and I don't envy you." Nate grinned. "You will be getting a threatening televid call, I assure you."

Great. Hopefully, them not telling the man right away wouldn't anger him. Payton and Nate both swore it would be better for Nate to inform Payton's parents in person. Simon sure hoped they were correct.

"Relax, Simon. Raleigh may be scary, but like me, he's a good man to have on your side." Nate chuckled.

"Will he be on my side?"

The humor drained from Nate's face and he was suddenly all business again. "Yes. After he calms down. He's also a very intelligent, reasonable man. Just make sure Payton is taken care of."

"He will not leave either here or the palace without an armed escort. Not even after we find who had my parents killed."

"Good." Nate nodded. "He's not going to like that, but I expect you to make certain he abides by it anyway. I'm still looking into my IN sources. So far I've found nothing about the assassination, but I'm willing to bet that it's related to this mess with the IN."

"Excuse me, Colonel," Dunston interrupted.

Uh-oh. Simon had told Dunston to secure the room. He wouldn't interrupt if it were unimportant. "Yes, Dunston?"

"You gave Payton admittance to everything in the house, correct?" Dunston's voice wavered.

Simon frowned. He couldn't ever remember hearing that

hesitant tone from his butler before. "Yes. Why?"

"He is accessing my hard drive and using the Englor Marine encryption program."

Simon groaned. "Bloody hell." *Why?*

A bark of laughter brought Simon's attention back around to Nate.

The admiral made no attempt to hide his mirth.

Grinning, Leland nudged his son with his foot. "Nathaniel."

"He did assure me he'd crack that message." Nate smiled up at Simon.

Message? Simon didn't remember anything about a message. Payton better not have lied about anything else.

The admiral shrugged. "It doesn't matter whether you gave him access or not. He'd get in. Did I forget to mention he's a genius when it comes to computers?"

Pride swelled in Simon's chest, overcoming the annoyance. He'd known Payton was brilliant. It was odd, he couldn't remember ever taking pride in someone else's accomplishments. No, that wasn't true, he'd always enjoyed seeing the men under his command succeed, but this was different. He found himself wanting to take credit for it. Like somehow because Payton was his, it gave him bragging rights. "So I've noticed. He's brilliant at everything he does. If he's an example of Regelence's artificial procreation technology, I see why the IN wants it."

The smile slid from Nate's face. "Speaking of Regelence men, I've got a ship to catch. Not only do I need to fill Steven and Raleigh in on what's happened and check with the Regelence scientists, if I don't get going I'm liable to be hunted down by an angry Regelence artist." He nodded and stood, a smirk appearing again. "I'll be in touch. Let me know if you learn anything new."

Simon rose and walked around the desk. The other five men rose as well. "Lord Deverell." Simon offered his hand to Nate.

Nate chuckled and shook his hand. "Reminding me of my Englor ties, Colonel?"

"No, just wondering how much longer you'll be an admiral."

"As long as they let me. I believe in keeping my friends close and—"

"My enemies closer," Simon finished for him. "Me too. Thank you, Nate. As soon as I—or Payton"—*since he's withholding information again*—"learn anything new I'll let you know. Let's cross our fingers that Parliament votes down the proposal to dissolve the Marines."

"Let me know when the vote is. I'll submit an absentee ballot or I can be here to lend support should you suspect the vote will go the other way." He gave Simon a pointed look.

Simon nodded his agreement, knowing exactly what Nate was saying. Simon would do whatever it took to ensure that the Marines remained, but he wanted to try it the legal way first.

With his advisors following, Simon opened the study door. "Gentlemen, I'll be in touch. I've a consort to keep out of trouble."

"Good luck with that." Hawthorne chuckled. "I've met all the Townsends and I can assure you mischief finds them whether they look for it or not." He glanced over at his son. "Should we tell him Payton's nickname is Lord Plague?"

Lord Plague? Terrific. Simon shook his head. He didn't want to know. "In that case, I'm going to go make sure he shares whatever it is he's learned by using the encryption program." He shook hands with all his advisors and hugged Aldred goodbye.

His trek up the stairs was one of the slowest he could remember. He needed to apologize to Payton, but he was still a little cross. There was obviously something else Payton wasn't telling him.

It was his own fault, not Payton's. Simon should have paid more attention. He'd gotten so caught up in the politics of what would become of the Englor Marines, not to mention trying to find out what the IN was up to, that he'd ignored the signs. And there had been signs. One thing was certain now. He'd get an alliance with Regelence. Which he desperately needed. If his assumption was correct, the IN had his parents murdered. Why? What did they want? He sighed. He was going to do his damnedest to find out. And he was going to need the Englor Marines. But even the Marines could not stand up to the IN on their own. They would need the help of the Regelence Navy and the Regelence Marines.

Simon got to the top landing of the second floor, feeling the weight of Englor on his shoulders. The man who could help him carry the weight was down the hall.

He glanced down at the foyer in time to see the door close behind his advisors. The footman turned and disappeared down the hallway toward the kitchen. What kind of mood would Payton be in? Was he still mad?

Pinching the bridge of his nose, Simon headed toward his room. There was too much to do to sit around and fret over everything. Besides, it wasn't his style. He had a problem. He had to solve it. It was his job. End of story. *Now to figure out what all needed done and in what order.*

He needed an heir. Simon grinned. The child would be completely his and Payton's, and that would go a long way in soothing the people of Englor. How could they not accept their next king's parent?

The palace had to be gotten in order. Not just security either. Moving back there was not something he was looking forward to. He hated that place. It was too big and too daunting. It was cold, like a mausoleum. He didn't want his kid to grow up like he had. Logically he knew part of it was his parents, but that place...

He got to his bedroom door and opened it cautiously. The only sound came from the fire crackling in the fireplace at the foot of his bed. Payton was nowhere in sight. Simon frowned. Dunston had said Pay was in his...their bedroom.

Simon closed the door and crossed the room. "Pay?"

No answer.

Damn, it was chilly in here. Simon rubbed his hands on his arms, looking around. There was a black leather-bound book and com-pad on the still unmade bed.

The closer to the balcony curtains he got the colder it

became. The heavy drapes moved just a tad. "Payton?" Simon pulled the dark green velvet back, revealing an open French door.

Payton sat huddled in his coat on the stone balcony rail, staring down at the garden. Snow drifted down, coating his dark hair like diamonds sparkling in the sunlight. He sat so still, with his knees drawn up and his arms wrapped around them. His head rested on his raised knees.

In this type of weather he shouldn't be sitting on the railing, even if it was over a foot wide. What if it were icy? "Pay?"

Payton turned his head to face Simon, resting his ear on his knees. A fog of hot air billowed around him. His yellow eyes nearly glowed in the bright sunlight. There was a shadow of stubble on his cheeks and his hair was mussed. He wore the clothes he'd had on last night, but even still, he was breathtakingly handsome. "Did Nate send my things?"

"They arrived this morning before I met with my advisors. We need to talk."

"Then talk." Payton turned his head back toward the garden, all but dismissing him.

"Is there something else you want to tell me?"

"Don't play games with me, Simon. What do you want to know?" Payton frowned and kept staring out at the snow-covered garden. *Just tell him, Pay. You're just trying to start a fight.* He knew Dunston had told Si he used the encryption program. Yet another thing he hadn't told Si...*yet.* He'd planned on telling Si about the message from the beginning, he'd just been biding his time, and he'd wanted to know what the message said first. He was not going to let Si yell at him for withholding information. He'd had his reasons. Besides, Nate could have told Simon last night when they were so buddy-buddy on the Lady Anna, planning Payton's life for him.

Payton gathered up some snow on the ledge next to him and threw it into the yard. Okay, fine, he was pissed at being caught keeping information to himself again. *Damn it.* He'd never been a liar but he sure as hell was making himself look that way to Si.

A groan sounded behind Payton. It seemed resigned rather than angry. "What did you use the encryption program for?"

It was on the tip of his tongue to snip at Si and tell him that he could use whatever he wanted because this was his house now too, but he bit it back. Taking out his anger on Si wasn't going to help anything. He'd been wrong for not telling Si who he was and for not telling him about the message.

Payton sighed, feeling about two feet tall. "Nate's son confiscated a message on the ship he and Aiden were taken hostage on. It was a message to you from Benson that Caldwell apparently stole. I've been trying to crack it since this whole thing started. I figured out it was Englor encryption, but I couldn't break the code." Which was another thing that made him angry, he wasn't used to not being able to solve puzzles on his own.

"What did it say?" Simon's tone was even and a little flat. Payton supposed that was at least something. He'd be yelling if he were Si.

Payton dropped one foot over the side of the rail. "There's an IN agent on Englor. Which we already suspected. Benson didn't know who, but he'd overheard Caldwell."

"Did the message say anything else? Hint at why the IN wants the Marines?"

Payton shook his head, continuing to stare out into the snow-covered garden. It was dismal. Kind of like his life right now.

"I bet this all ties into my parents being killed too. Aldred seemed to think my father was leaning toward throwing his backing to keep the Marines. I don't want you going anywhere without a guard, Payton. And you really shouldn't be out here on this balcony."

Great, he was going back to being chaperoned all the time. Payton stuck his hand out, catching the falling snow and watching it melt instantly. He was tired of the snow already.

"Is there anything else you need to tell me? Or are we done

with the secrets now?"

I don't know, are we? What did your advisors say earlier? Did it even matter what Simon's advisors had to say about their marriage? It was a done deal and they couldn't change it. Unless they expected Si to get the marriage annulled. Payton felt the blood drain from his face.

"Why don't you come inside? Besides the obvious danger, it's cold out here." Almost as an afterthought he added, "Please."

For a brief second, Payton just sat there, then he nodded absently. Swinging his legs over the railing, he stood and brushed past Si into the room, suddenly feeling the cold air. Funny, he hadn't thought it was that chilly when he'd gone out to have a look at the grounds in the daylight.

"Pay?" Simon closed the balcony door. "Listen. I never planned on— I never thought— Oh bloody hell, will you look at me please?"

Payton took off his coat and laid it across the bed, feeling defeated. He wanted to know what Simon's advisors had to say, but he refused to ask. It was no secret that Si hadn't wanted to marry him. He'd planned on marrying the Duchess of Kentwood and keeping Payton as a secret lover.

Payton swallowed the lump in his throat. Getting mad or fighting an annulment wouldn't change Simon's feelings. If Si truly didn't want Payton— The rest of his anger slipped away. Whatever happened, happened. He was tired of fighting.

"Please." Si rested his hand on Payton's shoulder.

How could he stay mad when Si sounded so lost? Payton turned toward Si and was immediately struck by how worn out he looked. Had he even slept last night? "I tried to let you off the hook. There was no need for you to marry me."

Si scowled at him. "I know bloody well that I didn't have to, you reminded me of that at least twenty times on the ride to the Lady Anna, and at last three times after." Si sighed, his shoulders heaving. "I'm trying to apologize for what I said last night. I didn't mean that. I have no intention of acting as your guardian, Pay, you're a grown man and can do whatever the hell you want. I was mad and— I'm sorry. Things got way out of hand."

Nodding, Payton glanced around the room, looking anywhere but at Si. "I'm sorry too. I should have told you who I was, I just didn't think it mattered. I was going back to Regelence and—"

Simon caught his chin, forcing him to make eye contact. "It was important, whether you went back or not, it was important. I wanted—want to know everything about you."

"What did your advisors say?" *So much for not asking, Pay.*

"Oxley seems to hope our marriage will start a trend. All of them were pleased that we'll be getting an alliance with Regelence as a result."

Ouch. Payton winced. The cold feeling tried to creep back in. Si seemed so sure. Almost like he'd thought of it as well. Payton had gone from unwanted spouse to political pawn in the span of a few hours. Could Simon have planned—? No, no, there went his overactive imagination again. Si hadn't known who Payton was until Nate had informed him.

"I like the scruffy look you have going on here." Si ran his fingers over Payton's jaw, his gaze following them. His voice was deeper, huskier.

The sound made Payton forget all about his rocky relationship. He loved that lust-induced voice. He shivered. Si was his, at least for the moment, and he could do whatever he wanted with him. What a thought. Focusing on Si's full, kissable lips, Payton bit his own. His cock twitched to life.

"What are you thinking?" Si's thumb traced Payton's bottom lip and he dipped his head closer. He licked Payton's lips. "What's with this naughty little grin?"

Moaning, Payton lifted his face until he could feel Si's breath cooling the trail his tongue had just made. "I was thinking that you're mine now and I can do whatever I want to you." Galaxy, was that his voice? It sounded so rusty and unused. Like he'd just woken up.

Si groaned and slammed his mouth down on Payton's, his

hand sliding around Payton's back. He crushed Payton to him and thrust his tongue inside. The muscled length of his body was absolute heaven, stealing Payton's breath and reminding him of last night before they'd been interrupted. Si was already erect against Payton's stomach.

Payton whimpered, his own cock hardened. There was so much wrong. So much they needed to work out. They needed to talk. *Pull back, Pay.* His cravat was tugged off and thrown onto the bed. Si stepped back, putting space between them and breaking their kiss. He practically ripped Payton's waistcoat and shirt off, then he jerked Payton's trousers open. Button's flew off in every direction, plinking and rolling on the hardwood floor. Payton's cock strained against his underclothes.

"Get these off and get on the bed." Simon tapped Payton's hip and began pulling off his own clothes.

Payton froze, watching the muscles of Si's chest flex as they were revealed to him. Si's face and neck were flushed, his erection evident through his trousers. Lifting his head as he dropped his shirt to the ground, Si met Payton's gaze before his attention fell to Payton's open trousers. "Now."

Spurred into motion by the growly need in Si's voice, Payton kicked his shoes off. He turned toward the bed, and seeing his com-pad and journal, he took the time to set them on the nightstand. He sat on the edge of the bed and pulled his stockings off. By the time he stood and reached for his trousers and underpants, Si was gloriously naked, hard and all hands. He helped Payton divest himself of the rest of his clothes and shoved him backward onto the bed.

Payton landed with a bounce, his cock slapping against his stomach and splattering moisture onto his belly. Before he knew what hit him, Si was on top of him, pinning him, mouth covering Payton's.

Si's hand wormed between them, catching Payton's cock. He growled and bit Payton's bottom lip. "Fuck, you make me insane. Want you so badly."

Gasping for breath, Payton squirmed, trying to get his hands on Si. His cock was so hard he felt as though he were going to burst. He'd never felt this intense, blinding arousal. He wanted to bite and scratch and—Galaxy, he needed Simon. Bucking his hips into Si's tight grip, Payton managed to dislodge his consort and tumble him to the side. Immediately he reached for Si's erection and squeezed.

Snapping his hips forward, Si never faltered in his motions. He kept stroking Payton's cock. "Yes. That's it, don't stop, Pay." His chest muscles looked so round and hard, Payton's mouth watered even as he moaned at Si's ministrations.

Payton sank his teeth into the bulging pectoral muscle as he jerked Si's heavy prick. It wrung a ragged cry of pleasure from Simon. After that it became almost violent, both of them trying to get at each other. They were both panting and sweating, and somehow Payton ended up on the bottom again with Si sitting on top of him. He peered down at Payton, his sweaty red hair matted to his face.

"Oh." Payton's testicles pulled tight, sensation shot down his spine and his orgasm ripped through him, bowing his back off the mattress. Heat splashed on his stomach and his arm. For several seconds he couldn't feel anything but the overwhelming pleasure, then the warm musky smell filled his senses and he collapsed back on the bed. His eyes clouded with tears and his body shook.

Si groaned above him and Payton blinked, focusing on the wide blue eyes staring down at him. He hadn't even realized he'd let go of Si's cock until that very moment. Si had grabbed it himself and stroked, once, twice. He fell forward bracing himself over Payton and came. His face scrunched together and then relaxed, a deep, shuddering breath left him. It was like all the stress of the past few days evaporated from him. Payton had never seen a more beautiful sight.

Fighting back tears, Payton caught Si behind the neck and tried to tug him down on top of Payton. He felt utterly worn out. He'd needed that in the worst way, but now he was all shaky, emotional. He didn't like the feeling at all.

Si's eyelids fluttered open. A small smile crept across his face and he pressed his lips to Payton's. The kiss was slow and sensual, their tongues lazily exploring.

Payton just went with it and let himself be swept away. He clung to Si, holding on tight. He didn't want to think right now, instead he let the light floaty feeling of Si's kisses take him away.

"Fuck, I needed that." Caressing Payton's cheek, Simon gave him one last soft kiss on the lips before getting up. "I've got to go to the base." His voice was soft—it sounded almost sad.

Sitting on the edge of the bed, Si stretched his arms over his head, his wide muscular back to Payton. Damn, that was nice. Even as sated and relaxed as Payton was the sight made his pulse race. He grinned and rolled onto his side. This marriage thing definitely had advantages. He trailed his fingers over Simon's lower back and down one firm arse cheek. *Dust, he's gorgeous.*

"Mmm...you're making me want to get back in bed."

"Then do it." Payton propped his head up on his hand.

Shaking his head, Simon stood. "I've got too much to do." He grabbed his underclothes without turning and pulled them on, covering up his luscious arse.

Payton sighed and watched the play of back and shoulder muscles as Simon tugged on his pants. It was a pity to cover up such perfection, not to mention, Payton was happy and comfortable and didn't want to move, but Si was right. They did have a lot to do. "What's the plan?" Payton sat and looked around the room for his strewn clothing.

"First I need to get Parliament's support to keep the Marines on Englor." Simon groaned and walked over to where his shirt lay on the floor. He picked it up and put it on. "I have to go clear some things up on base. General Davidson is coming in from the other base for a meeting. I plan on speaking to him about the IN merger and get his take on things." Buttoning his shirt, he bent over and kissed Payton on the forehead. "We need to move into the palace."

Payton smiled and looped his arms around Si's neck, trying to pull him back onto the bed. "What about the IN? We still need to find out what schematics they—"

Si kissed him and stood, tucking his shirt in. "Just leave that to me. See what you can do about arranging us an appointment with the Regelence procreation clinic and redecorate the palace. I've already talked to the head of the royal guards about security." He gave an over-exaggerated shiver. "I hate that place. It's so bloody cold."

Payton froze. What did he—? "An appointment? Why? Can't Nate or one of my parents talk to the scientists about the process?"

"Nate's going to look into it as soon as he gets back. He seems to think something in the process makes you stronger and more agile—"

Payton snorted. He'd apparently not gotten those traits.

"He's right, Pay. You're a lot stronger than a man your size should be. And you're damned quick. With a little training you'd make a hell of a soldier." Simon fetched his stockings and shoes, sat on the edge of the bed and began putting them on.

"Regardless, why do I need to make an appointment if Nate is going to speak with the scientists?"

"For an heir, of course."

Falling back on the bed, Payton tried to catch his breath and stared at the canopy. He wasn't ready for kids. He wasn't even—

Simon stood, bent over and kissed Payton on the mouth, oblivious to Payton's inner turmoil. "I'll meet you at the palace this evening. If you need help redecorating, call Dru."

Dru? Simon's fiancée? Payton laid there, a million things racing through his mind as Simon walked off.

Chapter Fifteen

I swore I'd never become some lord's brainless arm ornament and political host, but I've become far worse. I'm a glorified housekeeper and sperm donor.
—from the journal of Payton Marcus Hollister

Planet Englor: Hollister Palace in London, Moreal

He felt rather like a lab rat in a maze, or how he assumed a rat would feel. Payton jogged up a flight of stairs and faced yet another hallway that looked exactly the same as all the others. It had pale gray marble flooring and walls painted in alternating glossy white and flat white vertical stripes with glossy white wainscoting below. Wincing, he suppressed the urge to rub his hands over his arms. Hollister Palace was a lonely, cold and saturnine place, a showpiece rather than a home.

Raised in a gothic-style castle decorated in jewel tones and heavy mahogany furniture, he preferred dark colors that made a bold statement but felt cozy at the same time. His shoulders slumped as he continued down the hall. He missed Townsend Castle. Maybe it was the unsettled things between himself and Si, but he was starting to feel more than a little wary. It was bad enough he had been regulated to househusband, but this place was making him homesick.

As he turned the corner a maid was just exiting one of the rooms. She took one look at Payton, her face hardened into a scowl and she quickly averted her gaze. Hurrying to the next room, she closed the door behind her with a loud, very-final-sounding click.

The staff was really beginning to get on his nerves. He'd caught several of them watching him, before disappearing as soon as they noticed him looking back at them. Baxter, the butler, was downright belligerent and the housekeeper was avoiding him. The only one who'd welcomed him at all was a footman named Harry. Sighing, Payton continued going floor by floor and room by room. If the staff didn't watch it, he'd fire them all and start anew.

He headed toward the last door on the right. This was his last floor and he'd be done familiarizing himself with the palace. His time would be better spent looking up information on the movement to disband the Marines.

Opening the door, Payton froze. The room was blue, not the dark blue of Si's bedroom but a bright royal blue, with white puffy clouds painted high up on the walls. There was a small red table and chairs and yellow shelves filled with wooden soldiers. Payton shuddered, but unable to help himself, he stepped inside.

It was a nursery. *For an heir, of course.* Si's statement rang over and over like a death knell. Payton shook his head, trying to get the words out of his head, but there was no use, he kept them. At this point he couldn't decide what upset him most. The fact he'd been told rather than asked to produce an heir or that Si had spoke in such a matter-of-fact tone, like it wasn't a big deal. He'd received no vow of love. Maybe that was what rankled? Sure, he hadn't expected a declaration, but he'd always assumed he'd have one before he was asked, or rather told, to produce an heir.

This nursery wasn't unlike the nursery in Townsend castle, but for some reason it didn't seem very cheery. The far wall had a series of three windows with red curtains. Dust motes floated in the sunlight streaming in from the middle window, the only one with the curtains pulled open. Toys were scattered across the tiny table. The room looked...lonely.

"Your Highness, the decorator you asked me to locate is

here."

Payton jumped at the pleasant voice behind him. *Harry, the footman.* Payton was seriously considering promoting the man. To what he didn't know, maybe Harry could replace the absent housekeeper, Mrs. Cobbs, who Payton had asked to meet with him over two hours ago. "What do you think, Harry, should we have him start with the master suite?"

"I was informed you were to make the decisions, not the footman," Baxter the butler informed them in his snooty holier-than-thou voice.

Payton really hated that voice. It had done nothing but give him grief since he arrived.

Unclenching his jaw, he met Harry's gaze. "Is he always like this?"

"Yes and no, Your Highness. He's always, er..." Harry waved his hand side to side and lifted his pert nose into the air. He really was a cute kid. Well, not so much a kid really, he was about Payton's age.

Smiling, Payton waved his hand in the same motion Harry moved his. "Snobby?"

Harry nodded, his curly chestnut hair bobbing. "Yes, but he seems to have taken exception to you, because he's not usually quite so..." Again Harry whirled his hand in a circle.

"Hostile?" Payton supplied.

"Yes."

"Harry, you are needed in the kitchen." Baxter sounded like he too was clenching his teeth. Which was impossible since he was a computer.

"I don't think so, Baxter. You will find someone else. Harry is now my assistant, until I say otherwise." Payton beamed, making sure he was in full view of the palace's cameras. Juvenile it may be, but he was not going to be browbeaten by a computer. Speaking of...he really wanted to rifle through Baxter's memory. If he let Harry handle the decorating, er, decorator... "Harry, can you tell the decorator I want something similar to Hollister House. I think it's obvious that the colonel likes darker colors, and I certainly do." Which was why he'd requested the decorator who did Hollister House for Simon.

"The proper address is His Majesty, not the colonel," Baxter clipped out. "And from what I hear Hollister House is too dark and looks entirely too much like a bachelor pad. Eventually, His Majesty will come to his senses and marry a nice young lady and produce an heir."

"Don't mess with me, Baxter." Payton pointed at the camera. He was tempted to have the entire palace redone in black, just to spite the butler, but then that would be torturing himself as well.

Stifling a giggle, Harry blushed and his violet eyes twinkled. "Right away, Your Highness." He left the nursery.

Payton turned his attention back to the room, feeling like his heart was in his throat. *The nursery.* Of all the places he could have gone without seeing, this was it.

He walked over to the table and picked up a doll dressed in a blue uniform. An Englor Marine. The doll was made of plastic—it was really more of an action figure than a doll, the black hair painted on rather than actual hair. The gray eyes and painted-on lips were wearing off, indicating that the action figure was well loved. The Marine even had a colonel's insignia on his shoulders. Payton grinned. Seemed as though Simon was destined to be a Marine from an early age.

"His Grace the Duke of St. Albins is here to meet the new queen. What shall I tell him, Your Highness?" Baxter announced, startling Payton.

Keep it up, you jackanapes. I have no problem taking out my anger on your personality drive. "Tell him—"

"Baxter said you were up here and I thought I'd join you. I hope you don't mind."

Payton's heart skipped a beat at St. Albins voice. Not only had he not expected the interruption, he was nervous. He had no idea what to say to Si's uncle. What if he didn't approve of Si marrying Payton? Would he want Payton to get an annulment? The last time the duke saw Payton, he'd been bare-arsed naked in Si's bed. Payton bit back a groan and hoped he wasn't blushing when he turned.

St. Albins stood in the doorway smiling. He was a big man like Si, but he didn't look very intimidating. The man had permanent laugh lines at the corners of his eyes. It went a long way in relaxing Payton. If the man was smiling, he wasn't going to start telling Payton how he was no good for his nephew, right? "Of course not, Your Grace. I just wasn't expecting you. Baxter just informed me of your presence. I hope you weren't waiting too long."

"Aldred. Please. We're family now." He walked into the room, making the floor creak. He glanced down and smiled, then bounced a little, making the floor squeak again. "I'd forgotten all about the squeaky plank." His gaze met Payton's and his eyes twinkled. "We used to have to step over the spot to sneak out."

Payton grinned, his worry easing a bit. St. Albins didn't sound angry. "There's a spot like that in the nursery at Townsend Castle as well. It didn't matter though. Even if we made it past Christy, Jeffers would tattle on us."

Aldred laughed. "Ah yes. Russell never let us go far either."

"Russell?"

"Yes. Russell was the butler when I was a boy. Tell me, how many brothers do you have? There is a girl, isn't there?"

"I've four brothers, and the girl is my eldest brother's ward."

"Ah. I see." St. Albins dipped his head toward the Marine toy. "I'd forgotten all about the colonel."

"Oh." Payton went to set it back on the table, but Aldred stepped forward and held out his hand. Payton handed the toy over.

Aldred smiled, studying the toy. "I had him made for Simon for his fifth birthday." He chuckled, moving the colonel's arms, making him salute. "I should have realized then he'd been destined for the Marines. He dragged the toy everywhere with him." Turning the toy around, Aldred tugged on its uniform coat, straightening it. "I'm surprised it's in such good condition as much as Simon played with it." He set the doll on the table.

"Did Simon always want to be a Marine?"

"I don't believe so, no. I don't believe the idea of being a Marine came to him until he was about eighteen." Aldred leaned against the door. "I still remember the night he told me he was joining the Marines. I nearly swallowed my tongue. There was some scandal involving a lord and his footman. The queen was of course very opposed to the idea and quite vocal about it, saying the men should be hanged or some such. Simon overheard her and it had a lasting effect on him. He told me he wanted what was right for his people and that if he were going to learn to be king he was going to need better role models than his parents. He's always taken his responsibilities seriously, but something about hearing his mother that night really hit him. He enlisted the very next morning."

Payton grinned. That sounded very much like the Simon he knew. "He'll make a good king." He said it more to himself, but Aldred nodded.

"He will. He's prepared himself for it for as long as I can remember. His people have always come first and he'll do anything to ensure Englor's continued existence." Aldred's face held a soft, fond smile. It was obvious how much he loved and respected his nephew. Payton couldn't help but like the man. Aldred's expression reminded him a bit of how his father and sire looked when they spoke about Payton and his brothers.

Aldred picked up a wooden horse lying on the table next to the Marine. "Simon has qualities my brother never possessed. He reminds me of my own father in some ways. He's idealistic, but he's also a realist. He can be ruthless when he needs to be, but he's also very kind and understanding. He listens, and I guess the biggest thing is that he cares." Aldred shook his head, chuckling softly. "But enough about Simon. I came to see you."

"Me?" Payton stood there for several seconds, at a loss for words. He was much more comfortable talking about Si than himself. What if he said something wrong? What if Aldred didn't like him? Aldred was Si's only family and Payton wanted the man to like him.

"Yes, you." He ran fingers over the horse's back and looked at it, then blew the dust off the figure. "I came to welcome you to the family and see if you needed anything." Aldred set the horse down, before smiling at Payton. "And I wanted to offer you my congratulations."

The breath he hadn't realized he'd been holding left him, and Payton smiled so big his face hurt. Aldred seemed quite genuine and the rest of Payton's unease melted away. "Thank you. Something tells me that your welcome is going to be one of the few I get, and it's very nice to hear. I was afraid—" He shook his head. There he went again saying whatever popped into his head. "Thank you, Aldred, it means a great deal to me. Would you like some tea?" Galaxy, had his voice cracked or was it just the blood pounding through his ears making it seem as though it did?

"Oh no, you aren't getting away with not answering. Let's go get some tea and biscuits." Aldred crooked his finger and stepped outside the door, over the creaky spot. "Now tell me, what were you going to say?"

"I was going to say I feared you would not be happy with me being your nephew's consort." Shutting the door, Payton followed Aldred down the hall to the stairs.

"Nonsense. Simon chose you, and that's good enough for me. I want the boy happy. You make him happy, and not just because he's now assured an alliance with your home planet. Tell me, have you had problems with the staff?"

Payton's steps faltered. He could swear his heart stopped for a moment. Was Simon using him to get an alliance? He'd said earlier that his advisors were pleased about the marriage because of the surety that he'd get a treaty with Regelence. The night of their wedding came back to Payton with new clarity. Simon had insisted on marrying him after he learned who Payton was, even though it was obvious he didn't want to. Payton had tried to let him out of it. *Did Si take his responsibility serious enough to play the martyr?*

Aldred stopped and arched a brow at Payton.

Oh galaxy. Pretend everything is okay, Pay. Smiling, he

hurried to catch up and tried to cover his unease, even though it felt like his heart was going to pound right out of his chest.

"The staff *has* been giving you problems then. I'll speak to them."

"No. Not really. They just avoid me. Except for Baxter and Baxter is rather—"

"Shall I have tea prepared in the Queen's Parlor for you, Your Highness?" Baxter interrupted.

Belligerent. Baxter is a dust for brains, good for nothi— Payton swallowed the lump in his throat and tried to concentrate on the conversation. He could get through this. "Tell me, Aldred. Does Baxter have any sentimental value to you or Simon?" So what if Simon only married him for the good of Englor? It was no worse than what Payton originally thought. *Given the choice, having someone be forced to marry you or wanting to marry you, wasn't it better than they wanted you? Even if it were for altruistic reasons?* Payton should be happy that he was wanted. He could help Simon with a noble cause. Maybe Simon could grow to love him.

"Good lord, no. I can't stand him and Simon barely tolerates him at all. Simon's mother brought him with her when she married my brother."

"Baxter?"

"Yes, Your Highness?"

Payton may not be able to do anything about his marriage and the fact that Simon had married him out of loyalty to his planet, but he could do something about Baxter. "Send tea and biscuits to the *study* and...you're fired."

Payton hit the enter button and stepped back from the terminal. "Dunston?"

"Hello, Your Highness. I'm online and all security measures are in place." Dunston's voice came through the palace speakers loud and clear.

Yes. That had been easy. He'd only had to take the palace computers offline for roughly a minute and a half. He'd contacted Dunston on his com-pad and informed him of his new position, then simply erased Baxter's personality file, linked the palace computer to Hollister House and gave Dunston full access. Now Dunston had all of Baxter's memories and his own personality. He was in full control of the palace. "Welcome to Hollister Palace, Dunston."

"Thank you, Your Highness."

"Payton, please. You call Simon Colonel, it's only fair that you should call me Payton."

"Your wish is my command, Payton." Dunston actually chuckled.

Grinning, Payton stepped back to the keyboard. "And who all has full access to you at this point?"

"Only yourself and the colonel."

"In the event of an emergency, please allow the Duke of St. Albins access as well."

"Done."

Payton headed toward the control room door, scanned his thumb and waited for the door to open. "Dunston, familiarize yourself with the palace staff and the routine and notify me of any changes you need made. Do you have the security taken care of?" The door opened, allowing him to exit before closing behind him.

"Yes, Payton. Both Hollister House and Hollister Palace are secure. The guards should be changing in fifteen minutes. And Colonel Hollister is still on base."

Payton turned to make sure the light over the door turned red, indicating it was locked, and then made his way up the basement stairs, which he noted were also white and looked like the rest of the hallways in the palace. Reaching the bottom floor, Payton couldn't help but feel relief. Now he had someone in the palace he could trust. He'd been given full access to Dunston this morning at Hollister House and quickly ascertained that he was not only likable but trustworthy. *Wait.*

"How do you know Si is still on base? Do you now control all of the royal lifts as well?" Jeffers, Townsend Castle's computer, didn't control the lifts, but he could speak to them. Perhaps—

"I do, but I was tracking him through his dog tag, Payton."

"Oh." Payton frowned. He'd known the tags were used on base to log soldiers into buildings and such. The buildings had a computerized sensor similar to the smaller handheld ones used to identify the dead on battlefields, but... "I thought the dog tags were for identification and recording their movement on base only. Are you saying the dog tags have GPS and can locate military personnel anywhere without the tag sensors?"

"Yes."

This could be bad. If Dunston could track Si, then the IN could track him as well. Si probably had no idea the dog tag could be used to track. Payton certainly hadn't known it could, at least not from any location.

Payton felt like someone zapped the energy right out of him, Si was in more danger than Payton had first thought. The IN almost certainly had the king and queen killed and them being able to track Si at will was a very bad thing. "Dunston, can you disable his dog tag?"

"I can, but it could easily be re-enabled, by myself or the military."

It had to come out. "Would you be able to tell if anyone else is tracking him through it?"

"No, Payton, but if I disabled it, I would be able to tell if anyone re-enabled it."

"Very well, disable it and remind me to speak to the colonel about it when he gets in." Simon didn't need it to gain access anywhere, it was simply a way for the military to identify his remains or track his movements on base. At least, that's what the IN had always claimed.

After giving Dunston the codes to his com-pad and setting up a syncing schedule, Payton decided to check in on the decorator then retire to Si's room to go through Baxter's memories on his com-pad. "Dunston, look through Baxter's memories and send my com-pad Englor's Constitution or Parliamentary Sovereignty. Whatever I need to learn about the planet's government."

"Right away, Payton," Dunston answered.

Just getting rid of Baxter made the place feel warm, more inviting, but he needed to check on the decorator's progress. He'd been instructed to use only staff for the job and there was plenty to accomplish most tasks. They'd been working nearly four hours already. Payton rolled his eyes, thinking about the maids and footmen's reactions when he'd instructed them to help. With the exception of Harry and his girlfriend Maria, none had been too happy. Hopefully, the staff was more amicable to the decorator than they were Payton. Jogging up two flights of stairs, Payton was almost to his destination when an angry female voice halted him on the landing of the third.

"Excuse me, young man."

Surprised at the bellow, Payton turned, even knowing it wasn't directed toward him.

At the bottom of the stairs stood a short woman in a blue morning dress with her gray hair swept back into a severe bun. She appeared to be in her mid-fifties, or thereabouts. Her hands rested on her ample hips and she glared up at Payton with her sharp chin lifted high.

Glancing around, Payton saw no one else. Surprised, he pointed to himself. "Were you speaking to me?"

"I most certainly was." She started up the steps toward him. "What have you done with Baxter?"

Ah, Mrs. Cobbs, the housekeeper. If he'd known that was all it would take to get her to meet with him, he'd have done that first thing this morning. "Mrs. Cobbs, I've been wanting to speak to y—"

"Answer my question." She stepped onto the top step and faced Payton. She was actually shorter than him. Up close he could see the stiff set to her jaw and the faint tick in her cheek. Fury poured off her in waves.

Payton didn't know quite what he felt. Anger? Humor?

Both? No one had ever spoken to him like this. It wasn't that he thought he was better than anyone else, but he'd done nothing to warrant this treatment. He wasn't even sure how best to deal with this situation. His Cony would just fire the woman on the spot.

Payton smiled, hoping it would calm the woman down, and spoke softer than usual. "Mrs. Cobbs, it's nice to finally meet you. I'm afraid that Baxter and I had a difference of opinion and I feel Dunston will be a much better fit for His Majesty and me. I tried to speak to you about the run of the household this morning, but—"

"Don't you take that tone with me." She jabbed a finger in Payton's face, making him back up a step. "I want Baxter back immediately."

My tone? What tone? Blinking back his surprise, Payton shook his head. "Baxter will not be back, I'm sorry. I'm sure that Dunston can manage anything that Baxter did." He was quite proud of himself for that response. He'd comported himself reasonably without snapping or yelling. Cony would have definitely fired her already, but Payton was willing to give her time. It was an adjustment for everyone and—

"Now hear this. I don't care who you are. I've worked here for going on forty years and I run this household. His Majesty will eventually come to his senses, kick you out and marry a nice lady and fill the palace with heirs, but until then—"

"You're fired! Collect your things and leave the property immediately." So much for reason.

She gasped and sputtered. "You can't fire me!"

"I just did. You can leave the easy way, or I'll have the guards escort you."

"We'll see about this. I will be talking to His Majesty." She turned and stomped down the stairs without another word.

Dust. Now what was he going to do for a housekeeper? *Nothing can be easy, can it?* This just wasn't his day. Payton sighed and leaned against the wall. He was trying, really he was. He wasn't entirely happy about his new life, but he was determined to make it better. This househusband thing wasn't his cup of tea, but he could do it. He knew he could. Simon needed him.

"Payton?" Dunston's smooth voice asked hesitantly, no doubt having heard every word and recorded it on audio and video alike.

"Yes, Dunston?" Payton shoved away from the wall and headed toward the master suites.

"The Duke and Duchess of Kentwood are here to see you. I've had Her Grace seated in the parlor and allowed His Grace to go to the nursery and play. I hope that is all right."

The duchess was here? Payton stopped so abruptly his shoes slid on the polished marble floor. What did she want? Was she here to lambast him for stealing her fiancé? Did she even know Simon and Payton were married?

"Payton, should I send her away? She was on the guards' approved list of visitors from the colonel."

There was a list? Well that made sense, he supposed, since they were under heightened security. "No, no, Dunston, I'm on my way now. Will you make sure Mrs. Cobbs leaves without incident?"

"I will have her escorted off palace grounds if need be."

"Thank you." Turning, Payton headed back downstairs to the parlor. His stomach was queasy. It wasn't every day, thank goodness, that a man learned he had to produce an heir, decorate a palace and deal with a difficult staff. And now he had to face a jilted fiancée. What next?

By the time he got downstairs his hands were sweating and his pulse racing. *Get it together, Pay.* The parlor door opened for him, revealing Dru sipping tea on the love seat by the cream-colored marble fireplace. She looked lovely and elegant and fit right in this pastel, feminine room. Guilt tried to seep in, but Payton pushed it away.

When she glanced up and spotted him, her face lit up. Setting her cup down, she got to her feet and held her hands out to him. "Your Highness. How are you?" She seemed genuinely pleased to see him.

How odd. It wasn't what Payton was expecting, although when he thought about it she'd been very pleasant the last time they met. Perhaps the rumors about her and Si were just that, rumors. He hadn't actually asked Si if he'd proposed to Dru or even if she was his mistress.

Catching her hands in his, Payton offered her a tentative smile. "Hello, Your Grace."

"I came to offer you my help. Si dropped by my place this morning and told me everything." She tugged on his hands and pulled him down onto the love seat with her. "I know you were raised to do this kind of thing, just as I was." She chuckled and shook her head. "A prince no less. But I thought you might like some company." She looked around and gave a mock shudder. "I've always thought this place was so unfriendly. And since you don't know very many people..." She let go of his hands and shrugged. "I thought I'd see if you needed help with anything."

Whoa. The smile froze on Payton's face. Was she offering because Si had told her to? Or was she truly trying to make friends? *Does it matter?* It wasn't like he could be rude and send her away. She was Si's friend, whatever else she was or wasn't. And at this point it would be really nice to have someone around who wasn't a computer or scowling at him. "Thank you."

"You're very welcome. You do realize that by tomorrow rumors of your marriage will likely be all over Englor, don't you?" She patted his hand.

"Yes." Payton swallowed the lump in his throat. He wasn't sure he was ready for that. Somehow he'd managed going the whole day without thinking about it until now. He'd been too busy trying to get the palace in order.

"Are you going to host a ball in celebration of your marriage?"

"A ball?" Oh galaxy, he hadn't even considered that. Technically they were in mourning, but under the circumstances it seemed like something he should do. Would Si even want that? He didn't seem like the ball sort. Payton certainly wasn't, but then his circumstances had changed. He'd become the consort of a very important man who would need to use balls and dinners to gain support from Parliament if he wanted things to run smoothly.

Oh, Payton, you are a genius. A ball could be just the thing to help Simon gain support in Parliament over the Englor Marines. Security was an issue, but if they kept the guest list small and only to influential Parliament members... "Dru? Do you know about the proposal for the IN to absorb the Marines?"

She made a face and tsked. "They're idiots. If Englor gives up the Marines it will leave us vulnerable to attack."

Payton nodded. Good. She was a smart lady and not some arm ornament like most young ladies—or young lords on Regelence—of the ton. "Yes they are. Do you think you can help me arrange a ball and invite the important members of Parliament? The ones Si really needs to win over?"

"Oh, Payton, that's a great idea. It will kill two birds with one stone. Let me host it at Blake House. In honor of yours and Si's marriage."

Payton barely got out a nod before Dru practically bounced on the love seat and immediately set to work.

His head spun watching Dru. Getting up from the love seat, she paced back and forth in front of the fireplace, too much energy to contain. It took Payton a few minutes to register her thought process because she jumped from one thing to another. It was exhausting and fascinating.

Dru had Dunston take note of this and take note of that. They went over everything. Colors, flowers and guest list. She even managed to teach Payton about some of the ton. Which ones were going to be hard to convince about the Marines. Who would not accept his marriage to Si, which were pretty much the same people who would go against Si on the Marine issue. She also told him which ones she thought could be won over eventually.

By the end of the hour, she had Payton biting his bottom lip and pacing in the opposite direction as her in between bouts of laughter. He'd forgotten all about the leery feeling he'd had when he came into the parlor. Having planned the ball with

Dru, Payton felt much better. Dru did not act like a woman scorned. In fact, he found her company very pleasant. It snuck up on him. He'd gone from being wary of her, wondering if she was planning on stabbing him in the back, to glad she was here to help.

"What about food, Payton? Anything in particular or shall we leave that up to the housekeeper and the cook to organize?" Dru stopped her pacing back and forth and turned, her lavender dress swirling around her legs then unwrapping.

Oh dust. He'd forgotten about Mrs. Cobbs.

"Uh-oh. That doesn't look promising." Dru propped her hand on her hip, studying Payton.

"What?"

"You're droopy."

Droopy? Payton realized he was standing in Dru's path, his shoulders and head slumped. He smiled and stood up straight. "I fired the housekeeper."

"Oh." Dru pursed her lips and tapped them with her finger. "Okay, so get the housekeeper from Hollister House to come here and hire someone else for the townhouse."

"Good idea. Dunston, did you get that?"

"Yes, Payton, I'll contact Mrs. Gilliam directly," Dunston replied without missing a beat.

"Mama, Mama." A dark-headed little boy flew into the parlor, hitting Dru's legs and getting lost in the voluminous lavender material. Payton spotted the colonel clutched in one small hand and smiled.

She laughed and patted his back. "Oliver, I want you to meet Si's consort."

The little boy stepped back and turned around. His bright blue eyes were nearly the shade of Si's. Was he Si's? The boy looked like Dru, but those eyes. It was startling. Payton realized he was staring. He held out his hand and smiled.

Oliver let go of Dru's skirt and offered his own hand. "Hello. I'm Oliver, what's your name?"

Payton clasped the tiny hand and shook it. "I'm Payton. It's nice to meet you, Your Grace."

"Pft." Scrunching up his nose, Oliver pulled his hand back and waved it in dismissal. "You can just call me Oliver."

Payton laughed, charmed despite the niggling worry in the back of his head.

Dru pushed the little boy's shoulder. "The proper term of address for Payton is Your Highness," she corrected.

Oliver's blues eyes widened and his lips rounded into an O. "You're a prince?"

"I am, yes."

"He's Si's...husband," Dru offered, blushing.

Taking pity on her, Payton explained his title or what he thought it was. "On Regelence my title would be King-Consort." He looked back at Oliver. "But I *am* a prince as well."

Oliver frowned. "You aren't a girl."

"Oliver," Dru gasped.

Payton laughed and dropped down to Oliver's level. "No, I'm not. Is that okay?"

"Yes. I'm glad you aren't a girl. Girls are stinky." He glanced up at Dru. "'cept for you, Mama." Turning back to Payton, he grinned. "Si is my friend. Does this mean you're my friend too, since you're married to Si?"

"Oh absolutely," Payton agreed.

The rest of the afternoon went by quickly, but Payton couldn't help but wonder once again about Oliver's parentage as Oliver waved to him from the front steps. Payton picked up the doll Oliver had left on the sofa and headed upstairs to his and Si's suite. What if the boy was truly Si's child? Did it matter? He knew it didn't. Men had children out of wedlock all the time in historical England. Except that was a new concept for him. On Regelence men did not have children until they were wed. He knew it shouldn't bother him. Dru seemed perfectly fine with things and Si hadn't said anything about a son, well not counting telling Payton he needed to make an appointment for one this morning.

Just ask him, Pay. Just come right out and ask him if he and Dru are lovers. What are you afraid of?

After closing the bedroom door behind him, Payton flopped onto the bed and stared at the ceiling. He didn't want to know. What if Si said yes? What if Oliver were Si's true heir?

Payton could almost picture a child of his own and it terrified him. A child, or heir as Si put it, was a lot of responsibility. But did Si really want a son or did he only want to continue his line? Would any other parent have worked or did Si want the child to be both of theirs? Payton wished he knew. It would help him decide. No way would he bring a kid into this galaxy that wasn't wanted. He might give on a lot of things, his own happiness even, but his future son deserved two parents who loved him—like Payton's parents did Payton and his brothers—not a father who wanted to make sure his bloodline was carried on. Whether it was a noble cause or not.

After pulling the pillow from the top of the bed, Payton stuffed it under his head. He swung his feet idly off the side of the mattress. He loved Si and would do what he could to protect Si and make him happy. Even help Si with being a good leader for Englor, but he wasn't having a kid with a man who didn't love him. He'd thought he could do this without being loved in return, but he was wrong. Maybe in a few years, Si could come to care for him... Payton blinked back tears. Si wouldn't have even married him if it weren't for him being a prince. Maybe Si could make Oliver his heir.

"Payton!" Dunston's voice echoed through the empty room, making Payton jump.

"What is it, Dunston?" Payton dashed his hand across his cheek, wiping away the tears, and sat up.

"I found something in Baxter's memory that you will want to see."

Payton stood, already on his way to the basement and Dunston's control room. "What is it?"

"A plan for a weapon to be mounted onto a battleship. It says property of the Englor Marine Corps, but it wasn't stored here by the colonel. It was stored here by the queen."

The schematics. Payton took off running.

Chapter Sixteen

Simon stepped into the palace, feeling like he'd been on his feet for forty-eight hours straight. He'd met with General Davidson most of the afternoon. Then met up with Roc and Wycliffe at Gentleman Jackson's for a brief workout and to go over what he learned at the meeting. He'd thought about going to Aldred's to tell him about the meeting with Davidson as well, but he was too tired.

The sudden changes that had occurred in his life over the past two days had finally hit him. It felt as though he was drowning. There was so much to do and every bit of it seemed urgent. He'd hoped pummeling Wycliffe in the boxing ring would help reduce the frantic feeling racing through him, but it hadn't. Instead he now had a headache from introducing his face to Wycliffe's fist and his brain was still in what seemed to be permanent overdrive. Even now he had a list of things he needed to do, but he was tired and hungry. Maybe after he ate and took a nap he'd regroup and call a meeting to brief Aldred, Oxley and Hawthorne on what he'd learned from the general, which sadly wasn't much.

"Good evening, Colonel. I've been instructed to inform you that Payton is waiting on you in your suites and you are to join him right away," Dunston announced in an overly cheery voice.

"Tell him I'm on my up now, Dunston. Has he—?" *Wait. Dunston?* Simon stopped at the foot of the stairs and looked around. Yes, he was in the palace. He frowned. "Where's Baxter?" Not that Simon particularly cared, it was only a matter of time before he pulled the plug on Baxter himself.

Dunston made a nasally sound.

Was that a snort? Simon shook his head and climbed the stairs. He wouldn't put anything past Dunston.

"Baxter no longer works here."

"Oh." Simon grinned, wondering how long it took his tolerant spouse to get a gut full of Baxter's superior attitude. "Has Payton eaten dinner?"

"No, Colonel."

Damn, he hoped Payton hadn't been waiting on him. Guilt pushed at him. He should have called Payton during the day and told him when he was coming home. This marriage stuff was going to take some getting used to. "Can you have the cook make us something and have it sent up?"

"Right away, Colonel."

By the time Simon reached the second floor, he was wondering if he should have Payton include elevators into his redecorating. Simon hadn't even put his uniform back on, just thrown his greatcoat on over his sweatpants and T-shirt and hauled his arse out to his lift, complete with armed guards. What a pain in the arse armed guards were. Necessary, but a pain. Simon wasn't used to people accompanying him everywhere he went. He wasn't letting up on the guards though. He was fairly certain he could handle himself, but if he were going to insist Payton be guarded twenty-four hours a day, he was going to have to be fair. It was only a matter of time before Pay started balking about being under constant surveillance. By having guards himself, Simon would have more leverage for the argument to come.

He opened the bedroom door and found Payton sitting in the middle of the bed in just his loose white shirt and gray trousers with a personal computer sitting between his outspread legs and the ever-present black leather-bound journal lying beside him. He was slouched over, typing away on a holographic keyboard. A slow smile spread across Simon's lips and his cock twitched to life. Galaxy, Payton was good for what ailed him.

Wrapped up in what he was doing, Payton never even looked up as the door clicked shut behind Simon.

Leaning against the closed door, Simon watched unnoticed and let the rest of his tension fall away. His mind stopped whirling on everything he had to do and focused on the man before him. Would he ever stop getting that fluttering little happy feeling down deep when he saw Pay? He should have just come home after the meeting and aborted the attempt to unwind at Jackson's.

Payton's toes wiggled as his fingers raced over the holographic keys projected onto the bedspread. His bottom lip was let go, replaced by a grin, then he sat up straight, studying the display. "I found the schematics."

Simon started, not realizing Payton knew he was there.

Turning his head, Payton leaned back on his elbows and blew a lock of ebony hair off his forehead. "Don't you want to know what they're for?" Pay frowned, his brow scrunching a little. "Why do you have a black eye?"

As if Payton noticing it made it wake up, Simon's eye began to ache again, throbbing over his headache. He touched it and shrugged. "I was helping Wycliffe with his right hoo— Did you say you found the schematics?" Hurrying forward, Simon shrugged his coat off.

Payton laughed. It was a bubbly, joyous sound and it went right to Simon's cock. Payton nodded, looking rather pleased with himself. "I wondered when that would sink in. Here, look." He turned his screen toward Simon. "Your mother stored it in Baxter's memory and Dunston found it this afternoon. She didn't trade it according to what Dunston found."

Climbing onto the bed, Simon picked up the ten by twelve inch folding screen, making the holographic keyboard display vanish. There on the screen was a diagram of a cannon. Above it were the words *Cabochon Cannon*. At the bottom of the page it had EMCRD, *Englor Marine Corps Research and Development*. It appeared to be a weapon for a space destroyer. The Marines had only a handful of ships. With the IN defending their planet there had been no need to produce them. It was something they'd have to rectify—they needed their own fleet of ships. He toed his athletic shoes off, but continued to read.

"It's a directed-energy weapon made to fit onto a Destroyer."

What? "You mean like a particle beam?" That wasn't possible. The IN had experimented with particle beams several years ago, but the technology just wasn't there. They hadn't been able to get the weapon into a usable size. Simon's head whipped around to Payton, who was still smiling.

Payton nodded. "I'm no weapons expert, but it looks real enough to me. It uses a cabochon-cut gemstone to direct the beam. From what I've read, only a specific stone native to Englor works."

Simon sat there with his heart in his throat. This was huge. If the gemstone were native to Englor, then no one else had the technology unless they had that stone. "What gemstone?"

"An Englorian Yellow Sapphire."

The Englorian Sapphire was a dark yellow color, nearly the exact color of Payton's eyes. "They're rare." Which was good, the harder it was to make, the better. If the IN, hell if anyone got a hold of this, it could mean... Galaxy his head hurt, he didn't even want to think about what it meant. Ships, maybe even whole planets, exploding into a zillion pieces with one shot from the weapon. It was a horrific thought. Simon felt like someone reached into his chest, grabbed his heart and squeezed. He looked back at the screen. "Are you sure my mother was unable to pass this along to anyone?"

"According to what Dunston found, yes. She hid them in Baxter after obtaining them. She apparently realized what she had and was having second thoughts." Payton ran his fingers over the corner of Simon's eye. "Does that hurt?"

"A little." He turned to Payton and handed him the screen. "This would explain why the IN wants the Englor Marines."

"I would say so, yes." Payton took the screen and turned it off. "What did the general say?"

"That it was someone in the IN pushing for them to be

absorbed, not the Marines. Which, in light of this new discovery, I have a better understanding why." He needed to meet with General Davidson again as well as General Beauchamp who was in charge of Research and Development. He had to inform—

Payton scooted off the other side of the bed, taking his computer and journal with him. Storing them in the nightstand drawer, he looked up at Simon and licked his lips. It was an unconscious act, meant to moisten his lips, but it had Simon's cock twitching into a full-blown erection.

Growling, he held out his hand. "Come here." Everything else could wait. Whether it was just his normal lust for Pay or the realization that if the weapon ever got into the wrong hands it could mean the end of the universe as they knew it, he didn't know, but he needed Payton.

Blinking and scrunching his forehead, Payton took his hand and crawled across the bed on his knees. The confused look did nothing to douse Si's arousal. Instead it reminded Simon of his innocence. "Wh—?"

Simon grabbed a handful of thick black hair, knowing how turned on Payton got when his hair was pulled, and slammed his mouth down over Payton's. Galaxy, this man made him need.

A low throaty growling noise escaped Payton and he opened right up, meeting Simon's tongue with ardor. He was either getting the hang of kissing, or perhaps he was so aroused he didn't feel the awkwardness.

Smiling against Pay's lips, Simon pulled back. He stared down into dazed yellow eyes the color of Englorian sapphire. "I want you to lick my arse." He stood and shucked his clothes, not even paying attention to where they landed. When he stood in only his jockstrap, he looked back at his consort.

Payton's eyes widened in shock, then glazed over with lust. He moaned long and low. It sounded desperate and went right to Simon's cock. Damn, he loved how vocal Payton was. Payton didn't even try to hide his reactions. It was incredibly sexy, not to mention good for the ego.

Grabbing Payton's hair again, Simon kissed him. After letting go, he turned around until his legs touched the edge of the mattress. Looking over his shoulder, he watched Payton whimper and drop to his hands and knees on the bed.

Payton was tentative at first, pressing his lips softly to each of Simon's cheeks. Slowly, he got his knees under him, and his hands found their way to Simon's arse, squeezing. His tongue snaked out, swiping up the crease over and over. Spreading Simon's cheeks apart finally, he swirled his tongue around Simon's hole. Groaning, Simon bent over further. This was what he needed. He didn't want to think about the million things he had to do, or the reason why the IN wanted a weapon of mass destruction. He wanted to lose himself in Payton, if only for awhile.

Continuing to lick at Simon's hole, Payton made sexy grunting sounds. Galaxy, the man was amazing. Innocent to the core, yet such a hedonist he couldn't help himself from plunging right in.

"More." Fuck, he was driving Simon mad. It was obvious he'd never done this, and was still a little timid, but that turned Simon on more. He'd never cared for virginal partners, but there was something about knowing Payton had never done this with anyone else that brought out his possessive streak. Payton was his and only his. The niggling doubts he'd been having all day about Payton not wanting to marry him vanished.

Payton's tongue pushed into his hole just a bit, making Simon's cock jerk and his thighs tense. A drop of sweat dripped down his nose and onto the hardwood floor. "Fuck, Pay. Do it again. Fuck me with your tongue. Get me good and wet because your cock is going in there next."

There was a sharp intake of breath, then the words seemed to spark a fire in Payton. His moans grew more needy and his hands tightened almost painfully on Simon's arse. He dove in like a man possessed, fucking Simon with his tongue, while wet smacking sounds filled the air along with Payton's vulgar groans and grunts.

The rimming lasted only a few seconds before Payton's

mouth disappeared and latched on to Simon's balls through the jockstrap. He sucked the material. His mouth pulled on Simon's balls, slurping the sweat off the thin, yellowed cotton.

Bloody hell! Simon's prick began to leak, his balls drawing tighter. Who would have thought such an innocent would be so fucking oral...and naughty?

When Simon stood up and turned around, Payton's bottom lip actually pouted out. Perspiration ran down his face, soaking the inky black hair at the temples.

Simon grinned, pulled the jock off and held it up. "You like this? You like this sweaty jock?"

"Yes."

"Lay down." Dropping the jock on the bed, Simon threw his leg over Payton and straddled him. He stayed on his knees above Payton, just admiring for a moment while Payton got settled. "Get your trousers off."

Hurrying to comply, Payton unsnapped the placket of his gray trousers and shimmied them off, all the while staring up at Simon. Gripping the edges of Payton's partially opened shirt, Simon ripped, exposing his chest before backing up to help Pay pull his pants free of his feet.

Payton's prick was hard and leaking. The semen stood out clearly on the black trail of hair under his navel. Payton was so slim and sleek. His collarbones and hipbones were very prominent. Lying down like he was, his ribs even stuck out a little. Simon growled, barely keeping from flipping him over and pounding his arse into the bed. He ran a hand down Payton's stomach. "Such a fine man." *Mine.*

Payton snorted.

Well that would never do. Payton obviously underestimated his own appeal. "I happen to like your body."

Payton opened his mouth, to argue Simon supposed. Only Simon didn't give him the chance. He picked up his jock and stuffed it in Payton's mouth.

Eyes wide, Payton whimpered. His prick flexed. Oh yeah, he liked that. Simon's own cock throbbed as he grabbed

Payton's cock and positioned it at his hole.

Simon hadn't done this in a long time, actually he could count on one hand the number of times he'd bottomed, but this was different. Payton was his and Simon wanted this. Wanted to share everything with him.

"Don't move until I tell you."

Payton reached up for the jock in his mouth and Simon shook his head.

"Leave it."

Payton moaned and nodded.

Bearing down, Simon took Payton inside him. It burned, and even with Payton's spit and Simon's sweat it wasn't near wet enough, but it felt good. Just the thought of what he was doing made him hotter. He didn't want to stop. He pressed down, enjoying the stretch, and stared into Payton's wide eyes. It was one of the most intense things he'd ever done. A surge of emotion bubbled up inside him as he watched Payton's fingers white knuckle as he gripped the comforter. He wasn't letting Payton go. Ever.

Payton's breath sped up and the lusty noises began to pour from his throat.

Simon closed his eyes and concentrated on taking Payton in. Payton's prick wasn't small. He needed it to be slicker. Slowly he rose up, causing the thick prick to slip out of him. He scooted backward and bent over, taking Payton's shaft into his mouth. He got it good and wet, sucking. The sweet taste of Pay's pre-ejaculate filled his mouth. *Mmm...*

When he pulled off Payton's prick, Payton was quivering. Damn, it was a pretty sight. Simon's stomach tensed in anticipation. Before he scooted back up, he raised his head and let saliva drip out of his mouth onto the head of Payton's cock, wondering how his naughty little consort would react to such a vulgar display. He was beginning to realize the cruder he got the more turned on Payton became.

Payton didn't disappoint. He squeezed his eyes shut and his arse raised off the bed, thrusting his prick up and making it slap against him.

"Bloody hell, you're something else." Simon maneuvered himself back over Payton. This time when he sank down on Payton's cock, it slid in easily. It barely even burned this time. He sank lower, until his arse touched boney hipbones. He stayed there for a few moments, enjoying the feel. Shifting backward, he rested his hands on the bed between Pay's legs. A tingle shot right through him and he moaned as Payton's cock pushed hard against his gland. Fuck, he didn't remember this feeling quite so good. Supporting himself on his hands, he lifted off Payton a little, giving Payton enough room to move. "Fuck me, Pay."

Whimpering, Payton thrust his hips up. He gasped, his eyes going wide. He thrust again and set up a nice tempo.

Simon kept himself in check and didn't ground himself down on Payton's cock, but he wanted to. It felt amazing. Even his headache had receded in favor of the immense pleasure.

It didn't take long before Payton's hips sped and he was really pounding into Simon from below. His face showed all the strain and his rhythm faltered. He was close, but so was Simon.

"As soon as you come, I'm going to let you suck my cock. Right before I blow, I'm going to grab a fistful of those black curls so you can't move away and I'm going to come on your pretty face. Then I'm going to let you lick the come off my arse. How does that sound?"

Payton reacted exactly as Simon knew he would. His whole body went stiff as he screamed into the jock and came.

It was all Simon could do not to follow. He squeezed his eyes shut. No way could he look at the beautiful man beneath him and not come. He was dying to feel those full lips around his cock and see his semen splattered all over the pale face.

As soon as Payton's body relaxed again, Simon moved forward, letting Payton's cock slip out of his arse. He pulled the jock out of Payton's mouth and straddled his face. Come was already beginning to run down his thighs. He didn't even have to urge Payton to him.

Payton moaned, grabbed two handfuls of Simon's arse and

began to lap at his hole.

"Fuck me!" Simon closed his eyes and grabbed his prick, squeezing a little. This wasn't going to work. He was too close. Moving back, he looked down into amber eyes glazed over by lust. He caught Payton's hair in his hand, bent forward and guided his cock into Payton's mouth. "Suck me."

Taking the head of Simon's cock in, Payton moaned. He sucked and bobbed his head back and forth, propping himself on his elbows. Within seconds, Simon's balls drew up. Lightning sizzled up his spine. He pulled Payton off his cock, pumped twice and shot.

Come landed on Payton's chin, in his open mouth and on his cheek. His eyes blinked open, peering up into Simon's, looking like a debauched angel. He was so intensely sexy, Simon's cock jerked in response.

Letting go of Pay's hair, Simon scooted backward. He fell forward on one hand and licked the semen off Payton's face, then kissed him. After a lingering kiss he rolled to his side and pulled Payton into his arms, trying to steady his breathing. Payton felt so right in his arms, even with everything that was wrong. He rubbed Pay's back and kissed his temple.

Simon lay there for the longest time, until finally a soft snore escaped Payton. Grinning, Si stared at the ceiling. They would make this work. They'd get their heir, gain support from their people and they'd figure out what the fuck the IN wanted with a particle cannon and perfect soldiers, but first...first, Simon was going to rest. As his eyes fluttered closed, his stomach growled and it occurred to him that they still hadn't eaten dinner. *Nap, food, make an appointment with the generals, and inform my advisors what Payton found...and get word to Admiral Hawkins, make sure—*

Payton shifted a little in his sleep, his nose rooting into Simon's neck. Smiling, Simon yawned and rubbed Payton's linen-covered back. *Mmm...* Having Payton to come home to was going to make ruling a planet a whole lot easier than he thought.

"Colonel?"

Simon woke with a start, then realized it was only Dunston calling him. He laid his head back down and tried to erase the last remnants of sleep from his brain while taking inventory of the room. The fire crackled and glowed, casting dim shadows on the walls. In the distance he could hear the clip-clop of horse hooves outside the palace gates. His stomach growled, reminding him he hadn't eaten, and there was a warm body draped over his chest. *Payton.* Simon smiled and pulled his consort closer. Funny how it was so easy to think of him as a consort now, when just yesterday he'd been furious with Pay for lying to him. "What is it, Dunston?"

"Sorry to wake you, Colonel, but—"

Payton stirred, raising his head from Si's chest. Blinking open sleepy eyes, he yawned. "Wha'?"

"Shhh... Nothing." He pushed Payton's head back down, reluctant to give up the cozy feeling of Payton snuggled against his side. "Continue, Dunston."

"Payton asked to be informed if your dog tag was reactivated." Dunston's voice seemed loud in the quiet of the room.

Why was his dog tag—? Simon frowned, convinced he was still drowsy and hearing things wrong.

Payton bolted to a sitting position, rubbing his eyes. "Can you tell who has reactivated it?"

"I cannot," Dunston answered.

"Dust." Payton yawned and glanced down at him. "I had Dunston deactivate your dog tag."

"Why? It's for identification onl— Why are you shaking your head?" Simon sat up, propping himself against the headboard.

"The IN can use it to locate you. Dunston has been using it to track where you are all along."

"Not exactly, Payton," Dunston added. "I didn't know that I

could track him from it until I gained access to Baxter's memories. Baxter had codes to the colonel's dog tag that allowed me to locate him today. According to what's stored in memory, the late king installed the codes shortly after the colonel enlisted into the service in order to keep track of him when he was off of Englor soil. From what I can tell, it has not been used in several years, at least not from this computer. I can't say whether the IN or Englor Marines have tracked the colonel before, only that with this code it's possible."

Bloody hell. Simon didn't know whether to be mad or stunned. He was a little of both actually. Maybe a little afraid too. He certainly didn't like the idea of the IN being able to track him. *Damn it.* Why did it seem like things were piling up on him? *What else can go wrong?*

"They can track everyone ever enlisted in the IN." Payton's voice was barely a whisper.

"Yeah," Simon confirmed. If what Dunston said was true, the IN could track all Englor Marines and all of Regelence's Navy and Marines, because all three of those militaries trained with the IN for two years at the start of their careers. A hollow feeling settled in the pit of Simon's stomach and it had nothing to do with hunger. He swallowed the lump in his throat. Simon knew Payton was thinking the same thing. They sat there for several seconds just staring at each other, the impact of it sinking in.

Finally, Payton's stomach growled, interrupting the silence, and he looked down at it. "Dunston, have dinner sent up please."

Simon looked down too, but his gaze traveled further, to where the sheet was just slipping off Pay's slim hips and pooling at his groin. Even with everything going on Payton had the means to distract him. It was both frustrating and a bit of a relief. He was certainly going to need distracting from time to time.

Payton never even noticed though. He slid out of bed, grabbed his short drawers and began putting them on. The sight of his little pale arse peeking out from under his white lawn shirt as he struggled into his underclothes was enough to make Simon want to pull him back in bed. By the look on Payton's face when he turned around, something told Simon it would be a lost cause. Payton had his lip between his teeth and his brow furrowed in concentration, clearly his mind already working out something or other.

Heaving a sigh, Simon got out of bed. It was just as well, he needed to talk to Aldred about the schematics Payton had found and about the dog tags.

Payton got his trousers on and headed into the washroom. "Do you have a straight razor?"

Tugging on his sweatpants, Simon followed his consort. He reached the washroom just as Payton pulled a straight razor out of the vanity drawer. He leaned against the doorframe. The thought of Payton shaving was...well, intimate. Simon's cock began to fill. Who knew such domestic things would have this effect on him? Maybe Pay would trust Simon to let him do it. "What are you doing?"

Payton set the razor on the green marble countertop and began digging through drawers. "Get me two towels."

Simon grinned and pushed off the wall. He liked the take-charge, bossy side of Payton. It was quite a change from the shy young thing that had the urge to cover himself every time he was naked. Taking down two towels, he brought them over and offered them to Payton.

Shaking his head, Payton gathered up the razor and what looked like a bottle of disinfectant then started toward the bedroom. "Bring those and follow me."

A sick feeling washed over Simon. Why did he need all that in the bedroom? If he were going to shower and shave... "Pay..." Simon followed him into the bedroom to find Payton in the middle of the big four-poster bed, on his knees waiting. The unease increased. "What are you going to do?"

Motioning toward the mattress with the closed razor, Payton gave him a look as if to say, "Are you daft?" He held out his hands toward the towels, opening and closing his fingers. "I'm going to get the dog tag out of you, of course."

Of course? Tossing the towels at his spouse, Simon shook his head and backed away from the bed. His cock, which had been semi erect at the thought of Payton shaving and naked in the shower, deflated. "Oh no. I don't think so." Yes, he needed the thing out, but he'd call the family physician. His husband was a crazy person. This was some sort of perverted attempt to get back at Simon for the guardian comment. It had to be.

Payton patted the deep blue comforter on the bed. "Come on. Just climb up here and lie down. Don't be a baby. You're worse than Muffin trying to get out of a bath." Payton set the razor on the mahogany nightstand next to the corked glass bottle of disinfectant and crawled across the comforter toward Simon. "It's not that deep. I can get it out in a matter of seconds."

Was it his imagination or did those yellow eyes he normally thought sexy look a little on the psychotic side? Simon shook his head again, backing up until the heat of the fireplace made his arse feel like it had caught fire. A drop of sweat dripped down his temple. He was running out of room. Any further back and he'd be *in* the fireplace. "Pay…"

Payton slunk off the end of the bed and caught Simon's hand as Simon's back hit the mantle. "Come on, it won't hurt that bad. And you aren't leaving the palace with it still in your shoulder. You're the one harping on security."

Says the psychopath with the razor. Simon let himself be led to the bed, convinced this was a bad idea, but Payton was right. He couldn't afford to let the IN track him. His parents were already dead and Simon was not ready to join them. And who could he trust right now? Could he trust the family physician? A frisson of dread came over him, deflating his protest. He didn't want to die and he didn't want to leave his planet without a ruler. If he couldn't ensure his own safety, how could he ensure Payton's? "Okay, do it."

Taking a towel off the edge of the bed where Simon had tossed them, Payton spread it across the comforter.

Simon lay down with his chest on the white towel and buried his face in his arms.

Something cold—it felt like the razor—was placed on his back, and Payton nudged him with the bottle of antiseptic. "Hold this for me."

Without looking up, Simon opened his hand for the bottle and held it upright. Payton slung his leg over Simon, straddling him, and his fingers began to poke and prod at Simon's right shoulder. "There it is, I can feel it." He took the antiseptic. The cork was removed with a pop, then cold liquid poured over his shoulder and slid down his armpit before Payton blotted it off with the other towel. Payton replaced the bottle in his hand and the razor was picked up and flicked open. Payton's negligible weight shifted forward. Taking a deep breath, Si braced himself for the pain, but it never came. "Pay?"

"Yeah?"

"Are you going to cut it out?"

The bed bounced slightly as if Payton were nodding.

"Okay. Go ahead." Simon took another deep breath and made himself relax. Another few seconds went by and nothing happened. What was Payton waiting for? He seemed anxious to operate only moments ago. "Pay?"

"Don't rush me."

Simon rose up enough to look over his shoulder.

Payton's lip was between his teeth and he held the open razor out away from himself. He looked worried. Glancing up, he met Simon's gaze and offered him a weak smile. He looked adorable and miserable at the same time.

Now he's having doubts? Fighting off the urge to smile, Simon asked, "What's wrong?"

"I don't want to hurt you."

It was on the tip of his tongue to remind Payton he hadn't seemed to mind a few moments ago when he was taunting Simon with being a baby. Simon grinned, unable to help himself. Payton's hesitance was sweet and actually made Si feel a little better about the situation. "I can handle it. You see that scar on my lower back?"

Payton's gaze shifted, taking in the four-inch scar above

Simon's left arse cheek. He nodded.

"That's from falling off a horse when I was twelve. I was waiting by the palace steps for Aldred so we could go on our morning ride in Hyde Park. Aldred was mad at my father and slammed the door on his way outside. It scared my mount and he bolted. I wasn't expecting it and I landed on the corner of a concrete step. Nothing could hurt worst than that."

"See this." Payton's weight settled on Simon's lower back and his left leg thrust out to the side. There was a thin horizontal line up the side of Payton's calf. "When I was eight, Aiden and I found a couple of Cony's swords lying on his and Father's bed and we decided to play with them. I knocked the sword out of Aiden's hands and the blade cut me wide open. We got in so much trouble over that. I swear the beating I got was way worse than the cut."

"You see the scar here"—Simon let go of the bottle long enough to gesture at his right side—"this was from the battle of Chuzofield on Planet Galvon during my service with the IN. I was sliced by an enemy saber trying to rescue Roc's sorry arse from a Galvonic Guard. We were without medical aide for eighteen hours and it got infected. I was in the infirmary for a week. *That?* Hurt like bloody hell."

Payton nodded, closed the razor and set it aside, before peeling his shirt off his left shoulder. "You see this?" He pointed to a starburst-shaped scar on his deltoid, a grin on his face. "Tarren shot me with an arrow about three years ago. We'd shut down Jeffers to get some time without a chaperone. We went hunting—it was Aiden, Colton, Tarren and me. Tarren was pretending like he was going to shoot Colton in the arse for calling him a brat, and his hand slipped. *That?* Hurt coming out more than it did going in. I swear Father was trying to make it hurt more just to punish me."

Simon smiled, grabbed the bottle of antiseptic and lay back down, resting his head on his forearms. The love in Payton's voice when he spoke about his family went right to Si's heart. He wanted to hear that same tone when Payton spoke about him. As a child, he'd longed for that kind of affection. Aldred loved him, Simon knew that, but he wanted his own family. He wanted to witness what was in Payton's voice firsthand. He wanted to be a part of something like that. "Cut this thing out of my shoulder. And tell me about your family."

"Okay." Payton picked up the razor again. "Here goes. Are you ready?"

"Yes."

"What do you want to know about my family?" Payton's fingers danced over his dog tag, finding it under Simon's skin.

There was a pressure against his shoulder when the razor's edge touched him. Then the air hit the cut. *Ow.* Simon grimaced, but held real still. "Why do you call your father Cony?" A trickle of blood ran down Simon's side.

"I don't call my Father Cony." Payton blotted the wound with the spare towel. "I call my sire Cony. It's a nickname Rexley gave him as a baby and all of us have called him that."

The ache in his shoulder intensified as Payton poked around it. Si couldn't tell what he was doing, but it sure didn't feel very good. More blood dripped down his side, almost tickling in contrast to the pain. He squeezed his eyes shut tighter and tried to concentrate on the smooth low voice above him.

"On Regelence we refer to our parents as Father and Sire. Whomever has the higher title is referred to as Father and the other parent is Sire."

"So our son would call me Father and you Sire?" Was it his imagination or did Payton stiffen?

"Yes, if we had a son. Give me the bottle." Payton's hands left him and tugged at the glass.

If? Simon opened his eyes and turned his head to ask Payton if he had made the appointment with the Regelence reproduction clinic, and spotted a small cylindrical piece of metal about six millimeters long. "Is that it?"

The cold liquid hit his back, stinging a little.

"Yes. That's it." Payton blotted the incision and tossed the razor beside Simon on the towel. He threw his leg over Simon and crawled off the bed. "Stay there. I'm going to find a bandage."

"Bottom drawer on the left side of the vanity." Simon closed his eyes again and frowned. Payton had seemed to close up at the mention of a child. *Why?* He knew they needed an heir. With the situation as it was, Simon's heir was Aldred. Payton came from a big family he loved. Simon couldn't imagine him being opposed to children. If he could, Simon would wait awhile, but given the circumstances, that wasn't practical. And he couldn't deny that the idea of a miniature Payton running around keeping the household on their toes appealed to him. He grinned. It would be scary trying to protect a son and Payton, but it would be fun too.

In no time Payton was back taping him up.

As Simon opened his mouth to ask Payton about the appointment for an heir, there was a knock on the door. That interruption was followed by Payton explaining to him the firing of Baxter and Mrs. Cobbs. They went over the decoration plans that neither of them cared much about, and Payton's plans for a ball to gain parliamentary support. Simon wasn't exactly thrilled about the ball, but even he had to admit it was a good idea, so he reluctantly agreed.

Simon was exiting his lift and on his way to Aldred's townhouse door before he realized he hadn't had a chance to ask Payton about the appointment for an heir or his feelings on it.

The door opened and Dudley's smiling face appeared. "Colonel, should I inform His Grace you're here?" He reached for Simon's coat, bumping his incision. Simon hissed out a breath and shrugged his coat off, then handed over his hat and gloves.

"No. Where is he? I'll just go find him."

"I believe he's in his bedroom." Dudley turned, already putting Simon's things away.

"Thank you, Dudley." Simon started up the stairs, wincing at the sting in his shoulder. He was glad that blasted tag was gone, but it sure didn't feel too good. Maybe he should have called the family physician, but he really didn't want anyone to know about the tag being removed. The IN would figure it out after awhile, but Simon wanted to keep it to himself as long as he could. The less the IN knew the better. He didn't want them realizing he was on to them.

He was anxious to give his uncle the information he had and return home. He wanted to talk to Payton about the heir situation and go over security details for Payton's upcoming ball. Simon raised his knuckles to knock on his uncle's bedroom door as he pushed it open.

The smell of sex hit him before the blurred movement caught his attention.

Clayton, Aldred's valet, was sprawled across the bed, naked hands frantically reaching for the covers. Aldred's dark head was bent over Clayton's groin, a look of shock in his wide gray eyes when they met Simon's.

Oh damn. Simon gasped and closed the door. *Aldred and Clay?* How had he not seen it throughout the years? They were in love. Had been since they were young. It was so obvious now, the closeness, the shared smiles and discreet touches. Simon had known Clay used to sit and talk to Aldred when he'd get home from a ball, long after he'd helped him disrobe. His bed in the little room that was connected to Aldred's was always made like he'd never slept in it, and judging from what Simon now knew, he hadn't. Even Clay treating Simon as more of a nephew made sense.

Chuckling, Simon leaned against the door. A wave of pleasure bubbled up inside him. He'd always wanted Aldred happy and he adored Clay. He'd begun to worry Aldred would remain single and lonely for the rest of his life, but now that he knew... He dropped his hand and knocked on the door without ever removing his back from it.

"What?" Aldred growled, and flung the door open.

Simon fell on his arse right into the room. He was so pleased he barely felt the pain in his shoulder as he lay down and looked up at his uncle.

Aldred was now wearing a pair of trousers, glowering down

at him.

Tipping his head backward, Simon watched Clay struggling into his shirt, looking rather pink in the face. Simon winked at Clay and glanced back at Aldred. "I expect you to do the honorable thing and get married now that you've compromised Clayton."

"Excellent idea, my boy," Aldred said over Clay's immediate protests.

Chapter Seventeen

Dru is a force of nature.
—from the journal of Payton Marcus Hollister

Payton took a drink from his champagne glass. He'd only just gotten a few moments to himself. Not counting Si, he was the beau of the ball, so to speak. Standing on the edge of the elegantly decorated ballroom of Blake House with the hordes of laughing, dancing people made him glad he'd agreed to let Dru host the ball. He'd been schooled to host balls and dinner parties, but he had no practical experience. There was no way he could have thrown together something like this in such little time. Dru, on the other hand, was a pro.

The Marchioness of Philbert spotted him and her ruddy face lit up.

Dust. She was a nice lady, but she'd cornered him twice already. Before she could get her petite form in motion, Payton smiled and waved then took off across the ballroom, pretending to be a man on a mission. With any luck she wouldn't follow. So what if he looked like a coward. He was tired of hearing about Fefe and her best-of-show award. Really, how grand could a poodle be? The woman was worse than Tarren when it came to dogs, but at least Tarren had manly dogs like retrievers, wolfhounds and shepherds.

As he darted around a group of giggling debutantes he marveled at the work Dru had accomplished. The ballroom was decorated in dark green ribbons and cream-colored carnations that went well with the black marble floor in Dru's ballroom. Nearly the whole assembly wore black in mourning for their late king and queen, but from all appearances, the ball was a smashing success.

Walking past the refreshment table, he spotted Si and smiled. He'd missed Si the past couple of days. It seemed every time Payton turned around Si was meeting with his advisors.

Si held court in the ballroom corner away from the orchestra with a champagne glass in one hand and the other waving madly, as he made a point. A group of lords encircled him, giving their rapt attention. If it weren't for Si's formidable height, Payton wouldn't be able to see him at all. As it was Payton could only see his gleaming red hair and an occasional glimpse of his handsome profile when the men around him shifted about. He had his audience completely engrossed in whatever it was he was telling them.

A gloved hand landed on Payton's arm, nearly tipping his champagne, and wrapped around it in a soft grip. "Are you hiding?" Dru asked.

"If I were hiding I'd be behind that"—he pointed to an overlarge bushy plant in the far corner under the balcony that held the orchestra—"plant. It's rather a great place. I bet there's lots of room behind it. See how the pot is narrower at the bottom? More room for your feet, but you must be careful that they aren't sticking out."

Dru smiled. "You've given this a lot of thought."

"I've given it a lot of practice. I hate balls and dinner parties."

"Really?" Dru looked at him, her delicate eyebrow arched. "I'd have never known. You're a natural. You've been rubbing elbows with people all evening. You've caused quite a stir actually. People seem to be accepting you rather well."

She was right. Even the news, or rather rumors—since they planned on making the official announcement tonight—of his and Si's marriage didn't seem to be hurting his popularity, or Si's for that matter.

"It's amazing what a lofty title will do for one's popularity. It would seem that regardless of what they think of my planet or our"—Payton held his hand to his mouth in a mock whisper as one lady had done to him earlier—"our strange notions, they all want to talk to a prince."

Dru giggled, then slapped a hand over her mouth. "Someone actually said that to you?"

Grinning, Payton nodded. "The Countess of Crocksil." Oddly, he hadn't been offended since she'd said it without malice.

"Let me introduce you to some people." Dru tugged on his arm, heading toward a cluster of arm ornaments. "These are the women you need to get along with."

"You want me to talk to the arm ornaments?"

"Be nice, Pay, or I'll take you to the matrons." She cut a glance at the side of the ballroom where all the marriage-minded mamas were gathered, watching over their flock.

Giving a mock shiver, Payton took a fortifying drink from his champagne flute and urged her toward the crowd of ladies. "By all means, lead me to the ornaments. Those matrons scare me. They've been staring at me all evening."

Dru leaned in close to his ear. "That's just because they're jealous, darling. You managed to land the hottest piece of arse on the planet."

Payton actually stumbled, spilling a bit of bubbly, not knowing whether to laugh or be concerned that she'd sounded so confident in her pronouncement of Si's skills in the bedroom. Having spent time with her, Payton was beginning to think that the rumors of her and Si were indeed rumors, but then she'd say something like that and... What if? No, he wasn't going to ask. He shouldn't *have* to ask. "Wycliffe is right, you are scandalous."

"Bite your tongue. I'm just spirited." Dru waved at a lady standing in the group of arm ornaments and suddenly they were both engulfed by the women.

Payton smiled, trying to look pleasant as he was introduced. A footman walked by with a tray and Payton set his empty glass on it. He really wasn't sure what Dru hoped to accomplish. He knew an arm ornament when he saw one and all these ladies were young debutantes who'd landed titled, probably older men. Like their Regelen counterparts, they were more than likely interested in fashion and entertainment.

"Tell me, Your Highness, how do you like Englor? Is it very different for you?" Viscountess Gerber, a tiny blonde with huge green eyes, asked.

"It's not all that different actually. Like Englor, Regelence is a regency society."

After that they wanted to know all about Regelence, and Payton was all too happy to oblige. He loved his planet so it was no hardship talking about it, and he figured he could educate people. Perhaps he could help eliminate some of the prejudices.

Much to his surprise, he ended up having to eat his words because they weren't the frivolous bits of muslin he'd judged them to be. They were surprisingly sharp and not as giggly as he feared. They even grasped the strong military influence on Regelence. Eventually, Payton found himself talking about politics and learned that every last one of them agreed with he and Dru on the Marine merger.

They were just getting into a discussion on moral reform when Dru excused them and pulled him aside. "Well done. They will all go home and talk to their husbands about the merger. If you want anything accomplished, you go through the ornaments. I'm not sure how things work on Regelence, but here being an arm decoration has its advantages. You know the old saying, 'Behind every good man is a go—'"

"Good consort," Payton finished for her. "Yes, I know the saying."

Dru chuckled. "Actually, it's behind every good man is a good woman, but consort works too."

"You think they will help the cause?" Payton glanced around, trying to spot Si.

"Oh absolutely. He's over there by Wycliffe, Lord Sheffield and Lord Townes." She tipped her head toward the refreshment table. The song ended and Dru's voice dropped to a whisper.

"He seems to be having a bit of luck himself, from the looks of it."

Si stood in a group of three men, one of which was Wycliffe. Whatever Si was saying, he had all three of the men's undivided attention. In fact one of the men was nodding in agreement as Si spoke. He was so handsome in his black eveningwear. If Payton didn't know better, he'd have called him refined. Not that Si wasn't, but he had a wild side as well. A wild side Payton had seen in depth. Just the thought of it made his heart race.

They headed toward another group of ladies, this set a little older than the first, but before they got there they were brought up short by Si's booming voice.

"Ladies and Gentlemen," Si addressed the crowded ballroom, "I know most of you have heard the rumors of my marriage to Prince Payton Townsend of Regelence." He held up his glass and looked toward Payton.

Payton and Dru stopped, as did everyone else. There were murmurs among the crowd and everyone turned to stare at Payton.

His stomach grew queasy and he felt like his heart was going to beat right out of his chest. What if they protested after Si told them? What if all the progress they seemed to have made tonight unraveled in light of the announcement? Part of him was proud that Si was claiming him publicly, the other part though wondered if they should wait.

Dru handed him a full champagne flute that she snagged from a passing footman's tray. "Relax and smile," she said through her teeth as she smiled. "It will be all right. Trust me."

Galaxy, he hoped she was right. Payton pasted a happy expression on his face and held his glass up toward Si.

Their eyes met and Si winked, his grin growing wider. Some of Payton's tension eased.

"The rumors are true." There was a collective gasp, then Si bowed his head to Payton and raised his glass again. "Prince Payton is my consort."

Payton felt as though he were a bug on a microscanner.

The crowd began talking at once. He waited for the outcries and the hostility, expecting them any moment, but they never came. There were a few negative comments, but not nearly as many as he'd expected.

"A toast to our new King and his consort," someone shouted. It sounded like Nate's dad, but Payton couldn't be sure.

To his surprise what looked like the entire assembly held up their glasses, and there were several refrains of "hear-hear" and "congratulations." Someone patted him on the back, followed by several other men offering their good wishes. Payton took it all in, smiling and saying thank you at the appropriate moments, but his attention was fixed on Si, who had gotten rid of his drink and was making his way across the dance floor.

Si too was being hailed by the crowd and congratulated, but his eyes were on Payton.

Dru took back Payton's glass. "Go get him."

Almost out of instinct Payton put one foot in front of the other and met Si in the middle of the dance floor. The unease of moments ago faded into the background of his mind. The look on Si's face gave him hope. Si *did* care. His eyes held the same gleam Payton had witnessed before they were forced to marry. Before everything got so complicated.

Like magic, the orchestra struck up a waltz and the crowd seemed to part around them.

Clasping Payton's hand, Si put it to his waist, then grabbed the other one. "Shall we?"

"Do you think that's a good idea?" Payton glanced around the room trying to gauge people's reactions. An announcement was one thing, a public display was another entirely. That he even cared what these people thought was a testament to his feelings for Si.

"I don't see why not. They'll have to get used to us dancing together eventually." Si gave him a lopsided grin that was both charming and amused. "Besides, most of the ones who would oppose have already left. Didn't you notice the small exodus when I made my announcement?"

He hadn't noticed, but then Payton's eyes had been glued to his handsome consort.

After the first few minutes, Payton began to relax and enjoy himself. He'd watched his consort from afar all evening, admiring his commanding presence and how his people responded to him. Now he had Si to himself for at least a dance.

Gazing into the shining blue eyes, Payton felt like he'd been struck. The intensity of the stare and wicked little grin Si wore had Pay's cock threatening to rise. Si licked his lips and Payton's attention zeroed in on that kissable mouth. Gads, he had to get it together or he was going to embarrass himself. Everyone was watching them. "How is your shoulder?"

"It's a little sore, but not overly. Thank you for taking it out. I meant to tell you the other night when I got back from Aldred's but you were asleep."

Payton quashed down the feelings of regret that statement evoked. "You're welcome. I didn't think it was safe for it to remain in you." Simon spent more time with his advisors than he did with Payton. In the last two days, Payton had seen him a total of three hours and most of those had been in passing or eating. Si had mentioned something about Aldred and his valet over dinner the other night, but he'd changed the subject every time Payton brought up the investigation. It felt like Si was trying to cut Payton out of everything Si considered dangerous and Payton was not happy about it. If he could get Si alone, they were going to discuss it, but here wasn't the place.

"I wanted to wake you last night, but you looked so peaceful." Si's gaze trailed down to Payton's lips, then back up to his eyes. "Perhaps I can persuade you to stay awake tonight." His voice dropped into a seductive whisper. It was almost the same deep tone Si used to talk dirty to him in the heat of the moment, and all thoughts of cornering Si about the investigation fled in favor of cornering Si for an entirely different reason.

Swallowing, Payton felt his cheeks heat. *Find something else to talk about, Pay. If not, you're going to have everyone talking for sure.* "Do you think you gained any votes for keeping the Marines on Englor?"

"Changing the subject, Pay?"

He bit his bottom lip and nodded. "If I don't I'm going to make a spectacle of myself."

The smile Si gave him was wicked. "A very nice spectacle." Pulling Payton even closer, he leaned forward and dipped his head down close to Payton's. The fresh woodsy scent of him drifted up, teasing Payton's nose and doing nothing to eliminate his problem. "I want you, Pay. Do you know what I'm going to do to you after we get out of here?" Si whispered, his voice even lower now.

A squeak sounded and for a minute Payton thought it was him. Then he heard Dru say, "Sorry." Turning his head, he saw Dru, true to her shocking self, dance by with a pretty young debutante with a mass of curly blonde hair.

Chuckling, Si looked at the couple as well. Then he focused his attention back to Payton. "Don't dance with Dru, she's hell on the feet."

"I heard that, Your Highness," Dru mumbled.

Si waltzed him around the floor several times before Payton noticed Hawthorne and Oxley had joined them as well as St. Albins and Lord Jared Hawkins. Payton's rising libido took a backseat to the warmth around his heart. As he waltzed with Si, other couples began to join them, some same sex, some mixed. It was only a small gathering, but any support was something. Payton hadn't expected to have any, knowing how some Englorians felt about same-sex relations, but now...he had hope.

"Mmm... I love it when you smile like that. I don't know if we'll make it back to the palace. How do you feel about making love in the lif—" Simon glanced over Payton's shoulder and threw his head back and laughed. "Oh dear."

"What?" Payton tried to turn his head to see.

"Roc and Wycliffe are about to start beating each other to a bloody pulp right here on the dance floor."

Si's best friends were waltzing, or rather attempting to.

Simon was right, it looked more like fisticuffs were about to commence. They were both trying to lead. Roc had his hands on his hips, shaking his head no, and Wycliffe was tugging on him, nodding yes.

Payton chuckled. "Who's going to win that battle?"

Si grinned. "I've no idea. I guess we'll find out tomorrow when we see who has the most bruises."

A movement caught Payton's attention over Si's shoulder. It was only the veranda curtain fluttering. "Are Roc and Wyc—?"

Lord Markham pushed the curtain aside. Payton stumbled.

"Pay?"

Another man with brown hair stepped through the curtain and handed Markham something. He looked vaguely familiar, but Payton didn't catch a good glimpse of him.

Si turned them, blocking Payton's view.

No. Payton tugged, maneuvering out of Si's grasp. *That man. Where have I seen him before?*

"Payton, what's—?"

Tall, thin, brown hair... Blond hair, not brown. "The hair is wrong." Payton stared at the curtain dancing in the breeze. Markham gazed about and ducked out on the veranda, following— "Caldwell."

"What?"

Payton looked up at Si's worried voice and realized they were standing still in the middle of the dance floor. "That man who was with Markham."

Si glanced at the undulating curtain. "Just a moment ago?"

A chill raced up Payton's spine. "Yes."

"That was Baymore."

"No. That was the man who kidnapped Aiden and Trouble. That was Caldwell."

Payton laid his forehead against the shower wall, letting the hot water fall around his shoulders. The sick feeling that he'd gotten when he saw Caldwell was still with him. Was Markham the operative on Englor Benson had warned Si about? Rolling his forehead on the cool marble, Payton clenched his fist.

The door clicked open behind him and a cool breeze hit him before the door closed again.

"Stop letting it bother you. Even if we would have gone after him, he likely had someone waiting for him." Si kneaded Payton's shoulders. "Besides, an all-out search would have alerted Markham that we are on to him. The way we handled it was for the best. Let's see what we can find out before we start taking prisoners." He paused for a moment before continuing working Payton's shoulders. "I should have realized it sooner. He lied about seeing the horse nearly run Dru and I down." His voice sounded contemplative.

"What?"

"Dru and I were nearly trampled in Hyde Park the morning after I met you. Markham brought my horse back after he bolted and said he'd seen what happened. He couldn't have seen it around a blind bend in the trail. The only way he could have known is if he'd planned it."

That didn't make Payton feel any better. *Okay, perhaps I'm a lot on edge. Simon is all right. He's right here.*

Payton shrugged, his neck muscles on fire. He hadn't realized he was this tense until Si started massaging him. Why was it he was the one ready to torture answers from someone and his big bad Marine was willing to bide his time? Even now Payton wanted to lash out.

He heaved a sigh and tried to relax. If he were honest, his frustration stemmed from Si as much as the situation. Why couldn't things be easy? Why couldn't Si have married him because he loved him? So far Payton had avoided further talk about an heir, but he knew it was coming. Si was all about what was good for Englor. It was admirable, but it hurt. Payton hated playing second best to a planet and possibly a mistress and love child. He felt...tired. He just wanted to sleep for a month and forget everything. Life was so much simpler on Regelence.

A kiss landed on the back of his neck. "I've got people watching Markham and trying to locate Baymo— er, Caldwell. They aren't going anywhere. I'm going to get someone to go through Markham's townhouse, his country estate and his office in the House of Lords. No one really knows where Bay— Caldwell resides, but we'll find him eventually. It's best to let them both think we aren't on to them, until we get more evidence." Fingers trailed over his shoulder blade, almost tickling, and another kiss caressed his neck. "You weren't hurt." It sounded like an accusation.

What? Payton frowned and the anger he was attempting to let go of tried to make a resurgence.

Si ran his fingers over a spot above Payton's right scapula. "The night I met you. You had a bandage here and said you'd been cut with a sword."

"Oh. That was my dog tag. Nate and Brittani got one for me to tape on."

"I'm glad you weren't really hurt." Si bit his neck. It was probably in reprimand, but it didn't feel like it. A tingle ran up Payton's spine and raised goose bumps on his arms. His cock began to fill as Si laved the spot then bit it again. "I don't want you hurt, Pay. I want you to stay away from Markham."

A barrage of feelings overwhelmed Payton. Anger, happiness, hope and despair. He didn't quite know how to deal with them. He didn't like being told what to do, but the idea that Si cared enough to want him safe... Or did he just want him out of the way? Tears welled up in his eyes, which made him even madder. "Si—"

Nibbling his way down Payton's shoulder, Si wrapped an arm around Pay's waist and pulled him closer. As he slid his other hand down and grabbed Payton's prick, his erection nestled in the small of Payton's back and the hair on his chest and legs tickled Payton's skin.

Payton wanted to be mad, but his stupid cock hardened and his body relaxed, reveling in Si's caresses. It felt good to be held. He leaned his head back on Si's chest and let the hot water beat down on him.

"Want you, Pay. Love the sounds you make." Si's breath blew over his ear, making the goose bumps intensify as he slowly stroked Payton's cock.

"Mmm..." Payton nestled his arse against Si's thighs, the last of his anger leaving him. He wanted Si too. He wanted to feel Si inside of him and forget everything else. He wanted all the other things in his life to go away, at least for awhile. Nodding, he tilted his head, giving Si better access. "Yes..."

Si continued to kiss his neck and touch his body, in no hurry to move on. The water rained down on them, feeling like a caress. Payton became aware of the steam around them and the pitter-patter sound of water hitting the floor. All of it made him more aroused and more focused on his lover. After a few minutes, Si let go of Payton's cock and explored, rubbing Payton's thighs, cupping his testicles.

It was incredible, and Payton squirmed, enjoying the feel of Si's cock pressing into his back.

By the time Si's hand made it around to squeeze Payton's arse, Pay was boneless. He needed this.

The tip of Si's prick trailed down Payton's back as he put a little distance between them. He hated even the small separation of Si's body even though he could still feel Si against him.

"Shh... I'm not going anywhere." One finger found Payton's crease, sliding up and down, as Si's other hand squeezed Payton's cock. He pressed inside as he licked a long line up Payton's neck. "Can't wait to be inside here."

Payton moaned and Si pushed deep, hitting that spot that felt so nice. Si barely let him catch his breath before he inserted another finger and began to stroke Payton's cock again. Teetering on the edge of ecstasy, Payton writhed between the two sensations. It was hard to determine which felt better, but finally he decided it didn't matter as long as Si kept doing both.

By the time Si got around to replacing his finger with his cock, Payton was near begging. Already he was close to orgasm.

His cock throbbed and his testicles were tight. When he felt Si press the tip of his cock against his hole, Payton shoved back, eager for the feel of it.

Simon hissed out a breath. "Bloody hell you're tight." The hand that had been working Pay's cock faltered in its movements.

Si's prick entering him burned a little, but Pay knew how good it was going to feel. He bit his bottom lip and relaxed, letting the stretch become sensation rather than pain. He wasn't disappointed.

"Galaxy, Pay." Simon's voice rumbled in his ear and his other arm wrapped around Pay's waist. Simon fucked him in long slow strokes, hitting his prostate, and continued to work Payton's cock.

Nodding, because it was the only thing Payton was capable of at the time, he pushed back, making Si go deeper.

They both gasped.

"Love the way you feel in my arms, wrapped around my cock." Si hugged Payton closer to him with the arm around Payton's waist, then he kissed Payton's neck.

Keeping his eyes closed, Payton turned his head and searched blindly for his consort's lips.

Payton found himself pushing back into all of Si's thrusts, panting, "Harder." Simon gave him exactly what he asked for, fucking him with fast vigorous jabs.

In seconds pleasure overwhelmed Payton. He squeezed tight and thrust into Si's fist twice more before he exploded into climax. Payton opened his eyes and yelled as semen splashed onto the tiles in front of him only to be washed away by the water.

Si followed him, stiffening behind him and letting out a strangled moan of his own. Releasing Payton's prick, Si pulled him closer, his head falling onto Payton's shoulder. Payton closed his eyes and dropped his hands to his sides.

For several seconds they stood there propping one another up, listening to the water fall and the sound of their labored breathing. Payton was so relaxed he could almost fall asleep where he stood. He ran his hand over Si's wet hair. "Thank you."

Turning his head, Si kissed Payton's neck. "My pleasure." He kissed Payton's hand too before pulling away and allowing his cock to slip from Payton's body.

Payton shivered.

Si patted his arse and retrieved the soap from the ledge by the showerhead. From the sounds of it he was washing himself. After a few moments, his hands touched Payton's shoulders.

With his bones melted, he stood there and let Si wash him. It was nice, Si's calloused hands on his skin. He could be so gentle or he could be rough and he seemed to have an uncanny ability to tell which of those Payton needed at any given time. Maneuvering Payton under the spray of water, Si kissed his nose.

Payton grinned. He probably looked ridiculous but he didn't care.

Si chuckled and turned the water off. "Stay right there."

When the door opened a breeze hit Pay, but instead of being cold it felt good. He heard Si come near again, then a towel ruffled his hair. It slipped down his body, drying every inch of him.

Si swept Payton into his arms, cradling him against Si's chest.

Payton groaned, unable to decide how he felt about being carried. It seemed so girly, but he had to admit it was also nice. Besides, he wasn't sure his legs would work.

"Stop frowning and indulge me, will you?"

Resting his head on Si's shoulder, Payton allowed himself to be carried to their bed. After settling them both, Si ran his fingers through Payton's damp hair. It was nice, relaxing.

Payton felt better than he had in days. The underlying tension between himself and Si the last few days had pretty much vanished. He was feeling much less like a second choice for a spouse, even if Si did spend more time with his advisors than he did Payton. "I want to go with you to the parliament when you go to speak against the merger."

"Why do I have a feeling it's not to watch me win over the House of Lords?"

Payton chuckled. "Well that too."

"But?"

"I want to go through Markham's computer."

Stiffening slightly, Simon groaned. "I told you I'm going to have someone else do that." He caught Payton's chin, forcing him to look Simon in the eye. "It's dangerous."

"Yes, but just being myself at this point in time is dangerous. I'm trying to stand in the way of the IN, and I'm not exactly the consort Englor imagined for their king. And Caldwell has no doubt realized who I am now. He knows I can identify him." He rose up on his elbow so he could see Si better. The sooner things got solved with the IN the better off they'd all be. "It'll be perfect. You'll be there talking to Parliament, making sure Markham isn't in his office, and I'll let myself in and highjack his computer for a few minutes."

Simon pulled him forward, planting a hard kiss on his lips. "No."

Anger welled up inside Payton and he tried to sit up, but Si held him down.

"I don't want you hurt. How many times do I have to tell you that? It's my job to keep you safe."

Of all the arrogant— "I don't need you or anyone else to protect me. I'm quite capable of taking care of myself." Once again Payton tried to sit up, only to have his head held against Si's chest. *Damn it.* Si and his strength were ruining Pay's pique.

"Pay, please." Si kissed his forehead. "For me." Stroking Payton's hair, Si kissed him again, and again.

Of all the dirty tricks... Payton felt like pouting. Si was using Payton's feelings against him. It wasn't fair. Knowing it would do no good, Payton let the argument melt on his tongue. He could practically hear his father's voice in his head saying, *"Pick your battles, Payton.*" He relaxed and stopped fighting Si to sit up. "Fine."

"Really?"

"I said fine," he gritted out between clenched teeth.

Si kissed his forehead. "Thank you."

Lacking the energy to fight, Payton closed his eyes. He couldn't help but wonder if Si were trying to protect him or keep him out of the investigation, but for now he chose to believe it was what Si claimed, to keep him safe. Did that mean Si did love him...just a little?

Payton sighed and rubbed his fingers through the hair on Si's chest. Si needed his help and he was getting it, like it or not. Payton *was* going tomorrow. It was easier to ask for forgiveness than permission.

Chapter Eighteen

Someone should tell Roc that yellow and black makes him look like a bumblebee.
—from the journal of Payton Marcus Hollister

From where he sat in the balcony of the meeting chamber of the House of Lords, Payton gave one last glance down at the assembly hall, making sure Si wasn't looking his way. It was almost a shame to leave the view. Si looked so commanding and powerful down there in his Marine uniform, speaking to the Lords of Englor.

Not only was the view nice, but Payton had learned quite a bit about Englor's government, just by watching. Similar to Regelence, Englor had a unicameral parliamentary system where Si, as King, acted as the executive branch of the government. To feel completely comfortable with his new home, Payton still needed to learn more, but now was not the time.

Giving his consort an admiring look, Payton stood. As interesting as it was, he had work to do. He made sure Markham was still in his seat, then leaned to his left and whispered to Roc, "I'm going to the water closet. I'll be right back."

"Oh okay." Roc stood.

No, no, no. What is he doing? A sinking feeling settled in Payton's stomach. "Where are you going?"

Roc ushered him out of the row of seats onto the purple carpeted stairs. "I'm going with you."

"Why?" Payton kept walking up the stairs, his mind working furiously on how to get rid of Si's friend.

Roc shrugged and kept walking, coming up alongside Payton. "I'm supposed to watch you."

Bloody hell. Fury bubbled up inside of Payton, making him clench his jaw tight. Si had told Roc to watch him. Si didn't trust him. Payton straightened his spine and kept going. Then he realized Si had good cause not to trust him and his anger deflated. It wasn't fair for him to be mad at Si, since Payton *was* going to search Markham's office computer and had planned on doing so all along.

Payton reached the top of the balcony, then began the descent down the stairs to the ground floor. He looked over at Roc and grimaced.

Roc wore a black morning coat, a pair of charcoal-colored trousers, a nice white cravat, and the most horrendous bright yellow waistcoat known to man. It fit Roc's personality, but it was not good for blending in. *Oh well.*

Reaching into his morning coat, Payton felt for his mini com-pad and congratulated himself on remembering that he'd brought the smaller folding computer to Englor with him. His regular com-pad would have never been able to fit inside his coat pocket. He made it to the lobby, pleased to find it empty, and headed toward the water closet.

In the washroom, he glanced around to ascertain that there were no cameras or anyone else in the room. Once Roc cleared the door, Payton locked it behind them and pulled his com-pad out of his pocket. This shouldn't take him long. He'd already studied a map of the building and knew exactly where Markham's office was in relation to this washroom. He'd bring the cameras down for a minute and a half in order to get there, then bring them back up. That shouldn't be long enough to cause too much alarm. It would look like a glitch.

"Whoa. What are you—?" Roc shook his head. "Pay, I can't let you—"

Payton sighed and looked up from his screen. He didn't want to make Roc mad at him, but he *was* going to break into

Markham's computer. "You can't stop me, Roc. You can either come with me or go back to your seat, but I'm going." He hoped his tone was gentle enough not to make Roc mad, but firm enough to let Roc know he meant what he said.

Roc glared at him, his hands going to his waist. He opened his mouth to argue, but Payton held up a hand, stopping him. This was wasting precious time.

"You can tell Simon I gave you no choice. I'll take the blame."

"Right." Roc snorted. "I'm bigger than you, Pay. I can stop you."

Payton hated to do it, and he hoped Roc would forgive him, but he looked down his nose at Roc, challenging him. "Can you?"

"Yes."

"Assuming you can physically stop me." And Payton wasn't about to concede the point. He may be more brain than brawn, but he wasn't without skills. "I'm not above kicking and screaming at the top of my lungs. So you need to decide what you'd rather have to deal with. Me causing a scene the likes you've never seen before? Or Si?"

"I— You— Uh—" Roc groaned, then finally his shoulders slumped. "Fine. Theoretically he didn't say to stop you, just to watch you."

"Oh good, a technicality. I love those." They'd gotten him out of more than one tight spot. Payton looked back at his screen, tapped into the Parliament Building's camera loop and shut it down. Galaxy, he loved this. It was nice to know things. "Let's go. Stay close, look inconspicuous and walk fast." Payton unlocked and opened the door.

Roc stayed right beside him, peering around corners.

Surprisingly they made it to the office without incidence. The corridors were empty, with everyone in the meeting. It was almost too easy.

Pulling his com-pad out of his coat, Payton leaned against the closed door and turned the cameras back on.

"What do you want me to do?" Roc asked.

Shoving off the door, Payton took the cable out of his other pocket and headed toward the big golden oak desk. "Lock the door and look around, see if you can find anything of interest."

Nodding, Roc went to work searching through file cabinets.

Payton set his com-pad on the desk, then ducked under it to plug into Markham's computer.

Tap tap tap...

What is that? Payton froze, his head still under the desk. It sounded like someone drumming their fingers. Glancing up, he found Roc tapping on top of the file cabinet with one hand and rifling through it with the other. "Shhh..."

"Sorry." Roc looked at him and winced.

Shaking his head, Payton went back to work. He needed to make an image of everything on the computer. Typing as fast as he could, he got the program up and going. Now he could read through files as it copied.

Thump, thump, thump... Roc was tapping his foot on the carpeted floor. The sound was muted and probably no one else could hear it, but...

It was like working with Tarren. The man couldn't be still to save his life. How had Roc gotten through boot camp without the drill sergeant killing him? "Roc," Payton whispered. "Stop that."

Roc froze then turned, giving Payton a glaring view of his hideous bright yellow waistcoat. "I didn't mean to," Roc very nearly whined.

Oh yes, he even sounded like Tarren. Payton blinked, trying to get his eyes to adjust to the waistcoat against the dark colors of the rest of Roc's clothes and the wood bookcases that surrounded the room on three sides. It was worse than the crimson one Roc had worn to the gaming hell. Apparently, the man had the notion that as long as he wore black trousers and jacket, a white shirt and cravat, he could add any color for his waistcoat.

"This shouldn't take too long. I'm going to look through the files while we're waiting. I already set up a program that will send me any new information he receives, then we'll go." He looked back down at his com-pad, made sure the files were copying and opened the recovery program.

Rrowl, click... Roc shut the door in the file cabinet. "I was hoping to get to knock someone over the head or something," he groused.

Scanning down the screen, Payton stopped abruptly. *Vretiel.* He opened the mail and found it was one he'd read before on the IN Intelligence server. Markham was Vretiel. *Markham* was the operative on Englor.

Closing the mail, Payton skimmed through the rest until he came to a mail titled *Markham,* sent to someone named Michael. Opening it, Payton scanned through what looked to be the Earl of Markham's genealogy. At the bottom of the note was a short sentence that said, *Markham and heir dispatched, I'm in position.* "He killed the old Earl and his heir and took the heir's place."

Roc whirled around. "What?" He came forward and braced his hands on the desk. "You mean the current Markham?"

"Yes." Payton kept typing.

"What are you doing, exactly?"

"Taking an image of everything on this workstation, that way I can get deleted mail and such."

"But if it's deleted, isn't it gone?" Roc's tawny eyebrows rose in surprise, then he began to pace back and forth in front of the door.

Payton shook his head. No way was he going to try and explain this to Roc. When he'd done so to Tarren it had been a circular conversation and in the end Tarren still hadn't gotten it. "No. But most people don't know that and even less know how to recover that information."

"So I shouldn't put things on my computer I don't want people to know?"

"Essentially." Which was why Payton recorded his journal on paper. If he wanted to get rid of it, he'd burn it. Of course he could do the same to his com-pad, he supposed.

"Hrmph." Roc cracked his knuckles as he rerouted his pacing in front of Markham's desk. At least he'd stopped tapping his fingers on the file cabinet.

Looking back over the data he was gathering from Markham's deleted files, Payton spotted the word Regelence. The information was spotty, something about Azrael not knowing Remiel, who was in the castle. Payton frowned. Who the hell was Azrael and Remiel, and why did those names sound familiar? Was one of those Caldwell's code name? Or was Caldwell's code name *the valet*? *Azrael, Remiel, Michael and Vretial.* Payton rubbed his temples. *Come on, Pay, where have you heard those—?*

Rrowl, screech... Another file cabinet opened, then there was a clomping noise.

Jolted out of thought, Payton glanced up. Roc was frozen, staring at the door. The clomping sound wasn't in the room. It got louder and Payton caught his breath, realizing what it was. Someone was walking down the corridor outside the office.

Roc held his finger to his lips and pointed at the door.

Payton nodded.

The footsteps grew loud like they were right outside the door, and stopped.

Payton's heart felt like it was going to pound right out of his chest.

The steps resumed and Payton let out the breath he was holding. He and Roc remained motionless, staring at each other for another few moments, until the footsteps receded to nothing. It took several more seconds after that for Payton's heart to stop pounding.

Roc went back to searching the file cabinet.

Okay, where was I? Ah. Azrael, Remiel, Michael and Vretial. Angels? Payton shrugged. Maybe they were demons. He'd have to check when he and Roc got done here. Not that it really mattered, they were all IN Intelligence code names.

Going back to the com-pad screen, Payton flipped through

deleted files again. There were several from Michael. Payton skimmed through them until he saw mention of the queen. He read the words "met with unfortunate accident." *The bomb?* He searched further, looking for a date. That was the bad thing about recovering deleted data, it didn't always give you a full picture of the deleted file.

Rrowl, clink... Roc shut the cabinet door and heaved a sigh.

Payton went back to reading. The date was on the day of the king and queen's murder. *Good. More possible evidence.* "Got it."

"What?"

"Reference to the king's demise."

Roc smiled. "Are you sure?"

Nodding, Payton looked back at his screen.

"Good. That's evidence of treason. I'll have Markham followed when he leaves here. Maybe we can catch him *and* Baymore, or Caldwell, whatever."

Payton was glad to see that Roc was onboard with this mission, but he wanted to argue and tell Roc to have Markham arrested immediately. However, he understood the need to let the IN think Englor was still ignorant of their plans. As far as they'd been able to find out, Baymore had no holdings. No one knew where Caldwell was. And if they could catch Caldwell as well...

Roc was right, they needed to get a hold of Caldwell too. Markham didn't know they were on to him, so the chances were good he'd lead them to Caldwell.

Payton was actually getting excited. No way was Si going to be able to stay mad in light of this new info. Maybe now he'd stop trying to cut Payton out of the action and realize how much help Payton was.

Out of his peripheral vision, Payton spotted a blur of yellow, black and white. Galaxy, he hoped they could get out of here unseen. He typed in the word Regelence and started a search. "Good idea. Can you have marines follow him?"

"Yes, Si has a small group that's been working on this

already. I'll get in touch with them after this." *Clack, clack, clack, clack, clack...* "Oops." Roc hurried to still the clacking silver triangles and round gemstone toy on the big oak bookcase across from the desk.

"Roc," Payton ground out through gritted teeth.

"Sorry." Roc looked up at him, a blush on his cheeks. "Didn't know it was going to make noise."

Payton checked his com-pad to see how much longer the download would take. Already he had enough evidence to link Markham to the death of the former Earl and the Queen and King of Englor. *Beep.* The program finished. Payton unplugged his cable, shut down Markham's computer, leaving it like he'd found it, and folded the cable up and stashed it in his coat.

"Done?" Roc asked.

"Yes." Payton pushed back from the chair and picked up his com-pad. They'd need it to get out of here. He shut off the cameras and tucked the com-pad into his pocket.

Roc hurried to the door and peered out. "The coast is clear."

"Okay, lead the way. Walk casually."

"Gotcha." Roc opened the door and closed it behind Payton. "I can't believe how easy that was."

"Don't get complacent, it's not over yet." And with Roc's very noticeable waistcoat... Payton hurried his steps. "Stop before we get to the lobby area, and wait till I tell you."

As they got to the last hallway, voices reached them along with loud applause. It sounded as if the meeting was about over. Suddenly the noise got louder, people talking, their voices growing closer.

"Bloody hell. The meeting let out. Hurry, Pay."

A guard walked past their hallway. *Dust.* Payton froze. Roc urged him forward. The nervous feeling from earlier returned. How could the guard possibly miss them? Roc's yellow waistcoat was like a beacon it was so bright.

Someone else passed the hallway, never even looking down it. *Thank Galaxy.*

Payton stepped closer to the wall but kept walking like he belonged there. The noise of the crowd dismissing from the auditorium grew louder. Keeping his stride steady, Roc vanished around the corner.

Payton followed him, relieved to see a crowd of men directly in front of them. He and Roc blended in with the crowd and passed the guard that had passed them seconds ago. Another guard came running up to the first, no doubt letting him know the cameras were out. Payton nudged Roc's arm. "Go."

"Are you okay? I was supposed to take you back to Si, but—"

"I'm fine. Go. See to Markham. I'll go find Si."

Roc nodded and walked away at a fast clip toward the front doors.

Making his way across the crowd, Payton headed toward the auditorium. It was like trying to swim upstream, but he finally made it to a spot where he could stand behind a very large leafy potted plant beside the side door of the auditorium. He looked around and didn't notice any cameras or guards near, so he took out his computer and brought back up the building's cameras before quickly tucking his com-pad away again.

The lords who were exiting were beginning to gather in groups and discuss the meeting. Payton took a deep breath, getting his heart rate to slow down.

Leaning against the wall, Payton closed his eyes for a few moments. He wondered how it went. Was Si able to convince them to keep the Marines?

"Your Majesty?" someone said.

Payton's eyes snapped open, searching for Si, then realized that whoever had hailed him had done so from inside the meeting chamber. Excitement bubbled up inside him and the last bit of adrenaline rush subsided. He was anxious to tell Si what he'd found and to ask how the meeting went.

"Gentlemen." Si's voice was loud and clear, like he was right around the corner from Payton.

Payton watched the lords of Englor mill about, some talking, others leaving. Batting at the potted plant, he started around it to find his consort. He hoped Roc was able to get his men on Markham before Markham left the building.

"Nice speech, Si. I'm glad you were able to convince them. The planet is much better off with our Marines," a different man said.

Yes. Payton resisted the urge to punch his fist into the air. It sounded like Si was successful. They'd have a lot to celebrate when they got home. Payton stepped into the huge dark-purple-carpeted chamber with rows of tables and chairs around the perimeter.

Payton's eyes zeroed in on Si. He stood a couple yards away with his back to the door. His shoulders looked wide in the formal Marine uniform jacket. Payton swallowed back an appreciative sound, but it didn't stop his fingers from clenching, wanting to run through that russet hair. Several other men gathered around Si. None of them noticed Payton.

"I thought you were to marry the Duchess of Kentwood?" one lord in a brown morning coat asked.

Si chuckled and shook his head. "Ah, the Duchess of Kentwood. Dru is lovely, but I assure you my consort has his own charms."

There were a couple of lewd remarks about Dru and Payton.

Payton blushed and wondered if he should just wait outside. No one had seen him yet. He could just slip back out and—

"Drucilla Blake didn't come with a Regelence alliance," joked another lord.

A knot of dread formed in the pit of Pay's stomach. He swore he could hear blood drumming through his veins, even louder than when he'd heard someone walking outside of Markham's office earlier. His mouth went dry as he focused on the back of Si's head.

Si's red head bobbed slightly as he nodded his agreement.

"Very true."

The men laughed, but Payton barely heard them. He turned and walked out of the House of Lords with his consort's words echoing over and over in his head.

Chapter Nineteen

"Relax, Simon. He's at the palace." Aldred reached across the lift and patted his leg. "You did good today. The Marines are staying on Englor where they belong without you having to resort to force and abuse of power."

He had done good, but somehow without Payton there to share in the victory, it fell flat. Simon affected a smile he didn't really feel. "Thank you." Pay not being there when he was done not only took the wind from his sails, it worried him. Payton had as much at stake as Simon did. Payton had worked so hard on that ball, so Simon could mingle with the House of Lords and have a chance to persuade them to his line of thinking. So why had Pay left? And where the hell had Roc gone? "Are you sure the guards saw him get into our lift?"

"Yes. One of them stayed behind specifically to tell us they were taking him back. They were going to send another lift back for you, but I told them I'd take you home." Aldred was quiet for several seconds, then furrowed his brow in thought. "Maybe he went to call Admiral Hawkins and tell him the outcome of the vote."

No, that didn't sound right. Dread knotted in his stomach. Pay knew Hawthorne would call his son. Frowning, Simon pushed the blue lift curtain aside and looked out at the snow-covered city without really seeing it. He teetered back and forth between worried and hurt. Something wasn't right. Payton couldn't still be mad about Simon telling him he couldn't break into Markham's office, could he?

"Clay won't marry me," Aldred groused.

Pay hadn't said anything about hacking into that computer this morning when they were getting ready to go to the meeting. He hadn't even taken his com-pad to the Parliament Building. *Huh? Clay?* "What?" Simon let go of the curtain and turned to see his uncle's frowning face. "Why not?"

"Says because I'm a Duke and he's a nobody. A nobody? Can you believe that? Like I'd love a nobody for going on thirty years," he scoffed.

"Well, then I'll make him a Marquis. Problem solved." If only Payton not being where he should be was as easily solved. Feeling antsy, Simon shifted in his seat. He was used to giving orders and them being obeyed.

Aldred threw his head back and laughed. "That might work. The threat of having to manage an estate might make him relent without a title."

The lift stopped and Simon jumped to his feet before the door slid open. What if Payton hadn't come back here? The unease in his stomach escalated.

"You have it bad." Aldred chuckled. "Congratulations, boy. I'm proud of you."

Stopping as the door raised, Simon turned around and nodded. "Thank you, Uncle. Let me know if I can help in persuading Clay. I'm serious about the title."

"I know you are, but I doubt it will be necessary. I'm more stubborn than he is. It might take me a month or two, but I'll wear him down." He winked. "Open lift door, steps down. Now go find out why your consort left without you."

Giving a terse dip of his head, Simon stepped out of the lift, hurrying up the front concrete steps toward the white Doric column portico. Why were there so many steps? Did everything have to be so damned grand?

The front door of the palace opened and one of the footmen greeted him, taking his cape, gloves and hat. If the man moved any slower... "Is Payton here?"

"Yes, Colonel."

Simon took a breath and made himself slow down. Payton was here, in one piece, and that was all that really mattered. Why he left could be sorted out later. "Thank you." He spared a quick glance in the parlor to ascertain Payton wasn't there, before heading up the stairs. It took effort, but he made himself walk instead of run. "Dunston? Where is Payton?"

"Payton is in the gym, Colonel."

Gym? They had a gym? *When did this happen?* "Where exactly is that, Dunston?"

"Third floor, first door on the left, before the master suites, Colonel."

"Thank you, Dunston." Unbuttoning his jacket on the way up, Simon climbed the stairs. His unease from earlier was subsiding a bit and anger was creeping in. Why was Payton here working out? Was this his revenge for Simon not letting him break into Markham's office?

The smell of new paint tickled Simon's nose, burning a little. He got to the top of the third floor landing and stopped, staring. It was different. No more cold marble and stark white. He hadn't been up here in...years? He and Payton had been living out of Simon's old suites.

As he stepped onto the new hardwood floor, he grinned, forgetting all about being mad for the moment. The wainscoting was stained mahogany and the wall above it a deep burgundy color. It was warm, cozy and the dark colors made the hall look smaller, not so daunting. It fit him...them. It fit Payton too.

Opening the gym door, Simon was once again surprised. There were mirrors along one wall and the others were painted a nice deep blue. The floor-to-ceiling windows were covered with gauzy white curtains that let in light, but kept the room private. Several pieces of weight equipment sat in front of another wall as well as free weights. A punching bag took up one corner, a speed bag and some potted plants the others. *Payton made us a gym.* Simon smiled.

In the far corner of the room, Payton stood with his back to Simon, admiring a rack of foils, sabers, epees and rapiers. His boots and stockings were at the front of the room by the mirrors, but the maroon morning coat, cream-colored waistcoat and cravat he wore to the Parliament Building were hanging over a workout bench.

Feeling like a great weight had been lifted from him, Simon let himself enjoy the view for a few moments, glad Pay was safe. He hadn't realized until just then how scared he'd been that something had happened to Payton. *If...* A wave of panic hit him, clawing at his chest, but he quashed it and shook his head. He didn't know what he'd do.

Payton picked up a foil and slashed it through the air. There was a tension to his shoulders, hinting at his mood, but even still he was graceful. A thing of beauty, like an approaching storm. It was hard not to admire, even though you knew it was likely to erupt any moment.

"Why did you leave?"

Gasping, Payton spun around brandishing the foil, pointing it at Simon. His lips were set in a hard line and his expression appeared somewhere between irritation and surprise. "You scared me."

"You scared *me*. I thought something had happened to you." He walked into the room, laying his jacket over a leg press machine on his way to Payton. "I thought you'd be there until the end."

Turning around, Payton plucked another foil from the rack with his right hand. "I was. Congratulations on your victory." He tossed the new foil, handle first, at Simon.

Simon caught it, frowning at the clipped tone in Payton's voice. "You mean our victory. I couldn't have done it without you."

"Me?" Payton stepped forward, pointing his foil at Si as he touched his hand to his own chest. "I did nothing but help Dru plan a ball. You didn't need me." Was it Simon's imagination or did Payton's spine stiffen?

Before Simon could decide, Pay brought his weapon up, saluting, then stepped into an en garde stance. "In fact, you don't need me at all, you've got Dru and your advisors." He slashed his foil through the air. "And your alliance."

What? Simon frowned, still coming closer. Payton was the only comforting thing in his life right now. How could he not know that? "Pay, don't be ridicu—"

"En garde." Bare feet slapping against the wood floor, Payton advanced, taking Simon by surprise.

He barely got his foil up for a parry in time. "Bloody hell, Pay."

Payton went on the attack, giving Simon no choice but to block. He hardly had time to catch his breath, much less question his opponent. Payton came at him with a vengeance, backing Si clear across the room.

With no time to think, Simon focused on the fast and furious sword work and fought with pure instinct. As it was he scarcely had a chance to counter. Payton's speed was impressive. It was beautiful and frightening at once. His face never displayed any emotion, but Simon sensed the tempest of emotions warring within him, by his pretense of near disinterest. Payton was never detached. He was a passionate man whose feeling always showed, whether it be biting his lip in concentration or blurting out things he was thinking. Something was bothering him and he was keeping it in check. Simon wanted to know what it was, but Payton never gave him the chance.

In no time they were covered in sweat, and the only sounds were their panting breaths, the shuffle of their feet and the clink of metal on metal. The room was becoming stifling and the musky scent of sweat permeated the air.

Payton allowed himself to be maneuvered back to the middle of the room but otherwise gave no quarter. His skill was magnificent and Simon couldn't decide if Payton had been taking it easy on him the last time they fenced or if it was anger guiding him now. Whatever the case, his passion was an incredible turn-on and breathtaking in its beauty. Even with the fierceness of the engagement, Simon's cock was hard. As soon as he got an opening he was going to end this and fuck the anger out of Payton. Then they'd talk and work things out.

Apparently, Payton had gotten it in his head that Simon

didn't need him. Where he got that idea Simon had no clue, but he'd set things straight after he showed Pay he was wrong.

Simon parried, blocking a rather violent attack, and nearly lost his footing. His eyes widened in shock and a frisson of surprise came over him. His mind immediately set about righting his mistake, but it was too late.

Taking advantage, Payton knocked the foil from his grasp, sending it sailing across the floor.

Simon gasped, unable to decide whether he was irritated at losing or excited that he had. He was not used to being defeated and while pride surged through him at Payton's victory, uncertainty also niggled at him. His body, however, had no qualms about what it thought. His erection throbbed and his stomach tensed. The barely contained violence in Payton's gaze was like an aphrodisiac, ratcheting up his arousal.

Payton placed the rubber tip of his foil to Simon's chest. "Strip." His gaze trailed down Simon's body, lingering on his erection, and he licked his lips. The perusal was pure sex and from anyone else it would have been insulting, but from Payton...

Grabbing the foil, Simon yanked it out of Payton's hand and tossed it aside. Crowding close, letting Payton feel his erection, Simon caught a handful of Payton's inky black hair and slammed his mouth down on Payton. Their teeth clicked together and it hurt. The taste of blood cascaded over his tongue, adding to the sensation. The kiss was brutal, more of an assault than a show of love, but his need for Payton was so demanding he was past being gentle.

Payton ripped at Simon's clothes as he thrust against Simon's thigh. His prick felt like a brand. Loud eager grunts and groans made the sound of fabric rending barely audible.

Neither of them said a word, just pushed, shoved and bit at each other until they were naked. Somehow or other they ended up on the floor rolling around and wrestling to be on top. Even as small as Payton was, it was no easy task. He gave Simon hell. He couldn't remember ever feeling this savage, almost-blinding passion for anyone else. All he knew was his need for this man. It was rough and lacking finesse, but was one of the most exhilarating things Simon had done in awhile.

Eventually, he relented and let Payton be on top. As fun as the tussle was, he was tired of the wait. He tugged on Payton's hair again, making him arch his neck, then captured that long pale throat with his teeth. Payton keened and thrust his hard, hot prick against Simon's.

Simon shoved back until they were both rubbing against each other in a race for completion. The sweat of their bodies and the precome slicked their way. "Oh fuck, Pay."

Jerking his head free, Payton peered down at Simon with burning yellow eyes and a smear of blood on his chin. Whether the blood was Payton's or Simon's, Simon didn't know but it was sexy as hell. He grabbed two handfuls of Payton's delicious arse and moved them together faster.

Payton's eyes went wide and his movements grew erratic. Staring into Simon's eyes, he shuddered and stilled. Heat poured over Simon's stomach as a ragged cry tore from Payton's lips and his pale muscles tensed. It was incredibly sexy. Payton shouldn't look so lovely with his face strained, but he did. *Mine.*

Balls drawing tight and a flutter in his stomach, Simon stared, absolutely awed by the vision above him. He thrust up against Payton once more, then his own orgasm poured from him. It was amazing and scary at the same time—he felt like he was going to fly apart. Adrenaline surged through him along with his orgasm, seeming to draw it out.

When the last of the tension left him, he marveled at Payton. After all they'd done together, Simon shouldn't be surprised his consort was capable of such unrestrained passion, but he was. Pleasantly so. He cupped Pay's cheek, his eyes fluttered, lethargy pulling at him along with contentment. He had everything he needed right here. Together there was nothing they couldn't do.

Grunting, Payton swooped to capture Simon's lips. The kiss was still savage and more teeth than lips, but it was also full of feeling. Payton may be upset, but he loved Simon, he couldn't hide that, not from Simon.

Simon rested his hand on the back of Payton's neck, gentling the kiss. Sighing, Simon closed his eyes, relaxed and feeling at peace. Payton was here, in his arms where he belonged, safe.

He must have slept, because the next thing Simon knew he was lying in the middle of the gym with a blanket over him instead of Payton. It was a sorry substitute and Simon mourned the loss. "Pay?"

Feeling like someone had beat him with a stick, he sat up and stretched. His muscles ached, his lip hurt and he had semen flaking off his stomach, but he smiled anyway. That had been amazing and just what he'd needed. Hopefully it had been what Payton needed too. Squinting, Simon glanced around. Where was Payton? He'd obviously covered Simon up, but he and his clothes were nowhere to be seen and they still needed to talk.

Simon stood, bringing the blanket with him to wrap around his waist. The palace seemed awfully quiet. Of course, it always did because it was way too big, but something was...off. The hair stood up on the back of his neck and his stomach flip-flopped. Trying to push the feeling aside, he made his way down the hall toward the stairs. His and Payton's room was on the floor below this one. Well at least until the master suites were ready.

When he reached their open bedroom door there was no sign of Payton anywhere.

"Pay?"

Simon stepped on the end of his blanket on his way into the room and had to tug it back up. Payton better not be on the balcony in the cold. It was too dangerous. He hitched up his slipping blanket again and went to the French doors. Pushing the curtains open, Simon realized not only was Payton not out there, but it was dark. How long had he slept? "Dunston, where's Payton."

"He's not here, Colonel."

What does he mean Pay isn't here? Wherever he was he damned well better have taken a guard with him. Simon frowned. "Where is he, Dunston? And did he take guards with him? When will he be back?"

"He didn't say where he was going, but I got the distinct impression he wasn't coming back. I'm not sure if he took guards with him. He did leave you a message on the nightstand and he uploaded several files for you that he retrieved from Lord Markham's computer."

Shock set in first. Payton hacked into Markham's computer? Then a wave of sorrow hit him and he flopped onto the bed, staring at the note. Payton was gone. Simon's stomach fell to his feet and bile rose up his throat. He'd known something was bothering Payton, but he'd never thought...

The slip of paper blurred before his eyes, and a pain lodged in his chest. For the first time in years, a tear streaked down his face. Helplessness overwhelmed him as he stared at the note. He didn't want to read it. If he didn't read it then it wasn't real, only that wasn't how Simon handled things. He dealt with problems as they arose. He was good at taking charge and solving problems, that was what the Marines had trained him for. How could he have been so wrong? Funny he could handle his parents' deaths and the sudden burden of power thrust on him, even the realization that the IN wanted a weapon of mass destruction that Englor had, but Payton leaving... He couldn't handle that.

"What? What do you mean I'm under arrest? For what?" Markham spat out, struggling against the Marine Police holding his arms. A lock of dark hair fell over his forehead, covering one glaring eye, making him look like a deranged madman.

Simon felt hollow inside as he watched. He should hate this man, but he felt nothing but impatience. He'd wasted two days having guards watch Markham. Two days and Caldwell hadn't shown up. Simon wasn't willing to wait any longer. "For treason. You're being charged with the murder of the King and

Queen of Englor as well as the murder of the former Earl of Markham."

Markham laughed, still tugging his arms, trying to get free. "You have no proof."

"I have all the proof I need, Vretial."

"I have no idea what you're talking about." Markham went suddenly still, allowing the Marines to turn him toward the townhouse and press him against the wall. Simon had to give him credit. He never batted an eye or gave any indication that he knew the name.

Motioning to two other guards to advance on the steps, Simon glanced to make sure the guards armed with fragger rifles were out of reach of Markham. Cornered Markham may be, but he was an IN spy and dangerous, which was why Simon had brought ten marines, arming four with fraggers.

"I'll be out in a matter of hours." Markham's face was mashed against the brick wall as the policeman cuffed one hand.

A crowd was beginning to gather and Simon sure hoped the people stayed back. He didn't want anyone else hurt. He didn't trust Markham. No one made it to the esteemed position of IN intelligence without having a few tricks up his sleeve. Simon half expected the missing Caldwell to intervene. Simon wasn't going to feel safe until Markham was locked up.

"Will you leave now? You look like hell." Roc came up beside him, dressed in uniform. "Not only do you look like you haven't slept in two days, it's dangerous for you to be out in the open like this."

He hadn't slept, not since Payton left, but that was beside the point. He'd see this through. "I am a Colonel in the—"

"You are also the King of Englor."

Out of the corner of his eye, Simon saw a flash of blue as one of the marines went down. Markham swept the other marine's feet and vaulted over the front porch railing.

"Shoot!" Simon rushed forward just as the shots were fired. His heart pounded. The sound of the crowd screaming and Roc yelling seemed far away.

Markham went down with a sickly thud against the pavement and an armed Marine police officer beat Simon to him. The soldier landed on Markham, wrenched his hands together behind his back and cuffed him.

Roc came up beside Simon. "Get out of here."

"Not until he's cuffed, shackled and the armed outriders are in place to escort him to the tower." Simon looked down at Markham, who was coming to from the stun setting on the fragger. It should feel good to have this man in custody finally, but somehow without Payton here, the victory fell flat.

The marines wrenched the spy to his feet, and he let out a strangled cry. As he passed Simon and Roc with guards surrounding him, he snarled. "You'll never get away with this. I'm going to make your life a living hell."

It already is with Payton gone. Markham and the IN could do their best, but they couldn't hurt him more than that. For a split second, Simon let that sink in and considered leaving Payton on Regelence, thinking maybe he'd be safer, but that was ridiculous. It didn't matter where Payton was, he'd always be in danger.

Simon watched the marines load Markham into the armed lift and motioned to his bodyguards. Before he got in his own lift he looked back at Roc. "Turn him over to General Davidson. He and his men will get him to talk."

Roc nodded. "Are you going back to the palace?"

Simon climbed into his lift without looking back. "I'm going to get my consort."

Chapter Twenty

"Your Majesty, if you'll follow me, I'll show you to the parlor. Lord Plagu—uh, Payton, Lord Payton is in a meeting with King Steven and King-Consort Raleigh at the moment, but Jeffers will inform them of your arrival as soon as they're done." Thomas—at least that's what Simon thought the man had said—handed Simon's hat, gloves and coat over to a small man who stood silently behind him. "Rickles here will take your guards downstairs to get something to eat."

Lord Plague. A grin tugged at Simon's lips despite himself. The nickname was said in such a fond manner. Which wasn't at all surprising. Anyone who knew Payton... The truth in the name seemed to hit a little too close to home though. Galaxy knew Simon had been plagued since he left.

"That's fine." Simon nodded to the two armed guards, giving his permission. He wasn't likely to encounter any assassination attempts here from anyone other than Payton. Simon winced as he watched the guards leave with Rickles, then turned his attention back to the under butler. "Thank you, Thomas."

Finally. After a hellish nine days, he was going to see Pay. On the way to Regelence he'd gotten the call from Roc saying Markham was safely locked away but there was still no sign of Caldwell. It only increased Simon's need to get to Payton. Caldwell wasn't likely to turn up on Regelence, but with Markham in custody, the IN was liable to start suspecting something. For some reason Simon had convinced himself that if he were with Payton, Payton would be protected better, even though he knew that wasn't true. The cold reality of the situation was that maybe Payton didn't need him.

The ever-present butterflies he'd had since Payton left intensified along with his doubts and worries. He'd never been a man to doubt himself, but then maybe he'd never had anything as important at stake. It was an odd feeling. One he didn't particularly like, but... *What if Pay refuses to come home?* No, he wasn't going to think like that. Simon was going to do whatever it took to get Payton to come back to him. He'd grovel, beg, plead...anything. And if that didn't work, he'd resort to kidnapping. It would probably negate an alliance with Regelence, but as long as he had Pay he didn't care.

As Simon glanced around he found himself impressed and missing Payton even more. This place was Payton. It was beautiful. Massive, powerful and masculine with its stone walls and dark colors. If not for the modern conveniences, Simon would have sworn it was built a millennia ago. The place obviously honed Payton's own likes and dislikes, because Hollister Palace, under Payton's direction, was beginning to resemble it. With any luck, by the time they got home, the palace would be finished.

As they passed a narrow corridor into a larger area, Simon's heart dropped to his feet and back up again. *Pay.*

There at the foot of a massive staircase, looking up, stood Payton with his back to Simon.

Simon's breath caught. Damn, Payton was a sight for sore eyes. He wore a light gray morning coat, charcoal trousers and black riding boots. His shoulders looked wider. Had he been working out? It actually hurt a little to think of Pay working out without him, but it was a miniscule feeling compared to the relief of seeing Payton again.

Without thought, Simon found himself drawn forward. He reached out, but right before he touched Pay, he froze. What if Payton didn't want to see him? What if he—?

Simon wrapped his arms around Payton, buried his face in Pay's neck and inhaled.

Payton stiffened.

Simon did too, fearing rejection. His heart pounded so hard it hurt, his vision clouded over. What would Payton do?

Inch by inch, Payton's tension bled away and took Simon's doubts with it. As Pay leaned back into Simon's embrace, the stranglehold on his chest released, allowing him to breathe again.

He smells different. Simon wrinkled his nose. No he didn't, it had just been so long. Simon inhaled, filling his senses with his consort. It felt so good to hold him, to know he was near. Simon brushed a kiss over his neck. "I missed you," he whispered into Payton's ear.

"You just saw me five min—"

A low growling sound came from the landing above them.

Payton's head tilted up and he gasped.

The next thing Simon knew a sharp little elbow landed in his stomach and a foot swept both of his out from under him.

He landed on his arse. Pain shot up his back and down his legs and he couldn't catch his breath. *Ow.*

Someone laughed, followed by the sound of footsteps hurrying down the stairs.

Gasping for air, Simon looked up into a pair of glaring gray eyes. It was not Payton. He was nearly as handsome, and he did look an awful lot like Payton, but the eyes were wrong, as were the cheekbones. Pay had higher cheekbones. This man was the same height as Payton, but his shoulders *were* wider. And Simon had been right. The smell was wrong. He'd never really paid attention to how people smelled, but he knew Pay's scent, just like he knew hundreds of other intimate details about Payton.

"Nice takedown, boy, but you've just assaulted the King of Englor," Nate said, barely containing his mirth as he continued down the stairs.

"Oh dust." The young—not Payton—man offered Simon a hand. "I'm sorry, Your Majesty. I thought you were— Then I looked up and realized it wasn't— Oh never mind. I'm sorry." He grimaced.

Simon stared at the younger man, who had to be one of Payton's brothers, finally getting his lungs to take in air. He glanced down at the offered long-fingered, elegant hand, then hauled himself up on his own. "My apologies. I thought you were Payton." His cheeks heated and he shot a glance to the admiral, who was dressed for riding.

Nate stepped off the bottom step and squeezed the younger man's shoulder. "It's about time you came to collect your consort, Simon." He grinned and looked down at the other man. "Told you he'd come."

"Yes you did, sir." The younger man smiled and placed his hand on top of Nate's where it rested on his shoulder, then his fingers drifted up to toy with Nate's beard.

Sir? Bloody hell, it was Aiden, Nate's consort. *Good going, Si. Not only do you molest your brother-in-law, but you had to pick the one married to the scariest damned man you know.*

"It's nice to make your acquaintance, Your Majesty." Aiden bowed.

"Simon. Please." Simon bowed in return and offered his hand. "Please forgive me. From behind, you look very much like Pay. You're Aiden, I presume?"

Chuckling, Aiden nodded and shook Simon's hand. "I am. Nice to finally meet you, Simon." Letting go of Simon's hand, Aiden sobered and cocked a brow. Simon got the impression he was being sized up. Aiden's eyes narrowed slightly. "I'm going to assume by you being here that Nate is correct and you do love my brother?"

Simon swallowed, not sure how he felt about the inquisition, but if it would get him in to see Payton sooner... He glanced up at Nate, who was grinning broadly, and suppressed a groan. Nodding, Simon met Aiden's gaze. "I do."

"Then everything I've been hearing from Payton about you marrying him to get an alliance is false?"

"Yes. I—"

"Ease up, boy. He needs to be confessing this to Payton,

not us." Nate jostled his consort then kissed his cheek.

All Simon could do was stare in awe. Anyone who could make the fierce Admiral Hawkins look so—so, love struck deserved to be admired. *Poor Nate.* Simon knew the feeling.

Grabbing Aiden's hand, Nate jerked his head, indicating Simon should follow. "Come along. We'll take you to Payton before we go riding." Nate looked up at the slack-jawed under butler, whom Si had completely forgotten, and waved him away. "It's all right, Thomas, carry on."

The unease started up again as Simon followed. *Now. Finally.* He only hoped Payton would forgive him for being a blind fool. Simon rubbed his arse and winced. With any luck, Pay's reaction would be less violent than Aiden's. But at this point any reaction would be better than none. Simon had learned the hard way that an unresponsive Payton did not bode well.

As they rounded the corner, three teenagers and a little girl stood with their ears to a door. There were two ebony-haired teens, obviously Payton's siblings from the looks of them, and a pretty blond, who was holding the redheaded girl's hand.

Nate groaned and all four of them looked up at him with wide eyes.

The blond gasped, "Oh shit," followed by the little girl turning toward him and pointing her finger. "Jeremy..."

Jeremy smiled at all of them and shrugged. "Whaaat? We were just—" His face blanched and he tugged the girl down the hall.

The smaller of the two remaining teens pointed at the taller one. "It was Colton's idea."

Colton sputtered for a few seconds before turning on the smaller man and doubling up his fist. "Tarren..."

Tarren took off down the hall where Jeremy and the little girl had disappeared.

Colton gave chase.

Glancing back at Simon, Aiden laughed nervously, a blush staining his cheeks. "Um, please ignore them."

"Yes, please do." Nate chuckled and shook his head. "Come on." He opened the door and stepped aside.

A man's voice Simon didn't recognize trailed off, but Simon didn't catch what he was saying. Simon's mind was already going a mile a minute, wondering how Payton would react. Stepping forward, Simon looked into the open door. *Payton.* He stood there with his back to Simon, but Simon knew it was him.

How could he have mistaken Aiden for Pay? Sucking in a breath, Simon clenched and unclenched his hands. He wanted to reach out, yet he didn't. His stomach fell to his feet and a drop of sweat slid down his temple. Simon was sure his heart stopped. He was scared in a way he'd never been scared before. His whole life rode on this.

"Welcome, Your Majesty."

Simon started at the unexpected greeting and noticed the stiffening of Payton's spine. It was like a knife to the gut. What had he expected?

Wiping his sweaty hands on his trousers, Simon swallowed the lump in his throat. He glanced up at the man sitting on the edge of a desk directly in front of Payton. He wasn't sure what made him think so, but he suspected he was looking at the King of Regelence.

Simon knew he was being rude by not greeting the man, but he couldn't seem to make himself react. He was vaguely aware of another man standing from a love seat and going over to the desk, but he returned his attention back to that beloved dark head of curls in front of him.

As if in slow motion Payton turned around. Simon couldn't even blink. All he could think was *This is it.* Everything hinged on the next few seconds. Payton would either send him packing, or he'd welcome him. Simon was terrified. He felt as though he were about to cast up his accounts. It was funny actually, no danger he'd faced as a marine in all the horrors of war he'd seen had ever made him feel like this. He wasn't afraid of dying, but the fear of Payton's rejection...

Payton's yellow eyes widened, then a smile flitted across his face.

Simon smiled back. His heart felt like it was going to beat right out of his chest. He made his way to Payton and stopped in front of him with only a few inches separating them. He inhaled, taking Payton's scent into his lungs. The rightness of it hit him. He'd missed that smell.

Payton's gaze lifted and his smile fell. "What are you doing here?" Reaching out, he nearly touched Simon's chest, then dropped his hand.

"Your letter said if I ever needed anything..." He clasped Payton's hand, bringing it to his chest, needing the touch.

"You could have called and I'd have seen to it. You didn't need to come all this way." His teeth covered his bottom lip.

Until that moment Simon had had his doubts, but that telltale sign... Pay was as nervous as he was. Tears gathering in his eyes, Simon nodded and touched Payton's cheek. It was like drowning. He gazed into those Englorian yellow sapphire eyes and gave in to the inevitable. He was so lost. "Yes, I did. I had to come because what I need is you."

Chapter Twenty-One

He came all the way to Regelence for me.
—from the journal of Payton Marcus Hollister

"What are you writing?"

Payton closed his journal and glanced up at his consort. "Just writing in my journal." He set it on the nightstand by the bed. "Did you get the alliance ironed out with my father?"

"I did." Si tugged his cravat loose and began unbuttoning his evening coat. "He's a hell of a negotiator, but I finally wore him down." Tossing his coat onto the chair by the bed, Si started on his waistcoat. He'd been here for two whole days already, but Payton couldn't seem to overcome the oh-Galaxy-he-really-came-for-me feeling.

"He is. What did he give you a hard time with?" Getting his knees underneath him, Payton crawled to the edge of the bed and tugged on the ends of Si's cravat, making him come closer.

"You."

Payton kissed him and frowned. "Me?"

"Yes. I told him I was only agreeing to an alliance if you came as part of the deal."

"What?" Confusion and happiness warred within Payton. "What do you mean? You actually had him put it in writing?"

Nodding, Simon shrugged his waistcoat off. "That's exactly what I mean."

Pulling Si's cravat off, Payton tossed it aside and sat back on his heels. His nightshirt stretched tight at his shoulders and he had to shrug to loosen it. "Why? Why would you want that in the alliance?"

Simon took his shirt off, then sat on the bed next to Payton and began removing his boots and stockings. "Because this way no one, including you, can claim I married you for an alliance."

"But—" Payton got his feet out from under him and turned sideways to see Si better. "Are you saying you didn't marry me for an alliance?"

Kicking his boots aside, Si caught Payton's chin, forcing him to make eye contact. "No. I did not marry you for an alliance. The fact that marrying you almost certainly guaranteed me one was a bonus. It was also a way to justify it to my people, but I'd have married you anyway."

Payton didn't know what to say. He just sat there with his mouth hanging open. His chest hurt, and it had nothing to do with fear or anger. It was hard to breathe. Simon had wanted to marry him for him. It was more than he hoped for and everything he dreamed of.

Chuckling, Simon kissed him again and let go of his chin, standing. "I didn't mean to leave you speechless." He unbuttoned his trousers and shucked them and his underclothes. "I thought you knew that. I'm sorry that I was so busy with everything else I didn't see your doubt sooner." Standing in front of Payton gloriously naked, he reached out, a small smile on his lips.

Glancing at Si's hand, Payton put his own hand in it and looked up into Si's face.

Si drew Payton up, let go of his hand, grabbed the hem of his nightshirt and tugged it over his head. "I love you. I have for awhile." He wrapped his arms around Payton's waist and pulled him close, bringing their naked skin into contact. "I loved you way before I married you, Payton. Why do you think I got so mad when you kept trying to talk me out of it?"

Payton's mouth was dry. A tickle feeling started in his stomach, and the sound of blood rushed through his ears. His eyes filled with tears and he blinked them away. He'd had no idea. He figured Si cared, but... He wrapped his arms around Simon's waist and buried his face in Si's chest, holding on for dear life. The hair on Si's chest tickled his nose, and the sound of Si's heartbeat thudded steadily under his ear. It was perfect, and now that Payton had this, he was never letting it go.

Maneuvering them to the bed, Si got them lying down with Payton on top of him. "Pay?"

Still awed, Payton sat up, straddling Si's hips. He stared down at the man beneath him, amazed this strong, handsome, smart man loved him. *Get it together, Pay, you're acting like a ninny.* He nodded. Why was he nodding? Si had broken his brain.

Grinning, Si ran his hand down Payton's cheek. "Say something. Tell me that you forgive me and you'll come back to Englor with me."

Again Payton nodded, leaning into Si's touch. "Yes. I'm coming back to Englor with you. I love you too." More than he ever thought possible. He was going to spend the rest of his life with this man, raise a family with him... It was a good feeling. Payton smiled, resisting the urge to laugh, he was so happy. *Wait. Family?* Yeah, yeah he could do that. Was anyone truly ready for a family? At least they loved each other.

Payton realized his head was bobbing up and down and forced himself to stop. He was still scared, but they'd get through it together. Simon was right. Englor needed another heir. Aldred was a great man and would be an excellent leader, almost as good as Si, but the likelihood of him outliving Si— "If you want we can stop by the procreation clinic before we leave."

Si shook his head. "No. I won't ask that of you. Not yet. You aren't ready. And besides..." He grinned. "I can make Oliver my heir."

Payton stiffened. He'd decided that it really wasn't important, that he wasn't going to ask, but...

Chuckling, Si pulled him down, kissing his forehead, then let him sit back up. "You should see the look on your face. Relax. He's not my kid. I adore Dru, she's a wonderful friend, but good galaxy, the thought of her like that—" Simon shivered.

"Oliver's father was my mother's cousin. I'll talk to Aldred about making Oliver his heir, until he convinces Clay to marry him and they have their own children."

Tension eased from Payton's shoulders and he felt suddenly silly and petty, but it didn't keep him from grinning at his relief. He liked Oliver and he liked Dru. And as awful as it was, he liked them even more knowing their true relationship to Si. A picture of Oliver popped into Payton's head, with his cute little grin and his big blue eyes so like Simon's. The image morphed into a little redheaded boy with those same eyes and Si's nose. Oliver was a good kid, he looked up to Si and— No, Payton wanted *his* son to be *his* consort's heir.

"What's the serious look for, Pay? You're biting your lip." Si ran his thumb over the side of Payton's lips, freeing it.

It tugged at Payton's heart that Si knew him so well. He smiled down at his consort and nipped his fingers. "You're right, Englor needs an heir. We'll make the appointment."

"But—"

Payton shook his head and put his fingers on Si's lips, silencing him. "We'll figure the rest out along the way."

Growling, Simon kissed Payton. Si's tongue traced Payton's teeth, then his lips before pulling back. He grinned up at Payton. "Have I told you how much I missed you?"

He had, several times. He'd showed Payton too. Payton shivered, remembering the other night when Si had *shown* him rather well. "Mmm... Yes you have. But I don't think I quite got it. Maybe you should show me again."

The next thing Payton knew he was on his back in the middle of his bed with Si straddling him and pinning his hands above his head. Payton gasped, caught by surprise. When the world stopped spinning from the abrupt move, he blinked up to find Si leering at him.

"I have a better idea." Judging from the gleam in Si's eyes, Payton was sure whatever his idea was it was a good one. Payton's cock flexed involuntarily and renewed its interest. He bucked his hips up, making sure Si felt his cock as well. Smiling wider, Si pushed down. "Oh good, I think you're going to like my idea."

I think so too. Payton squirmed, trying to get his hands free.

Cock bouncing in a mesmerizing sway, Si moved to contain Payton. Payton couldn't take his eyes off it. His whole body clenched in anticipation, not caring what Si had in mind as long as he did it soon. "If your idea is fucking me, I think that's an excellent plan."

Laughing, Si let go of his hands.

Payton took full advantage of the freedom and grabbed Si's cock. It was so hard and hot. It felt amazing and Payton's body responded in kind, tingling in anticipation. He wanted Si. His mouth watered to taste him. It seemed like forever since he'd had his mouth wrapped around that beautiful fat prick. "Please?" He licked his lips and surged his hips upward, trying to get Si to move forward.

Groaning, Si batted his hand away. "I— Yeah. Good idea." He babbled almost incoherently, his eyes focused on what Payton was doing. Scooting up, he dropped one hand to support himself, gripped his cock and aimed it at Payton's mouth. The tip tapped Payton's lips, giving him a taste of slightly sweet precome.

Mmmm... Swiping his tongue across the head, Payton got a better taste. It made his own cock leak. *Galaxy, he is amazing...and mine.* The way he stared down at Payton, braced on one hand and holding his cock with the other was so possessive. It made Payton's stomach clench and his testicles draw tight.

"Ah fuck." Si tapped his cock against Payton's face. "Suck my cock, Pay." He gave Payton no choice but to do as he commanded. He plunged down, fucking Payton's mouth.

The act was so raw and masculine and naughty. Payton moaned around the mouthful of cock. The tangy salty flavor of sweat burst over his tongue, and he grabbed Si's arse, digging his fingers in, wanting him. *More.*

Payton shivered as one of Si's hairy thighs brushed past his side as he laved the head of Si's cock again. He thrust up and his prick slapped against his belly. It left a wet spot but did nothing to ease the aching throb.

"You look so bloody good with your mouth wrapped around my prick. Love the way you make those noises."

Payton moaned at the praise, trying to imagine how he looked from Si's point of view. Did he look as wanton and needy as he felt?

Si pushed deep, hitting the back of Pay's throat, then froze and shuddered. He stayed there for a few seconds until Payton couldn't breathe, but before Payton could panic, Si pulled back, letting his cock slip from Payton's mouth. He slid down Payton's body and his saliva-soaked cock left a trail of moisture on Payton's stomach. If possible the air hitting the wet path made his skin even more sensitized and raised goose bumps on his arms and legs.

Staring down at Payton with an intensity that made him quiver, Si smiled, nice and slow. It was full of love and lust. He thrust his hips against Payton and their cocks slid together.

Pushing up to get more of that lovely friction on his prick, Payton moaned and wrapped his arms around Si's wide, muscular back. "Please."

"Oh yeah. Gonna fuck you." He nipped Payton's lip then soothed it with his tongue. *Oh nice.* Si's body stretched out and his muscled abdomen rippled as he leaned forward toward the automatic lube dispenser on the headboard. The smattering of hair on his chest looked gold in the lamplight, and his nipples were hard, begging to be nipped at and sucked. Payton tried to sit up and do just that, but before he could, Si was back with lube in his hand.

"Are you ready for me, Pay?" His eyes seemed to sparkle and he trailed his fingers down Payton's cheek, holding his gaze for several seconds. The gaze was intense and full of love. Payton's heart melted. He'd seen the look before, but now he recognized it for what it was. "I love you."

Simon sank down onto him with a moan. He captured Payton's lips in the tenderest kiss. It was slow yet intense. There was a purpose behind it and Payton felt as though he were drowning. It seemed to last forever, both of them giving and taking and exploring. They ended up on their sides with Payton's leg over Si's hip, but they never stopped kissing, loving each other with their mouths.

Something slick slid over Payton's crease before dipping in and pressing against his hole, then Si broke their kiss. He stared into Payton's eyes and eased his finger into Payton.

Payton fought the urge to close his eyes—the penetration seemed so...intimate—but he didn't. He didn't want to miss anything. He'd never expected to have this kind of relationship with anyone. He'd always dreamed of it, but he never hoped. Tears clouded his eyes, and he blinked them away and gazed into Si's blue blue eyes.

"I love you too." Si thrust deep several times and added another finger. His mouth covered Payton's again, stealing Payton's breath.

Kissing back, Payton tensed a little. He was getting used to the invasion. It was more pleasure and anticipation than pain now.

Simon cradled him close, sliding kisses down his neck and on his collarbone. He added a third finger, hitting Payton's gland every now and then. Every time it started getting intense and Payton was on the verge of orgasm, Si drew back, fingering him leisurely. He rocked his hips against Payton's, leaving a trail of precome on his belly as he continued to place little love bites all over the skin he could reach by mouth. "Love the way you moan for me." He slid down, latching onto Payton's nipple, pulling hard.

Payton arched into Si's mouth with a guttural moan. Fire zipped down his spine. It was like his nipple and cock were attached.

Releasing his nipple with a pop, Si also removed his fingers from Payton's body. He hitched Payton's leg further up on his hip, then reached down and positioned his cock against the slick hole. He didn't push in. He teased, brushing the head of his prick over the sensitive skin. Finally, he let go, and his cock slid up and down the seam of Payton's arse while he fondled Payton's testicles.

It was maddening and so arousing Payton wanted to scream. It wasn't enough. He needed more. Payton tried to push down as the head of Si's cock skimmed over his hole, but Si moved back, chuckling. The sound was rusty, attesting to Si's own arousal.

"You want my cock?"

"Yes," he gritted out. He slid his hand behind him, reaching for Si's cock.

Si caught his hand and nipped his neck. "You want me to fuck you?"

Payton groaned in frustration.

"Say it, Pay. Beg me. Tell me what you want. I want to hear you—"

He's going to kill me with pleasure. Growling, Payton jerked his hand loose, grabbed a handful of red hair and pulled Si's face close. "Fuck me before I beat you to death, you evil tease." He ground his mouth down on Si's, cutting off his laugh.

Si shoved into him so hard it was nearly painful, before giving way to blinding pleasure. Si never stopped kissing him. He ate at Payton's mouth, his mirth completely gone. Hooking his arm under Payton's knee, he thrust, fucking Payton deep and hard. "You like my cock in your tight little arse?"

Barely able to catch his breath, Payton nodded. He clung to Si, trying to help move, but couldn't get any leverage. He was at Si's mercy. And it was exactly where he wanted to be. "Yes, oh galaxy yes." Si had his hips canted in the perfect position, his cock dragged across Payton's gland on every thrust.

Payton stayed on the verge of climax for what seemed like forever. He begged, his fingers leaving half moons on Si's shoulders. Si never stopped moving. He continued to thrust into Payton over and over. Both of their bodies coated in sweat. The sharp musky smell of sex filled the air around them, along with their panting and the slap of skin against skin.

"Touch yourself for me. Make yourself come, Pay." Si's voice sounded far away, foggy through the haze of desire.

Why hadn't he thought of that? Payton let go of Si's

shoulder and gripped his own cock.

"That's it."

He gazed up into Si's face as he worked his own prick and Si pounded into him. It was probably the feel of the warm hand around his prick that finally did it, but there was something in that gaze too. Something that tipped Payton right over the edge. His whole body tingled, feeling like he was going to break apart, and just like that he came.

Hot semen splashed over his hand and stomach. He was vaguely aware of Si still watching him as Payton closed his eyes.

Si cried out, thrust hard and stilled. Heat filled Payton along with a sense of utter exhaustion. He rolled onto his back, gasping for air. He was hot and so boneless he couldn't move if he wanted to. For several minutes he lay there in the silence, listening to Si's heavy breathing.

Simon's hand nudged his and then his fingers twined with Payton's.

Turning his head, Payton grinned, feeling a sense of peace he couldn't remember ever feeling before. He was physically and emotionally drained, but in a very good way.

Si stared at the canopy, sprawled out on the bed with sweat coating his incredible body. A lock of red hair fell onto his forehead when his gaze met Payton's. "You're way more than I ever dreamed I'd have."

A grin flickered across Payton's face and a warm feeling settled into him.

"What?" Si squeezed his hand.

"You are exactly what I always dreamed of."

Epilogue

At a week old Garrett is already way too attached to his pacifier. I suspect we are going to have hell getting it away from him when the time comes. I tried to tell Cony pacifiers were a bad idea, but Cony rolled his eyes and gave me the "when you were a baby" speech. I agreed just to get out of hearing that speech.

—from the journal of Payton Marcus Hollister

"He looks like you."

"What?" Payton lifted his pen and looked up from his journal.

Si sat with his elbows braced on his knees with Garrett's head in his palms. His tiny little body was bundled into a blanket and stretched out on Si's forearms. He looked like a cocoon. *Impressive.* Si was becoming quite good at swaddling. It was hard to get the blanket tight enough. Every time Payton did it, Garrett flailed his way out of it and got mad and started screaming because he was cold.

Closing his journal and setting it aside, Payton slid down the sofa until his shoulder was resting against Si's arm.

Garrett was sound asleep, but every time his mouth went lax and his pacifier began to slip he started sucking on it again. *Silly baby.* Tugging the blue stocking cap off the baby's head, Payton unleashed a spiky mess of beautiful bright red hair. "He did not get that hair from me."

"No. I suppose not." Si's head tilted. "At least he didn't get the Hollister ears."

Mmm, speaking of ears. Payton caught Si's earlobe between his lips and tugged. Si's clean masculine scent was slightly masked by the smell of baby powder, but it was there, flooding Payton's senses. "I happen to like your ears."

"I don't have Hollister ears." Si leaned his head closer to Payton, giving him better access. "Mmm... Do that again."

"What, this?" Payton got to his knees, resting his hand on Si's thigh, and stuck his tongue in Si's ear. Maybe he could talk Si into going upstairs.

Si moaned and closed his eyes. The sound elicited a jolt of arousal from Payton.

Galaxy, that was sexy. Payton scooted as close as he could, wrapping his arms around Si's chest. It was a little awkward with Si holding the baby like he was, but Payton managed to get himself pressed up against Si's side.

Moving Garrett into the crook of his arm, Si freed one hand. Finding Payton's lips, he pulled him to straddle one of Si's thighs, wrapped his arm around Payton's back and grabbed his arse.

The new position brought Payton's erection into contact with Si's hip, and his own thigh awfully close to—

"Watch the knee." Si blinked up at him, his lips already slightly red from their kiss.

"This knee?" Carefully, he snugged his knee up against Si's testicles.

Squeezing his arse, Si growled and kissed him again.

"Ahem."

Dust! Payton froze. He should move, but if he did he'd be rather indecent and rather obvious.

Apparently, Si was of the same mind regarding his own obvious erection because he tightened his grip on Payton's arse, keeping him from moving.

Cony came into the room, frowned at them and shook his head, then his attention focused on Garrett, who still slept in the crook of Si's arm. A big happy grin lit his face and he walked over and plucked the baby from Si. He headed toward the door, then turned back and walked around the sofa when he saw Father coming in the room.

"Give me that baby, Raleigh. You monopolized him last time he was awake. I've promised to take him to see the portrait gallery." Father rounded the sofa, completely ignoring Payton and Si, arms outstretched toward Garrett.

Cony actually snorted and turned his back on Father as he made his way toward the door with Garret clutched to him like a prize. "You are not going to bore my grandson with your stuffy ancestors. He'd much rather see my weapons collection."

Payton scooted closer to Si, pressing his cheek to Si's as they both watched his parents leave, still fighting over Garrett. *They have lost their minds.* Cony hadn't even given him a lecture on proper behavior. *Amazing.*

"You don't think they're going to start playing tug-o-war with the baby, do you?" Si kissed his cheek.

Chuckling, Payton kissed Si on the nose. "No. But we may very well start a war when we take Garrett home with us." He straddled Simon's lap fully, tilted Si's face up and kissed him.

Si grinned and nipped Payton's chin. "We'll have them sign a peace treaty before we leave."

"Good thinking."

About the Author

To learn more about J.L. Langley, please visit www.jllangley.com. Send an email to J.L at 10star@jllangley.com or join her Yahoo! group to join in the fun with other readers as well as J.L. http://groups.yahoo.com/group/the_yellow_rose.

Talk about a compromising situation!

My Fair Captain
© *2007 J.L. Langley*

A storm of political intrigue, murderous mayhem and sexual hungers is brewing on planet Regelence.

Swarthy Intergalactic Navy Captain Nathaniel Hawkins ran from a past he had no intention of ever reliving. But when his Admiral asks him to use his peerage, as an earl and the heir to a dukedom, to investigate a missing weapons stash, he's forced to do just that. As if being undercover on a Regency planet where the young men are supposed to remain pure until marriage isn't bad enough, Nate finds himself attracted to the king's unmarried son.

All Prince Aiden Townsend has ever wanted was to be an artist. He has no interest in a marriage of political fortune or becoming a societal paragon. Until he lands in the arms of the mysterious Earl of Deverell. One look at Nate's handsome face has Aiden reconsidering his future. Not only does Nate make a virile subject for Aiden's art, but the great war hero awakens feelings in Aiden he has never felt, feelings he can't ignore.

After a momentous dance at a season ball, Aiden and Nate find themselves exchanging important information and working closely together. They have to fight their growing attraction long enough to find out who stole the weapons and keep themselves from a compromising situation and certain scandal.

Warning, this title contains the following: explicit sex, graphic language, violence, hot nekkid man-love.

Available now in ebook and print from Samhain Publishing.

Enjoy the following excerpt from My Fair Captain...

The window to Nate's left shattered.

Shit. Nate hit the ground, landing flat on his stomach. A white polo ball rolled across the wood floor and onto the rug, coming to a stop inches in front of Nate's face. *What the...* He picked up the ball, got to his feet and crossed to the broken window.

"Hello there." A young man with wide shoulders and a friendly smile waved from atop a sorrel horse. "Sorry about that. I didn't hit you, did I?"

Nate shook his head. "No, you didn't hit me." He held up the ball. "Would you like this back?"

"Yes, please. Are you the earl?" the horseman asked.

"Yes, and who might you be?" Nate tossed the ball out.

"I'm Prince Colton. Pleasure to meet you, milord." He tipped his head and heeled his mount off toward the ball.

Colton? The second to youngest prince. Judging from the looks of him and the similarity to the other two gentlemen Nate had seen since his arrival, he realized they were probably siblings. Good Galaxy, the royal family was a handful. He was starting to get a suspicion as to why Jeffers was shut down.

Stepping away from the window, a rustling sound made Nate stop mid-stride. Leaves rained down and a grunt came from above. "Bloody black hole and imploding stars," a soft masculine voice hissed.

Way up in the tree closest to the window, a boy balanced precariously on a thin tree limb. He reached toward a flat computer screen of some sort that had snagged on an adjacent branch. At his unbalanced angle a fall seemed imminent. Likely a shout to be careful would bring the teen plummeting to the ground, so Nate raced to a set of French doors on his left. Hurrying outside, he got to the base of the tree just as the branch the kid balanced on snapped.

"Whoa." The boy wobbled and fell against the limb holding

the computer, knocking the device loose. "Dust!"

The flat screen clipped only one bough before falling free. Nate caught it before it hit the ground.

The young man gasped, his gaze meeting Nate's.

Nate started. The boy—no, that wasn't right, he was young, yes, but not a lad—was absolutely gorgeous. Nate stared into the big gray eyes, mesmerized. The man was simply beautiful. He had a small frame that had, at first, deluded Nate into thinking him a child. A mass of ebony curls surrounded a handsome face, and a full bottom lip was caught between even white teeth.

"Uh, thanks. I, uh— Whoa." The man's booted feet slid off the tree, leaving him dangling from his hands ten feet in the air.

Nate set the computer screen down and held his arms out. "I've got you. Drop."

"Uh…"

"Drop."

"Okay. Please don't miss." The man let go with a reluctant whimper.

The negligible weight landed in Nate's outstretched arms. He bent his knee slightly to keep from jarring the young man. Nate glanced at the handsome face and his gut clenched. Up close the man's eyes were the color of molten steel. He had flawless ivory skin and full lips. The heat of his body pressed against Nate's chest made his cock stir. The man was slim and not very tall, but he had broad shoulders that spoke of nice muscles under the well-tailored clothes. What he wouldn't give to see this slim body completely bare of clothing and those pretty lips wrapped around his hard cock. Closing his eyes, Nate concentrated on getting his pulse back to normal. He was here on a mission, not to get involved. Besides, this was most likely his hosts' offspring.

He opened his eyes in time to see a pink tongue dart out and wet the beguiling lips. Nate's cock—fully erect now— strained against the placket of his pantaloons.

The man's gaze roamed over Nate's face as long, elegant

fingers came up to trace his beard. "Who are you?" he asked in a seductive whisper.

Nate hadn't even realized he'd leaned forward until the smaller man jerked, nearly spilling himself out of Nate's arms. Setting the man on his feet, Nate watched him straighten his waistcoat. When he brushed off his trousers, he seemed to realize he had a problem.

Good, the young lord wasn't unaffected, just surprised. Not, of course, that it mattered. Nate wasn't interested. *Yeah, right.* He bowed. "Nathaniel Hawkins, Earl of Deverell."

The younger man's gray eyes shot wide and he hastily tried to hide his obvious erection. He squirmed before spotting his computer. Picking up the screen, he held it in front of his groin and met Nate's gaze. His enticing mouth formed an "O", followed by an inhalation of air, then the man blinked and shook his head as if to clear it. "Thank you for rescuing me, milord. I, uh, got my screen caught on the way up."

Nate was about to ask the man's name and why he was in the tree in the first place when an older version of the young man appeared in the window. "What in stars happened to the window? Aiden?"

The younger man, Aiden, frowned. He darted his gaze to Nate and gave a barely perceptible shake of his head. "I didn't do it, Cony. I was trying to get a different perspective on the garden." Aiden glanced back at Nate, his eyes pleading, and bowed. "Thank you again, milord."

Before Nate could respond the vision bounded off toward the back of the castle. How odd. Apparently the imp didn't want Nate to mention his fall from the tree. Or did he not want Nate to mention who broke the window?

"Lord Deverell?"

Nate dragged his attention from Aiden's retreating backside and turned toward the window. "Lord Raleigh?"

Raleigh smiled. "Yes, please come inside. You wouldn't happen to know what became of the window, would you?"

GREAT
CHEAP
FUN

Discover eBooks!

THE FASTEST WAY TO GET THE HOTTEST NAMES

Get your favorite authors on your favorite reader, long before they're
out in print! Ebooks from Samhain go wherever you go, and work with
whatever you carry—Palm, PDF, Mobi, and more.

Samhain
Publishing
LTD

WWW.SAMHAINPUBLISHING.COM